Also by the author

THE ATTEMPT
TANGIER BUZZLESS FLIES

THE FLIGHT OF
THE PELICAN
John Hopkins

NORTH POINT PRESS · SAN FRANCISCO · 1984

Copyright © 1983 by John Hopkins
Printed in the United States of America
Library of Congress Catalogue Card Number: 84–060684
ISBN: 0–86547–169–x

The author would like to thank Lawrence Wright Music
Co. Ltd. for permission to quote from
"Stardust," 1929 Mills Music, Inc. Words by
Mitchell, Parish, music by Hoagy Carmichael.

Published in England by Chatto & Windus, London

For Ellen Ann,
Jonathan, Beau, and Cabell

Contents

PART ONE

I

Sunday Lunch

The last thing the family had expected that day or any other was
word that Ben Bradshaw's yacht, the *Pelican*, had been found in
Panama. Jonathan Bradshaw's father had been missing and pre-
sumed dead for twenty-five years. Naturally the news which
arrived just before Sunday lunch was a shock to everyone. What's
more, Jonathan's mother refused to argue in front of the servants; so tempers flared and were clipped mid-sentence whenever the pantry door swung open.

'You're not going to bring him back into our lives now!' Henry
Harrison, Jonathan's stepfather, jumped to his feet, waving the
carving knife. 'I won't allow it!' he shouted, pointing the knife at
Jonathan. 'Take off after Ben Bradshaw and I'm crossing you off
my list!'

Tilly the Portuguese maid wisely decided to disappear. The
pantry door thumped a few ominous beats and stopped. For a
moment the dining room of the rambling grey shingled house on
Martha's Vineyard was silent. Through the open window the
breeze brought the rattle of sailboats moored in Edgartown
Harbor.

'Calm down, Henry!' Granny Terry exercised her seniority.
Banging a braceleted fist on the table, she brought order to
Sunday lunch. 'And for heaven's sake put down that knife!' Her
cheeks were flushed pink as her flowered dress and lipstick.
Although her face sagged with eighty years, her eyes retained a
youthful expression. She was still a pretty woman.

Henry grumbled and turned his frustration on the roast beef.
They watched in alarm as he hacked at it. Normally Jonathan's
step-father was an amiable, retiring man. Square-faced and
stocky, he still had a head full of reddish white hair. He might be
the dictator at Harrison & Co. in New York, where he'd made a
fortune in publishing, but he couldn't handle emotions. Today he
was so agitated he'd forgotten to take off his golf hat. Nobody
dared tell him.

'You better listen to him, Johnny,' advised Bea, Jonathan's
mother.

Bea and Granny cast worried looks at each other and then at Henry. Henry was a rich man, very rich, and generous. They were grateful for the financial security he supplied. Before Jonathan's father had vanished twenty-five years ago, there'd been nothing but chaos.

Henry pointed the knife at his step-son. 'I'll tell you one thing – I've tolerated a lot from you, but I'm not tolerating this!'

Even Granny agreed that Henry coped with Jonathan as well as could be expected. He'd only come unglued once. That was three years ago after the automobile accident. He was smoking his pipe when the car hit a patch of ice and went off the road. He broke his leg and knocked half his teeth out. For a month he was in the hospital with the leg in plaster and his jaw wired shut. Taking advantage of a captive audience, Jonathan went to the hospital every day and leaned over Henry's bed for a couple of hours, theorizing on what was wrong with their lives. Finally Henry grabbed his crutch and bashed him over the head. Everyone was horrified, but Jonathan's psychiatrist argued that it was a sign of love. They all tried to forget the incident, and no one ever spoke of it. Now they feared Henry was reaching the breaking point again.

Henry plunged the knife into the meat, causing them all to wince. 'Your mother and I won't stand by and watch you run away, too!' he roared, then stopped himself. Bea and Granny were making frantic signals across the table, and Henry realized he'd said too much. To cover his mistake he added, 'I mean, we won't let you run off on some dangerous wild goose chase.'

'Hold on, Henry. Let's clarify that statement.'

Jonathan pulled an unlit cigar from his mouth and looked incredulously around the table. His face was unlined but for one deep vertical crease between the eyebrows, hollowed out by years of intense effort to understand: his mother, his family, his life. Now the strong face drooped around the thick blond moustache. It had always been a sympathetic face – handsome features that had suffered trying to get to the bottom of things. His brow furrowed; for several moments his stare was fixed inwardly on his thoughts.

'Do I understand you correctly, Henry? For twenty-five years you've all been telling me Dad's dead. Now the insurance company phones and says the boat's turned up, and suddenly you're acting as though he's been alive all this time. What's going on?' he asked, hammering in each word with the cigar. They stared at the smashed cigar on the table cloth. Jonathan swept away the tobacco with the side of his hand. 'Run away, *too*? So you think Dad ran away?' Jonathan looked at them each in turn. 'Was all that weeping and sobbing at Dad's funeral a fake?'

Everyone was stunned by this accusation. On the tall pole outside, the American flag could be heard snapping in the wind.

'Jonathan, I won't have you saying that!' Bea gripped the arms of her chair. Her lips trembled. 'You know that's unfair. It was perfectly ghastly for all of us. Ben tore our lives apart when he disappeared. *Nothing* was faked.' Her voice was harsh and clipped as it always was when she was under stress. 'If he's alive and you bring him back, he'll ruin us all over again. Dead or alive, he's been gone too long, and you know it.'

'You can't go anywhere,' Henry growled. 'You're broke.'

'I've still got the Lincoln letter,' Jonathan said.

'Oh no!' Bea cried. 'Please don't sell that. It's all you have left.'

'Take it easy, Mom, take it easy. What about humanity and sentiment? What about love and emotions that motivate us and separate us from . . .' Jonathan looked under the table and nudged a snoozing hound. 'Our pets?' He laid a new cigar on the ashtray. 'Let's assume for one moment that Henry's right, and Dad ran away. Can't you see in your heart and imagination that I might want to pursue the remote chance that my father's still alive? That I want to know the truth?'

'The truth is you just want another distraction from getting your life together.'

Henry's voice trailed away. Bea and Granny glared at him.

Jonathan leaned on the table and covered his face with his hands. 'Jesus Christ, Henry. You're a publisher, aren't you? Can't you see the irony and poetry of this gesture? The celebration of life . . . that I should sell the last thing I have left from Dad to find out if he's still alive? Mom's talking as though the letter's more important than the man.'

Henry Harrison stumbled where he stood and stepped on the kitchen buzzer. 'In this case it certainly is!'

'Henry, for heaven's sake give us some wine. We need it.' Lifting her glass, Granny winked at Jonathan and smiled.

Poor Henry, relieved to have something to do, began filling the glasses. Everyone looked grateful when the pantry door opened, and Tilly peeked in to see why she had been summoned.

'We haven't finished eating yet, Tilly,' Bea said, trying to sound a cheerful note.

The door closed again. Jonathan took the opportunity to apologize. 'Look, I don't want to ruin Sunday lunch . . .'

'You already have,' Henry grumbled.

'Henry!' Bea scolded. *You're* ruining Sunday lunch. Look at that roast beef.'

Henry's jaw moved, but he didn't speak. He kept sawing at the meat to conceal the fact his hands were shaking. Sometimes it seemed to Henry that Jonathan had been created to drive him mad. His life was a constant effort to control himself with his forty-two year old step-son, who sat across the table looking like an unmade bed. On days like today the very sound of Jonathan's voice was like a steel band tightening around Henry's head. To begin with, in the twenty years since his graduation from Princeton, Jonathan had never had a job (discounting a two-week stint in the men's department at Brooks Brothers during last year's pre-Christmas rush.) Not a *real* job. Jonathan had 'served' in the Peace Corps during the 'idealistic' sixties. But Henry suspected this heroic gesture was enforced by a desire to avoid the draft. Whatever the case, Jonathan had returned from two years in Bolivia suffering from disappointment, disillusion and dysentery. For years thereafter, the family had been subjected to lengthy readings from his 'white paper', scribbled on yellow legal pads he carried everywhere, an anti-communist tract entitled *An Alternative Message and Vision for the Agrarian Peoples of South America.*

Since then, Jonathan had lost every penny he'd inherited from Granny Bradshaw dabbling in the stock market. Whenever he needed money, Jonathan would haul a Bradshaw antique to Parke Bernet to auction, until nothing was left. For Bea's sake Henry listened politely to Jonathan's schemes and loaned him money in exchange for promises to find steady employment. The loans were never paid back and the promises never kept. For several years now Jonathan had been on Henry's 'list', which meant he received monthly cash handouts to keep him going. Before that he would disappear for months at a time, driving his mother mad with anxiety. Naturally she took it out on Henry.

Jonathan kept no fixed address. One entire winter he'd slept in that old Ford of his parked on the streets of New York City. Back home he came in spring like a stray cat, broke, with a carload of mouldy laundry. He dressed in front of the washing machine, made a pass at the new maid, and created such chaos the staff threatened to quit.

Henry had been told that Jonathan 'worked' upper Madison Avenue in the mornings, Lexington in the afternoons, looking for someone to marry. (Immediately eliminating those who showed interest.) He instinctively shunned any girl introduced by his mother or friends. He liked them of his own choosing – strangers drawn to him without knowledge of his background. Jonathan described himself as a romantic, believing in love at first sight. He was convinced he'd meet the girl of his dreams in some chance encounter. In anticipation of this he'd taken out a life insurance policy to benefit his wife-to-be. It mystified Henry how Jonathan could attract anyone going around with his shirt-tails hanging out, tie yanked open and shoelaces undone. Nonetheless, Jonathan surprised him by bringing home women whom Henry found charming. Despite his exhausting life-style Jonathan had kept his boyish, blond, blue-eyed good looks. If less fit, he didn't look much older than when he was captain of the hockey team at Princeton.

'Jonathan, stop chewing that cigar and eat your roast beef,' Granny scolded in her nursery voice. 'Let's not fight during Sunday lunch. Believe me, Ben Bradshaw's not worth it.'

'May I quote you on that, Granny?' Walter Harrison, Henry's son, walked in through the pantry door, eating an apple. He was wearing tennis clothes. 'Happy Fourth of July, Johnny. The yacht club's buzzing with the news about Ben.' He sank into an empty chair. 'Or rather about his boat.'

Granny and Bea exchanged desperate looks. Would the speculation start all over again, making them the target of gossip on Martha's Vineyard? Had Ben skipped out on his family? Why did he have so much money on board? What about the debts he left behind? Why was the Coast Guard unable to find a single scrap of Ben's sixty-foot yacht? Was the *Pelican* hijacked by dope runners or gun smugglers? Was Ben really dead? In addition to all the other things people had said when Ben Bradshaw disappeared, it was rumoured that Bea had had a nervous breakdown. Henry looked at her with concern. He worshipped her and had never left her bedside when she was ill.

Jonathan stared at his step-brother in consternation. 'Jesus, Walt, you waltz in with that smug Wall Street smile on your face when you know perfectly well the *Titanic's* sinking in here. Don't you have any compassion?'

'No more compassion than you showed last night. That 'losers' convention' of yours kept the kids awake until dawn. What kind of circus are you running? Naked dancing by the driftwood fire, beercans flying from the guest house windows, cars arriving at all hours of the night . . .' Walt filled his wine glass.

Henry groaned. Jonathan looked at his stepfather apprehensively. 'Take it easy, Walt, take it easy. It's Fourth of July weekend, isn't it? Americans are supposed to be celebrating the independence of their country. Dancing and drinking beer are accepted forms of celebrating.'

'I appreciate your patriotism, Johnny, but we are not amused when little Walt says he found Uncle John and a girl rolling around naked on the beach this morning.'

Henry sank lower in his chair. Jonathan forced a cough. 'Come on, Walt. You know how kids exaggerate.'

'Don't ruin Sunday lunch, Walt,' Granny snapped. 'Jonathan's entitled to a little fun.'

'I see you've got Dad all worked up. He still has his golf hat on.' Walt winked at Jonathan as Henry removed the hat.

'Jonathan's determined to go looking for his father,' Bea sighed. Her bright green dress made her look younger, too. Her face was lightly freckled, and her blond hair was pulled back like a girl's. If somewhat weathered, Bea was considered a beauty, even now.

'Great – I can use the guest house for Labor Day weekend.'

'Walt, this is *serious*. It could be dangerous chasing Ben's ghost.' Granny's face was getting red.

Walt laughed. 'No more dangerous than sleeping in a car in New York City. So when do we leave on this great adventure?'

'Today.'

Granny and Bea gasped. 'You're not leaving today and that's that.' Bea was trying to get her composure back, but tears glistened at the corners of her eyes. Normally in moments of crisis Bea retreated upstairs, where she could stretch out on the heart-shaped cushions and weep. Today she seemed determined to stand her ground. She put her hand to her heart. 'Please don't do this to us.'

'By the way, who's going to pay for this little expedition?' Walt asked. 'Sounds expensive.'

'I will, like always,' Henry muttered.

Jonathan looked with astonishment at his step-father. 'Henry, I just told you I'm selling the Lincoln letter!'

'You mean you actually found that letter that's been missing for a couple of years?' Walt asked.

'Tilly found it.' Henry refilled his glass. 'When she threw out those damned papers of Jonathan. We had three bedrooms full of yellow legal pads and they were driving us out of the house.'

'Henry!' Jonathan put his head in his hands in exasperation. 'That's my *novel* you're talking about.'

'By novel,' Walt asked cynically, 'do you mean that mountain of worthless stock certificates, eviction notices, betting stubs, food stamps, bounced cheques, telephone bills and parking tickets going back ten years?'

Jonathan blinked several times, trying to bring Walt into focus. 'You know perfectly well my novel is my life. Look at Tolstoy. Weren't the little bits of paper in Tolstoy's briefcase important?' Jonathan forced a cough. 'Do you think Tolstoy's family came to him and said, "Look here, Leo, we've got to clean out your desk"? Written on the back of one of those parking tickets might be an idea that will win the Nobel Prize. I told Tilly to leave everything alone.'

'Don't complain about Tilly.' Bea said. 'She just ironed forty-five of your shirts.'

'Don't complain about Tilly. She *works* for a living,' Henry said.

'Jesus, Henry, you just threw away my life! *My life*. Doesn't a person's *life* mean anything to you?'

'You're throwing away your own life if you ask me.'

'Nobody asked you, Walt,' Granny snorted.

During the ensuing argument, Henry sat quietly and tried to breathe slowly and deeply, as the doctor advised. The steel band around his head was tight now. Maybe those rooms full of papers really were Jonathan's novel. With him anything was possible.

For example, Jonathan was a celebrity, of sorts. Through a chance, late-night encounter in a bar with a drunken female TV producer, whom he had impressed with his 'alarming sense of reality', Jonathan had been invited to appear on the Johnny Carson show. For an hour one Monday night he amused New Yorkers with tales of how to sneak into the Grosvenor, the Brasilian, and other big charity balls. On one occasion he took with him twenty friends, including one congressman, all properly attired in black tie. He revealed which art galleries and museums gave the best food and free drinks on opening nights and how to get in uninvited. He discussed plans to open a smart decorating shop he would stock with the discarded rubbish he'd collected off the sidewalks of Madison and Park. Torn Chesterfield couches, expensive chopping blocks, damaged Chippendale. He described how he succeeded in picking up socialites in the Holland tunnel during rush hour. Invariably they were on their way to some exclusive party where he would subsequently appear. Jonathan had become a fixture at many of the most chic occasions of the year. He turned up at Norman Mailer's or Sargent Shriver's. Henry wouldn't be surprised if he turned up at the White House one day.

The hit of Jonathan's TV appearance had been his blueprint for a Meaning of Life Conference to be held on Granny's farm in New Jersey. Immediately following the programme NBC's switchboard had been swamped with calls. Jonathan's idea created such a stir among New Yorkers that the Mayor got involved and announced he wanted the conference to take place in Central Park. The Mayor and the Governor of New Jersey (both friends of Henry) subsequently became embroiled in a public wrangle over where the conference ought to be held. An avalanche of mail drove the family berserk. Jonathan finally backed out because he'd lost control of his idea, and the conference was called off. But he became an instant celebrity. He still signed autographs in singles bars. A rival publisher of Henry advanced him fifteen hundred dollars to write *A Freeloader's Guide to New York*. He spent the money but never wrote the book.

Granny cleared her throat. 'Jonathan, please don't do this to us. It could be dangerous and foolish. For years we've believed something terrible happened to Ben, and it could happen to you, too. Worse. Your father always courted disaster. If he's alive today I guarantee there'll be a mess.'

Jonathan's cigar ashed on the tablecloth. His mother groaned as he swept it away with his hand, leaving a grey smudge. 'So you all think I'm following in his footsteps, do you? You think my life's a mess!'

'We don't mean that,' Bea pleaded. She still prayed for a miracle that he'd get married and pull his life together. 'I wish you'd never quit your job. You only quit because we were happy.'

'I quit because your millionaire friends were slapping me on the back on New Year's Day because I got a temporary job at Brooks Brothers. You would have thought I'd just returned from planting the flag on the moon.'

'They wanted to congratulate you . . .'

'That's why I quit! Because you were crying with joy when Brooks Brothers asked me to stay on for the January sale and because all those bank presidents and industrialists were so *sincere*. My father was captain of the Princeton tennis team. My grandfather was an admiral. My great, great grandfather was a general in the Union army and a friend of Abraham Lincoln, and the Chairman of the Board of I.B.M. was wishing me luck selling ties and underwear at Brooks Brothers. That's why I quit. *Your* tears of happiness and *their* sincerity threatened me with *total loss of self respect!*'

'Johnny . . .' Bea's voice softened as she wiped away the tears. 'I know what you're trying to do, but look at it from my point of view.' She glanced at Henry slumped in his chair. '*Our* point of view. If your father's alive, I don't want to know. If he left us, I don't want to know why. I don't want to think about Ben Bradshaw because we've suffered enough. We have new lives and we don't want to know. For five years every time the phone rang I thought it was Ben. That's over now. Pain and time have deadened all my feelings about him. He means nothing to me now. He's just a bad memory I wish I could forget.'

'Jonathan, let the insurance company handle this.' Henry supported Bea in his most sober man-to-man voice. 'I'll speak to Senator Hollenberg about it. Maybe the State Department can help. We're already going to have to deal with the insurance company over the boat. Leave this to the lawyers. If you bring your father back, someone's going to have to pay back his life insurance, and it won't be me.'

Walt put his elbows on the table and leaned toward Jonathan. 'Let's face it, Johnny, nobody's ever known for sure whether

Ben's dead or alive. Now that the *Pelican* has been found, let's say he's a little less dead than he was before. Dead or alive, he left a mess behind. And it's typical of you, who refuses to work for a living, who sponges off Henry's generosity, to make people even more worried by threatening to go off and search for your father. I know what's driving you to do this. You view this as a mission that will somehow absolve you of the mess you've made of your life.'

Jonathan plunged the cigar into his mouth and stared at them all. 'None of you think he's dead, do you?' He pushed his chair away from the table. 'All these years you've been afraid he's alive! You've never given him credit for being anything but a bastard.'

'Why should we?' Walt asked blandly. 'I thought everyone agreed on that subject at least.'

'All my life, I've never heard a good word spoken about my father. You only remember the bad things.' Jonathan searched his mother's and grandmother's faces. 'He was a war hero, wasn't he? He came home with a purple heart.'

Walt threw back his head and laughed. 'Some purple heart. Wounded in action, all right. You know what kind of action?'

'Walt!' Bea exploded. 'Stop it!'

'The day after Manila was liberated, he threw a cocktail party in his hotel room. He was standing in the window with a martini in his hand and got hit by a stray sniper bullet.' Walt laughed again. 'Some hero. He only got the medal because his father was an admiral.'

'Hush up, Walt. This isn't your affair.' Granny's face was trembling with rage.

'Well, he wanted to know the truth.'

'Not from you!'

For a minute everybody stared back and forth between the step-brothers with varying degrees of horror and pity.

Suddenly Walt jumped to his feet.

'I hope he's *alive!* I hope you find him, Johnny, and bring him back. He can tell his old buddies down at the club how he bilked the insurance company out of a million dollars. Good old Henry'll cave in and pay it back, won't you, Dad? What's another million to you? After all, you married his wife even before he was pro-nounced officially dead. Maybe you can set him up in business. Publish his memoirs! Oh no, I've got it! He can be master of ceremonies at the Meaning of Life Conference! Good luck, Johnny! Good hunting. Bring 'im back alive! What's another nightmare to this family?'

Everyone remained frozen in his chair as Walt stomped from the room.

'I better go talk to him,' Henry said wearily and followed him out.

The tension immediately lifted. Bea put her hand over Jonathan's. He sat speechless, staring at the tablecloth, trying to understand Walt's attack on his father. Bea was listening like an Indian to the noises from outside – Walt's tantrum and Henry's low ineffectual drone.

A conspiratorial grin spread over Granny's face, and she winked at Jonathan. 'Who does that self-satisfied Walter Harrison think he is? Anyone who jogs thirteen miles a day has got to be a nut.'

'Mother, please don't make things worse!'

'I should have crushed him like a bug!' Granny said.

'Who, mother?' Bea's voice expressed alarm. She and Jonathan looked in amazement at Granny, who was grinding her thumb into the top of the table.

'Ben Bradshaw – that's who! A chain of diet clinics for rich dogs! Snail farms in Florida! Chick peas for the starving Egyptians! Underwater 3-D photography! Pre-Columbian art from Mexico! One reckless irresponsible scheme after another. He's been a knife in my stomach for forty years! I couldn't forgive him when he was dead! I certainly won't forgive him now if he's alive. He's come back from the grave to cause us more trouble. You listen to me, Jonathan.' She pointed a finger at her grandson. 'Do you want to know what kind of man your father was?'

The old lady, whose complexion was normally a soft pink colour, had again gone bright red in the face. 'The audacity of that man! In good faith he persuaded me to invest in his real estate venture – a big sum of money. And my lawyers discovered it was to start a summer camp for lesbians in upstate New York!'

Bea laughed. 'But, mother, it was only a joke.'

'You may think it's funny, but we don't.' Granny appealed to Henry who had just reappeared, looking disgusted. 'I swear Ben was handing out brochures on the streets of New York. He and some women who looked like football players. They were going to have guard dogs and towers to keep away the press.'

Henry shook his head and crumpled into a chair – a despondent sight in madras trousers and a red golf shirt.

'I'm telling you – I've made up my mind,' Jonathan said. 'If Dad's alive I want to see him. If he's dead I want to know what happened. I'm leaving.'

'I can't stand any more of this!' Henry ran from the room. The screen door slammed. Jonathan hurried with his mother and grandmother onto the porch, where they watched Henry dash headlong across the beach and plunge into the ocean with all his clothes on.

'*Now* you've done it,' Bea said.

Jonathan went to the guest house and began packing his suitcase. His mother sat by the window and cried.

'Don't you see how you're upsetting everybody? Look at your poor stepfather out there. He's completely distraught, and our lives are in turmoil again.'

'I don't want to ruin your life with Henry.'

'That's exactly what you're doing. Your insistence on going through with this.'

'I don't want to threaten him any more than he already is, but everyone's going to feel threatened until we find out the truth.'

'I wish that boat had never turned up.' Bea regarded her son sadly. 'Jonathan, if your father's alive, then all the rumours are true. He deserted us and cheated the insurance company. He didn't want anything to do with us then – what makes you think he wants to see you now? You stopped being his son twenty-five years ago.'

'I thought he got shot while he was leading a patrol behind Japanese lines.'

'Granny and I wanted to protect you. We didn't want to ruin all your memories. It's true, it seems we only remember the bad things. There were good things, too . . .'

The wind hissed through the window screen. Jonathan was folding his jacket and said nothing.

'That's not the way to pack a suit.' His mother, in resignation, dried her eyes. 'Let me do it.'

He tried to stop her, but it was too late. Lifting the jacket from the suitcase, she discovered the revolver.

'Oh my God, a gun! Mother, he's got a gun!' But Granny was

too far away, coaxing Henry from the waves. 'You're not taking *that!*' She tried to grab the revolver, but Jonathan slammed the suitcase shut. Clutching the jacket, she shoved Jonathan onto the bed. She tried to punch him but missed. The power of his mother's fury alarmed him. Her eyes were shining and fierce. 'What are you going to do with that gun?' she demanded. He ripped the jacket from her and her anger abruptly subsided. She seemed stunned and sat heavily on the bed. 'Oh my God, don't take a gun . . .'

Jonathan grabbed the suitcase and ran for the car. He drove to the dock, arriving just in time to leap aboard the departing ferry. His mother and Granny followed in the station wagon, kicking up a cloud of dust as they raced after him. As the ferry cleared the breakwater and headed out to sea he could still see them on the dock – a pink blob and a green blob hanging onto one another and waving frantically. Their cries, carried by the wind, were lost in the rush of waves.

2

Puerto Gusano

The light notes of a marimba mingled with the odour of cookfires borne upon the air from the shore, and by degrees the freighter swung around into the breeze.

Jonathan Bradshaw passed his suitcases down to the waiting boatman. He then stepped into the canoe, which tipped dangerously with each movement.

'Tread lightly on my boat, stranger,' said the boatman in Spanish. He was a black man of colossal build. He was naked to the waist and wore only a pair of shorts.

Pushing off from the ship, he inserted a long tapering oar into a chock in the stern. Standing erect and using an easy sculling motion, he propelled the canoe noiselessly away.

A vast hush prevailed over the water. Except for a pair of lateen sails and solitary fishing canoes that might have been floating logs, the sea was vacant. A flight of egrets in ragged undulating V formation was etched against the towering banks of pink cumulus piling up on the horizon.

As he scanned the shore, Jonathan's fingers tapped the shiny black wood from which the canoe had been fashioned. Beyond the jetties and fringe of beach he made out the shapes of houses half hidden among the thick foliage and palm trees. The twin belfries of a church drew down a swirl of vultures. On a sandy hook of land opposite the town stood the high towers and gleaming storage tanks of an oil refinery. Great gouts of flame shot up into the evening sky and were reflected on the oily waters of the bay.

This was it. Jonathan nervously lit a cigar. There was no turning back now. The family was undoubtedly pulling every string to locate him, but it was unlikely that Senator Hollenberg or even the State Department could track him to this forgotten banana port in South America.

Two weeks had passed since the uproar. The family hated unpleasantness at Sunday lunch. Jonathan smiled although nothing had been funny that day. Nothing that is except the last glimpse he'd had of his mother and grandmother in their pink and green flowered dresses. They were holding onto their floppy sunhats for dear life as they chased him top speed onto the dock at Vineyard Haven. The ferry was just pulling out.

'Johnny – Johnny!' they'd shouted in unison, jumping out of the car. 'Where are you going?' They still couldn't believe he was leaving. 'Tell us where you're going! Tell us where you're going!' They were running along the docks as the ferry picked up speed.

'To look for Dad!' he'd called from the rail. 'To find out whether he's dead or alive!'

The ferry was heading out to sea. The pink and green blobs on the dock were growing smaller.

'But where –*where?*' Their voices were nearly indistinguishable from the plaintive cries of the seagulls that floated above the ferry's wake.

'Panama! South America! Who knows where? *China!*'

He could almost see their mouths drop open. *'China?'*

Jonathan's reverie was shattered by the shrill whine of a machine drill. The canoe was gliding beneath the solemn grey cylinders of the refinery.

'Hey!' he said to the boatman. 'I thought this was going to be a tropical paradise.'

The boatman pointed at the sky. 'Paradise there, not here.'

Jonathan stared at the storage tanks and leaping flames. 'No-no-*no!* This is supposed to be a typical jungle Shangri-la where men flee to embrace nature, native girls and rum bottles. This place looks like . . . the New Jersey industrial zone, with *vultures.* Hasn't anyone around here heard of ecology?'

The sun set abruptly and the water, which a minute before had been coloured a milky green, turned black. The tropical night came on with a rush, and the boatman began to use his oar as a pole. The water was full of phosphorous, and jumping fish made shimmering splash marks. Bottom animals swirled beneath the surface, leaving eddying chains of luminous beads.

An ancient pier loomed in the darkness. Propelled by a sluggish wave laden with seaweed, the canoe glided past the hulk of a half-sunken lighter, with barnacles and weed clotting about the deck machinery, and bumped against a piling. From the outline of a dilapidated steam winch, loading booms canted at crazy angles into the water. An old boiler lay on its side, and coils of rusty cable webbed the oily deck. The air was warm and moist and permeated by the rank odour of creosote and iodine and decaying vegetation.

Jonathan reached up, found a handhold and pulled himself onto the pier. The boatman handed up the suitcases.

A few feet away a match was struck and a candle glowed.

'Well, *well!* Look who's here! We haven't seen one of your kind around here in a long time!'

Swathed in yards of Java print, a large and very handsome black woman was seated on the pier. Piles of shiny fruit ranged about her gleamed dully in the candlelight.

'Excuse me, *señora,*' Jonathan forced a cough. His Spanish was a little rusty; he hadn't used it since the Peace Corps. 'Can you please tell me how much I owe this guy? He doesn't talk much.'

'How about a coconut, boss? Very fresh, very nice.'

'*Gracias.* I'm sure they are. Listen, *señora,* what's the local currency? All I've got are dollars.'

'Mm!' She smacked her lips. 'All Mister Gentlemen got is *dollars!* Ripe avocados? – black man's butter.'

'Can a white man eat it, too?' Jonathan dug into his pocket and produced a bank note. 'How about five dollars – will that do?'

The woman stared at the bill. For a second he feared she might try to snatch it from him.

'Hey! For the boatman, I mean!' He rushed to the edge of the pier and looked down. '*Señora,* what's the fare?'

'I got toothsome pineapples, limes and lychees, mangoes and passion fruit – they're mighty juicy.'

'Thanks, but I had my dinner aboard ship . . . Hey, he's gone!'

'And I got cocos and oranges, guavas and cashew fruit. You like bananas – yellow, green or red? How about a bunch of bananas?'

'Listen, *señora,* the boatman's departed. Doesn't he want to be paid?'

'Take a mango, boss. Come on and try it!'

'I don't want to seem ungrateful, but my stomach's full.'

'Well, ain't you a lucky one.'

Fearing that he had offended her, Jonathan patted her arm. 'Back in New York I used to live with a girl who went on a mango diet. Ha ha. It sort of put me off them.'

The woman heaved herself to her feet. With the material

rustling around her as she moved, she came forward and held up
the candle and smiled. She had perfect white teeth and sculpted
lips the colour of aubergine. High, swelling cheekbones gave her
an oriental look. She exuded the odour of orange juice and pipe
tobacco.

'My oh my, you *are* a sight for sore eyes. Look at that pretty
white shirt and the necktie and everything complete. Why don't
you tuck in your shirttails and look neat?' She was fingering his
lapels. 'Don't you know we've been waiting a long time for you to
come back?'

'No, no, come on – you must be mistaking me for someone else.
I've never been here before. I used to raise chickens in Bolivia.
Some people think that I look a lot like Jack Kennedy. Maybe I
remind you of him.'

'You look kind of familiar.' She was gazing into his eyes and
looking him up and down. 'You sure this is your first trip out?'
She was gently patting his chest. She was even stroking it. It felt
good. Jonathan suddenly experienced a wave of warm feelings
for her.

'Sure is a pretty suit, boss.'

'It's an old suit that belonged to my father. I wore it because . . .
white is supposed to reflect the heat.'

'Maybe it does, but if you feel uncomfortable, you can always
take off your shoes and strip down to your drawers like sensible
folk. Ha ha.'

'If I don't go around in my drawers, will people think I'm not
sensible?' Jonathan held up a pair of boots he'd been carrying. 'As
a matter of fact . . .'

'Boss!' she exclaimed and roared with laughter. 'What kind of
shoes are those?'

'Hey, take it easy. These are combat boots. What's so funny
about combat boots? My father wore them when he parachuted
behind Japanese lines in the Philippines. I thought they might
come in handy down here.'

'Uh huh.'

'So, anyway, I think I'll put them back on now.'

'Good idea. This old deck's full of splinters, and I know you
white folks don't like to get splinters in your feet.'

'Do black folks *like* to get splinters in their feet?'

'If the feet are tough, they don't feel the splinters, but from the looks of yours . . .' She lowered the candle and was inspecting Jonathan's feet, which were very white. 'Each little splinter is going to make 'em mighty sore.'

'Wait a minute, don't do that! A woman's not supposed to look at a strange man's feet like that.'

While Jonathan was lacing up his boots, she turned to her pile of fruit and selected an avocado. A machete blade flashed in the candle light.

With a deft stroke she halved the fruit and popped out the pit, which bounced off the pier and landed in the water with a splash of phosphorous. She squeezed the avocado, and the ripe fruit, whole in two parts, jumped out of the skin. She handed them to Jonathan resting on the skin.

'Eat it, boss, it's good. That way you won't get your fingers sticky.'

She picked up a coconut. Twirling and bouncing it in one hand until she had a firm grip, she whacked off the top with a few swift machete strokes. She handed it to Jonathan and made him drink. When he'd finished, she cracked it open and showed him how to scrape out the jellyish meat with a sliver of husk.

'Is it good, boss?'

'We could make a fortune in New York. I know a place in the Village that specializes in Piña Coladas. With you standing behind the bar lopping off the tops of coconuts with that machete . . .'

'When sailors hit the shore, they go for the fruit.'

'My father was a sailor, not me.'

She took the broken husk from him and tossed it away into the night. It landed in an explosion of phosphorous.

'No, I can see you ain't . . . but if you ain't . . .' She held up the candle again. 'What are you?'

'By profession you mean? I'm self-employed. My stepfather would say unemployed. I don't have an occupation but my pre-occupation is tragedy.'

'Never heard of that kind of business, boss.'

'My stepfather thinks I'm a no good bum because I don't go off to an office every day. To him tragedy is when you don't have a job. What he can't understand is that for me tragedy *is* a full-time job. I've been too busy worrying about my life to work.'

She looked confused. 'Tragedy . . . can you make a decent wage off it?'

'My family wishes I could.'

She laughed. 'I hope you didn't come all this way looking for work, did you?'

'No, I'm not job hunting.'

'Because there ain't no work around here since Peaceful Banana pulled out.'

'I've come looking for my father. In Panama I learned he might have been here at one time. He was connected with that banana company you were just talking about.' Jonathan sucked in his breath and forced a smile. 'His name is Ben Bradshaw – ever heard of him?'

'Lord – you Ben Bradshaw's son?' She grabbed him by the shoulders. 'Let me have a look at you.' She made him turn around, planted a kiss on his cheek and laughed. 'I thought you looked familiar. I'm Bertha.'

'You know him!' Jonathan vigorously pumped her hand. 'For twenty-five years no one's known anything about my father. We even had his *funeral!*' He was jubilant. 'I've barely lifted my *foot* from the *boat* when the *first* person I meet on the dock *knows* him. It's like *War and Peace* ending on the first page! Jesus Christ! I thought I'd have to spend years hacking my way through a tropical rain forest, living off the last remnants of civilization . . . All these years we thought he was *dead.*'

'Dead? Not that I know of. I reckon he's still alive . . .' she answered doubtfully. 'Can't say for sure.'

'Wait a minute. A man is either dead or alive. There's nothing in between. Or is there?'

'I haven't seen him in a long time. I haven't heard he's dead – so . . . he must be alive.'

'That's a strange way to conclude a man lives . . . so anyway, is he here?'

'Oh, if he's alive he must be here . . .'

'He's here!' Jonathan tucked in his shirttails. 'Let's-get-*going!* Can you take me to him? Jesus Christ!'

'. . . and yet he ain't exactly here either.'

'Well, a man can't be in more than one place at a time, or can he? Where is he?'

'In the swamp.'

'What's he doing in a goddamn swamp?'

'That's where he lives.'

'Is he being held forcibly, or does he live there by his own will?'

'Oh, I guess he's made his own choice.'

'Look, where's this swamp?'

'Where the town ends, the swamp begins.'

'Well, that can't be far away. Can we go there now?'

'We can go, but you won't find your daddy.'

'Why not?'

'The swamp is big, that's why.'

Jonathan stood with both hands in his pockets, nervously jangling change as he talked. 'Wait a minute.' His brow furrowed as he tried to think. 'What is he, a recluse? Or is he in hiding?'

Bertha was hastily gathering up her fruit. 'Grab those suitcases and I'll take you to someone who'll tell you everything you want to know.'

'Maybe I should see the police . . .'

'That's exactly who you're going to see.'

She placed the fruit in the basket, blew out the candle and balanced the basket on her head. 'Come on.' She led the way. 'First of all we'll get you settled and taken care of.'

'Thanks, Bertha. I can hardly believe it! But I'm worried, too. This is beginning to sound too easy . . .'

'What did you think – that folks wouldn't look after Ben Bradshaw's son?'

'I mean, I could hardly expect this kind of reception – to learn immediately he's alive. You know I haven't seen him since August 13th, 1956, the day he pulled up anchor in Vineyard Haven. We thought he was just sailing down to Florida for repairs and a winter berth, but he never came back.' Jonathan trotted along at Bertha's heels, chattering away. 'The hurricane season was coming on and everybody thought the boat was sunk in a storm and my father drowned. There was a search, but his body was never recovered and not a scrap of the boat was ever found.'

Bertha turned around to answer, and Jonathan, who had been following right behind, bumped into her.

'Sorry.'

'Nothing wrong with that boat when it came in here. One morning we opened our eyes, and there it was, floating like a dream in the harbour. Nobody around here had ever seen the likes of it before. Or your handsome daddy. No sir. That's the day I'll never forget.' She pinched his hip. 'You got good-looking legs like your daddy?'

'Hey, take it easy! So anyway, where was I? It took seven years before he was declared officially dead. Even then nobody was sure. People insisted the boat must have been hijacked by dope smugglers or gun-runners from Cuba and my father murdered. Other people said, 'No' – he'd deliberately run away to start a new life. There was talk about his affairs – business and women. My mother and grandmother were miserable for years, and I guess I never got over it. The tears, the humiliation, the prayers, and he's been here the whole time.'

At the end of the pier they passed beneath a sign nailed to a palm tree. It was feebly illuminated by a single naked light bulb. Jonathan stopped and frowned as he read:

> GUSANEROS
> Your town welcomes you.
> STRANGERS
> Puerto Gusano welcomes you.
> Please register with the police.
> Beware of brazen thieves, pickpockets,
> beggars, prostitutes, 'official guides', etc.
> Do not feed stray dogs. They may have rabies.
> Taking photographs of crippled children
> and dead bodies floating is strictly
> forbidden.
> Do not wander beyond the town limits.
> In case of difficulty consult the
> Chief of Police.

'Hey, Bertha, come back here! This place makes Spanish Harlem sound tame. What kind of town is this with . . . *dead bodies floating?*' Jonathan punched a button on his digital watch. Bertha gaped as the red numerals appeared. 'I'm doing this to remind myself that I'm still living in the space age.'

'You're a good boy to come looking for your daddy.'

Jonathan hurried to catch up. 'My mother doesn't think so.'

'She doesn't want him back?'

'No, she doesn't want to *know* . . . The memories are too painful. As far as she's concerned, he's *dead*, but I had to find out.'

They left the rotting pier and followed a path that wound among shanties erected on stilts, some on dry land, some over the water. By lantern light people could be seen lounging in hammocks. Naked children rolled in the puddles and played hide-and-seek among the hibiscus bushes and palm trees. Mostly women were about, preparing the evening meal. The lilting voices of the native girls, as they conversed from house to house with much laughter interspersed, lent an air of carefree gaity to the scene, the poverty of their dwellings notwithstanding. The sea lapped easily against the shore, and the smell of woodsmoke wafted on the breeze.

'Now *this* is more like it.'

'More like what?'

'More like the tropical paradise I'd imagined my father might be living in,' Jonathan said.

'If you call being poor paradise you've never been poor. But it was more of one before your daddy came.'

'What do you mean by that?'

She gestured disdainfully in the direction of the refinery flares. 'I mean before they built Santa Petrolina.'

'I was going to ask you about that . . . Hey, Bertha – wait.'

Crossing a bridge over a canal, they entered town by a dusty, poorly lit street, where crowds of small children milled in the reddish gloom. Sugar cane vendors loudly hawked their wares. Monkey vendors, parrot vendors and a vendor of ibises displayed sad animals as they went past. Beggars and shoeshine boys circulated in the mob and waited outside cafés, where the dark-skinned, straw-hatted male population drank beer from large green bottles.

Jonathan was suddenly besieged by a group of urchins who seized his suitcases. A tug-of-war ensued, with him in the middle trying to hold onto both bags at once. The struggle raised a cloud of dust.

'They only want to carry them for you, boss!'

'Oh sorry. Go ahead, kids.' He turned to his guide. 'I thought they were the brazen thieves the sign mentioned!'

The children had begun to fight among themselves over who would carry the suitcases. As Jonathan was attempting to arbitrate, a painted lady surged forward and blocked his way. She was tattooed all over and displayed two rows of silver teeth. Hissing and sucking, she grabbed his arm and pointed to a little doorway he hadn't noticed before. But Bertha stepped between them and sent the whore scampering away to the raucous laughter of the others.

Jonathan was examining the red marks on his wrist. 'Bertha, you better tell them to add 'beware of tattooed women' to that sign. She sunk her nails right into me. I hope *she* doesn't have rabies.'

The children were still kicking and punching one another for the right to carry the suitcases. Jonathan made no further attempt to intervene. He stepped back and let the big ones win.

'Hey, meester!' Leading a mangy anteater by a string, a grinning street photographer ran up to Jonathan. 'Have your photo taken with this wild animal!'

'That wild animal needs a wheelchair.'

The grin faded. 'Only cost five cents, *señor*.'

The man's sinking spirits moved Jonathan. 'OK, OK – later,' he promised.

'Later?' The grin reappeared. 'OK! Good! That's great! See you later! Wow!' He skipped away dragging the anteater. 'He wants me to take his picture *later!*' he shouted to everyone in the street.

Jonathan watched him go. 'Someone ought to put that poor anteater out of its misery.'

'Your daddy brought it here on his boat. It used to have a long bushy tail like a feather.'

Jonathan looked incredulously at the animal. 'My father had an *anteater* on his boat? Why?' he asked, running after her.

Turning down a side street, Bertha pushed through swinging doors beneath a sign which read HOTEL PARADISE. They found themselves in a bare entrance hall illuminated by a single neon tube around which a swarm of insects danced and died. The sole piece of furniture was an ancient rolltop desk where a Chinaman sat, doing accounts on an abacus.

Bertha lowered the basket of fruit from her head and set it down. 'Foo – got a room for Mr Gentleman here? This is Ben Bradshaw's son!'

'Great to meet you, Mr Foo.' Jonathan extended his hand. 'There's a Foo's restaurant on Madison and 93rd Street – any relation?'

The Chinaman looked up, removed his spectacles, squinted, and slowly got to his feet. He was a correct and dignified old fellow, the colour of old linen. He bowed over his abacus. 'Very great honour, sir.' His hairless scalp appeared almost translucent. A few hairs were still growing – sparsely, as reeds will stand in water. He still took the trouble to comb them. The freckles on the top of his head floated like islands on a saffron-coloured pond. 'Your father, here . . .' He touched his heart. 'We keep loving memory . . .'

'Loving memory?' Jonathan turned a worried face to Bertha. 'He's not *dead*, is he?

Bertha shook her head. 'He just means we remember and miss him. Your daddy used to be Foo's number one customer.'

'Is that right?'

Ben Bradshaw had been in this very hotel; Bertha and Foo were his friends; to them he was flesh and blood, not just a memory. As Jonathan stood there trying to absorb all these facts, he looked down and spotted a skinny arm slither under the swinging door and grope about near his feet. The hand found his suitcase handle; slowly and cautiously it began to drag the suitcase out the door. Jonathan raised his foot and placed it gently but firmly on the arm, pinning it to the floor.

'Oh! Ouch!'

'Hey, buddy.' Jonathan addressed the terrified face of a young boy that appeared beneath the door. 'I think you made a mistake. That's *my* suitcase.'

Jonathan lifted his foot and pulled the boy to his feet. His matchstick legs were engulfed in a pair of voluminous khaki shorts. His chest was bare and his head had been recently shaved.

'You don't want to steal *that* suitcase, *amigo*.'

'No, *señor*, no!' The boy shook his head emphatically.

'Do you know what's in that suitcase?' Jonathan asked.

The boy was expecting to be thrashed. His dark eyes registered the anticipated hurt. His breath came and went in short, wet pants.

'That suitcase is filled with one hundred dollar bills, USA.'

The boy stared at the suitcase. Bertha and Foo moved in closer. For a moment it seemed that all three might dive for it.

'With that much money you'd probably fly down to Rio and spend it all on fast women.' Jonathan patted the boy's shoulder. 'I'm saving you from a bad sunburn and maybe a hangover.'

Jonathan looked expectantly from the boy to Bertha to Foo, but no one laughed. No one moved or breathed.

'Hey, take it easy, everybody. I'm just joking.'

Bertha began to fan herself. 'Boss, don't joke about money. Not in this town.'

'What is this – a town without a sense of humour?'

No one laughed. They couldn't take their eyes off the suitcase.

'Look – calm down, everybody. There's nothing but old clothes and bug spray in there. I'll show you if you don't believe me.'

The boy glared suspiciously at Jonathan.

'Hey, I didn't mean to disappoint you.' Jonathan fumbled in his pocket. 'How about a cigar?'

The boy held out his hand. Bertha slapped it.

'*Sin verguenza!* You steal his suitcase and smoke his cigar?'

'*Sin verguenza?*' Jonathan laughed. 'Is that your name?' I never met anyone called "shameless" before.'

'That's not my name.'

'What is it?'

'El Ratero,' the boy muttered.

'That means pickpocket, boss.'

Jonathan extended his hand. 'Pleased to meet you. I'm Jonathan. If you're supposed to pick my pocket, why are you stealing my suitcases?'

'If you're supposed to be so rich, why are you so poor?' the boy answered back.

'What do you mean by that?'

'You, rich man with old clothes in your suitcase.'

'I'm probably poorer than you. I'm broke and out of work. At least you're self-employed, while I'm living on the last remnants at the bottom of the barrel. Maybe I can be your . . . assistant. What about it?'

El Ratero, whose coffee-coloured face bore an expression of permanent pout, laughed begrudgingly. 'Everybody from the US is rich,' he insisted.

'Not me.'

'I'm an orphan,' El Ratero announced plaintively. 'Here in Puerto Gusano we're all orphans.'

'I'm an orphan, too. I haven't seen my father in twenty-five years. I should fit right in, don't you think? Now, how about a job?'

'Can you shine shoes? Catch iguanas?'

'Everyone I've seen so far is barefoot. You wouldn't start me off in a bad job, would you? I haven't worked in ten years.'

El Ratero looked concerned. 'Ten years and no job?'

'See, you don't have it so bad. Look at me. My family's rich, there's a building at Princeton named for my great-great-grand-father, but I'm permanently out of work. I have to sleep in my car.'

'You have a car, I sleep in a tree.'

'What are you, a bat?'

El Ratero dropped his stern demeanour and let out a squeal of laughter.

'See – you're the lucky one,' Jonathan said. 'You can't get parking tickets in a tree. Now what about this job? I'm desperate.'

El Ratero thought for a minute. 'You can sell cardboard.'

'That sounds better.'

'A penny a kilo. Go to the dump in the morning and pick it out of the garbage.'

'I think I'd rather catch iguanas. How'd you get started?'

'I used to work for a man named Sam,' El Ratero mumbled. 'Scaring off vultures while he drank whiskey in the park. He never paid me. Then I picked the bananas that fell from the wagons . . . when I collected a bunch I sold them . . . 30 cents a day. I gave my money to friends for safe keeping, but they never gave it back. So I had to spend all my money on cigarettes and the film . . . Peaceful Banana left – no more wagons, no more bananas. At night I stay on my branch and smoke the weed to keep warm. If I win today – OK. If I lose today – OK.' He concluded his sad litany with a shrug.

'What about tomorrow?'

'No more slop time!' El Ratero blurted out. 'Tomorrow we're going to whip these river peasants into shape and make something out of this counterfeit paradise! More Bach and less bananas! More Proust and less pissing around! We've got the lungs of the earth right here in the Amazon, and we're going to let the rest of the world know about it!'

'Hey! What's this kid talking about?'

'He gets that from Mr Hak.'

'Who's Mr Hak?'

'The Chief of Police,' El Ratero retorted. 'He's wasted in this hick town.'

'Your daddy's friend, boss. He's the one to tell you about Ben

Bradshaw. El Ratero, this is Ben Bradshaw's son.'

'Ben Bradshaw's son? Ben Bradshaw's *impotent*.'

'What?' Jonathan shouted. 'My God! Jesus! I don't . . . how? What are you *talking* about? Who is this kid? I'm . . . *Ben Bradshaw's son!*'

'Hush up, Ratero. You don't know what you're talking about.'

'Benjamin Winchester Bradshaw. Superstar time.' El Ratero snapped his fingers in the air and performed a little dance step. 'Best looking man I ever saw! Zroom! Zroom!' He throttled the handlebars of an imaginary motorcycle. 'BMW 500! Capetown to Cairo!' He pretended to aim a rifle. 'Boom! Boom! Elephant fall! This wormhole is the closest thing to a home town he's ever known!'

Jonathan stood with his hands in his pockets, brow knitted, trying to piece together what the boy was saying.

'I travel two thousand miles looking for a man who's been missing twenty-five years and a fast-talking *sin verguenza* who lives in a tree tells me my own father's impotent! Where did you get that idea? How do you know about that motorcycle trip and the safari in Africa? What's a juvenile delinquent doing name-dropping? Proust and Bach?' He looked at El Ratero. 'You can't know my father – you're a child!'

'I may be a child, boss, but I've lopped off the fingers of a man with a machete.'

'Not my father's fingers, I hope.'

'Ben Bradshaw raised coffee and cannabis on a plantation near town. He told his man to set fire to the weed if the planes flew too low. His man panicked and set fire to the whole thing! Ah! Ha! Ha!'

'Shoo now, El Ratero! You've talked too much. Scram before I tell Mr Hak you tried to steal a suitcase belonging to Ben Bradshaw's son!'

'*Aujourd'hui*, Bradshaw!' The boy fled.

'What does he mean by that?'

'El Ratero don't know nothing, boss. He hears a lot of fancy languages from Mr Hak. He says things and doesn't know what they mean. Don't pay any attention.'

Foo led them upstairs to a large airy room, screened in on two sides. The bed was hung with mosquito netting. He pressed a button and an overhead fan began to revolve.

Bertha, hands on hips, was surveying the room. 'Very nice, Foo. He gave you the best room, boss.'

Jonathan put down his bags, and they stepped out onto the wooden balcony which ran around the hotel. One side overlooked the main street, leading to Cathedral Square. The twin bell towers of the church rose above the massive foliage of the mango trees which grew so thickly the church appeared to be located in a wood. Above the canopy of trees the brightly lit rim of a ferris wheel turned and stopped and turned again.

The swamp came right up to the back of the hotel. A solitary bulb illuminated a bridge. The oily waters of a canal gleamed with reflected light. The night rang with the voices of crickets and the plangent mewing of frogs. Far out on the horizon the towering pink thunderhead had turned ash white, like the face of a corpse, when the sun went down. The clouds were veined with silent lightning which, long after darkness fell, continued to flicker. The dark hulk of Jonathan's freighter stood alone in a pool of light. The blazing towers of the refinery lit up the night with lurid effect. Red smoke and flames were reflected in the windows of the houses. A pall of reddish mist hovered over the town. Jonathan sniffed the air and made a face. The breeze had shifted, bringing from the refinery a chemical stink.

In one corner of the balcony, from which one could look up and down main street and across town as well, stood an instrument mounted on a shiny metal tripod. Bertha removed the cover, revealing a modern and very powerful telescope. She was examining it closely but did not touch it.

'What's that for?' Jonathan wanted to know. 'Looks like you could see ants crawling on the surface of the moon through that thing.'

'Sometimes Mr Hak comes up here to sit and watch. This is the only three storey building in town. He can see all over from here. If one man comes down one street, and another man comes down another, and the men got hatred between them, Mr Hak can jump down quickly and stop the fight.'

'Who's this Mr Hak who keeps law and order through a telescope?'

Bertha grinned at Jonathan's ignorance. 'Mr Hak's the number one man around here. His family came from Europe five generations back.' A dreamy, wistful expression crossed her face, and she looked very pretty. 'He's special – you'll see. Right, Foo?'

'Oh, yes.' Foo nodded gleefully.

'The Chief of Police knows everything. He's the one who's going to tell you about your daddy.'

After Bertha and Foo had gone downstairs, Jonathan laid a suitcase on the bed and opened it. Out tumbled the revolver. He hid it beneath the mattress, and went downstairs, to discover that Bertha had gone.

'Hey, Mr Foo, is my father in danger? Is he in trouble? What's all this swamp business? Why do I have to go to the police? Has he become a disreputable type? What's the true story?'

'My English is badly, but I tell one story.' The memory of what he was about to say made the old man giggle. 'Your father organize race – very big race.'

'What kind of race? A horse race?'

'That's it – whores race.'

'What?'

'Whores race. All whores participate. Umberto's orders. Your father draw line across street with stick. Whores line up, all naked, down on hands and feet, ready to run like monkeys. Your father – he has candles from church and American cigarette lighter. Zippo. Many people watching, many petroleros – all drunk. Many bets. Whores drunk. Your father – he walk behind whores and light candles one by one. One candle up each whore's ass. Some grunt, some curse. They all ready to run but do not move until all candles lit. When all candles in place he holds up gun. Smith & Wesson .38. On your marrk . . . boom! Whores begin to run like monkeys. People cheer, people shout, but whores run too fast, and candles go out. All whores must return to the line. Father takes out Zippo and relights candles. On your marrk . . . boom! Whores run again but slow. First whore through Ricardo's door wins prize – a case of beer. Many bets, many judges. We had good time. Your father pay for all.'

'Now, *come on*, Mr Foo!' Jonathan shook his head in disbelief. 'You can't just casually tell me a horrible story like that about my father. That's *obscene*. That means that while my mother was lighting candles in church and praying for his soul, my father was down here lighting church candles and shoving them up whores' asses and making them race for beers! Jesus, if I'd told that story on the Johnny Carson show, they would have thrown me in jail.'

3
Cathedral Square

A few minutes later Jonathan was standing beneath a long white banner strung between lamp posts where main street entered Cathedral Square.

* * * * * * * * * * * * – BOYS – * * * * * * * * * * * *		
Were you born in	Your name will be put on the list in	You will be conscripted in
1967	1980	1981
1968	1981	1982
1969	1982	1983
* * * * * * SECURITY OF THE FATHERLAND * * * * * * RIGHT, HONOUR, AND RESPONSIBILITY OF EVERY CITIZEN		
* * * * * * * Register with Chief of Police * * * * * * *		

Small boys were hurling missiles up into the branches of the mango trees. Sticks and stones and mangoes were raining down. The boys scrambled after the green fruit bouncing along the sidewalk and fought over them under the wheels of passing wagons.

Ancient houses leaned out over the street. From balconies swung cages full of parrots, whose excited screams and answering calls reverberated among the fading pastel facades. In the street around Cathedral Square the evening promenade was in full flow. Dozens of noisy prostitutes were walking arm in arm. Their bright coloured toenails flashed over the mosaic sidewalk. Red, blue, orange, and mauve lights kicked and flashed across the uneven stone tiles where black mosaic fish jumped among black and white mosaic waves.

The appearance of Jonathan raised a cacophony of yells and catcalls. He came to a small plaza before the church where scruffy

adolescents and dirty little children were arranging beds for the
night. With fingers that seemed numb or drugged with fatigue
they were unrolling sheets of cardboard on the cobbles. Bundles
of rags and newspapers fastened with string served as their
pillows, and the foliage of the trees formed the roof above their
heads.

Although the doors stood open, the church looked abandoned
or closed. The cavernous entrance was obstructed by a huge,
crudely wrought metal grate whose lower portion was whitened
by wax that had cascaded from thousands of candles. Placed
in niches as high as the hand could reach, they were flickering like
so many little stars. A pitiful effort had been made to decorate the
ugly grate with bunches of flowers, coloured paper streamers,
and offerings of fruit.

Jonathan peered through the barricaded doorway. Within the
recesses of the church, a madonna was wreathed in cobwebs, and
the stone floor was dusty and littered with bits of desiccated fruit
and flower stalks.

Incense wafted from a censer attached to the grate and spread
across the square where the sleeping bodies lay. Above these
prostrate forms the ferris wheel turned and stopped and turned
again. At each stop two or three children climbed wearily down.
To Jonathan they looked exhausted; the ride on the ferris wheel
had failed to raise their spirits. Nevertheless, there was a long line
of glassy-eyed children waiting patiently to take their places.

Drawn up beside the church, a battered circus wagon had been
painted to resemble a lurid jungle scene swarming with gigantic
snakes. Hideously fanged, they seemed to be holding the old
wagon together by the constricting force of their coils. An equally
florid sign announced:

MISS BETTY Y SUS SERPIENTES BOA

The wagon door was flung open, and an ancient vendor of
lottery tickets appeared. Staggering from foot to foot, he came
down the steps and poked his way with a stick across the plaza
toward Jonathan.

'A million! A million! A million!' he cried.

It was a priest. Filthy and dressed in ragged habit with collar
askew, he held his arms out rigidly, like a scarecrow. The fluttering lottery tickets were attached to his sleeves and lapels with

clothes-pins. They adorned his chest like a row of coloured battle ribbons.

'A million! A million! A million!' His raspy voice was not unlike the wailing of frogs that inhabited the myriad canals.

The tip of his stick found the toe of Jonathan's boot. 'Who's this? A stranger! Whoever you may be, I have a feeling you're here to hurt us!'

'No, no! Padre, you've got it all wrong. I'd like to *help!*'

'Then buy a lottery ticket and contribute to the Children's Fund.' He waved his stick at the children bedding down on the pavement. 'For the sake of those whom life has cheated.'

Jonathan dug into his pocket and produced a bill. 'Say, what's happening here, padre? In Bolivia it would take an earthquake to close the church. And why are these children sleeping in the street? This looks like a playground in hell. Hey!'

The priest grabbed Jonathan's sleeve and dragged him between rows of sleeping children. 'Father Odorico, at your service! Since I have no other service!' He shrieked with laughter.

'Take it easy, padre. This is my father's suit. He had it made in Hong Kong right after the war.'

The girls were on one side, boys on the other. There was a semblance of order: the square looked like a makeshift field hospital that had been set up in a disaster area – one that had not yet been supplied with cots or blankets. Some children were still wandering aimlessly around. The old man knew each by name. While Jonathan watched, he went down on his knees and gently coaxed some of the sleepers to move over in order to make room for the others. Patting bundles of newspapers, stroking sheets of cardboard as though they were the most comfortable beds in the world, he bade the little ones lie down.

'Look at their hollow eyes, sir . . .'

'Hey!'

Odorico yanked so hard on Jonathan's lapel that his jacket ripped somewhere. 'Have you felt the pleading looks of silence that have been fastened to you since you entered their small world? We shepherd them through the day, but when night falls, no one picks them up and takes them home. That difference is in their eyes.'

'Take it easy! You'll wake them up.'

'Have you looked closely at them, sir? Look at the rings under

Robertito's eyes,' the priest wheezed. He forced Jonathan down to look at a sleeping boy. 'Like most of the others here, he already works for his living. From five o'clock in the morning until midday he goes about the town, carrying a basket and twig broom, following the carts. Have you not noticed, sir, the spotlessness of our streets? It's a public service initiated and organized by the Chief of Police to keep the children occupied.'

'What about child labour laws?' Jonathan asked. 'Do they have them in this country?'

'It's the Chief of Police's belief that children would rather work than play. In the afternoon they go to the beach with rakes and shovels to bury as much of the refinery mess as they can, but those black tides keep coming ashore.'

Jonathan stood with his hands in his pockets, looking at the children. He felt helpless and saddened by their plight.

'There must be something that can be done, padre. The adoption agencies in the United States are crying out for kids like these. If my mother and grandmother could see all these children, they'd be horrified. They'd see that they were put with loving families in the States. Or they'd adopt them all themselves. Maybe I can . . .'

'It's the curse of Santa Petrolina!' The old man grabbed Jonathan by the shoulder and pointed his stick at the red flames of the refinery. 'The men who fathered these unfortunates live and work out there. Foreigners. Petroleros. Outsiders who care nothing for our town. The Chief of Police permits them to come ashore after dark to visit the mothers.' He waved his stick at the prostitutes. 'Santa Petrolina has attracted to our town an army of itinerant women who have in turn produced all these illegitimate children. The women come, the women go. The men work for six months or a year, and leave, go home. We get stuck with the orphans.' He paused for a moment. He was gasping for breath and held Jonathan's lapel in a tight grip. His hands shook. His head was pressed against Jonathan's chest.

Jonathan recoiled from his foul breath. Odorico's ravings frightened him. 'What about birth control? I realize this is a Catholic country, but surely some dispensation can be made.'

'You see my church? You see the bars across the door? People can look inside, light candles on the steps, inhale the breath of the church . . . no more! *They* closed the church! *They*'ve given the

Holy Mother the last rites. *They* kicked out Peaceful Banana! *They* want us to worship Santa Petrolina!'

'Who's they? Who are you talking about – the government?'

'Ask the Chief of Police,' the old man growled.

'Say, padre, I've got an idea that might work. We could have a Meaning of Life Conference down here. You could make a fortune for these kids. The potential is amazing. You've got every social problem – pollution, orphans, whores, the church is closed. I could get my mother and grandmother to . . . Ow! Hey!'

The priest had smacked him across the shins with his stick. He swung again, and Jonathan jumped aside.

'Ask the Chief of Police who closed the church! Ask *Hak* who's responsible for the children!' the priest shrieked after Jonathan. 'Ask *Hak!* Ask *Hak!* Ask *Hak!*'

4
Ricardo's Happy Hour Café

Across a sandy space and partially concealed by a clump of palms stood a long low structure on stilts. One part had been built on dry land and the other – from all appearances a later extension – on a jetty over the bay. Some pilings had sunk or settled, the roof sloped precariously seawards, and the place looked like a chicken coop about to be launched into the water.

As Jonathan climbed the wooden steps, straw-hatted men lounging by the door moved aside to let him pass. With cigar stub tucked firmly under his moustache and hands plunged deep into his pockets, he smiled to show that he was friendly.

Inside was all cobwebby. A long low zinc counter ran along one wall, with bottles of rum and packets of cigarettes ranged on glass shelves against the mirror. Opposite stood a display refrigerator loaded with cabbages and pink eggs. Axe handles and narrow-necked jars filled one corner near the door. Coiled ropes of black tobacco gave off a pungent odour.

A few tables and chairs haphazardly occupied the intervening space. Suspended from naked rafters overhead were dozens of dusty hams. Some hung so low that Jonathan had to duck his head and dodge among them.

The night was hot and the place all but deserted. At the sea end of the long room the barman was conferring in a confidential manner with a tall and handsome man who Jonathan immediately guessed to be the Chief of Police. An unlabelled bottle of rum and a jar of hot peppers sat on the counter between them. Both appeared to be slightly drunk. They stopped talking when they caught sight of Jonathan.

'Mr Bradshaw. Welcome to Puerto Gusano.' The Chief of Police spoke perfect English. 'Umberto Hak, at your service.'

He energetically pumped Jonathan's hand. 'Ricardo, get off your butt and fix this man a decent drink! Mr Bradshaw, meet Ricardo, best bartender this side of the Roosevelt Hotel, down-town New Orleans.'

'Hey, yeah, it's good to be here,' Jonathan shook hands with the barman, who had a malarial complexion, a large Adam's apple, and bulging grey fish eyes.

'Now, what'll it be?' Hak's hand fell heavily on Jonathan's shoulder. 'How about the house speciality – rum collins made with fresh lime juice and a maraschino cherry? Ricardo, where's that bottle of cherries?' he demanded in a loud voice.

The Chief of Police's feet were firmly planted, and one hand rested on his hip. His shoulders were thrown back, and he cocked his head in an attitude of extreme self-confidence. He was smoking a cigarette and gesturing with it as he talked. Despite the heat he was dressed in a rumpled tweed jacket and bow tie, and, Jonathan noted with amusement, he wore old saddle oxfords. Thick curls included, he was well over six feet tall. His appearance resembled that of a college professor whose wardrobe has not been replenished in twenty years. Despite a troubled look that flickered about his greenish-brown eyes, he managed to radiate an exaggerated vitality. Jonathan guessed him to be about forty-five years old.

After rummaging behind the counter, Ricardo produced a bottle of musty-looking grey cherries.

Umberto unscrewed the top and sniffed. 'Aha – still as good as new! Ricardo, this is Ben Bradshaw's *son!*'

Ricardo set two drinks on the bar, fished a pair of cherries out of the bottle with his fingers and dropped them in. Wiping his hand on a dirty rag, he offered it a second time.

'Pleased to meet you, sir.' He placed his hand over his heart. 'Your father . . .'

'*Ricardo!*' Umberto drank off half his drink and set down the glass with a bang. 'Put some more rum in these things! What's the matter with you?'

Ricardo filled both glasses to the rim.

Jonathan picked the cherry from his drink and dropped it in an ashtray. 'You know, I never have been particularly keen on grey cherries.'

'Now listen, Mr Bradshaw.' Umberto turned a powerful gaze on Jonathan. 'Doesn't your family live in one of the largest houses on Martha's Vineyard?' He put his cigarette to his lips, drew on it, snatched it quickly away and blew out a cloud of smoke.

'Yeah, well, we live in New Jersey. My grandmother has a summer place on the Vineyard. Do you know my family?'

'Didn't your father tell me it was a particularly historic, rambling estate?'

'I guess. People call it the Old Terry Place. But you're probably thinking of my grandmother's place out in New Jersey. It's on this dirt road where all the gentry live next door to each other. Wait a minute though. You act like this is an important question, Mr Hak. Isn't it supposed to be rude to ask someone how big their house is?'

'Does your grandmother still have her old butler? Didn't she employ about twenty servants at one time?'

'Mr Hak! How did you ever . . .? I guess you must know I'm trying to find my father, and Bertha said . . .'

'Ben said your mother was one of the prettiest women ever to graduate from Vassar.'

'Smith. He did? Yeah, that's what people say. Is Dad around . . .?'

'Has she lost her looks?'

'*I* don't think so. No, no she hasn't. But getting back to Dad, is he . . .?'

'Wish I'd seen her.' Umberto was looking at himself in the mirror. He ran a hand through his hair. 'Isn't she an artist?'

'At Smith she used to paint murals, you know like the ones you see at the Indoor Tennis Court in Far Hills. Have you been there at any time? . . . It has these murals with ivy trailing down, and languid ladies. . . .'

'Didn't Ben tell me she stopped painting when they got married?'

'She did for a while. Then she wrote a book about the family called *War and Pizza*. A family history – very baroque, like a Russian novel. You know, where the peasants are singing in the fields as they bring in the hay, and you can hear people weeping because someone's giving birth and someone's dying somewhere else.'

'Does her story start when they were living in the Hyde Park Hotel in London?'

'*That wasn't my mother*, Mr Hak! I don't know where you get your information. That was my father's . . . but anyway, to answer your question: no, it begins in the womb, because Mom says she can remember being in the womb.'

'And since your father left?'

'Yeah, well, now she does these terribly anguished paintings with suns and children and blood. She puts about a hundred layers of paint on the canvas until it's as thick as a dictionary. The other day one of them fell off the wall and we all ran down thinking that the piano had collapsed.'

'Ben told me people said your grandmother ruled New York with a velvet glove.'

'She was famous for her Sunday lunches. She'd invite all these artists and writers from the Century Club and people who were in the news, and have a fancy lunch in her garden or conservatory. One day she was sitting next to this man who had just done this big survey on world population control and he asked her how she liked oral sex.'

'Ah! Ha! Ha!' Umberto slapped Jonathan on the back. Then he became serious. 'That's terrible.'

'Yeah, well, I don't think she ever felt the same about her Sunday lunches again.'

Umberto was looking at Jonathan in the mirror. Jonathan caught his eye. 'Uh, Mr Hak, I'm going to speak directly into the mirror now. Couldn't we *please* talk about my father? You must know how desperate . . .'

For a moment the two men puffed away and stared at each other in the mirror.

'I don't think I've been anywhere in the world' – Umberto glanced at Ricardo, then back at Jonathan – '*anywhere* – where you could walk into a house and be so knocked over by the charm. Maybe I'm naive, but Ben's house had a distinct charm about it.'

'Jesus! Dad's house? Where is it? Some kid told me he raised cannabis and coffee.'

'*Gone!* Nobody there. You can't even get to it.' Umberto took a long drink and smiled at Jonathan. 'I had my driver take me up there the other day. You know, for old times' sake. We stopped in the middle of the jungle, and I said, "What are you doing?" And he said, "This is it." You could see where there was once a driveway through the trees. We'd all taken it thousands of times. Well, it's solid jungle now. Some cane-cutters came down the road. Said the house wasn't there any more. What wasn't dismantled piece by piece by the natives was swept away in the floods. I'm not surprised – leave a house empty for seven years in this wilderness, and it's gone.'

'Nothing left?' Jonathan asked. 'What about Dad?'

'I couldn't even see it. You'd have to take a machete to get to where it was. Here and there a coffee tree growing. Gone – like your father.'

'Gone? Mr Hak, please stop beating around the bush. *I'm looking for my father!*'

'Do you think you're unique? Do you think you're the only one with that particular condition?'

'What do you mean – *that particular condition?*'

Umberto was shaking his head. 'Trying to find a father.'

'*Wait!*' Jonathan grabbed his shoulder. 'What do you mean *the only one* with that particular condition? Do you want half of New York to have it? Or one quarter of New York? I happen to have it. I don't know how many other people have it.'

Umberto waved a hand to silence him. 'What I'm trying to tell you is, we have a serious problem in this town. You've seen our children, haven't you? They're all fatherless like you. The responsibility for their well-being is on my shoulders. It'd be a disaster if they started drinking.' He looked at his drink, frowned at it and downed it in one gulp. 'They've got things to learn, they have to raise themselves from the mud of this hick town. It's not going to be easy. No families, no money – drink would be the end of their hopes and mine. So I have a strict rule.' Umberto was sucking an ice cube. '*Expulsion.*' He slurred the word. 'One drink and they're *out!*'

'Out of what?' Jonathan asked.

Umberto threw back his head and laughed. 'Out of my house! Out of my life! Out of my town!'

Out of your mind? Jonathan thought. He smiled nervously at the Chief of Police.

Umberto spat the ice cube back into the glass. 'You know what's out there, don't you?' he asked in a hollow voice. His arm swept an imaginary horizon. 'The Great Swamp! A vast territory of quagmires and lagoons, full of quicksand and wild animals, totally uninhabited but claimed, naturally, by all the neighbouring republics and included arbitrarily on their maps. So far there've been only two defectors.'

'My father?'

'Yes, your father and one other . . .' Umberto slammed his glass on the bar and Jonathan jumped back. 'You see, Mr Bradshaw,

I've sacrificed a lot,' he said fiercely. 'People tell me I'm wasting my life here, but I've got a town to run. A town full of orphans. My family came here five generations back. We're the only ones who know how to get things done. I'm the last one left, and the responsibility of many lives – homeless and otherwise – is mine. Kids want discipline. I can teach them things they wouldn't learn from anyone else. Can't I, Ricardo? My kids drink tea poured from silver teapots. Their cookies sit on Crown Derby.'

'High tea served in the street? Sounds pretty fancy.' Jonathan took from his hip pocket a packet of cigars which he'd sat on and crushed. 'Seems a strange way to deal with the problem . . .'

He spent several seconds trying to reconstruct a smashed cigar, then lit it. 'Mr Hak, I've been thinking about the children I saw in Cathedral Square, and about what you're saying. Anyone who saw those children would want to help them. I know that Mom and Granny and their friends would, and hell, I feel like I ought to roll up my sleeves and start frying hot dogs. The thing is people have got to know about the problem, this particular town and its problems. Not just an ad in *The New Yorker* that says, you know, five bucks can save José, and you see a photo of some poor starving kid. I'm talking about personal contact. It's slow and difficult to do things through official channels, and so forth . . . But what if you had a Meaning of Life Conference down here?'

'What the hell is that?' Umberto asked.

'It could mean anything. You get this New York socialite who's been in Oklahoma for the weekend taking peyote with the Indians because she wants to understand the culture and write about it "in depth" for Italian *Vogue*. She lives in a floor-through on Fifth Ave. between 86th and 87th, with pillars like the Temple of Karnak. She's sitting in her dining room which overlooks Central Park, giving two round tables full of art historians tenderloin tips, home-made pasta with pesto. Leonard Bernstein is going to play after dinner. She leans over the salad with walnut dressing and confides to the guy who wrote Somerset Maugham's biography that something's wrong with her life. You say, "OK, sweetie, take off the chinchilla sunglasses and take a look at the world." It turns out her husband is head of Channel Thirteen, the public service television. Before you know it he's filming *One Hundred Years of Servitude* – the crisis in Puerto Gusano. And the next thing you know everyone in Manhattan is driving around with bumper stickers that say SAVE PUERTO GUSANO. You could attract ecology groups, charitable organizations, lonely people who could adopt the orphans, give them homes . . . try to get private individuals interested in the cause . . . you could make a fortune off the tourism it would generate.'

'Hey!' Umberto clicked his fingers and performed a little dance step. 'Great! I like that idea, but . . .' He stopped and looked Jonathan up and down. 'Who's going to get this organized?'

Jonathan began tucking in his shirttails, 'Well, I . . .'

'What's your profession? Are you on Wall Street?'

'I used to sell socks.'

'Socks?'

'Yeah, at Brooks Brothers. It's a hotsy, totsy men's store on Madison.'

'I know what Brooks Brothers is. But socks?' Umberto looked as though he smelled something bad.

'They hired me for the pre-Christmas rush.'

'Mr Bradshaw, you must be joking. Your family are *millionaires*.'

'Is there some law saying millionaires can't sell socks? Millionaires like to sell socks as much as anyone else. Besides,' Jonathan turned to Ricardo, 'you have to be a chemical engineer to sell socks these days.'

'What?' Umberto sounded impatient.

Jonathan sipped his drink and leaned on the bar. 'Oh yeah, I thought like you – there were just socks. I didn't realize there are about twenty different polyesters with cotton 40 per cent, 30 per cent some other material.'

Umberto and Ricardo looked confused.

'Yeah. There's not just one sock. They've got a hundred and fifty different varieties of socks. Wool. Cashmere. All different lengths. You know, calf's length and so on. They'd say, "This is the wrong length." And I'd say, "Goddammit, what length do you want?" And there'd be about twenty people waiting in line.'

'I don't want to hear any more about that now. I'm talking about serious problems. Art – that's the only way to breathe, even if you're wallowing in mud. That's why I insist on doilies and linen napkins even though the kids don't own shoes.'

'You mean more Bach and less bananas?'

'Exactly. It's a relief to encounter an enlightened thinker for a change.' Umberto flashed a boyish grin and poked him in the ribs. 'Don't worry about offending me. I know what you Americans think of the third world.' He laughed. 'The *turd* world!' He slapped Jonathan on the back. 'Ah! Ha! Ha! But neither do I want to populate this town with cheerleaders, pompom wavers, and football players eating hotdogs off paper plates. If these kids are going to improve their lot, it must be done with creativity and vision. No slop-time!' He banged the bar and demanded another drink. 'My kids are going to know about astronomy and arabesques . . . music, theatre, dance . . . Even though they have no formal education, they *learn!* I'm not trying to produce Bachs or Shakespeares, I'm trying to produce happy individuals who know how to sew on buttons. This Meaning of Life thing might be a great idea . . . They've got to learn how to be happy on this planet, because the world'll be smaller when they grow up. They must be aware of other cultures and the expanding universe. I tell them about Einstein and Buddha and remind them to keep their elbows off the table.'

'Pickpockets with a Ph.D?' Jonathan was attempting to reconstruct another ruined cigar. 'Sounds more practical than the place I went to school . . .'

'Was it Hotchkiss, sir?' the Chief of Police asked. 'Like your father?'

'Yes, that's right.' Jonathan was taken aback by the eagerness with which the Chief of Police seized upon this piece of information. 'How do you know *that?*' he asked, shoving the tattered cigar butt into the corner of his mouth.

'Well, I'll tell you one thing,' Umberto smiled. 'They may grow up in this worm hole, but my kids say, "Yes, sir" and show respect. More respect than some adults show. Ask Ricardo.'

'Yeah, well, it's interesting what you want for your kids, because I spent a year in the Peace Corps in Bolivia, and there the children, and even their parents, had never heard of *anything*. I used to walk down the road, where some cannibals had just eaten some folks the week before, and no one knew or cared who I was or where I was from. They'd never even heard of the United States. They didn't have any idea what the United States meant to them. And I was supposed to tell them. I remember sitting in a hut in the middle of the jungle and hearing on my transistor radio that Kennedy had been assassinated. He was a friend of Dad.

There was no one I could talk to. No one even knew who Kennedy was. I was like a lot of people of my generation who identified with him, pinned my hopes onto him. My Dad was gone but here was someone who was everything I wanted Dad to be, that I wanted to be. Then a thousand days later, I heard those words, the President is dead . . . I sat for three days in that hut, listening to every broadcast, I didn't eat, I didn't shave, it was like losing Dad all over again. And somehow it made it worse that the people around me didn't understand. Didn't even know that I was there because of John Kennedy.' Shaking his head, Jonathan took off his coat and rolled up his sleeves, 'Practically the *first thing* that impressed me down here is that the kids on the street have actually heard of Proust and the Big Bang.'

'Yeah, well, I wish some people were more aware of what's going on *inside* this bar.' Ricardo, who pretended to be absorbed in wiping his glasses with a towel, had been listening to every word. 'Goddamned thieves,' he muttered between his teeth.

Umberto was distracted for a moment by his image in the mirror behind the bar. Running a hand several times through his thick mass of curls, he forced them upward to create a bushy effect which offset his rather heavy jaw. He simultaneously pursed his lips and sucked in his cheeks, which made his face appear leaner and younger.

'I'm here this evening to investigate the theft of hams,' he announced, 'but what concerns me most is the "cosmological problem". Did it ever occur to you, sir,' he went on, addressing Jonathan once more, 'that the universe is isotropic? Which means, of course, that the missing hams can't be far away.'

Jonathan stopped chewing his cigar and gazed at the Chief of Police with a confused, quizzical smile. 'My father's missing, too. Does that mean he can't be far away, either?'

'Long and lean and as hard as rocks!' Umberto slapped the ham above his head, snatched the cigarette from his lips and waved it. 'Just this evening I've noticed how gently they swing . . . like random pendulums, twisting slowly in the breeze set up by the fan. Or is it the sea breeze?' Through the window the blazing flares of the Santa Petrolina could be seen.

Jonathan sniffed the air. 'Smells worse than Elizabeth, New Jersey out there. Are those hams for sale?'

Ricardo glided down the bar and poured himself a drink. 'No, they're not. They belong to the customers.' He pointed his finger at Jonathan's nose. 'And if . . .'

'Hey, take it easy!' Jonathan leaned away.

'Ricardo . . .' Umberto's hand closed over Ricardo's finger and pushed it aside. 'Have you forgotten who this is? This is Ben Bradshaw's *son!* Where're your manners? And when are you going to shave?'

Ricardo muttered an apology.

'After all, he's here to investigate something, too.' Umberto, who was gazing into his empty glass as though it were a crystal ball, shot Jonathan a knowing glance. 'A man can steal hams or hearts. A town can be robbed of its pride or its purity, a person of his self-respect. Children can be robbed of their parents, husbands of wives, friends of one another.' He watched himself wave his arms about in the mirror, like an orator practising a speech. 'Don't look so serious, Mr Bradshaw. We know you're here to investigate not a robbery but a disappearance. Maybe both.'

He stopped talking for a minute and looked sympathetically at Jonathan. 'Yes, I know you're not in Puerto Gusano to visit the ruins . . .' The softness of his voice startled Jonathan. 'You've come to the right place.'

'Is he alive?'

'After a manner of speaking.' Umberto spat another ice cube into his glass.

Jonathan knitted his brow. 'Wait a minute – what's that supposed to mean?'

Umberto enveloped his shoulders in a rough bear hug, then let him go and patted him on the back. 'Of course, he's alive. He'd be a tough one to kill. They don't make many like Ben Bradshaw, do they, Ricardo?'

Ricardo passionately squeezed Jonathan's hand. 'Your father . . .' His eyes glistened with emotion. 'He was very correct . . . happy . . . intelligent. He came into this town – boom! There were many things in his life, but his conscience was clear. Everything was together . . .' Ricardo was flapping his arms to help himself speak. 'He was like a diamond between two stones – *hard*. Oh!' he groaned. 'I loved him *too much*.' He pulled open the front of his shirt to display a scrawny chest. 'His name is inscribed here, on my heart, like a tattoo!'

Jonathan gently pulled his hand away. 'I appreciate your admiration for my father, but he abandoned his family in the United States. His conscience couldn't possibly have been clear.'

Umberto frowned. 'More drinks!' he demanded, and slammed his fist on the bar. 'I'm going to give up drinking,' he added. He waved away Jonathan, who was about to speak, and said very firmly, 'Now listen to me. I don't want to talk about that now. I don't give a damn if you've got problems – we all have.' He picked a pepper from the jar and began to eat. 'Want one? Look – we've all got things we want to find out about. There's a time and a place . . .'

'That's easy for you to say. You haven't waited twenty-five years . . .'

Umberto smiled and slid another glass toward Jonathan. 'There's something *I* want to know about . . .' He paused for a second, as if unable to decide what it was. Finally he said, '*You.* Grab that drink and come over here.'

Carrying his glass and the jar of peppers, the Chief of Police walked with heavy, flat steps to a table near the window. He sat down and leaned back in his chair. 'Did you go to Princeton like your father?'

'Yeah. Sure . . . but I was so upset about Dad that Granny sent me for an extra year of prep school at Upper Canada College. We wore uniforms and had to polish our shoes and played hockey all the time. We weren't supposed to have any time to think about emotional problems.'

'And like Ben were you the captain of the Princeton tennis team?'

'I was captain of the hockey team. My freshman year we played St Paul's for Hobey Baker's hockey stick at Madison Square Garden. The old Garden. I scored the winning goal. It was Christmas vacation. Dad wasn't there to see it. All the other guys' fathers were there on the boards, cheering . . . Right after that I began to notice that when I was on the ice, I could see the hockey puck, but like it was flat. I lost my 3-D vision. I couldn't judge how far away from me it was. I started to fall down all the time, like I was drunk. Mom and Granny got worried and so I went to this brain specialist. They thought I had this brain condition, *cerebellum . . . deterioti.* And I started contemplating death. I'd sit in my grandmother's deck chair, slumped over thinking about death. And Mom and Granny would be standing at the window looking out at me, thinking, "He's so young" . . . and they'd be crying.'

'Were you the only one with this particular condition?'

'Well, what do you mean? You keep saying the *only* one. Do you want *all* of New York City to have it?'

'So did this have something to do with your father?'

'No. It turned out that the car I was driving was leaking carbon monoxide.'

'Are you a member of the Ivy Club?'

'Oh, yeah, well, when I was there Ivy was still the red-brick, preppy, F. Scott Fitzgerald ideal of the sophisticated Princeton social club. But hell, he was just some brat from the mid-west who wanted to be in the big time, and sort of romanticized all these institutions. We wore our hair short back and sides and we were supposed to eat by candelabra, and we had this rich, sort of staid, tradition. You know . . . Steve Rockefeller was head of the club. All the hockey players belonged. Dad had been a big figure there. I was able to hide my unhappiness behind my hockey success and because I was good-looking and my family had money. Everyone thought, "Hey, he's the perfect college guy, a star on the ice and with all the women." Which wasn't true at all. I barely had the nerve to ask a girl to go have a chocolate soda with me. When I got to Bolivia I didn't have any of those crutches to rely on. No one knew or cared. Anyway, just to show you how quickly things changed in the sixties. When I came back from Bolivia and went to some football game, I went to the Ivy Club and some black guy opened the door and said I couldn't come in, they were occupying it with some of the black sisters. Turns out they were holding the dean hostage in there. I said, "Jesus Christ, I can't even get in my own club, and they've got *women* in there?" He told me to go to his place, so I did. Here I was, sort of the cream of the white establishment, in this black terrorist's room with posters of Che Guevara and Malcolm X all over the walls, and I was wondering if the FBI would bust in and arrest me. That was when I started thinking about what was going on, and decided to go down to Selma, Alabama.

'I got my grandmother interested in starting an American quilt business down in Selma. You know, a cottage industry that would employ the starving blacks to make those beautiful red and white folk quilts. And my grandmother and her friends could think up the designs and sell them to interior decorators in New York. So anyway, she got the business going, but *The New York Times* wrote a big piece about how she was exploiting cheap labour down south. She had a hell of a fight with the publisher who was a friend of hers, but she pulled out. That's the only time I've ever seen her beaten.'

Umberto continued to eat peppers. 'You know your grandmother had a secret affair with a prize fighter,' he added laconically.

'No, I didn't know that. The kids on the street down here know more about my family than I do. What prize fighter?'

'She met him on a train in France. Gentleman Jacques – he was the toast of Paris. He wore an orchid in his lapel, and his muscles bulged under the pinstripes. Your grandmother couldn't keep her hands off him, but it didn't last.'

'Well, then, I guess there's somebody for everybody, even my grandmother.'

'Tell me more about your mother.'

'She married a tycoon. Henry's a genius when it comes to business, but emotional problems he sweeps under the rug. He runs a publishing empire in New York. Before that he made a fortune on Wall Street. *The Wall Street Journal* dubbed him "the tortoise of Wall Street" because he plodded along to success while all the quick starters failed. Everybody in the business world is terrified of him. Then he comes home and gets bossed around by the snapping turtle – that's my mother. He's the President of the New Jersey Racing Association. He has this fancy private suite at Monmouth Park with black butlers serving drinks and Maryland crab cakes. Basically, Henry's a good man caught in a difficult situation. He swore he'd cut me off if I came down here. Uh, Mr Hak . . . you're yawning. Aren't you enjoying this? You talk as though you're an old friend of the family.'

'I am – of your father.'

'If you're my father's friend, why are you throwing up this smokescreen when you know I'm desperate for information?'

'You don't seem to realize your father's been gone from your life for twenty-five years. You come here with certain preconceptions. Just *how much* do you feel your father owes you?'

'Jesus Christ!' Jonathan said. '*Of course* I realize my father's been gone for twenty-five years! But he's still my father. I think he would be interested in seeing me. I don't think that's an imaginary bond.'

'I know all about fathers and sons, Mr Bradshaw. I have a son of my own. And a town full of fatherless children. How did you know Ben was here?'

'The *Pelican* turned up in Panama. I went to see it. I met this beautiful junkie at the Panama City yacht club. She killed her father . . .'

'*Que barbaridad.*'

'She led me to the clue that brought me here. She showed me all the stuff that had been stolen off the boat. There was this hidden cash box with the words *Peaceful Banana Company, Puerto Gusano* on it. The irony of it was, she had *killed* her own father, and yet she helped me find mine. In a roundabout way she brought my father back to life.'

'How could you take up with a junkie?'

'She was beautiful. Besides, there's *somebody* for *everybody*, Mr Hak.' Jonathan said it with conviction. 'Didn't you? I haven't read it, but you know, Carson McCullers, *The Heart is a Lonely Hunter*. I saw the movie. Where the guy's without . . . can't hear or speak, blind and crippled. They stumble together and they fall in love. Their big toes interlock on some dirt street as they walk down. They say, "Hey, get your big toe out of my foot." And then they get to know each other just by happenstance because one is blind, deaf and dumb, and the other drives his wheelchair with his tongue and has to speak out of a larynx with a hole in it. And somehow they fall in love. They fall in love those two people. It's just like Joyce Kilmont. When I was a senior at Hotchkiss, her picture was on the cover of *Sports Illustrated*. She was an olympic skier. She had an accident and was crippled for life. And there I was arriving at the peak of my physical abilities and so forth.'

'You mean the peak of your sexual abilities?'

Jonathan paused. 'Sexual is part of physical, isn't it?'

'Men hit their sexual peak when they're nineteen.'

'Well.' Jonathan thought for a moment. 'I was a virgin. So I didn't know I had peaked because I had never peaked with anyone. So anyway, I identified with Joyce Kilmont because we were both crippled. My father had just disappeared, leaving me crippled for life. They made a movie about her, and she fell in love with this man. They got married. But the point of the story is, here I got crippled and I'm not married, and she got married, even though she was a quadriplegic. What's wrong with me? The question is: *what's wrong with me?*'

'So what is wrong with you?'

'What's wrong is what *I've been trying to tell you* by all this laying bare of my soul. I'm trying to generate your sympathy so you'll tell me where Dad is. What's wrong with me is I haven't been able to get married. I'm afraid of that kind of relationship . . . I'm afraid of being hurt and deserted again.'

'One more question, Mr Bradshaw.'

'Yeah?'

'Your prick . . . is it as long as your father's?'

Jonathan choked and sprayed the air with rum. He coughed for several seconds. When he raised his head, his face was bright red.

'What?' His voice came out as an unfamiliar croak. 'Mr Hak! What did you say?'

'Your prick – is it smaller?' Umberto held out his hands, palms vertical, about six inches apart, as though he were measuring a fish. 'Or longer?' He separated them until they were about two feet apart. 'Or is it about the same size as your father's?' He narrowed the distance to a foot. 'You know he has a shlong that'd make a donkey blink.'

'Mr Hak! Jesus!' Jonathan could not stop coughing and spluttering. 'I don't . . . Are you? I've never. Where did you! When did you *ever* . . . *EVER!*' he shouted. 'You're getting . . . mixed up. And after all this sort of sincere opening of one's heart. Which *totally* makes me seem . . . ridiculous! I NEVER . . . *No*-no-no-no-no-*NO!* Why are you interested in my father's cock? JESUS!'

All of a sudden Umberto tipped over backward and fell with a crash.

Jonathan leaned over him. 'Mr Hak! Are you pulling my leg again?'

'Damn it, Ricardo!' Umberto yelled from the floor. 'What's wrong with this chair?'

'Nothing – if you know how to sit on it. And not get so drunk.'

'I wouldn't if you'd serve some food around here. Fix me a *croque monsieur!*'

'Nothing here but hams – that is if they're not all stolen while you're rolling on the floor!' Ricardo brushed him off. 'You're supposed to be conducting an investigation!'

Umberto winked at Jonathan. 'When Ricardo shouts, I know he loves me.'

'Come on, Mr Hak – are you pulling my leg?'

'Listen – get with it. Let's have another drink.'

They returned to the bar. This time Ricardo appealed to Jonathan: 'It's the truth, sir,' he said in a more friendly tone. 'Someone's been stealing these prize hams from right over my head. It ain't as if two or three hams have been stolen, sir, or five or six. No sir. *Twelve!* These hams are worth a lot of money. People are angry, and I'm losing my customers. If this goes on much longer, I'm going to have to shut down.'

'The fascinating detail,' Umberto said, 'is that these thefts occur, *not* when the bar is closed and padlocked with the shutters slammed down, which Ricardo manages to do in such an intimidating manner, but during his happiest hours . . . that is, when this place is full, which is generally between midnight and four o'clock in the morning. My guess would be that the thief strikes closer to dawn than midnight, when people are sleepy and drunk.'

'That's right, Mr Bradshaw. I count these hams every night – twice. Once when I open and again when I close. Count them myself. And almost every night a new string is cut. Not at the back of the room, no sir, but *here*, above the bar, right where we're standing now. Someone standing *right at this bar* has been stealing these hams.'

'What's his trick?' Jonathan asked. All he could think about were the sexual implications of Umberto's question. He'd given up hope of getting a straight answer. 'He must be clever to get away with it.'

'That's the mystery Mr Hak's supposed to solve. I don't know how the bastard gets away with it, but he does – right under my nose and in full view of the owners of the hams. Why, the other night a man was standing right where you are now. I'd just served him a drink. He reached up with his knife, sliced off a piece of ham, trimmed the fat from it and ate it, and drank his drink – all the time talking with me and his friends from Santa Petrolina. I served him another drink, he reached up for another bit of ham, and the ham was gone! And he was surrounded by friends!'

'And subsequently created a row among friends . . .' Umberto added in an acid tone of voice. 'Accusations flew, followed by recriminations, followed by threats and insults, followed by bottles, followed by chairs . . . a real rumble.' He threw a few punches in front of the mirror.

'What do you make of it, Mr Bradshaw?' Ricardo asked.

'A bunch of brutal rednecks, derelicts, bums, who've never washed their hands or read a book in their lives!' Umberto bellowed. 'I've been banging their heads together for as long as I can remember, and believe me, it doesn't do a damn bit of good. Have you noticed, Mr Bradshaw,' he hissed, 'that the scum of the earth is virtually indestructible? Now what do *you* make of all this?'

'I don't know what to make of anything, Mr Hak, but I want to lay to rest this business about my father's cock.'

Umberto, who had creased a cigarette paper down the middle, thoughtfully tore it in half and began to laugh softly to himself. 'Order may be my profession . . .' He had shaken the tobacco onto the narrow bit of paper, not without spilling some, and was deftly rolling the cigarette between his fingers. 'And an idea for order may be my preoccupation, but *survival* . . . is the order of the day for most of us.' He was licking the edge of the cigarette paper. 'One way or another, all our acts are a form of revenge against . . . *that*. Santa Petrolina – our patron saint.' He made a motion in the direction of the open window. The refinery was ablaze with light; the night sky was yellow and orange.

Ricardo was looking at Jonathan. 'When we catch the son of a bitch he's going to pay the full price for those hams. More than the full price . . .' He made a knot in his towel and was twisting it. 'We're going to . . .'

Jonathan had to step backwards as the Chief of Police reached across the bar, took hold of Ricardo by the nape of the neck and pulled him slowly but firmly toward him. A glass crashed to the floor. The bottle was rolling along the counter gushing rum.

'Cut off his balls and feed them to the pigs?' he asked hoarsely. Ricardo opened his mouth to cry out in pain but made no sound. Umberto had taken a fold of neck flesh between his thumb and finger and was pinching hard. 'Is that your redneck, depraved notion of paying the full price?'

He let go, and Ricardo stood up. The bottle hit the floor but did not break.

'Ricardo . . .' Umberto said, 'I'm worried about you – I think you're beginning to strut with the other rats. Don't talk to me about feeding anyone's balls to the pigs! Disgusting! What century do you think we're living in? Now straighten up and get with it!'

Ricardo, who seemed shaken, nevertheless produced a match and struck it on the bar. 'Then you find the thief, Mr Hak,' he said holding a trembling flame to the meagre cigarette, 'and that'll be my "happy hour".'

'You see, Mr Bradshaw . . .' Umberto started again. 'We *think* we're living in civilized times, but there must be authority. Children need authority – don't they, Ricardo?' Ricardo nodded cynically. 'Children of all ages. Even if that authority has to be reinforced with *machine guns!*'

Umberto pulled himself up to his full height, pursed his lips and sucked in his cheeks. 'Now what would happen to this jerk town if I decided to walk out?'

'I've heard that one before,' Ricardo sneered.

'You see, Mr Bradshaw, there's no winning. They all know I've made too big an investment here – both time and emotion – to leave easily. They also know I'm suffocating in this cultural vacuum. Each additional day I stay here I throw away my chances to breathe the clean, pure air of New York, where I should be making a name for myself in the theatre. I don't know how many times your father urged me: "Get out *now! NOW!* Before it's too late." '

'Did my father want to go to New York with you?'

Ricardo snickered. 'He'll never leave because he can't make up his mind.'

'I make up my mind in one minute!' Umberto retorted angrily.

'Sure – then change it the next.'

'How can you say that? You know perfectly well I make quick decisions.'

'Sure – if it's where to have the next drink.'

Umberto gave Jonathan a wounded look. 'My problems are all our problems,' he said. 'What would happen to the children if I left?'

'What about my hams?' Ricardo snarled.

Jonathan feared the fight would erupt again, but Umberto only sighed and looked at himself in the mirror. 'There's no way to

win, but you'll see, Ricardo – I'll leave you all in the lurch one day.'
Jonathan watched him run his hands up the back of his neck and
through his hair, and purse his lips again. 'But first I have to get
myself into shape.'

'You're a good-looking guy, Mr Hak,' Jonathan said. 'You don't
have to keep staring at yourself in the mirror.'

Ricardo howled with laughter.

'I saw myself naked in the mirror this morning, and I was
horrified.' Umberto couldn't stop preening himself. He glanced
at Jonathan's waistline, and a sly smile crossed his face. 'How old
did you say you are, Mr Bradshaw?'

'Forty-two.'

'I think we both need to cut down on the booze . . .'

'Oh no!' Ricardo pretended to ward off an invisible devil. 'Not
another diet! He's *impossible* when he goes on the wagon.'

'Got to take a leak,' Umberto announced and walked heavily
away.

Ricardo picked a hot pepper from a new jar and leaned across
the bar. 'He's awfully nervous tonight, Mr Bradshaw.' he whispered, rubbing the back of his neck and nibbling the pepper as
though it were a carrot. 'That's why he talks so much. Why, I've
heard him lecture a lamp post on how the stars were born. He'll
stand beneath a tree and tell it where it came from. On nights like
tonight when he's feeling lonely, he'll board that ferris wheel and
ride round and round. Not a few turns, mind you, but hours and
hours. And he feels better afterwards. Yes, when he steps down
from the ferris wheel, he's got a smile on his face and goes on
about his business. I suppose seeing you tonight has triggered his
loneliness.'

'Yeah. Well – I'm very shocked by some things he said. What
sort of relationship did he have with my father?'

'They were great pals. Ben was a man Umberto could look up to
and talk to – talk about the world. The part your daddy came
from.'

'He said some very provocative things. I didn't know if he was
being serious or not.'

'Just wait. He'll open up when he's ready. Just hang around. It
may take a while, but he's the only one who can tell you. Shhh!'

Ricardo pretended to be swabbing the bar with his rag as
Umberto re-entered the room.

'Show Mr Bradshaw your axe handle, Ricardo!' he roared.

Ricardo reached beneath the bar but produced instead another bottle. Umberto grabbed it and poured out fresh drinks. He took Jonathan by the arm, led him to the window, and pointed across the red waters of the bay.

'A film was made of the construction of that refinery, Mr Bradshaw.' He leaned on the sill and stuck his head out the window. 'And I've got it. The children and I watch it in reverse. The film commences with the shiny steel city before us, the flames and the smoke, the workers busily turning giant valves, the tankers arriving and departing. It *concludes* with waves pounding on a wild and desolate shore. Think of it!'

'Why do you watch it in reverse?'

'To see time go backwards. I show it to the children. They always cheer when the birds appear. In the distance, where the refinery used to be, a line of half-naked men seem to be hauling in a net. But they are not. If you watch closely, you will see they are *returning* the fish to the sea. Then the men disappear, but the birds remain, presiding over the ceaseless rush of waves. They are our pelicans. Oh, how we miss them!'

'Are they missing, too?'

'The pelican floating up the water, sir, has not the sleek profile of a gull or duck,' Umberto resumed in a loud voice. 'The humped wing shoulders and arched neck and bill so long that its tip is not held out of the water combine to give the impression of top-heaviness. The birds in flight, however, surpass the others in gliding power. With a wing span so broad they have to flap but a few times to glide a long distance, low over the water – so low, with wing tips miraculously missing the swinging wave ends. And they are reckless divers. In my film, long lines of them fly backwards into time past, flapping together and sailing in fluid motion away over the undulating sea tables. There the film ends, with the pelicans disappearing, and the children sobbing. Which is not so much different from the beginning. The filth spewed out by Santa Petrolina has long since decimated our pelican population.' Umberto raised his glass. '*Vanished* – rather like your father has.'

'Yeah. Well. I'm trying to go back in time, too. Explore my father's past, just like your film. To return to my father . . .'

'Don't you recognize the importance of what I'm telling you?' Umberto was suddenly so cross that Jonathan shut his mouth.

'I've viewed that film over and over again, to study the process of time. Nothing we know corresponds to the passage of time. How do you define time, Mr Bradshaw?'

Jonathan thought for a moment. 'The space between tragedies.'

'No, no, *no*. What is the *essence* of time?' Without waiting for Jonathan to reply, he went right on. 'Time is defined by events we assume cannot be undone. That's the arrow of time. But what makes this process irreversible? Why can't we accept the reversed film as a record of a real event? That's what I'd like to know – why can't time be reversed? We can make the future be like the past, which is exactly as God intended it.'

'If you could do that, you'd be *God!*' As he said it, Jonathan realized he was quite drunk. 'These cherries aren't so bad after you've eaten a few.'

'And afterwards, *God*, free drinks for all!' Ricardo called from the bar.

'Free drinks for all . . .' Umberto glanced over his shoulder. 'You say it in such a sinister manner.' He was distracted by a noise outside the window. 'And here they come.'

It was the sound of approaching motors. Beneath the flames spiralling up from the towers and the billowing clouds of smoke, a flotilla of boats, still some distance away, could be seen bobbing on the orange waters of the bay. Ricardo, who had finished swabbing the bar, flicked a switch. On the end of the jetty a neon sign buzzed, sputtered, and came to life.

RICARDO'S HAPPY HOUR CAFÉ

Umberto returned to the bar and downed his drink. 'Do you suppose they're coming to collect their children?' He smiled wanly at Jonathan, whose attention was distracted by the appearance of the photographer. He had just entered the bar, leading the same bewildered anteater by a string.

'Meester, meester! Photograph now please? You said later. Now is later.'

Jonathan looked with pity at the shabby anteater. Old and blind, it cast about aimlessly with its long conical nose. Its claws, grown long with disuse, rattled over the boards.

'Yes, yes, yes! Let's have a photograph!' Umberto gathered Jonathan in with his arm and grinned, but neither photographer nor anteater was ready. The man slapped the animal on the nose to make it wake up.

'Hey, don't kill it! Take it easy.'

'He'll perk up.' Umberto made room for the anteater, whose long tail was in tatters.

'What was my father doing with an anteater on his yacht?'

Umberto raised two fingers. 'Two photos, please. This is Ben Bradshaw's son!'

The photographer held up his old Rolliflex. 'And this is Ben Bradshaw's camera! He gave me this wild animal, too. That's how I got started in business. Pleased to meet you, sir. I owe everything to your father. *Everything*.'

'When do we get to see these photos?' Jonathan wondered out loud.

'I'll send one to you,' Umberto said.

As the camera clicked, Jonathan laughed nervously. 'Mr Hak, you seem to be implying that I'll be leaving soon.'

A black man in a straw hat, in a great state of excitement, out of breath and carrying a sea turtle under his arm, dashed into the bar. Upon catching sight of Umberto he stopped, came forward slowly, and reverently laid the turtle at his feet.

'At last . . .' the Chief of Police murmured. As the turtle was still alive, he gently placed his foot on it to keep it from moving. Ricardo leaned over the bar, craning his neck.

Umberto had taken out his wallet. 'Bravo, Waldo! This is for my son, Mr Bradshaw.'

'A pet?'

'No. This is a great service.' He admired the turtle. 'A creature of such beauty can have no price . . . but how much do I owe you?'

Waldo had taken a step backwards and was standing at attention, straw hat in hand. He wore a tweed coat and grey flannel trousers that had been repaired many times. He was, if possible, a black caricature of the Chief of Police – dressed in even more rumpled, threadbare tweeds.

'Not a penny, sir. The fisherman said, just a few minutes ago he said . . .' He seemed unable to contain his excitement. 'If the cure works, if the blood is successful, if it smooths the skin, that will be reward enough. He will be most honoured and pleased . . .'

Everyone was looking at the turtle. It was a beautiful creature, with a shell of a greenish brown colour, like dark amber. With its flippers it was pathetically scraping the shrimp shells and bits of shattered glass that littered the floor.

'Well, in that case, will you join us for a drink? Waldo, this is Mr Bradshaw – Ben Bradshaw's son.' Umberto flicked a bill to the photographer who dragged his exhausted animal away.

Waldo, who was trembling all over and could not suppress a radiant smile, seized Jonathan's hand and squeezed very hard. 'Very pleased to meet you, sir. Most pleased. Your father – he's a fine man . . .' He glanced at Umberto for approval. 'Generous. He gave something to everybody. He gave Mr Hak his taxi – I mean, his car. Only one in Puerto Gusano!' He chuckled to himself. 'Mr Bradshaw's son – that's good! Blue eyes that look right through you.' He was sizing Jonathan up. 'Very proper. A gentleman – just like Mr Ben, only fatter and more worried.'

Ricardo poured him a glass of Coca Cola.

'I'm the one who should be holding Waldo's hand tonight, Mr Bradshaw,' Umberto said. 'Tonight is a very special night: his wife is in the clinic producing a baby!'

Waldo was jittering with joy and anticipation. He could hardly hold the glass in his hand. Umberto was gazing at him with an expression of paternal admiration. Even Ricardo was smiling.

'Well, what's the news?' Umberto asked sharply.

Waldo stopped bouncing and stood at attention once more. 'Uh, what news, sir?'

'Is it a boy or a girl?'

'Uh, I don't know, sir.'

'Well, don't just stand there! Go find out! What's wrong with you?'

He dashed off.

'Those clothes.' Jonathan smiled. 'Where did he get them?'

'Waldo's clothes,' Umberto responded soberly, 'your father bought at Brooks Brothers during his college days. He gave them to me, and I handed them down to Waldo.' He looked at his own sleeve. 'The moths have been at them.' Taking out a fountain pen, he spent a minute studiously inking in the lining of his coat through the moth holes to make the tweed look whole.

Ricardo refilled their glasses, set another jar of peppers on the counter, and moved down the bar. The sound of motors was growing louder, and the first boats were bumping against the pilings. Beneath the flashing light of the neon sign, men could be seen leaping onto the jetty. The room was filling with hard-hatted workers from the refinery, and with the odour of sweat and oil and cologne.

They were a dubious-looking lot – bushy, drooping moustaches, dark hooded eyes, long greasy hair, striped T-shirts, torn blue jeans, pockmarked cheeks, sallow skin.

'Cheap cigarettes, cheap booze, cheap women, cheap lives . . .' Umberto was muttering to himself. 'Scum!'

They were calling for drinks. Some had knives and were expertly slicing long strips from the hams. When they caught sight of the Chief of Police, the petroleros nodded in his direction and lowered their voices.

A fat woman in a red dress came in and sat down. She proceeded to open a white suitcase she had with her and rummage around inside. It was stuffed with raw vegetables – turnips, radishes, and bunches of carrots.

'Ricardo's sister,' Umberto winked at Jonathan. 'To keep an eye on the hams. Rosa – what's wrong with you?' He walked over and put his arms around her and lifted her off her feet.

Rosa beat at his sides, 'Let me go!' she yelled over his shoulder. 'Last time he hugged me my ribs were sore for days! Help!'

Umberto's eyes were closed. 'You don't get enough squeezes, Rosa.'

'Too many from you!' She pulled at his arms and attempted to straighten her dress.

Umberto rejoined Jonathan at the bar. 'That's my girl friend. Aren't you, Rosy?' he shouted. 'Give her a drink, Ricardo,' he demanded perfunctorily, as though he were ordering water for his horse.

'Huh! You've got too many girl friends!'

Umberto poked Jonathan in the ribs. 'She may not be pretty,' he whispered, 'But she gives a mean blow job. Sucks like an irrigation pump. The trick is to shut your eyes and pretend you're in Hawaii.'

Jonathan's face turned red.

Umberto had completely forgotten the turtle. He seemed surprised to see it again.

'This turtle, which until recently proliferated along these shores . . .' He gestured despondently in the direction of Santa Petrolina. ' . . . is the last resort. Spilling this noble creature's blood is going to bring some relief, we hope. A certain local, uh, witch woman, who has her headquarters in a doorway off Cathedral Square assures me that it is so.'

'A witch?'

'She demands a turtle from the sea. She's going to cut off this poor creature's head, drain its blood; and my son Salvador will probably have to drink it. She'll gouge out the meat, grind it up and mix it with her own powders, and smear it on his skin.'

Jonathan gasped in horror. 'What's wrong with him?'

'Vitiligo, the disorder is known as.'

'A friend of mine was cured of vitiligo with massive doses of vitamin B at the Princeton Bio Brain Center,' Jonathan suggested.

'Vitamins?' Umberto laughed scornfully.

'Wait a minute. Do you ever listen to Bernard Meltzer on the radio? Can you get him down here? If you have a problem you phone him. He had a big programme about vitamin therapy. I'm sure it works.'

'We'll take our chances with this witch-woman, who happens to be a close friend of mine.

'You know, on the way over here this priest grabbed me in the front of the church. He told me the refinery attracted the whores who produced all the unwanted children. He kept saying *they* closed the church and kicked out the banana company. *They* brought in the refinery. I was wondering who he meant by "they". He said to ask you.'

Umberto banged his drink on the bar. 'Odorico exaggerates!' A fierce, brutal look transformed his face.

'The way he said it . . . he seemed to be implying you were to blame.'

'I don't like to hear that filthy talk. Negativism and despair – that's his world, not mine. I don't give a goddamn who *they* are – I've got important work to do. I've got to make this town into something – a decent place for children to grow up in. I don't have time for his bitterness. Besides, he's crazy.'

'You meet some pretty colourful characters down here.'

'Horrible, vicious . . . and vindictive. I tell you I don't want to talk about it!'

'All right! Take it easy . . . I'm sorry.'

Waldo came running back. It was a girl.

'I have the most beautiful wife,' he announced. 'I have a brand-new daughter. Can you think that anyone could be happier than me?'

Umberto kept patting him on the back and refilling his glass with Coca Cola. Waldo was completely transported with delight. He was breaking matches in two and throwing the pieces into the air. Suddenly he realized his responsibilities.

'I go tell my wife's family this happy, happy news. Do not go away . . . please, do not. I come back . . . five minutes. I buy drinks . . . and you will drink with me to the health of my wife and *daughter!*'

He rushed off again.

Umberto was laughing and shaking his head. 'Fatherhood, I've discovered, is essential to the search for happiness.'

'I wish mine felt that way,' Jonathan commented bitterly. 'Tonight I learn he's alive. I also learn that while his family and friends lit prayer candles, he was busy lighting church candles up whores' asses!'

Umberto's eyes flashed. 'I don't want to hear talk like that!'

The turtle had begun to move again and had collided with the base of the bar. It scratched the floor with its flippers and shoved and shoved, but it was the end of the line.

Umberto took his foot away and was staring down at it.

'There's nothing I'd rather do this minute than return this creature to the sea, which it smells and hears and knows cannot be far away . . . where it belongs, which it misses, where it longs to be. But it is the turtle that will be sacrificed.'

Umberto was eyeing himself sullenly in the glass. Jonathan couldn't help thinking that more than anything else the Chief of Police needed to hear the sound of his own voice. Somehow it soothed him, as did his reflected image in the mirror behind the bar.

They were looking at a cardboard sign propped up between two rum bottles.

THIS ESTABLISHMENT COLLABORATES WITH THE ASSOCIATION OF ADOLESCENT AND SUBNORMAL CHILDREN OF PUERTO GUSANO

Umberto had poured himself another drink. 'Who was it who said: *It is through children that the soul is cured*? An idiot? Do you believe it, Mr Bradshaw? Do you believe it?'

They caught sight in the mirror of a small boy entering the room. He was one of the most impish-looking children Jonathan had ever laid eyes on. Bare feet notwithstanding, he was quite elegantly dressed in a light grey suit, pressed and neat, with a pink rosebud in the lapel. He wore a clean white shirt and necktie whose colour matched that of the rose. His hair was parted in the middle. It had just been combed or brushed – not a hair was out of place. Although he behaved as though he were older, Jonathan guessed him to be about ten years old. He was standing among the tables, very composed, coolly taking in the scene around him. But those big front teeth gave him away. He looked like a playful animal, ready for any sport. He was carrying a basket of roses on his arm. Attached to the basket was a scrap of paper, upon which some letters had been scrawled in a childlike, uneven hand.

SAVE THE CHILDREN

'Salvador, come over here!'

The boy walked obediently to Umberto, who ruffled his hair and straightened his tie.

'This is my son Salvador. Meet Mr Bradshaw and speak English.'

'Yes, sir.' Salvador, eyes lowered, extended his hand.

'Now remember,' Umberto addressed him with mock sternness, 'you're soliciting for charity – not begging.'

The left side of the boy's face was a map of blotches. The eyebrow and lash were white, and the ear was speckled.

'Salvador's quite a linguist. Aren't you? Say something in French.'

The boy was pointing impatiently at the crude doors that concealed the toilets.

'All right, but hurry up. Be sure to zip up when you're done. You've got to be tidy if you want to be the Chairman of the Board of Westinghouse.'

Salvador ran off. '*Aujourd'hui!*' he called over his shoulder.

'*Au revoir*, you rascal,' Umberto shouted after him. 'Little devil, he makes those mistakes on purpose. See what I mean, Mr Bradshaw, about the vitiligo?'

'He seems perky and hopeful and not in the least bothered by it,' Jonathan heard himself saying.

'Thank you,' Umberto beamed. 'He's a good boy.'

Jonathan, too, felt the urge to go to the toilet. By mistake he pulled open the door where Salvador was seated on a rough wood structure.

'*Bon appetit!*' the boy exclaimed.

When Jonathan came out, Salvador was already approaching the tables where the refinery workers were sitting. With great deference he selected a rose from the basket and placed it by the elbow of one of the drinkers. He then took a step backwards, assuming an attitude of the utmost correctness, with the handle of the basket looped over his arm and his hands clasped together. If, within a minute, the drinker hadn't picked up the rose or made a gesture that he would buy it, Salvador retrieved it and proceeded to the next table.

A hush spread through the bar. The petroleros were curiously sizing up the little missionary. Ricardo cast a worried look in the direction of Umberto, but the Chief of Police was mute. Ricardo's sister stopped chewing.

Salvador screamed, and there was a stampede from the bar. One of the petroleros had opened a basket while Salvador was offering a rose, and a long green snake dived to the floor. Salvador was running, and the snake was whipping its body through the chairs and tables. The drinkers were leaping out of its way. The shouting and laughter abruptly stopped when Umberto pulled out a revolver and shot the snake through the head.

The shot rang out so close to Jonathan's ear that he was nearly knocked over by the report. Stumbling over the turtle that had crept beneath him, he embraced a ham to keep from falling. The string broke, but he managed to stay on his feet.

'All right – that's enough!' Umberto barked.

He thrust the revolver back into his belt, where his old tweed jacket concealed it. Ricardo ran out from behind the bar and snatched the ham from Jonathan's arms. His lips were moving, but Jonathan couldn't hear. The pistol shot had temporarily deafened him. Salvador darted to his father's side. Umberto put his arm around him and paid no attention to Ricardo, who was waving his arms about and pointing to the stricken serpent writhing on the floor. A petrolero picked it up and slung it out the window.

'Ricardo,' Umberto ordered, 'put these drinks on my bill, and give us one more round.'

Ricardo put down the ham and angrily slammed a stack of papers, impaled on a nail, on the bar. '*This*, Mr Bradshaw, is not the Caracas telephone book – it's Mr Hak's "bill". Some date back to the age when reptiles ruled the earth.'

'From the look of this place they're ruling it now.'

'One day they will again!' Umberto shouted.

'It was different when your father was here, Mr Bradshaw,' Ricardo growled. 'Very different. He paid his bill . . .'

'He paid *everyone's* bill,' Umberto added.

'It's true,' Ricardo sighed. 'We had a good time. Your father was a true gentleman.'

5
Worm Hole by Night

A horn sounded outside.

'Waldo's back. This way, Mr Bradshaw. Puerto Gusano by night!'

A pair of headlights cruised through the palms and drew up before the café. It was eleven o'clock and Waldo was just returning from taking Salvador home. He jumped out and ceremoniously opened the door for the Chief of Police.

'What kind of car *was* this?' Jonathan studied the auto. 'Looks like someone took a can opener to it.'

'It was a fairly standard 1965 Pontiac before we removed the roof with an acetylene torch. Watch those edges, they're sharp. It was your father's idea to make it a convertible. He had it shipped here from the capital.'

'You should have seen the stares when Señor Ben drove through town.' Waldo smiled, closed his eyes, and blew a kiss. 'It was the only car in Puerto Gusano – still is! He had a big heart for us poor fellows.' Waldo slammed the door and grinned. 'Presents for everybody.'

The car crept forward, and they drove through the port. Brazilian schooners lay at anchor, laden with cargoes of bricks and pineapples, bananas and mangoes, drinking jugs and grimy barrels. Standing waist deep in water, naked men were casting lines into the void. Fish scales glittered on the sea wall, and the rank odour of fish and creosote pervaded the night.

Umberto had leaned back, put his hands behind his head, and propped his feet on the front seat. Waldo turned on the radio and was accompanying a popular song in a passionate tenor voice.

'Hello, Umberto!' A fisherman held up a fish. There were cheerful salutations from all sides, which the Chief of Police took much delight in acknowledging. He sat up and waved as the car rolled along at a steady five miles per hour.

Jonathan smiled at a notice attached to the dashboard.

WALDO IS YOUR DRIVER
NOT YOU

On either side were medals on magnets. One held the photo of a young girl, the other a patriarch with a long white beard. Jonathan asked who they were.

'That's my Angelita,' Waldo answered sadly. 'She died. A malady of the blood she contracted on the beach.'

'Another blessing from Santa Petrolina,' Umberto added.

'Gosh, Waldo, I'm sorry.' Jonathan regretted he'd asked because his question had upset Waldo.

But Waldo wanted to talk. 'She was engaged to marry a man who worked in an office . . .'

'You've got another daughter now,' Umberto reminded him. 'She'll grow up and marry a man who *owns* an office.'

'Yes, yes! Right, boss!' Waldo slapped himself on the side of his head. 'A new daughter – how could I forget?'

Jonathan pointed over Waldo's shoulder. 'Who's the old man in the other photograph?'

'A saint. My wife believes in them, not me. I believe in Mr Hak and Mr Ben.'

Jonathan laughed. 'My grandmother says the only saint in my father's life was his St Bernard.'

'Your father – he helped me.' Waldo snatched the hat from his head and clutched it to his chest. 'He rescued me when I couldn't brush my teeth . . .'

'What?'

'When Angelita died, I was a mess. I couldn't brush my teeth for a year. I couldn't do anything.'

'Well, you're not a mess anymore.' Umberto reached forward and gave Waldo's head a friendly scratch. 'Ben sorted you out and made you start thinking about the future again. Didn't he?'

'Yes, sir, Mr Hak!'

'That man was *amazing!*' Umberto emphasized his statement with a long, low whistle.

'You say *was*,' Jonathan noted with alarm. 'He's not dead, is he?'

'Not any more!'

Jonathan was confused by this remark, but Umberto wasn't paying attention. He was waving to someone in the street. 'Your father . . . God, I'd like to show these kids how to be like him. That man had one of the best heads I ever listened to. Superstar! He knew how to perform . . . how to be . . . how to get people to work for him . . . how to get people to find out what he needed to know.

I don't give a goddamn where he is now – wherever he is, it's superstar time.' Umberto paused. 'Waldo, run over there and buy some food. I'm starved.'

The car stopped, and Waldo leapt away into the dark. Umberto's eyes focused on Jonathan. 'What I want to know from you is . . . what is this *it*?'

'It?'

'Yes, what is this *it* everybody's talking about? It. It. It. Everybody's substituting art, Plato, sawed-off automobiles, Einstein, yachts, black holes, cocktail shakers, A-bombs, sea turtles, pelican bones, anteaters, ice buckets, rose gardens, and photographs to put on mantels – substituting for what? It. It. It. Nobody understands what I'm talking about – this goddamned *it!*'

'It?' Jonathan thought he was listening to a madman.

'We're substituting for what's missing . . . and *what's missing is love!*'

'*Here!*' Waldo thrust two sticks of sugarcane into their hands.

The car lurched forward again.

'Get going, Waldo! We've got a lot of ground to cover tonight.'

Waldo accelerated to about six miles per hour. They passed a man pushing a baby carriage full of live iguanas. He held one up hopefully as the car cruised by.

'Waldo,' Jonathan asked. 'Why do you drive so slow?'

'Because there's nowhere to go.'

'Oh!'

There was something white up ahead. As the car slowed, Jonathan peered around Waldo to see what it was. The headlights illuminated a triangular sail spread on the road. The cloth was so white that it seemed to glow in the dark. On it five black men were lying. Head to toe, their naked bodies bent or straight, with arms flung out in elusive, beckoning gestures, they made a configuration like a dark hieroglyph. Some looked ready to jump and others were running and they all could have been flying through white space when in fact they were sound asleep and even snoring.

Umberto leaned forward. 'Now, Waldo!'

The car let out a blast of horn as loud as a ship's siren. The sleeping men levitated like collapsed puppets whose strings had been pulled and were on their feet, swaying and staggering from surprise and fright.

'Well done!' Umberto pounded Waldo on the back. 'Caught you – you lazy bastards!' he shouted at the men. 'What do you mean by lying in the road? You want to die?'

The bewildered men stood in the dusty light. 'Good evening, Mr Hak,' they cried out plaintively. Their voices sounded like the moaning of sleepy birds.

'Get with it, men. Get your heads right.'

The car rolled forward and left its tracks on the sail. Umberto gazed at himself in the rearview mirror and was caressing the back of his head.

'I'm going to start looking good after the Night of Sacrifices.'

'Sounds sinister – what is it?'

'My annual party for the children – like graduation.'

'Are there schools in this town?'

'Want a job teaching English, Mr Bradshaw? Ah! Ha! Ha! The schools all folded when Peaceful Banana left. The Church ran a school until Odorico went berserk. Ben and I talked about turning his boat into a floating university, but there's no school like my school . . . first of all, I have to get into shape.'

They stopped at an outdoor restaurant near the market. The young black waitresses, when they caught sight of the Chief of Police, rushed forward to the car. They leaned in and kissed him gaily on the mouth.

Steaming plates of black beans and rice were served to them in the back seat of the car. Waldo went over and sat with friends at a table while they ate.

'I never expected to find a carhop in Puerto Gusano,' Jonathan said.

'Try this rum and cashew juice. Ice cold and delicious! Better than the whiskey sours at Galatoire's in New Orleans.'

Jonathan was sorry to see more drinks arriving, as Umberto's boozing made him all the more unpredictable. While they ate, they were serenaded by a group of minstrels plucking one-stringed twanging harps of African origin. They gave out some odd and eerie notes. But it was a festive interlude, and Umberto was in high spirits, laughing and joking with the waitresses and encouraging the musicians. The incident at Ricardo's seemed to have been forgotten.

Within a few minutes, Umberto was snoring, mouth open and head thrown back, as the car cruised through the park. Waldo switched off the motor, and they rolled to a stop next to a kiosk. Beneath the spreading branches of a colossal mango tree, beer was being served. The kiosk roof flared out into broad eves supported by iron lace girders. Close by, tables and chairs had been set out beneath a pavilion with a tiled roof. To one side stood a low, box-like structure of brick, whose odour rendered part of the pavilion most disagreeable – the public latrine.

The clientele consisted of straw-hatted black men smoking green cigars.

The breeze changed, rustling the thick foliage overhead, and Jonathan was nearly overpowered by the stench of the latrine that wafted through the pavilion. Waldo turned around in his seat and pinched his nose shut. Peripatetic shoeshine boys, vendors of candy and cigarettes and newspapers, beggars, prostitutes and aimless children circulated among the tables. (The beggars were periodically driven off by harassed, exhausted waitresses.) Whistling, quarrelling, biting down suspiciously on any coin that was offered them, the shoeshine boys in particular comprised a considerable force. They often conversed in whistles. Even the smallest, five or six years old, spat a great deal.

Umberto jerked awake. His face darkened when he saw an old woman ogling Jonathan. 'Now listen – I want to tell you something. I just had a dream about getting everyone who works out at Santa Petrolina registered when he comes ashore. Anyone who's not registered won't count. He just scratches.'

'Are you going to register them for the draft?'

'We're going to register their *pricks!*' He laughed out loud. Waldo grinned over the front seat. 'That's it – every petrolero's prick will be measured. We'll have a prick bank and start a mail-order business. We'll amputate, preserve, freeze in dry ice, and mail C.O.D.! We'll advertise the latest miracle of modern surgery. An illustrated catalogue. To the sceptical we'll send free plaster cast models of hard-ons. Who would say no to a mulatto prick one foot long? Only two sizes – big and *extra* big. All colours. Men tend to overlook colour, you know, but the women notice. You think I'm kidding? Where do you think all these children come from? Boom, boom, boom in the bushes. Born in the park and left to starve.' Umberto hammered his fist against the cardoor. 'By God, we'll profit from what's plaguing us! We'll sell their pricks!'

'You could advertise in *Screw Magazine*,' Jonathan suggested.

The car had drawn up beside a throne-like easy chair upholstered in a quilted material. UNTOUCHABLE MIRROR LUSTRE – 10 CENTS was engraved on a metal plaque that hung from one arm. Plastic roses wreathed the back of the chair, and a vase of plastic tulips stood on one corner of a trunk.

The shoeshineman, seated on a low stool, was bent over in hunched concentration. According to the brass badge pinned to his shirt pocket, Sox was his name, and his number was one. His mouth was full of nails, and he was hammering on a lady's shoe. A fat, brown, painted creature occupied the throne, dangling a plump foot in mid-air.

Umberto, forgetting his monologue, suddenly shouted, 'Sox, get over here! Customer!' He kicked open the car door, 'Sox – this is Mr Bradshaw – Ben Bradshaw's son!'

'Glad to meet you, Sox.'

Sox's face brightened. 'Señor Ben – he liked shiny shoes all right! He gave me these.' He proudly displayed a pair of patent leather evening pumps with a gros-grain ribbon. 'They've been shined over a thousand times!'

'And these are the boots he wore when he parachuted into the Philippines and won his Purple Heart,' Jonathan laughed. 'I bet they haven't been shined since World War Two.'

The fat whore who occupied the throne began to squeal for her shoe. One baleful look from Umberto silenced her, and she hobbled off barefoot. Jonathan was made to take her place.

'Many, many times your daddy sat here,' Sox was saying. 'He was always my first customer in the morning. With him I smoked my first cigarette and drank my first cup of coffee. While the gardeners were watering the flowers, while the air was cool, he would sit where you're sitting now, and we began our day together. One morning he said to me: "Sox, when I sit here in this South American plaza, I feel liberated. Those brushes of yours massage my feet and put me at my ease. This throne may be nothing but an old easy chair, but it lifts my spirits." '

'When I was in Bolivia I dreamed that one day I would come upon my father just as you described him, having his shoes shined in some South American plaza.'

Like an artist surveying a canvas, Sox sat back, drew on his cigarette, and contemplated Jonathan's boots. Following a quick

brush to eliminate superficial dust and dirt, he was applying a
water and alcohol solution with a toothbrush.

'I stay here day and night, night and day.' Sox was waving the
toothbrush in the air. 'I never leave the tree. Look at these
branches, mister. They go out twenty, thirty feet. This tree is like
a big house. It shelters all the children.'

Jonathan followed his gaze up into the network of branches.
Half concealed among the leaves, the faces of little children were
peering down. Straddling the branches, curled up in tree huts,
they looked like a tribe of friendly marmosets.

Umberto was waving back. The children were waking up,
whispering among themselves. The tree filled with a strange
rustling sound as they began to stir.

Jonathan thought he was dreaming. 'Have they really no place
to go?' he asked.

'Nowhere.' Sox was applying polish with another toothbrush.
'See the little houses they build among the branches? They *like* it
up there.'

'But children need families,' Jonathan said. 'We all do.'

The brushes churned over Jonathan's boots. The muscles of
Sox's flat, brown chest jumped and contracted as he worked.

One of the drinkers had risen from his table. Sox picked up a
large key to which a bit of wood was attached by a wire and
handed it to him. The man headed for the latrine.

'Ben gave him that key,' Umberto said.

'Cost you five cents to take a leak in there, mister!' Sox proclaimed. 'Take a leak in the park if you don't want to pay, but
there's a law against it, and if the police . . .' He winked at Umberto. Another man staggered out of the latrine and handed back
a key, with a coin. Sox pocketed the coin and waved the key.

'In this town there're more shoeshine boys than shoes. It's not
easy to make a living. But with *this*,' he said, shaking the key once
more, 'thanks to your daddy, I've been able to clothe, feed, and
look after myself, my wife, and all my children. And let me tell
you, mister, the family is big! This key to the latrine brought
an end to my worries! This,' he cried defiantly, 'is the key to my
life!'

'All right, Sox!' Umberto looked away; he seemed embarrassed. 'Enough.'

The motor roared. They left Sox putting away his brushes and tins of polish. The children in the tree waved silently.

'So you see, Mr Bradshaw, all these children belong to me and your father.'

'What do you mean?'

'We sired them. We brought them into the world.'

'Are you serious?'

'We're responsible for them.'

'*All* these children? I thought the petroleros . . .'

'They're ours – every last one of them.'

'So this is my family tree? I should take a photo and send it to my mother and grandmother. But I can assure you of one thing, Mr Hak – I'm his only legitimate son.'

They came out on the other side of the park where a band of boys was playing soccer.

'Let's watch!' Umberto and Waldo vaulted out of the car. The children were delighted. Jonathan, who'd had so much to drink he had to lean against the fender for support, had never met anyone so robust as the Chief of Police.

Umberto couldn't stop shouting orders. 'What's wrong with that boy? Pass the ball! Get with it!'

'*Goal!*'

Jonathan, meanwhile, was attracted by shouts of a different nature. Leaving Umberto and Waldo engrossed in their game, he wandered off down the street. A crowd had gathered about a wagon loaded with long, hairy pigs. The driver, a honey-coloured man, was standing on the box, beating his mule with a stick. As Jonathan approached he could hear the man cursing and grunting. He was putting all his strength into each blow.

'Uh! I'll make her move!' he shouted in a hoarse voice.

The mule never stirred, It was white and bony, with grey spots along its flanks. Jonathan grimaced as it stood there, shivering under the force of the blows and wearily shaking its head.

There were mostly women and children in the crowd. 'Stop it!' they were shouting. 'You're killing her!' The mule staggered and almost fell. Its hooves clattered against the cobbles. The farmer, who seemed to be drunk or insane, was sweating profusely. Dropping the reins, he took the stick in both hands and aimed a blow at the mule's head. Momentarily released from the grip of the bit, the mule lowered its head and the stick whistled above its ears. The momentum of the blow brought the farmer tumbling head first from the wagon. A shout of approval went up from the crowd.

The farmer jumped to his feet and began to pummel the mule with his fists. The laughter became general; but at the very moment when it appeared that the farmer's anger was spent, a group of petroleros arrived on the scene.

'You going to let that mule whip you, farmer?' one of them shouted.

'Hey, farmer, that mule ain't got no balls and neither do you!'

'Hey, farmer, show us what you do when you catch your wife in bed with another man. Show us a good beating!'

'Or maybe your wife beats you!'

The rising laughter threw the farmer into a frenzy. He dragged a spade from the wagon.

'Give it to her with the sharp end!' the petroleros taunted. 'Give it to her with the shovel end!'

Leaping back onto the wagon, he took the spade by the handle and raised it above his head. The women were screaming.

'That's it, farmer – show her you mean business!' the petroleros yelled. 'Give her a lesson she'll never forget!'

The spade came down, and a moan spread through the crowd. The mule stiffened and shuddered and collapsed. The blade had cut deeply into its back. The black blood welled up and flowed down both sides. People turned away and hid their faces.

There was a movement in the crowd. Umberto had just rushed up and was pushing his way through. Picking up the farmer's stick, he vaulted onto the wagon as the people fell silent. Only the farmer, who was still staring down at his fallen mule, seemed unaware that the Chief of Police was standing directly behind him among the grunting pigs.

Umberto struck him across the back with the stick. The farmer cried out and fell down on his hands and knees as the women and children cheered.

'How does it feel?' Umberto asked when the shouting had died.

Umberto raised the stick to strike again, but his hand dropped limply against his side. For a minute he surveyed the fallen mule, the grunting pigs and the farmer who lay at his feet. His gaze swept the upturned faces of the grandmothers, the prostitutes, the children and the petroleros. The chanting died as his shoulders slumped and his arms dangled in a gesture of utter defeat. His face assumed an expression of such loneliness and despair, that the crowd surrounding the wagon began to buzz with concern.

'I suppose you're going to tell me this is all *Mr Bradshaw's* fault,' he said in a loud whisper. The arm holding the stick began to rise ominously.

Jonathan was so astounded he took a step backwards, but there was no escaping. The crowd hemmed him in; every eye was on him.

'I suppose you're going to say *because he's here* – in Puerto Gusano, searching for his father who made such an impact on this town, overturning the stones of the past, that all the worms underneath are going to start wiggling free. And this sort of thing is the result.' The stick was pointing directly at Jonathan, whose face was burning. He was torn between embarrassment and fear; if the crowd turned on him, he would be beaten like the wretched mule.

'What's wrong with you?' Umberto's voice wavered.

Jonathan was about to burst into a complicated apology, but the indictment was not meant for him.

'Bravo! Right on! Long live slop time!' The Chief of Police bellowed. 'Degeneracy and poverty of the spirit! To hell with human dignity – let's wallow in the mud with these pigs!' He paused. 'What about your yearning for respectability?' Umberto's voice had once more dropped to a stage whisper. 'To die respectable men? I'll tell you people one thing – you haven't got a prayer. This place is a prelude to hell and you people are going to hear the whole sonata. Jerk time, baby!'

Umberto waved his arms. 'And all this because the chickens have come home to roost? The son of Ben Bradshaw arrives and you revert to being savages?'

Jonathan felt the people around him moving against him; more prodding from the Chief of Police and they might jump him at any second.

'Because Mr Bradshaw's here asking where's Ben gone and what's Ben doing and blah! blah! blah! – you're reminded of Ben Bradshaw and happier times. So you just throw in the towel and give up. You look at Puerto Gusano the way *he* does – seeing for the first time the barricaded church, the homeless children and the empty offices of Peaceful Banana. The burning skies and angry waters of Santa Petrolina! Well, I'll tell you people one thing – I've never felt guilty about *anything!* I swear to the Father, the Son and the Holy Ghost.' Umberto crossed himself; many people in the crowd did the same. 'Get your heads straight! You've got to stop turning sons of heroes into sons of bitches!'

The mood of the crowd abruptly grew less hostile; a hand reached out and patted Jonathan on the back.

'This nonsense has got to stop!' Umberto shouted. 'Go on – help that mule back to its feet. And don't blame Mr Bradshaw for being here. Don't expect him to do for Puerto Gusano what Ben Bradshaw did. Don't blame *him* for not being the man his father was or for not having the purity and vision his father had. For not being superstar like Ben Bradshaw. *He* hasn't ventured to the forbidden city of Smara or explored the coral reefs of the South Pacific. Don't blame *him* for not climbing the Acropolis or for never experiencing a sunset in the Sahara . . . Get with it!' He looked down at the farmer who was sweating and bleeding from the cut across his back. 'And get this wagon out of here before I fine you for creating a public disturbance!'

There was an appreciative murmur and applause. 'Mr Ben's son – glory!' someone shouted. 'Have a good time, sonny!'

The mule shifted its weight and raised its head. It seemed ready to stand. Up it came. Some people stepped forward to help the farmer. The animal stood so unsteadily they had to brace it from both sides to prevent it from falling again. The cobbles were slippery with blood.

'I want you to welcome Mr Bradshaw for the man he is, even without Ben's generosity of spirit, or the charm.' Umberto jumped down from the wagon and began to walk toward the car.

Jonathan ran up behind him. 'Mr Hak – what in the? Jesus Christ – for Pete's sake . . .'

'Come along, Mr Bradshaw. I want to hear more about your grandmother's love affairs.'

'We'll get to that in a minute. First I want to lay to rest this myth that I'm to blame for what happened to that mule or anything else. One more taunt from you and those people would have torn me apart.'

'What's wrong with you? Do you take everything personally? Get with it. Come on, I've got a lot to do tonight.'

6

The Wheel

As the car emerged from the trees, the ferris wheel came into view.

'Waldo, you buffoon, stop here!' Umberto commanded. 'We're going to ride!'

Waldo responded happily. 'Yes, sir!'

'This goon's got to learn English.' He slapped Waldo on the arm. 'Don't you?' They both let out raucous laughs.

Jonathan and Umberto climbed out of the car.

'The kids call him "Night and Day".' Umberto banged the door shut. 'On duty round the clock.' He smiled affectionately at Waldo, who was already stretching out in the front seat. 'That's where he sleeps. He likes it that way. Hey!' he bellowed, and Waldo snapped to attention. 'Where are those cashew daiquiris?'

Waldo opened the trunk and produced a silver ice bucket and cocktail shaker. He poured the daiquiris from a glass jar into the shaker, added some ice cubes, and began to shake.

Umberto took the shaker. 'See this?' He wiped the condensation from a spot in the middle of the shaker. The initials 'G.B.' appeared, engraved in silver. 'Know what that is, Mr Bradshaw? Know where this came from?'

'Oh, yeah, that looks like a wedding present. In America, that would be a typical wedding present. Silver. One of my roommates at Princeton was Andrew Jackson Donaldson Downie from Memphis. At his wedding I never saw so goddamn much silver. From all his relatives from Tennessee and Mississippi. Southerners like to give away silver.'

'Art deco – from the genuine cocktail days.' Umberto demonstrated how the cap pulled up, and he poured out two drinks. 'Belonged to your grandfather, Gardner Bradshaw. And that silver ice bucket was a wedding present your mother and father received over forty years ago.'

'Mr Hak!' Jonathan was incredulous. *'My grandfather?* Jesus Christ! Wait a minute. How did you get my mother's wedding presents?'

'Ben had 'em on the yacht.' Umberto shook the ice cubes and topped up their drinks. 'Your grandfather was an admiral . . . commander of the battleship *Oklahoma* when the Japanese bombed Pearl Harbor, right?' He smiled broadly. 'When the ship turned turtle, this shaker was the only thing from his cabin that floated free. Your father gave it to me. Come on. Get in here.'

They climbed aboard the ferris wheel.

Shaking his head in consternation, Jonathan sat down heavily on the seat. 'Mr Hak . . . I just don't see . . . the *Oklahoma*, Pearl Harbor. My *grandfather's* cocktail shaker? Gardner Bradshaw's initials. Are you kidding? I'm really shocked that you have our family *silver*.'

A bar was snapped across their knees. The motor was put into gear and accelerated, and immediately they were lifted upwards. The children who had gathered were waving as they were swept up into the night. Jonathan's brow furrowed as he tried to word his claim on the ice bucket.

'We got this thing off a circus.' Umberto gulped his daiquiri. 'Now there's a *real* drink. It was Ben's idea. The ship it was travelling on conked out and put in here. He persuaded them to come ashore and perform for us. The circus, as you can imagine, drove the children wild with excitement – they couldn't be kept out. The elephant, maddened by a hail of pebbles, broke loose and went on a rampage and had to be shot. A camel was stolen and roasted in the park. The circus, alas, was forced to retire. In their haste they left this machine behind. Ben bought it for a song. Four hundred bucks.'

They were hovering above the treetops. Far out at sea the lights of passing ships were visible. The lightning continued to flicker silently but closer, as the storm crept steadily toward the shore. In the midst of so much blackness, Santa Petrolina blazed like a volcano.

'The children continue to ride it,' Umberto mumbled. 'So do I. Out of smokes!' he suddenly yelled. 'Waldo!'

As the gondola swept earthwards, he flung some money away.

'Americanos – blond ones! And some cigars for Mr Bradshaw! Pronto!'

Waldo bounded from the car and caught the bills in mid-air.

The ferris wheel stopped, and children were climbing into the empty gondolas. Umberto waved at them. 'Chico, close the bar

properly and hang on tight! That's my boy!' he called down.
'You'll see, Mr Bradshaw, they'll all be here in a minute.'

The wheel began to move again, stopping occasionally to let
children on or off. Everyone was having a good time, especially
Waldo, who'd come back with cigarettes and cigars. Umberto
snatched them from his hand as they sailed by. Waldo lounged in
the car, admired by the crowd of children that seemed to follow
the Chief of Police everywhere. Deep in thought, Jonathan
slouched in his seat.

All of a sudden, Umberto slapped his knee. 'I knew it was too
quiet around here. *Music,* Waldo, *music!*' he shouted. 'What's
wrong with you?'

From somewhere ancient music was heard. Waldo had taken
an old victrola from the trunk, placed it on the hood of the car and
plugged it in somehow. Umberto listened intently. 'Louder,
louder!' The scratchy music filled the night. '*Stardust* – listen!'

'Sometimes I won-der why I spend the lone-ly night
Dream-ing of a song
The mel-o-dy haunts my re-ve-rie
And I am once ag-ain with you . . .'

Static drowned the words, but Umberto knew them by heart.
He was relaxed at last.

'Look, Mr Hak, about that cocktail shaker . . .'

'Shh. Can't you hear the poetry of this? Here is cool, soundless
oblivion where, while travelling with great velocity, one at last
comes to a standstill,' he said, leaning back in his seat.

Jonathan lit his cigar and shut his eyes.

'It *is* a comforting idea – that of the wheel . . .' Umberto, like a
man at ease in his own parlour, had crossed his legs and put his
hands behind his head. ' . . . that one is always moving, that one
can never be enclosed or stymied. To comprehend the movement
of the wheel, all that is required is an appreciation of the concept
of balance. To go around and around, to remake the world, to
make it like it was before. Are you listening Mr Bradshaw?'

Jonathan was looking down upon the tiny bodies of children
flung in rows on the ground. It was as though the ferris wheel had
just run over and flattened them.

'To be honest, Mr Hak . . .'

'Listen – now that's a *real* song.'

Umberto ran his hand several times upward through his mass

of curly hair. He seemed to be tugging on it. His face bore a familiar, troubled, faraway look that lasted so long that Jonathan thought he was deliberately exposing and indulging his pain.

'I'm not the sort of man you'd expect to find in a hole like this, am I?' he finally said. 'I'm not saying I'm ahead of my time, but I'm certainly ahead of *this*.' He lit a cigarette and waved it about. 'I'm going to tell you some things about myself and your father – things you must never repeat. You're someone who can understand love, art, theatre, Beckett, tragedy – especially Greek tragedy and the forces that are beyond man's control.'

Jonathan remained silent and respectful of Umberto's mood. He stopped chewing the cigar, and tried to figure out what he was talking about.

'You know the last act of *Orestes*, don't you?' Umberto went on. 'When the author employs a *deus ex machina* to bring a happy solution to a hopeless, murderous situation?' He was too absorbed by the sound of his own words to wait for a reply. 'He should have brought on loud, booming cymbals to announce the way out of this idle putrefied civilization. Throngs to jeer the heads of young heroes driven on the end of stakes!'

'That's you?'

'That's *death!*' Umberto nodded solemnly. His eyes were half closed. '*This God-forsaken place doesn't understand* what I'm trying to do. They're jealous of anyone who has the vision and imagination to try to improve things. They want to see my downfall – trampled, face down in the gutter. *Dead.*' He poured himself another daiquiri. 'Here.'

'No thanks.'

'What's wrong with you? This is an important conversation!' He grabbed Jonathan's arm. 'The night my wife left me . . .' Umberto squinted as though he was attempting to view something in the distant past. 'There were all those illiterate drunks and hopeless failures that wash up nightly to guzzle from foul-smelling bottles at Ricardo's. Sitting there on stools like so many hairless, decaying specimens in a taxidermist's window. Four or five of them in a row – hateful, resentful, negative, burnt-out cases. They all turned and looked at me as I entered. Word was out she'd gone, and I saw five smug cheshire grins – smiles on ravaged faces that had never smiled before – smiles of glee and satisfaction over my personal tragedy.' He sipped his drink and was silent for a minute. 'Then,

as if directed by Beckett himself, they all stood up and moved over
– offering me the stool of honour in their row of despair and
failure. Ben, Marie and I – we were an oasis in this cultural desert.
They were all jealous.'

'Marie?'

'My wife. You can't imagine how different it was then. Music,
art, creative ideas . . . constant repartee, humour. We were happy
doing things – living creatively and productively. There was a
purity and vision that guided our lives.'

'What kind of purity and vision?'

Umberto laughed. 'Ben was my friend. We shared the unique
experience of kindred souls who are attracted to each other by all
the energy of the universe. We were two Greeks – émigrés from a
previous, dazzling age.'

'If you're my father's greatest friend why are you throwing up
this smokescreen?'

'Do you realize how important those years were – what they
meant – and the tragedy that they had to end? That was big time,
baby.'

Umberto's face was lit by a smile. 'Ben Bradshaw on the deck of
his yacht. Three-thirty one sultry afternoon . . .' He slapped his
knee, delighted by the memory. 'I thought I was *hallucinating* – a
Greek god sailing into Puerto Gusano! Apollo himself. He was the
best looking man I'd ever seen. Tall, cleancut, blond – superstar!
Ben Bradshaw, tan and lean, hands on hips, Damn!'

Absorbed in Umberto's description of his father, Jonathan
shook his head slowly and chewed his cigar.

'I've seen him whirl a poisonous snake around by its tail and
make it dizzy, before grabbing it by the throat . . .' Umberto
spread the fingers of his left hand. 'This is his signet ring.'
Jonathan stared at the ring which Umberto wagged a few inches
from his face.

'The crest consists of a simple sunflower and the motto *Tibi
Soli.* It means, "To you, O sun", or, more appropriately, "To you
only".'

'I'm his son!'

Umberto withdrew his hand. 'He gave it to me. With those blue
eyes no one could read . . . straight nose and a mischievous
smile . . .'

Jonathan hardly heard him; suddenly he feared for his father's life. The appearance of the ring, which he recognized instantly, had startled him.

'Mr Hak, this whole thing is beginning to sound awfully suspicious. Why did he give you the ring?'

'I have a photo taken when he was a youth in France. Wasn't that when the admiral was having an affair with a chorus girl and sent the whole family packing to Biarritz for a year, just to be rid of them? And didn't they spend another year at the Hyde Park Hotel in London while your grandmother waited for the affair to be over, so they could go home?'

'I don't know anything about that.' Jonathan dismissed the question. 'Did my father ever talk to you about coming home?'

Umberto frowned at the remark. 'I'm fascinated by people who can get on with things,' he answered gruffly. 'The way I ought to be getting on with getting out of this town. My family may have been here five generations, but I don't belong. But then . . . what will they do without me?' he asked himself sadly. 'Everybody knows it's my drunken spirit that holds this town together.'

Umberto sat back in his seat and acknowledged the waves of the children. 'I used to puzzle over the phenomenon of a free man like Ben Bradshaw. Free of the chains of the past, free of the people he was born among, the people he happened to grow up with. A life completely of his own choosing.'

'Are you saying free of me and my family?'

'Ben needed Puerto Gusano and Puerto Gusano needed Ben.'

'What in the world for?'

'Ben sailed in here unencumbered by family. Making money didn't interest him, or to do or be what other people expected of him. He was beyond their reach and control, floating free of outside influence and in his own field of gravity, like a rocket or balloon launched into space. He didn't want to return to where there was no comprehension of what is valuable.'

'And what is valuable?'

'Art . . . purity and vision . . . to make life an adventure, not just making money and raising a family. He was in search of something different, strange . . . exotic.'

'What about the suffering of those he left behind?'

'I'm not talking about that.'

'I know you aren't, but I am, and it can't be ignored.'

'If all the orphans in this town spent their time trying to find their fathers, they'd never get on with anything. I'm telling you that Ben had a vision of how to be . . .'

Umberto furtively scrutinized Jonathan's face. 'Your father arrived here when Peaceful Banana's operations were still in full swing, and, as he was a natural engineer, he extended the network of canals that drained large areas of the swamp where the plantations flourished. He also designed a drawbridge that opens and closes on its own. The sailboats can pass through without the mast being lowered, and the sailors don't have to jump down. We had big ideas for this town. We used to lie on the deck, gaze at the stars, and dream. Listening to Handel and Bach.'

'Mr Hak, just because a guy gets on his boat and sails away, it doesn't mean he's looking for the Holy Grail. You give the whole thing a messianic ring. I know plenty of guys who went to the fifth floor of Abercrombie's and bought a safari outfit and headed out after the great white elephant . . . that doesn't mean they're on some holy crusade. Was your wife in search of some deep truth when she left you?'

'Marie, too, sensed the importance of knowing Ben . . .'

'Was Marie beautiful?'

'Of course, she was beautiful!' He looked angry for a moment. 'Do you think I'd have a wife who wasn't beautiful? In quest of something, too.'

'And what was her quest?'

'*Mediocrity!*' Umberto looked a bit confused when he said it. 'She taught me there was purity and vision in mediocrity, too.' He didn't seem to believe this, but went obsessively on. 'I mean, there are various plateaux of enlightenment, and to glorify the mediocre is a great talent. I wasn't up to it. I couldn't fulfil her needs. They were too simple. I was blind to her truth, and that destroyed our happiness. She was miles ahead of me – it moved everyone who saw us together to tears. People wanted to cry at the sight of our happiness and affirmation of life – and her purity.'

'I'm very sorry.' Jonathan tried to picture a town full of people sobbing.

'It was my stupidity and lack of vision. Then I got tired coming home at night to a house with no life and no sounds. So I moved them all in.'

'Who?'

'The kids. Simplicio, Eusebio, Mercedes, Dolores – all of them.'

'They live with you?'

'You'll see . . . Waldo!' he yelled.

'What about my father?'

'He left. *Waldo!*'

'If he needed Puerto Gusano so much, why did he leave?'

'Yes, man does feel a strange kinship with the stars . . .' Umberto once more changed the subject. 'They shine down upon him, they approve of him and protect him, they restore his sense of proportion and reaffirm his humanity . . .' The ferris wheel had stopped once more. They were at the top. It was late and most of the children were getting off. 'When I look up, I always look out – *there*.' Umberto swung his arm inland, in the direction of the swamp. 'On the odd chance . . . a lantern swinging, or the lamp of a boat weaving its way through the web of canals that he himself helped to build – a sign that Ben has finally decided to return.'

Umberto sighed and breathed a soft whistle. 'My life ended when he left.' He turned unsteadily toward Jonathan. He paused to think. 'The spirit of my life ended . . . *then*.'

'That's sad, Mr Hak. But you have a life now, don't you?'

Umberto was shaking his head. 'That will always be my life.' He held his head up with effort.

'Didn't Dad ever talk about coming back home?'

'*Yes he did!*' Umberto shouted. 'The same anger and rejection I felt when he vanished . . . Crap!! It's all crap . . . you, Marie, Bertha, children, the church, Santa Petrolina, Waldo's baby . . .'

'Are you trying to tell me my father's leaving you is a greater tragedy than his leaving me?'

'It's funny . . . this predicament of irreversibility.' Umberto never listened. 'Since we can't turn back, since we can't make things the way they once were, or undo what's been done, the only recourse is forgiveness. Waldo, *Stop this thing!*' he shouted. '*Stop the music! Stop this goddamned wheel! We want off!*'

'Mr Hak, you've avoided the most important question . . .'

Umberto shrugged. 'You can't.'

'Can't what?'

'Can't find him.'

A shiver passed through Jonathan. 'Why not?'

'Because . . . nobody will take you to him.'

'I'll go alone.'

'Impossible. Only Ben Bradshaw can get through the dogs.'

The ferris wheel stopped, and Waldo steadied the rocking gondola.

'What dogs?'

'Dogs that guard the entrance to green hell.'

'Mr Hak . . .' Jonathan's words were interspersed by nervous laughter. 'Mr Hak! Take it easy, take it easy. You talk like I've walked in here carrying my umbilical cord like a lasso. You've thrown up a smokescreen of poetry and vision, Greek civilization, Beckett and Bach, contradiction and words. I'm sure if we got all the witnesses in there'd be heated debate for and against the past, and so forth and so forth. What I want to know is where is the entrance to green hell. Where is Ben Bradshaw and who will take me to him – or how do I get there by myself?'

'Look, Mr Bradshaw. Can't you get it through your head that you can't find your father, and that he doesn't want you to, and that you'll only cause trouble by looking. What's wrong with you? You've admitted that your family didn't want you to come, either. Believe me, you'll create a disaster. *Waldo!* I'm sick of this redneck time. Let's move.'

7

Umberto's Nest

Umberto's house was set back from the street in a wild, untended garden. The palms reached roof level, where their fronds mingled with the foliage of the mangoes.

'Welcome to the jungle.' Umberto held back a hibiscus branch so Jonathan could pass. 'This garden is beginning to look like the virgin forest which begins right at the edge of town. The municipal gardeners are due to come tomorrow for the annual purging of weeds. They will do battle, not with snippers and trowel, but with machetes and axes. In two weeks' time you won't recognize this place – it'll be manicured and prepared to receive my guests for the Children's Day party. They all come and those lucky ones who have families bring them, too. It's the highlight of the year.

'This year I've decided to call the party "The Night of Sacrifices". Ah! Ha! Ha! Don't worry, it's not going to be some Aztec slaughter. No hearts will be torn from living breasts. *They already have!* No. What I mean is . . . each citizen is supposed to make some gesture, some small sacrifice that will help bring peace and well-being to our town. Such as to refrain from throwing garbage into the street, to befriend the neighbour you've been feuding with, to make a donation to the orphanage. And I hope you'll join us, Mr Bradshaw. Bertha's preparing curried goat.'

'Why don't you offer a look through that telescope as a door prize?'

'Brilliant idea! Just the kind of thing Ben would have thought of.' He clapped Jonathan on the back. 'Bravo!'

The path led to a large, rambling wooden house of two stories, yellow with blue shutters, built on low pilings. A screened-in verandah ran the length of the front.

'This year, we've got an added attraction. After the fireworks, which will bring everyone rushing out front, a chorus of children's voices will be heard from above. The lights will be turned on, and the guests will look up.' Umberto pointed to a balcony above the verandah. 'Quite a drop, isn't it? But they'll be safe . . . a row of angelic faces peering down at a world they've never known, hanging onto the balustrade for dear life, singing their hearts out. It will make the party. The children are in a great state of excitement and practice their song daily.'

The front door was the same light blue colour as the shutters. Umberto flung it open.

'*Soyez le bienvenu.* My humble nest – Umberto's hideaway.'

They passed through a verandah furnished with cane tables and chairs, and pillows of faded yellow and blue. A porch swing was suspended from the rafters, which had also been painted blue.

'Not everyone gets invited here, Mr Bradshaw. Make yourself at home. I'll get us a drink.'

He stumbled away.

Jonathan was ready to drop with exhaustion. But he could not get rid of a suspicion that the man who could be heard slamming the refrigerator door and cursing the heat might be his father's murderer. He passed a collection of hats and walked across the black and white tiles in the direction Umberto had indicated. In the dining room a slim antique grandfather clock stood alone against the white-washed wall. A pair of crystal hurricane lamps hung over a polished refectory table. Old prints of flowers and birds decorated the walls. The book shelves were full but orderly. Poetry occupied one shelf, drama another. Jonathan read some titles. There was Nietzsche and Bertrand Russell's autobiography. John Donne, Emerson's essays, Hart Crane, Tennessee Williams, Beckett, Dostoyevsky, the Greeks, and Octavio Paz's *The Labyrinth of Solitude*. The thicker reference books were ranged along the bottom.

'Goddamn – no ice!' came Umberto's voice from the other end of the house.

In a little hallway to one side, Jonathan glimpsed a yellow chest of drawers and a blue stairway. An odour of mildew and damp pervaded the house.

'Come on – we'll have to make do!' Umberto stomped in flat-footed. 'That damn fridge is fifteen years old, but it worked all right till tonight. Must be the heat.' He was carrying two cut glass goblets in one hand and a bottle under his arm. Throwing open a pair of double doors, he gestured cavalierly for Jonathan to enter the sitting room.

'Ah-Choo!' Jonathan went into a sneezing fit. 'This is a charming house.' He sneezed again. 'My grandmother rented a place like this one winter in Tangier. It never did dry out.'

'What'd you expect – a dump?' Umberto carried the bottle to a couch covered in blue linen and was tugging strenuously on the cork. 'The idiots who make these things nowadays . . . you have to be a Houdini to get 'em open . . .'

A large portrait of himself hung above the fireplace and dominated the room. His lips puckered and his cheeks were sucked in – exactly as when he looked at himself in the mirror.

'That's an impressive likeness,' Jonathan commented. 'Do you always suck in your cheeks when you know someone's looking? There's this girl caricaturist I know . . . I met her in The Madison Pub on 81st. She does drawings for the criminal court in the 63rd Precinct . . .'

'That was painted fifteen years ago – the good old days.' He poured out the drinks.

Jonathan continued to study the handsome bushy-haired young man in the portrait. A fixed, melancholy gaze took in the room. His left hand held the edge of his jacket – Napoleon-style. There was no ring on the finger. The background was a green prism.

Absent-mindedly, as he looked at the portrait, Jonathan allowed his hand to close about the satiny back of a carved wooden pig that stood on the mantelpiece.

'Look here, put that pig back in the same place,' came the order from the couch. 'It came all the way from Indonesia and doesn't like to be disturbed.'

'Oh.' Jonathan carefully replaced the pig among the smooth river stones and native pottery that decorated the mantel.

'Hey! – that's Dad.' He'd discovered a collection of silver-framed photographs perched on shelves among books and Indian figurines. 'And my mother and grandfather!' He picked up a photo of an elderly man in a topcoat and derby, escorting a happy young woman along a street in New York. 'You've even got photos of my grandfather!'

Umberto came up behind him, took the photo from Jonathan's hands and returned it to its place. 'Your grandfather was quite a dresser.' He handed Jonathan a glass. 'Look at those spats.'

'He always dressed up, even after he lost all his money in the Depression. Whoa! There's Dad – skiing in St Moritz. Just after he graduated from Princeton. I've got a copy of that photo at home. Look at those plus-fours . . .'

'Your father was an expert skier.' Umberto said matter of factly.

'Right, right.' Jonathan was studying a group of young men posing on wooden steps in a photographer's studio. Ben Bradshaw wore a tam-o-shanter and a rubber bear claw. 'That's Dad with his roommates at Princeton.' In another, more recent photo, an older Ben wearing canvas shoes, a faded blue shirt with a red bandana around his neck sat beneath a palm tree. Umberto, in a dark suit, stared balefully at the camera. Seated between them, with her hand on Umberto's knee and her eyes on Ben, was a tall black beauty. Her hair was piled up on her head and fastened with an enormous colourful scarf. She wore an evil-looking monkeytooth necklace and earrings. Her chin was held at a preposterous angle in the air, and her eyebrows arched.

'Who's *that?*'

'Marie.'

'Oh.' Jonathan realized Umberto was waiting for his reaction to the fact his wife was black. 'She's pretty. Are there more of my father?'

Umberto picked up a large leather album, and they sat down on the sofa together. In a minute they came upon a photo of a child about three years old, riding a tricycle. Jonathan was almost speechless. But most of the pictures were of Ben Bradshaw.

Jonathan coughed loudly. 'Jesus, Mr Hak, that's *me!* And I've *never seen* so many photos of my father!'

Many faded, yellow shots of the Bradshaw family were interspersed among more recent ones taken in Puerto Gusano.

'My God – there's Aunt Nina! And Uncle Jack!' Jonathan looked at Umberto in confused amazement. 'Really . . . Mr Hak . . . you know you have *all* our family photographs! Ones we don't even have!'

Umberto went on turning the pages. There was a Christmas tree and a table littered with glasses and the remains of a meal. Ben, Umberto and Marie were ringed by native musicians. Jonathan's father was leaning back in his chair, regarding the marimba players with a tanned, dreamy gaze. He was barefoot, and his head was shaved. Marie, who was smoking a cigar, couldn't take her eyes off him. Neither could Umberto. Behind them, a macaw perched on a hoop.

'He did that every year to make his hair grow back thicker,' Umberto commented. 'That was the last Christmas we spent together. My life ended then – in the spirit of our adventure.'

'What about *now?*'

Umberto waved the question aside. 'That photo was taken just before he disappeared.'

'How long ago was that?'

Umberto flipped the page. 'Seven years.'

'Dad's been in the jungle all that time?'

'Seven years dead.'

'Dead?' Jonathan glanced in alarm at the signet ring. '*Is* he dead?'

'Seven years *my life* has been dead. Look, there's a picture of your mother and her bridesmaids.'

'Wait a minute – Mom would give *anything* to have that photo!'

Umberto didn't seem to hear.

'Is that Dad on that donkey, with his head in a turban?'

'In Luxor. The Valley of the Kings. Do you see the art and imagination in your father's life? He gave experience a spiritual, holy quality . . .'

'Yeah – it seems a lot less holy to those he left behind.'

'Shh! Now look, that's Stravinsky's niece,' He pointed to the photograph of a woman with her arms crossed over her breast. Her mouth was open in surprise or excitement, her eyes huge like a gazelle's. 'A Russian ballerina. A disciple of Jouvet. Your father knew her in Paris. He learned a lot from her. Of course, she was much older . . . He paid for her funeral in Venice. She's buried on San Michele between Stravinsky and Pound.'

In almost every photo in which Umberto was present, he wore the same puckered, self-conscious expression that gave him a worried and determined air. Ben's thoughts, on the other hand, invariably seemed to be somewhere else.

The last page of the album was devoted to the *Pelican*. Jonathan peered closely at the mosaic of photographs. In many, Marie posed on the deck of the yacht as though she owned it. Whether holding the anteater on a leash, or gazing meaningfully at a parrot perched on her finger, or playing with white rabbits or monkeys, every gesture was extravagant. In one, a thick boaconstrictor was draped about her arm. Her breasts were pushed upwards and her ass stuck out. She always assumed a jaunty or provocative pose. There were numerous photos of Ben and Umberto, their bodies languidly displayed in bathing suits or shorts.

Umberto banged the album shut. 'Well, there you have it!'

'That's quite a trip down memory lane. If you don't mind my saying so, Mr Hak, for a man who doesn't like chains, you've got quite a collection.'

'Chains?'

'Back there on the ferris wheel you called my father's past his chains . . .'

'What's wrong with you? I don't like that negative talk.'

'I feel as though I've just peeked into my father's tomb.'

Umberto's face once more took on that pained, faraway expression. 'When the present seems empty and the future pointless, it's the past that reassures and confirms life. The past can never be changed and love and yearning remain yours forever.'

'Aren't you contradicting yourself?'

While Umberto put the album back in its appointed place, Jonathan noticed a silver cigarette box that bore his father's initials. He kept his mouth shut.

'Come on – I'll show you the rest of the house.'

They went into the bedroom. A row of empty perfume bottles stood in perfect order atop the dressing table. Two oil paintings supplied the only decoration. Romantic desert scenes.

'There's been love and passion in this room . . .'

The tone of Umberto's voice invited comment, but Jonathan said nothing.

'I still miss her. No warm bosoms snuggling against me. Her gentle fondling of my cock and balls in the middle of the night . . . I'd wake up, and she'd be giving me a blow-job.'

Jonathan nearly choked. 'Mr Hak, you shouldn't be telling me things like that!' He saw tears in Umberto's eyes and began to retreat toward the door.

'What's wrong with you?' Umberto gripped his arm. 'There's beauty in all that, and life. I believe people should express themselves . . .'

'Yes, but . . . your *wife*. That's very indiscreet.'

'Naked, she would beg me to join her here. If I was busy or tired, she was cast into a depression, suicidal frustration, a foul mood and a filthy frame of mind. She had to have it when she wanted it. I never got any sleep, but in the morning I felt rested and happy nonetheless. Night after night of succulent love-making . . . she loved to suck.' Tears were streaming down his cheeks. 'She made my body feel like one enormous cock.'

Jonathan didn't know where to look. 'I'd rather talk about something else, please.'

'My wife and I . . . those nipples gleaming like ebony in the candlelight . . . I didn't feel this constant anxiety of leading a stranger's life, the stranger within me. But love was accompanied by horrible dreams. She'd decorated the house with dead fish. They were hanging everywhere. Then the dogs – Marie had about twenty dogs.'

Shoulders slumped, Umberto sat heavily on the bed and buried his face in his hands.

'I was at the door, and she was inside with a pack of baying hounds. I told her to open it just a crack, but she deliberately flung it wide open, and the dogs charged – a seething mass of snapping, murderous hounds, growling and going for the throat! I was on my hands and knees, screaming! Then help arrived, and the dogs were killed or beaten off! I lay panting and exhausted on the ground! My mouth was full of hair . . . I'd bitten one of the dogs with my teeth! "You stupid bitch!" I yelled at her. I pushed her in the chest and knocked her down. She glared at me, wilder than any of her mutts. It was the dogs she loved, that attack together and kill in the moonlight!'

'God, what a nightmare!'

'What do you mean, *nightmare?* It *happened!* Not only that, she muttered obscenities when greeted in the morning. She knew how to ride horses, too. She stuck her feet straight into the air . . . her knees gripped my waist, her passionate mount. How she used to heat up this bed! A little oven. Her legs were powerful, they could grip like a vice. Squeeze, squeezing . . . bumping. Over we go. We would fly over the hurdles, her legs in the air kicking and squeezing hard.'

'Mr Hak. Jesus Christ.'

Umberto's shoulders were shaking; he was sobbing.

Jonathan crept from the room. He didn't know whether to sneak away, or wait until Umberto had composed himself and say goodnight. He picked up one of the silver-framed photographs of his father. Wherever Ben was, Umberto possessed his memory with manic ferocity and power. Jonathan rubbed his eyes. He was too tired to think.

Suddenly, Umberto reappeared dressed in his underwear. He came in yawning and scratching his genitals, as though he'd just woken up. He spotted the photo in Jonathan's hand. 'Listen here, put that back in its place. What are you doing – snooping around?'

He took the picture, looked at it briefly and laughed contemptuously. 'The elusive Ben Bradshaw gazing into empty space. Pictures taken on yachts, your mother's June wedding, Paris, Luxor, St Moritz, Princeton, Martha's Vineyard . . .' Hand on hips, he turned to face his own portrait. 'Just a lot of photographic nonsense – *bullshit!*'

'If that's the way you feel, why've you made such a shrine out of these photographs?'

'I'm trying to track the past.'

'We both are.'

'Get myself tracked . . .' Umberto had that wounded look again. 'Where'd he go? What's happened to Umberto?' He lowered his voice to a stage whisper. 'Doesn't do any good because it's always in the past. Ain't no future tracking. Future's washed up!'

'Now we've both got to track the future.'

'*I don't know how to track the future!*' Umberto laughed but there was no humour in it. 'The future's in the past! Got to get the kids! They're the future.'

He stomped across the tiled floor and began to shout at the ceiling. '*Salvador! Simplicio! Jaime! Wake up! Get down here!*'

'Shouldn't they be sleeping? I'll meet them tomorrow.'

'Just wait. *Eusebio! What the hell do you kids think you're doing? Sleeping! You've got things to learn!*' Umberto shouted up the stairs. '*How're you going to get anywhere if you sleep all the time?* Get down here! Get with it!'

There was the sound of voices and the tumble of feet on the floor above.

'I'm feeling pretty tired, Mr Hak . . .'

'Wait! *Sal-va-dor!* This is disgraceful! Get everyone going!'

The door at the top of the stairs opened a crack, and a face appeared.

'*Sal-va-dor!*' he bellowed again.

Umberto's son appeared in pyjamas.

'Get moving, boy! Wake everyone up! How're you ever going to make anything of yourself sleeping all the time?' Umberto picked up a brass bell and paraded through the house, ringing it as loudly as he could. Jonathan put his hands over his ears.

A small boy, rubbing the sleep from his eyes, came down the stairs. 'Are we going to see the film again, Mr Hak?'

'Simplicio, tell the others to wake and get down here! I want them to meet Mr Bradshaw from America!'

Simplicio grinned and ran back up the stairs shouting, 'Hey everybody, Mr Bradshaw's here!' He was a hunchback.

In another minute, the stairs were swarming with half-dressed, sleepy little children struggling to manage the steps. Some were dragging their hindquarters, or walking like insects on their elbows and knees, or scuttling sideways on their bellies like crabs. The ones who had use of their arms leaned on the banister.

Jonathan marvelled at their courage.

'That's it, everybody. Mercedes, what's wrong with you?' Umberto scolded. 'How're you ever going to be a ballerina if you move so slow?'

Mercedes, who had sound legs but tiny flippers for arms, bounded ahead of everybody. She smiled a happy smile and twirled around for Umberto and Jonathan to see.

Salvador came and stood like a little soldier at his father's side. 'OK, Daddy. Everyone's awake.' He was a few years older and bigger than the others and seemed to be in charge.

Umberto started picking up small bodies and moving them downstairs, not without giving each one a squeeze and a kiss. He held up a small boy he had plucked from the banister. He had only arms and his frail body terminated below the waist.

'See, Eusebio – the stairway's not so scary. Eusebio loves music. He's going to be an orchestra conductor one day, aren't you? *Won't you?*' He shook the boy for a response.

'That's right, Mr Hak!' Eusebio's mouth gaped ecstatically as he began to beat his arms about.

'Listen to him. It's Beethoven! Or is it Mozart?'

Salvador clapped his hands. 'Bravo, Eusebio!'

'Bravo, maestro.' Umberto gave Eusebio a big kiss on the cheek. The children adored the Chief of Police.

'Mr Hak, what will I do? What will I be?' Another looked up hopefully from the floor. His hands and feet were so withered that he was obliged to crawl about on his elbows and knees. He had long thick eyelashes like a doll's.

'Jorgito . . .' Umberto paused a minute to think. 'You'll be a famous politician and give speeches into a microphone and tell us all how to behave, how to be.'

'*Viva Jorgito!*' the children cheered. 'Jorgito for president!'

Umberto came into the living room holding a curly-headed little girl who was blind and paralyzed below the waist. He sat down and held her on his lap. She was sucking her thumb, and appeared to be half asleep.

'Dolores here is going to be an interpreter at the U.N. Aren't you?'

'Yes!' Dolores shouted.

'She's going to listen to all that rubbish everyone's talking and translate it clearly into five different languages.'

'Yes, yes, yes!' She kissed Umberto and passionately threw her arms around his neck.

Jonathan walked through the house greeting the children. They were crawling over the furniture and looking through Umberto's collection of photographs. He had to be careful not to step on them. A group was pulling books from the shelves and searching for illustrations.

'All right – everyone knows the rule! Everything must be put back *exactly* as you found it!'

In the dining room, Jonathan came upon the little hunchback pouring rum drinks for himself and two tiny friends.

'Hey, Simplicio, you shouldn't be doing that! If Mr Hak catches you, he'll kick you out of his house – out of his *town!*'

Simplicio pointed to the bottles of rum and Coca Cola that had been especially arranged on a little shelf one foot off the floor. It was the children's bar. They all giggled and raised their glasses.

'Big deal.'

Umberto walked over to a little boy with withered hands and picked him up by the scruff of the neck.

'You should see this kid draw, Mr Bradshaw! Brilliant! Holds the pen between his toes, don't you, Carlos? What's wrong with you, Carlos?'

'He's sleepy,' Salvador pointed out.

'Get with it, Carlos! Don't you know great artists never sleep? They work all day and lie awake all night worrying about failure and money!'

Carlos immediately brightened. 'Yes sir! Yes sir!'

The children, some with drinks in their hands, began to gather around Umberto, who sat on the sofa holding the album open to a photo of the *Pelican*.

'One day we were out on the yacht, a giant snake appeared in the river . . .'

'Ohhhhh.' They all shivered and looked terrified.

'An anaconda thirty feet long. Do you think Ben Bradshaw was afraid?'

'Noooooo.'

'Hell no, he wasn't. He jumped overboard and grabbed the snake by the head. Thick coils wrapped around his body. There was a terrible thrashing in the water . . .'

Jonathan, overcome with fatigue, stepped onto the verandah. The night had grown cooler, and a breeze stirred the branches of the trees. Lightning flickered eerily on the horizon and was followed by the ominous mutter of thunder.

8

Princess Beatrice and Furry Animal

A few minutes later he was making his way along a side street of the town – one of the maze of windy paths that intersected the system of drainage canals. The way was dusty and unlit, but the refinery flares cast Puerto Gusano in a perpetual sulphurous twilight. Toads grunted and flopped in the ditches.

Someone was coming along in the opposite direction. 'Hey, Bertha!' Jonathan called out. 'Jesus, am I glad to see you!'

'Oh, boss! You gave me a fright. Dressed in white like that – I thought you were a ghost! What're you doing over in this part of town?'

'I don't know – I must have taken a wrong turn.' He noticed she was carrying the shell of the turtle under her arm. 'I've just come from Mr Hak's house. I saw all those pictures of my father. He woke up the children. I thought I knew the way back to the hotel, but this trail just goes on and on . . .'

'Well, you almost landed in the swamp. Come on in.'

She led the way across a bridge and through a gate to a tiny house built on stilts. A hammock was slung between two roof beams on the porch. Within a desiccated blowfish suspended on a string in the doorway, a candle gleamed. A goat tied to the front step moved off into the bushes.

'Nice place you got here.'

'Why thanks. You like it over in this part of town? You came to the poor part.'

'You know, I used to wonder why I never felt right at my grandmother's apartment in New York. She used to have this big fancy place on Fifth Avenue between 91st and 92nd overlooking the Park. Finally I realized it's because you're supposed to suffer in New York. I told her, "Nobody's suffering enough here." '

Bertha hung the turtle shell on a nail. 'You ought to feel right at home here in Puerto Gusano,' she commented wryly.

'Can't some improvement be made in the situation?'

'It ain't as if we haven't been trying a long time,' she sighed. 'As

long as everyone else in the world, I reckon. We just can't seem to
make any headway.'

He was eyeing the turtle shell; it was dripping blood. 'Progress
is the word.'

'Is that the word? By progress do you mean Santa Petrolina? No
thank you.'

'Bertha, it's hard to believe the town doesn't profit from that
refinery in any way.'

Bertha spat into the night. 'You've just come from Umberto's
haven't you? You've seen his kids. That's how we've profited from
Santa Petrolina.'

'Why does Mr Hak fill his house with crippled children?'

She pounded her pipe on the rail, and the sparks cascaded out.
'He blames himself for everything that goes wrong in this town.'

'I've never known anybody so obsessed by children,' Jonathan
remarked. 'He even told me he's the father of them all – he and
my father!'

'Oh, he'll say anything this time of night.'

'Mama!' a voice cried out from within the house. 'Mama!'

'Just a minute, sweetheart . . . It's Santa Petrolina, boss. I pray
every night that steel city will sink out of sight and be gone, and
things'll be like they were before. If that's progress . . . why, the
stink that comes from that place . . . and the children and old folks
can't sleep because the fires burn all night and light up the sky.
Our tropical paradise, ha! – it's a mess that won't go away, and let
me tell you those flames are making people crazy!'

'Mama!'

'I'm sorry, boss, for carrying on like this, but it makes me so
mad I can't sleep. Now come inside and see something nicer – and
much prettier!'

She plucked the blowfish lantern from the door, and Jonathan
followed her into the house. It consisted of one pink room with a
plank floor. A chest stood against one wall. The walls were decorated with starfish and a seashell crucifix. The floor gleamed.
A hammock was slung from the rafters. There was a sweet odour
of woodsmoke and fruit. Everything was plain and bare and
immaculately clean. The cooking was done outside.

'This is Princess Beatrice.' Bertha handed Jonathan the blowfish and bent down and picked up a little girl about five years old.
'Isn't she cute?'

The child blinked her eyes and snuggled sleepily in her mother's arms.

Jonathan held up the lantern. 'She looks a lot like you.'

'She ought to – she's mine.'

'Beatrice – that's my mother's name.'

'Is it time to get up, mama?' The child was peering curiously at Jonathan. Her hair was braided into dozens of plaits that looked like the tails of tiny animals hiding in the wool.

'Not yet, baby. You go on and get some more sleep.' She placed the child back in the hammock. 'See what I mean? The children can't tell night from day.'

Jonathan returned to the porch and sat down. For a few minutes he stared off into the night and listened to the sounds of the swamp.

'Try this, boss.' It was a glass of aguardiente with a hunk of lime in it.

'Listen, Bertha, do you have to call me "boss"?'

'Well . . . ah!' Bertha eased her body into the hammock which sagged to within a few inches of the floor. The roof beams creaked. 'You're white and you're rich – that makes you boss, don't it?'

Jonathan laughed. 'What makes you think I am rich?'

'Your daddy had a big yacht, didn't he? He never stopped spending money. Don't get me wrong. Folks love that. Why, the moment he stepped ashore, the whole town started to jump. When he gave a party, everybody was invited.'

'Mama?' Beatrice was standing in the doorway.

'What is it, baby?'

The child came out and climbed into the hammock with her mother. Jonathan looked up apprehensively as the roof groaned.

'Can't you sleep, sweetheart? What you got there? Well, go on and show it to him.'

'What is it?' Jonathan asked.

The child got out of the hammock and padded over and stood by Jonathan's chair.

Something was moving inside her shirt. She gave it a shove and a little head popped out by her neck and regarded Jonathan with large, blinking eyes.

'What is it?'

'Furry animal.'

'Does it have a name?'

'Furry animal.' The child giggled. 'Here – you want to play with it?'

Before Jonathan could reply, the animal reached out and took hold of his necktie and gave it a hard yank.

'Hey, take it easy!'

Beatrice drew it out of her shirt and placed it on his arm. It was a gentle little thing, with tiny hands that gripped lightly but firmly, and a long furry tail. Its bulging eyes reflected the candle-light. The fur was as soft as down. It was a nocturnal animal of some sort – a kinkajou.

'Where'd you get it?'

'It comes from the swamp. Ain't he special?'

The kinkajou climbed up on Jonathan's head, where it pro-ceeded to clean itself.

Jonathan grinned sheepishly. 'It's pulling my hair.'

'He likes you, boss.'

'Don't call me that, Beatrice. Call me Johnny.'

All of a sudden the kinkajou leapt from Jonathan's head and dashed into the house. Beatrice and Jonathan ran after it. For the next few minutes they played hide and seek, in and out of the house.

'Having a good time?' Bertha called out.

'Whew!' Jonathan dropped into his chair.

'Are you married? You got kids of your own?'

'I've been too messed up to get married. I don't want to inflict my problems on someone else. Besides, I can't get married until I have a job. It's the only reason my stepfather respects me.'

'I wouldn't want to be your wife,' she said.

Jonathan took out his handkerchief and was wiping his brow. 'Why not?'

'You'd make me a jealous mother. Beatrice sure has taken a shine to you.'

'She makes me feel good,' Jonathan said. 'Better than I've felt all day.'

Beatrice came back with the kinkajou clinging to her arm. 'Don't you want to play no more, Johnny?' She climbed into Jonathan's lap.

'That's enough, baby.' Bertha took her daughter's hand and led her into the house. 'Now put that furry animal away and get some rest . . .'

The swamp jangled with choruses of crickets and frogs.

When Bertha returned, she was carrying a plate of tortillas and black bean mash. She spread the beans on the tortillas, rolled them up, and offered them one at a time to Jonathan. They ate in silence for a few moments.

'You fixing to go up river?'

'Mr Hak says it's impossible.'

'It ain't easy. You'll need a guide. Nobody here knows the swamp. You'll have to go to Nile Town for that.'

'Bertha, I know it sounds crazy, but . . . *did Mr Hak kill my father?*'

Bertha clapped her hands together. *'Lord God no!'*

'I got suspicious because Mr Hak's wearing my father's clothes. He's got his silver and his photographs. He's even wearing his ring. He's got *everything*. Don't you think it's strange?'

'Johnny, you got to understand – one day your daddy just took off. Umberto sort of inherited his things.'

'Why did he leave?'

'Well . . . only he can answer that.'

'Didn't anyone bother to go looking for him?'

'That's wild country he's gone to – swampy, and those hounds.'

'What are the hounds?'

'Those big dogs that live in the swamp. They're mean. Everybody's scared of them. That's why nobody lives there – nobody but Ben Bradshaw.'

'What kind of hounds?'

'Peaceful Banana brought them in to chase the niggers.'

'You mean they were slaves?'

'Just about. When Peaceful Banana pulled out, they let those hounds loose in the swamp. And now they've run wild – and bred, so they say, with wild animals, which made them bigger and stronger and meaner. I saw one brought in dead.'

'Sounds like Peaceful Banana was the biggest thing that ever hit town.'

'Sure was . . . so was your daddy.'

'Why did the company leave?'

Bertha began to jiggle her foot. 'Just pulled out, that's all. Went somewhere else where there was more bananas and more money. Left us high and dry.'

Jonathan got the impression there were other reasons she

didn't wish to divulge. He guessed that the company's departure and his father's sudden disappearance were somehow connected, but he was too exhausted to pursue the subject. They drank in silence while he finished the tortillas.

'It's awfully late . . .' Jonathan felt waves of fatigue rolling over him. 'I can't think anymore.' He got to his feet. 'I ought to go back to the hotel and get some sleep.'

'Come on and take your shoes off. Lay down here where it's more comfortable.' Bertha took hold of his arm and drew him down beside her. 'Now ain't that better? Big Bertha'll take care of you.'

Jonathan felt that a big cat was leaning on him – one that had eaten a lot of fruit. He was too tired to put up any resistance. Besides, he liked being cradled in Bertha's arms.

'Big Bertha . . .' He yawned. 'You know what Big Bertha is?'

'What is it – not me?'

'Big Bertha's the name of a cannon.'

'But, boss.' Her hand slipped down between his legs. 'It's you who got the cannon – the cannon, the cash, and the coconuts, too! Ha ha!'

When Bertha laughed, the hammock swung back and forth, and the roof beams groaned ominously.

'Hey, take it easy!'

'Kind of lonely on that ship, was it?'

She laughed again and kissed him on the mouth – a soft sucking kiss. Her hand slid up under his shirt, and she pinched a piece of backflesh between her fingers.

Jonathan kicked off his boots.

'I bet you have lots of girlfriends.'

'I recently had a Japanese girl try to haul me into bed with her . . .'

'*Ride 'er cowboy!*' hissed a voice from the darkness.

'Who said that?' Jonathan sat bolt upright.

'What's wrong now?'

'Didn't you hear that voice? Who's that?' Jonathan shouted into the night.

'I didn't hear nothing.'

'Bring that lamp, Bertha!'

'How can I move with you squishing on me?'

'Is that you, Ben?'

'He ain't here, boss. I keep telling you . . .' Bertha heaved herself out of the hammock and padded inside for the lantern.

'Maybe he's come back!' Jonathan was groping for his boots in the dark. 'Who else would say that?'

Bertha returned with the blowfish lantern. Jonathan took it and went out to the gate. 'Ben, is that you?' he shouted, holding the lantern aloft. 'It's me – Johnny!'

'See anything?' Bertha called from the house.

Jonathan was listening to the night but heard only the wailing of frogs. The goat was moving around.

'Night voices – I've heard 'em myself. People say there's spooks, but they don't do no harm.'

'That was no spook.' Jonathan sat down and pulled on his boots.

'Where you going now?'

'To find who said, "Ride 'er cowboy".'

9
The Storm

Within the half-cleared forest, miniature cabins nestled among the sprawling roots of the ceiba trees. Inside some dwellings lanterns glowed. Others were dark. It was late – long past midnight – and the sound of snoring emanated from laden hammocks. Winding paths led off in all directions, and the whole area was laced by canals and ditches. Night birds sighed, and toads gurgled and crawled in the mud as Jonathan crossed one rickety drawbridge after another.

Each bridge was illuminated by a feeble light. In the distance, he caught a quick glimpse of a man pausing briefly on one of the bridges. In another second he was gone, but there was no doubt who it was.

'Hey, Mr Hak! Wait!'

Puzzled and a little annoyed that the Chief of Police had followed him to Bertha's house, Jonathan gave up the chase.

For the better part of an hour he wandered blindly in the maze of paths and canals. Thunder rolled constantly, and a gusting breeze moved the branches of the trees. All of a sudden a pale shape loomed in the dark and glided through the trees ahead of him. He ran forward and came to the bank of a wide canal where a sailboat was passing. The sailors laughed at the figure in white waving his arms and shouting, 'Hey, wait, which way to town? I'm lost! What? Huh?'

The sailboat slid away and vanished into the forest, the glow of a cigarette marking its passage through the trees. Tiny waves lapped at Jonathan's boots. This was worse than trying to hail a cab in New York.

Before long he was approaching yet another bridge. On the bridge, which was still some distance away and partially obscured by reeds and banana leaves, he spied a man and a child. The man lifted up the child and placed him in what Jonathan thought was a box. By the time he reached the bridge, however, they too had moved off and disappeared into the night.

Standing on the bridge, he got his bearings back. The upper

story of the Hotel Paradise was visible through the tree tops. He'd been walking in circles, he realized, and hurried on his way.

A minute later he almost collided with a huge man standing in the path. He jumped back in fright before recognizing the muscular arms and massive torso. It was the same fellow who'd rowed him ashore – Bertha's brother.

At once he felt safer. 'Hey! *Amigo!*' he called out in an unnaturally loud voice, as though the fellow weren't standing two feet away. 'Can you lead me back to town?'

The giant turned slowly around beneath the huge cane basket he was balancing on his shoulder. *'Perdido?* Follow me, stranger,' he said in a deep voice.

They made their way along in silence. Soon they came out of the trees near the port. Jonathan realized he'd completed almost an entire circuit of the town.

As they passed between the first houses, the giant began to sing:

> 'Bread in the belly –
> Bread is life!
> Buy my bread –
> Give it to your wife!
>
> 'Give it to your wife –
> Answer to all life!
> Bread will keep her stout –
> She never will go out!
>
> 'She never will go out –
> You'll be free as air!
> Buy my bread –
> Answer to your prayer!'

When he finished, the giant burst into a cheerful laugh. 'You're here, stranger,' he said. With the basket still perched on his shoulder, he strode off down a side street and left Jonathan alone at the corner, staring into darkness.

'Thanks a lot for leading me out of the swamp!' he called after him.

The distant lightning flickers were closing in. Thick blue bolts stroked the earth and were followed by thunderous reports, giving the deserted streets the aspect of a town under siege. Trotting along the dusty street with the wind at his back, Jonathan spotted a familiar beacon flashing up ahead. The storm broke, the wind was causing a wild thrashing of palms, and he ran for it.

RICARDO'S HAPPY HOUR CAFÉ

Amid the general retreat from the stoop as the rain cascaded down, he dashed up the steps. The men at the door stepped aside to let him pass.

Ricardo was running about shouting and slamming down shutters. Grateful to have found a sheltered place, Jonathan pressed the button on his digital watch. It was nearly three o'clock in the morning, and he was in a daze of exhaustion. The rain was hammering on the roof, and a few leaks had developed.

When all the windows had been shuttered against the storm, Ricardo went behind the bar.

'What'll it be?' he asked impatiently.

'Do you know how to make *cachaça*? There's a bar in New York called the Brazilian Coffee Shop. They specialize in *cachaça*. I think it's rum and cashew juice, crushed ice, lime and sugar.'

'*No.*' He poured Jonathan a glass of straight rum.

With the Chief of Police not present, Ricardo was much less sociable than before. He was drunk and in a foul mood. Taking out a straight razor and a shaving bowl, he began to lather his beard in the mirror behind the bar.

'Do you always shave at 3 o'clock in the morning?' Jonathan asked.

'Did you find out where your daddy is?' Ricardo retorted.

'Not yet.'

That was the end of that conversation. Jonathan stayed alone with his drink at one end of the bar while the petroleros clustered at the other end near the door. Ricardo's sister was sound asleep in her chair.

After a while the rain momentarily abated and Jonathan was about to pay up and leave when he heard a familiar rumble. Bertha's brother entered the bar, still carrying the huge basket. 'Hey!' Jonathan waved. The others stepped aside to make way, but he didn't act friendly toward them. He ordered a drink in the middle of the group but drank alone. The basket was perched on his brawny shoulder, right up among the hams.

Ricardo noticed Jonathan's admiring gaze in the mirror.

'That's Panadero. We call him that because he delivers bread in that big basket. Built more like a tree than a man, ain't he?'

With Bertha's brother in the room, Jonathan felt more secure and poured himself another rum. He was about to go over and offer to buy him a drink but refrained. Their eyes had already met, Panadero nodded coldly and formally; evidently he wanted to be alone with his own thoughts.

Jonathan drank his rum and smiled. 'A man like that Panadero could handle any situation – doesn't even have to think about fear. It's not in his repertory,' he babbled. 'He looks like the Empire State Building.'

Ricardo frowned. 'What the hell are you talking about?' He was wiping his face with the same towel he used for everything.

'A man like that – see how those petroleros stepped aside when he came in? They respect him. He could handle them a dozen at a time, and they know it. He's like – Ajax.'

'Who's this Ajax?' Ricardo asked impatiently.

'A Greek.'

'We had some Greek sailors in here once – runts.' Using the same razor he had just shaved with, Ricardo expertly carved a long slice from his private ham which hung behind the bar. 'He lives in the forest mostly.' He pushed the meat into his mouth without offering Jonathan any and chewed pensively for a moment. 'He ain't afraid of the hounds.'

'I've been hearing a lot about these hounds.'

'He brought one in dead once. Killed it with an axe. I saw it with my own eyes.'

The reappearance of the razor unaccountably filled Jonathan with a dull apprehension. He downed the last of his drink; his money was on the bar.

'I thought you told me he carried bread,' he said.

'He does a little bit of everything – rows boats, carries bread, stevedores some, chops wood . . .' Ricardo frowned at Panadero. 'He always carries that basket at night – never seen 'im in here without it.'

Jonathan took a step away from the bar. 'It's a little late to be delivering bread, isn't it?' he said.

They simultaneously turned their heads in the direction of Panadero. The instant they looked, a small hand appeared above the rim of the basket. The hand held a pair of scissors. The scissors cut the string suspending a ham, and the ham disappeared into the basket.

Ricardo blinked and opened his mouth. '*Thief!*' he spluttered.

Edging along the bar, bottle in one hand with the contents spurting out, Ricardo was shaking his fingers at Panadero and bellowing at the top of his lungs. 'It's him! *Thief!* You steal my hams! I saw you do it! *Thief!* It's in the basket! I saw you do it!' The drinkers nearest were dumbfounded, and stepped back as a man: not one wished to be the first to tangle with the giant.

'*Thief!* Goddamnit, get him! Get him!' Ricardo roared.

Panadero's face twisted into a malicious grin that did not conceal his fear. It was he who made the first move. A man standing between him and the door was caught full in the face and knocked across the room. Nobody dared take him, and he was half way to the door. For a second it looked as though he might escape, when Ricardo's sister broke through the group, took Panadero by surprise and tackled him around the waist.

'That's it!' Ricardo bawled from behind the bar. '*Kill 'im! Kill 'im!*'

In the action the basket tumbled to the floor, and a child bounded out. Jonathan gasped. 'Beatrice!' And there was the ham. She could have gotten away, but she sought refuge behind Panadero. Jonathan dived through the crowd to save her, but a fist came out of nowhere and slammed him.

The petroleros now rushed against Panadero like hounds on the flanks of a stag. Ricardo's sister clung blindly to his waist and could not be dislodged. Her grip both embarrassed him and hampered his movements. Panadero was swinging in all directions, sending men flying when he made contact, and managed to fight his way to the door with Beatrice taking shelter behind him. But there were too many of them, and they all went down the stairs in a tumble.

'Beatrice, run!' Jonathan scrambled to get up, but he was being held down and men were leaping over him. Ricardo vaulted the bar, bottle in hand, and retrieved the ham. Jonathan wrestled free, ran out onto the porch and looked down. It was at least ten against one, all shadows twisting and rolling in the mud. Ricardo's sister sat on the bottom step, her face buried in her hands. Jonathan hurtled past her and flung himself into the mob, kicking and punching to break through. They were diving into Panadero like sharks, and those now joining the fray carried axehandles. Little Beatrice clung in terror to one of Panadero's legs as his great arms flailed and battered them down. Jonathan fought to get to her. 'Run, Beatrice! Get away!'

Panicked by the scene he had created, Jonathan was frantically pulling men away with both hands. He was about to reach Beatrice but had to grapple with a man with a club raised to strike. Panadero screamed, and a blue light flashed before Jonathan's eyes.

PART TWO

10

Doc and Adam

Jonathan opened his eyes. He was in bed. An old man was bending over him and peering at him through rimless spectacles.

'Hm. Jonathan Bradshaw . . . Any relation to Benjamin Bradshaw?'

Jonathan groaned. 'My father.'

'I thought so. A fair resemblance, which not even your youth can hide.'

'Where is he?'

'There now, don't move. It'll only hurt more if you move.'

Jonathan blinked and tried to focus. The memory of the fight in the rainstorm returned. 'What happened? Where's Beatrice?'

'You've received two nice blows on the back of your head, which says something about the courage of your adversary. Very clean wounds, which I've sewn up. A concussion but no fracture – you'll be all right after a few days' rest.'

'How did I get here? What happened to Beatrice?'

'Are you speaking of Bertha's daughter?'

'Yes, where is she?'

'At home with her mother, I should imagine. A knock on my door early this morning and there *you* were, like another abandoned child. Whoever brought you had disappeared. A good Samaritan, perhaps – that would be a welcome addition to our community.' The old man waved Jonathan's passport. 'Forgive me if I took the liberty . . . but as a matter of principle I prefer to know the identity of my patients. Please let me introduce myself. I am Doc – Professor von Bohlen, to be more precise.'

'German, huh? Thanks for patching me up. What happened to Panadero?'

'Are you speaking of the local strong man? Is that your friend?'

'There was a terrible fight at Ricardo's . . .'

'Ach! Every night there are fights at Ricardo's. I shouldn't worry about your friend – the man is practically indestructible. It's yourself you should be thinking of, Mr Bradshaw. You must stay here and above all, with that concussion, rest, and in the future refrain from engaging in bar-room brawls. In this town, they tend to be dangerous, as you've already discovered – not only bloody but deadly.'

'I've lived in New York City fifteen years, and I've never been in a fight.' Jonathan touched his wounds. 'The first night in Puerto Gusano I get my head bashed in.'

The old man got to his feet.

'I go to my clinic now. When I return, you will be feeling better, and we shall talk. Now take this pill.'

'Doctor, are you a friend of my father?'

'Yes, indeed I am.'

'Is he really in the swamp?'

'As far as I know he avoids humanity, for which he may have good reason.'

'Are there good reasons for avoiding humanity?'

'If you need anything, just pull this string. It's attached to the toe of my – uh – assistant. So. You will remain here until I return. Then we shall talk of your lost father. So. As they say in more civilized countries, *au revoir*.'

The old man glided out of the room and pulled the door behind him. Jonathan soon fell asleep.

Another storm woke him. Propping himself up on the pillows, he listened to the rain drum noisily on the roof. White curtains billowed in the breeze. Except for the polished wooden floor, the room was as white as an operating chamber. There was a library of accumulated medical texts in various languages. The bed was narrow and hard and overhung by a gauzy knot of mosquito netting. Doc had put him in his own bedroom.

Thank God Beatrice is OK, Jonathan thought; he felt safe in Doc's sanctuary. He pulled the string, and somewhere within the house a bell tinkled. There was the sound of quick footsteps – bare feet. The door opened, and something loped into the room on all fours.

'Jesus Christ!' Jonathan gasped.

Bent over from galloping about on his hands and feet, with a great mane of greying hair and a long beard, clothed in shorts and shirt – was *this* the doctor's assistant? He sat back on his haunches and looked at Jonathan. Their eyes met.

'Hey! I'm Jonathan Bradshaw. Good to meet you.' He managed a smile; whoever this fellow was, he didn't want to make him mad.

He just stood there and waited, head cocked to one side. Then Jonathan remembered he'd summoned him and that he was expecting an order.

He forced a cough. 'Could you please bring me a glass of water?'

No reply. Apparently he didn't know how to talk, or didn't care to. Jonathan made the motion of drinking, and he bounded away with a swift animal movement. In another minute he had returned with a tray holding a glass of water. He took a step back and stared at Jonathan while he drank. The animal intensity of the gaze made Jonathan feel so self-conscious he couldn't finish the water. There was an awkward silence during which he tried to befriend the fellow by offering him a cigar.

'Uh, do you assist in, uh, any of the operations around here?'

No answer. Jonathan smiled again. 'Just wondering.' He placed the glass on the bedside table. By now Jonathan was convinced he *was* a man, although he had a great deal of the beast in him. The movements especially belonged to the forest – supple, smooth, conveying the impression of great strength and speed.

A wave of exhaustion swept over Jonathan – the savage presence of this fellow was fatiguing. He lay back and pretended to arrange the bedclothes around him; when he looked again, the assistant was gone, the door shutting softly behind.

'Hey!' Jonathan called after him. 'Thanks for the water!'

An hour later he woke again.

'Oh, Doc. Thank God. It's you.'

'You've been perspiring, Mr Bradshaw. A slight fever, but nothing serious. This damp cloth . . .'

'Jesus, Doc, that assistant of yours would put anyone into a sweat.'

'Yes, you've met Adam and drunk one glass of water.'

'Did he tell you that?'

'He cannot speak, but by signs he has communicated all that happened.'

'Who is he?'

'Why he is one of us!'

Jonathan laughed. 'What do you mean, *one of us*? He gallops around on all fours.'

'He was not raised in the company of men, you see . . .'

'Where was he raised?'

'The Great Swamp, the fecund origin of us all. Your father found him and tamed him. Although Adam is eminently tameable, the veneer remains disappointingly thin, with the savage still struggling for space just beneath the surface. They were companions in the jungle until your father concluded he had taught him all he knew and so handed him over to me for further lessons.'

'Wait a minute! My father's been living with a wild man? What do you mean, *companion?*'

Doc laughed. 'He helped Adam. Above all, Adam wishes to be useful – active, that is, with a purpose. He desires to serve, and indeed he has made the perfect servant – undemanding, except in his desire to learn more, and totally faithful and obedient. All within limits, of course. One must know how to handle him in order to remain the master. All important! When Adam senses weakness, he is inclined to challenge it. But I have great confidence in him. In fact he is my only luxury – a devoted servant.'

'If he can polish silver, he'd be a big hit back home.'

'He can do almost anything, except talk. You're probably wondering why I, as a man of science, have not sent him off to be scrutinized by the scientific community of the so-called civilized world. No doubt he would create a sensation, especially these days, when we are examining our origins more carefully than ever before. You've heard of the Gazelle Boy of the Western Sahara, the Kangaroo Kids of Australia, the Fox Children of Malaysia . . . But that would be the end of him, of course.'

'Well, look at King Kong. You could make a fortune . . .'

'Far better to keep him here and make a useful fellow of him, which is precisely what he desires. In any case, your father made me promise not to send him away.'

'My grandmother always said that if Dad was still alive, he'd be hanging around with a wild crowd. I ought to send her a photo of Adam.' Jonathan laughed.

'I believe there was a conflict which precipitated Adam's arrival here – your father has a woman with him now.'

'That sounds a little more normal.'

'A native woman. Apparently it was either Adam or her.'

'I haven't seen the woman, but it would seem to me that Dad made the right choice.'

'He needs to be looked after. Your father, I'm sorry to say, is a sick man. He has yaws.'

'*Yaws?* Wait a minute . . . isn't that a form of syphilis?'

'A chronic, spirochetal infection. Morphologically and sero-logically indistinguishable from syphilis. It begins with a granu-lomatous lesion of the legs, which later spreads to the buttocks, often at the mucocutaneous junctions, and to the face . . .'

'Oh my God.' Jonathan winced. 'Poor Dad. it sounds terrible. Strangely enough, *just the other night* I was driving out to New Jersey listening to this radio programme put on by the National Institute of Disease Control, and I heard some guy talking about the problems they have with yaws in Haiti. How it infects the poor ignorant population who don't know about hygiene and never get to see a doctor. I remember distinctly he said it could be cured easily by penicillin. Then the next day at lunch I started telling my mother about it, and now you say my own father has it. Here I was listening to this radio programme about yaws, and my own father has it. *What's my father doing with something like that?*'

'The last time I saw him the infection was confined to the legs, although by now horny lesions may have developed on the soles of his feet. Perhaps that is why he no longer comes . . .'

'You mean he's not getting any treatment?'

'He used to reappear from time to time, secretly – in the middle of the night. I did what I could. After the woman joined him, he came no more. Of course penicillin will cause the spirochetes to disappear. Without it, the disease causes great suffering and eventually death. But the man is indifferent.'

'You can't just casually tell me my father's indifferent to suffer-ing and death.'

Doc shrugged. 'As I say, he comes no more, not since he took the woman . . . not in five years.'

'Maybe she's cured him.'

'Not without penicillin.'

'Maybe that's why he stays away – he can't move and he needs help!' Jonathan pulled himself into a sitting position on the bed. 'If he's not cured, he's got to come in for treatment.'

'True . . . but he will not, or cannot.'

'If he can't come, I'll take the penicillin to him.'

'Is that your intention, Mr Bradshaw – to bring him back?'

'Someone's got to help him. He's got to be cured.'

All light having left the room, the old doctor seemed no more than a shadow occupying the bedside chair. The door opened and Adam entered, bearing a lamp.

The doctor got to his feet. 'Don't be afraid – I must remind you, Adam takes poorly to fear.'

'Doc, this native woman living with my father – who is she?'

The doctor went to the window and stared out into the dark. The frogs were vocal. 'A native woman to be sure . . . a very beautiful one. She is Umberto Hak's wife, Marie.'

Jonathan flopped back on his pillow and groaned. 'Marie? Mr Hak's wife? Jesus, Doc, my father ran off with Mr Hak's wife?'

'I'm afraid it's true, Mr Bradshaw.'

Jonathan lay still for a minute, trying to think. When the doctor had left the room, he took the lamp into the bathroom. For several minutes he stared at his face in the mirror, trying to figure the whole thing out. Focusing a hand mirror he picked up from the dressing table, he was able to view the back of his head, the places where the hair had been shaved from the wounds, and the neat stitches. He splashed some water on his face and put on the jacket, dirty and streaked with blood as it was. He'd bled a lot.

The dining room table was set for two. Jonathan and the doctor took their places, and Adam served the first course, peanut soup. It was a moving experience to be waited on by Adam. He darted gracefully about the table and was very careful with everything. He trembled somewhat, Jonathan noticed, and from time to time his jaws clacked nervously.

'Doc . . . the thing that bewilders and mystifies me is Mr Hak. Last night in the bar he said some very provocative things. I was really shocked by his behaviour. I didn't know whether to take him seriously or not. He was drunk, and it was in public. He was quite explicit, yet he seemed to be mock-serious. I could still choose to accept it as a joke. There was that option. You know what I mean?'

'When Umberto is drunk his behaviour becomes outrageous and exaggerated. He constantly abuses his authority.'

'Well I felt like he was playing with me – like a toy poodle. He seemed to know everything about my family. Then he threw in another extenuating sexual dimension. Jesus Christ, he asked me if my cock was as big as my father's. I didn't know whether he was accusing *me* of being gay – like he was mocking me, or testing my virility in this macho town. I didn't know which.'

'Umberto has been under a great deal of pressure since Peaceful Banana left.'

'Is that it?'

'What you are witnessing, Mr Bradshaw, is the spectacle of a town in the process of losing its grip. Like an individual who has previously enjoyed only marginal good health under the most tranquil conditions, when threatened by events he does not understand and cannot control, he is likely to break down under stress. You have detected a mood of grim anticipation. Puerto Gusano is slowly being unhinged by Santa Petrolina.'

'Oh yeah? Then why did you come here, Doc?'

'I came under the auspices of the Peaceful Banana Company. A hospital was to be constructed, and I was hired as its chief practitioner and to get the project underway. Yes, I arrived with a set of blueprints in my pocket. They are still in my possession. But the company was obliged to remove itself. Virtually the entire male population of Puerto Gusano was left without work. The company had built, supported and financed all the schools. When the schools closed, the children were thrown into the street. And, of course, the hospital never materialized. I stayed on, doing what I can.'

'Why did Peaceful Banana leave?'

'Under political pressure from the capital. The banana plantations soon reverted to their former swampy state, and banana exports went into sharp decline. Our citizens reacted bitterly. Responsible politicians in the capital later admitted that it had been a hasty action, and in recompense allowed the oil refinery to be built across the harbour.'

'Is that when my father disappeared, when Peaceful Banana pulled out?'

'No. He lost his job like everyone else but stayed on for a while. It was typical of him to be quite happy doing nothing, just as he had energetically dredged the canals and designed bridges. It was only when he beheld the hideous impact Santa Petrolina was having on our town that he left. And since then Umberto has been wandering the streets like a minstrel, riding the ferris wheel, repeating his monologue of despair to anyone who will listen.'

'You mean I should feel sympathy for him?'

'And patience. Mr Bradshaw, I fear there's something I must tell you . . .'

'Huh?'

Doc suddenly changed his mind. 'Adam, bring the fish!'

The next course was grilled bass with a green coriander sauce.

'Delicious – does Adam do the cooking as well?'

'Yes.'

'Please tell him how good I think the food is.'

'Try to tell him yourself.'

Jonathan rubbed his stomach and smiled. Adam blinked his eyes and cheeped appreciatively.

'Hey, that's great. What other sounds can he make?' Adam's efforts had a cheering effect on Jonathan.

'He can imitate every animal in the forest.'

The doctor said something, and there followed a startling crescendo of sounds – mosquitoes whining, fish jumping, trees falling, innumerable bird songs, crickets, various unidentifiable hoots and screeches, even the sound of a motorboat. He managed to bring the forest right in the house.

'The way he portrays it, Doc, the swamp sounds like a friendly place to live in – not frightening at all . . .'

The doctor said something quite fast, and Adam suddenly barked, then erupted into a long, blood-curdling howl. Jonathan dropped his fork.

'The swamp dogs, of which you have no doubt heard,' the doctor said.

Jonathan was shivering. 'Excuse me, Doc, I think I'll go lie down.'

The doctor was immersed in his thoughts. 'As you wish,' he murmured. A few minutes later he appeared in Jonathan's room carrying a small glass of rum. 'Drink this,' he said.

'Does Adam ever leave the house?'

'Never. If he went out . . . the people would be afraid, naturally. They would probably try to kill him.'

The doctor was pouring Jonathan another drink. 'At the clinic I learned more unhappy news, Mr Bradshaw. A child was killed during that fight.'

'*Beatrice?*'

'I'm afraid it's true.'

'Oh my God! Bertha's daughter!' Jonathan's eyes filled with tears.

'Bertha's daughter by Umberto. He himself brought the dead child to my clinic. The skull was crushed . . .'

'Umberto's daughter?' Jonathan ripped the covers off and sat upright on the edge of the bed. He was trembling.

'During the fight, an errant blow accidentally struck the child on the side of the head. Unfortunately it was delivered by a heavy club . . .'

'It's my fault, Doc! My fault!'

'Perhaps you should not say such things, Mr Bradshaw. Umberto has a warrant out for your arrest.'

Jonathan covered his eyes and moaned.

'Please calm yourself . . .'

'I've got to see Bertha!' Jonathan got to his feet and began to pull on his clothes. 'If Umberto wants to arrest me, why hasn't he already? He must know where I am!'

'It was he who carried you here.'

Jonathan held his head in his hands. 'Look, I'm going out . . . I've got to find Bertha. What happened to Panadero?'

'*Out?*' the doctor snapped. 'Look, your head is sewn up with stitches already. Don't underestimate Puerto Gusano's capacity for violence. Everybody's talking about this, and a lot of people are blaming you for the murder.'

Jonathan suddenly turned very pale. The doctor stepped quickly and caught him just in time to keep him from falling.

'Adam!' Doc called.

Adam bounded into the room. Together they helped Jonathan back into bed.

Umberto's Office

When he awoke, sunlight was streaming into the room. It was already midday. The wind had shifted, driving the stench of the refinery out to sea. Following the rain, the earth smelled moist and fresh and clean. The notes of a marimba floated easily in the limpid air, and for a few seconds Jonathan felt at peace.

Then the weight of real events returned to press upon his head. Beatrice was dead. And Panadero? He shut his eyes again, only to remember that Umberto was out to arrest him.

Still fuzzy-minded from the sedative Doc had given him, he put on his clothes and slipped out of the house. This was the day to move, he thought. The day to get out of town. He was more anxious than ever to find his father. And he had to see Bertha. But first he wanted to slip back to the hotel, get some money and change out of his filthy, blood-stained clothes.

The white sand streets of the town were strangely deserted; the heat had driven everyone indoors. From directly overhead the sun flared.

The heat shimmered along the street; the silent wooden facades wobbled and seemed to fade away like old photographs. Jonathan shaded his eyes with his hand. What sort of police patrol was this – barefoot adolescents in straw hats and faded overalls?

He didn't care who they were, or what they wanted. If he didn't get inside Foo's right away he would faint. His wounds would reopen, and his blood would mix with this dust.

But they were closer to Foo's door than he was; they were deliberately standing in the way to coolness. What's more, they were mere children – pistol-packing teenagers.

'Meester Bradshaw . . .' An adolescent whine. They drew their revolvers.

Jonathan stopped, barely able to stand. 'Take it easy, *amigos* . . . let's go inside where it's cool and talk about this over a couple of beers.'

He attempted to dodge around them, but they blocked his path. One reached out and gripped his arm, but he shook himself free.

'Hey! This isn't Hollywood, kids.' Jonathan's joking tone was a bluff; these children with their pistols pointed at his stomach terrified him.

Two identical faces were looking him over. Identical boyish grins flashed beneath shadows of moustaches. Jonathan shut his eyes – he thought he was seeing double. In another instant he was tumbling over backwards. There was a rattle and glint of metal.

'Hey, take it easy,' he cried. 'Take it easy.'

They straddled him and put handcuffs on him. A foot on the back of his neck forced his face into the dust. Sweat trickled and burned his eyes. He was so dizzy he wasn't sure where he'd been hit. Somehow they'd kicked his legs out from underneath him. He felt too dizzy to put up any resistance.

'My head is sore,' he moaned. 'This sun – I haven't got a hat like you. Let me go inside and lie down.'

Still imagining that safety could be found within, he began to crawl abjectly toward Foo's door. He thought he caught a glimpse of the orb of the Chinaman's face floating in the gloom behind the swinging doors.

'Mr Foo!' he called out. 'Help! Tell these cowboys to let me go!'

The next thing he knew they had him back on his feet and were shoving him, stumbling and nearly fainting, down the street to the waterfront. With their pistols they prodded him up the steps of a crumbling warehouse whose eaves were decorated in iron lace, framing the rusted inscription –

PEACEFUL BANANA COMPANY
1911

They pushed him along a veranda whose floorboards had in places rotted away. He had to look where to step, or he would have found himself waist deep in wood. They propelled him down a corridor and made him sit on a bench.

At least it was a relief to be out of the sun.

Jonathan found himself looking glumly at a poster on the wall opposite that displayed pictures of 'terrorists'. The boys and girls in the photographs had faced the camera directly, even haught-ily. Even so there was an element of wistfulness in each of those frozen faces above the row of numbers. They were still very young, but their destinies were already upon them. Each bore a gentle alias, such as 'The Doll', 'Armadillo', 'The Monkey', 'Emanuelita', 'The Cigar', and so on. And the bearded ones resembled intense young teachers. The teachers and their pupils: how did they get to be branded 'assassins, anarchists, arsonists – wanted dead or alive'?

'Wasted lives – wasted youth! Are you one of those, Mr Bradshaw?'

Umberto was standing in a doorway, his fists plunged deep into his trouser pockets. His head was cocked slightly to one side, questioningly. He wore a black arm band over the sleeve of his dark blue pinstripe suit. His face was dark with fatigue: he seemed to be aware of the impression his tragic appearance was making on Jonathan.

'Mr Hak. Beatrice. I tried to save her. I'm sorry. Is Bertha . . .' He swallowed hard; he couldn't talk.

'Come in here and shut the door.'

Umberto turned his back, re-entered the office and walked to his desk with flat, heavy steps. Gripping a chair in one hand, he pursed his lips and stared out the window, as though he could not bring himself to look at his captive. He seemed to be waiting for something – a confession.

Umberto's office had nothing in common with the rest of the building. Here the floor was polished and shiny. There was a massive wooden desk and two comfortable-looking chairs covered in a pleasant blue and yellow material. Against one wall stood an imposing bookcase that contained, among many volumes, a thick biography of Joseph Conrad and several photographic books on Africa and South America. On the desk, a silver letter opener lay diagonally across a leather blotter. Rounded river stones held down stacks of papers. An ink bottle with a gold top served as the centrepiece. Everything was orderly, everything was in its place. 'Liberty and Order' proclaimed a green and yellow flag that hung above the desk. 'Onward! Upward! Forward! – Together!'

'I thought I explained to you that I have a constant struggle to hold this town together.' Umberto's fists were back in his pockets. His face had twisted itself into an expression that successfully conveyed hurt and betrayal.

Jonathan tried to avoid his piercing stare. 'That's right. You did.'

'I thought I made it clear to you that we're not governed by polite civilities around here, or even by predictable hatreds and violence. I thought I also explained to you that this is a town that has been robbed of its vision and purity and moral integrity. Eaten away spiritually by a plague of degenerates and prostitutes, and stripped of its beauty and natural resources, its physical innocence shattered for all time by the hellish flames and insidious odours of Santa Petrolina.' Umberto was leaning stiffarmed on his desk, his face close to Jonathan's and his eyes never leaving Jonathan's. 'I deliberately confided in you about the corruption of moral fibre, the thievery of self-respect, and the loss of good intentions!'

Suddenly the Chief of Police sank into his chair and raised his palms heavenward, beseeching.

'Just what are your intentions, Mr Bradshaw? To rob us of the little dignity and hope that remains?'

Jonathan coughed. His voice came out in a whisper. 'You know what my intentions are – to find my father.'

Umberto matched his whisper with another. 'You're free to do anything you like – as long as you don't hurt anyone. But you already have . . .' His voice trailed away as he shook his head hopelessly. His face was rippled with pain, his eyes were strongly projecting his anguish. At the same time he seemed aware of the effect this was having on Jonathan. Like an actor who has effectively conveyed his suffering, he turned his head away to be seen in profile. 'You've robbed me of my daughter . . .' He paused and looked mournfully out of the window. 'We buried Princess Beatrice this morning.' With his head still positioned in a profile of noble agony, his voice wavering melodically. 'Just as your father robbed me of my wife.' He passed his hand wearily through his thick curls. 'My little girl is dead.' He heaved a long, heavy sigh.

Jonathan felt crushed by the weight of Umberto's loss and by his accusations. His mind sought to phrase an apology, but everything seemed trite or inappropriate. He coughed again and shifted a sad, troubled gaze across Umberto. 'It's a tragedy I can't . . .'

Still in profile the Chief of Police seemed to be waiting for a confession.

Jonathan tried to explain. 'I saw a man put a child into a box on a bridge. It was dark, and I didn't realize it was Bertha's brother . . .' He was sweating. He wanted to free his hands to express himself. He was torn between remorse and guilt and a strong desire to clear himself. 'I ran into Panadero a few minutes later. I was exhausted. I didn't put two and two together.' He fumbled with his handcuffs. 'I didn't think.'

Umberto whirled around, his face that of a fierce judge. 'How many political assassins and well-meaning terrorists have spilled the blood of innocents? You saw their faces outside! How many little men who fired the first shot that sends civilization tumbling and millions of brave men to their graves . . .' – he picked up the letter opener and jammed it into the top of the desk – ' . . . have looked up in dumb disbelief after the damage is done and mumbled in vague comprehension, "*I didn't think!*" ' He rapped the signet ring against the desk.

Jonathan felt so weak in the knees he was afraid he'd fall down. 'Mr Hak, I've never felt so awful about anything in my life.'

'Just what are you doing here, Mr Bradshaw?'

Jonathan shifted his feet and blinked away the sweat that was pouring down his face. 'Your boys – they knocked me down in the street, they kicked me in the head, they put these on me,' he said slowly and raised his hands. 'They brought me here.'

'I don't mean *here*, in my office, Mr Bradshaw.' Exasperated, Umberto let his head sink into his hand. 'I know why you're *here*.' He breathed in and exhaled loudly. 'Why are you in Puerto Gusano? What's your real mission? Are you here for your father's sake, or your own? Are you trying to take something else away from me now? What more do I have? What more do you want? From me? From my country?'

Jonathan felt engulfed by the power of Umberto's personality, his pain and his questions. He tried to think clearly, but the breeze was moving the flag above Umberto's head. Through the window he could see some sinister, pterodactyl-like seagulls floating in the wind. They soared to great heights – so high that Jonathan glumly asked himself what they could be doing up there, except to enter into swirling battle with the vultures. Watching them, he experienced a dull envy for those wings, for that flight, for escape.

Umberto had covered his eyes with his hands and was quiet for a moment. 'I loved my wife, Mr Bradshaw,' he began again in a low voice. 'You know that.' He was quick to add: 'And she loved me. We were happy. My wife was young and we had a son . . .' He seemed to be listening to himself, as though it were a story he was hearing for the first time, and it interested him – as though it all sounded good to him. 'She made me happy. Yes, marriage was a revelation for me. I loved being married, as I loved her. I think I told you about it. We had adventure, there were wild passions and yearnings like you may never have known. We needed each other's flesh – breasts and balls and cock.'

Once again, Jonathan was at a loss how to respond to Umberto.

'How inspiring it all was – our truth – our purity – our adventure. You can't imagine – you've never been married – how wonderful it was, after a long term of bachelorhood, after so much loneliness, to be passionately in love with one's *wife!*' Umberto had a way of making people envy him – even his tragedies. 'We reached a spiritual union so perfect – so rare – a combination of enlightened souls, liberated minds, humour, vision, a state of living and being seldom achieved and not to be met with again, and yet satisfying our carnal needs, which even in their savage instincts our wild desires to kiss and lick and suck all the parts of our bodies – endlessly – were somehow *blessed!*'

Jonathan shifted his weight. His head sank lower.

'And Ben was with us – except sexually, of course. And I can't really blame him for what happened because I couldn't go ahead with the change of spirit that was necessary after the plateau we had reached. It had to go forward – to evolve – to change one's environment and needs. They could leave and I couldn't. I couldn't embrace the world outside Puerto Gusano because of the demands on me here. My responsibilities. This town needs me. The children. Law and order. Right and wrong. *I* had to sacrifice . . .' Umberto was enraptured by his own monologue; he seemed to be convincing himself of its truth. He ran his fingers through his hair several times, then looked at them, twisting the signet ring on his little finger with his thumb. 'I was the one who had to make the sacrifice,' he murmured again. 'That's why I really can't blame *them*.' A note of malice was entering his voice. 'It must take a great deal of *courage*, Mr Bradshaw.'

'What must?'

'What you're doing. Why don't you sit down?'

Jonathan gratefully collapsed into one of the chairs, and stared at his boots.

'*Courage* to come to a wild outpost of humanity like this, where only the most intelligent and talented spirits can survive the rot and stagnation. To search for a father you hardly know, who certainly wouldn't recognize you if he saw you, who doesn't even think of himself as your father, who probably hasn't even thought of you in twenty-five years.'

Umberto's hardening tone began to worry and frighten Jonathan.

'*Courage* to seek out someone who doesn't want to see you, who *never* wanted to know you, and who probably refuses to recognize you as his legitimate son.' Umberto got to his feet and walked to the window, where he stood, hand on hip, his back to Jonathan. '*Courage* to inflict your desires and needs on a man on whom you have no claim . . . by right of the intervening years of his life that have embraced a new world, a new life, new friends, a new vision – because he wanted no part of your world.' His voice rising, he turned to face Jonathan. '*Courage* to say to hell with the pain you may cause others in the course of the search – myself, Bertha, Beatrice, Panadero – in your blind, selfish determination to satisfy your own needs – needs which I must tell you, Mr Bradshaw, are stupid and hopeless! Impossible to fulfil. Destructive because Ben can't give you what you seek.' Umberto pointed into the air. 'And I must stop you from inflicting more pain on those who don't want you!'

'Mr Hak!' Jonathan's mouth was open, but no other words came out.

Umberto was shouting. 'You come down here with your shirt tails hanging out, your belly showing, with a cigar in your mouth, sweating and innocently demanding to see a father who left you twenty-five years ago! He would have gone back if he'd wanted to see you! He didn't. It's my duty to stop your yankee arrogance and your innocence and your foolish courage from hurting anyone else! Haven't you done enough already? Don't you find your selfish courage rather diabolical?'

'Wait a minute. Let's get the record straight. You knew all along who was stealing those hams. Bertha had to know – you *must* have known!'

'Mr Bradshaw . . .' Umberto looked frustrated. 'This has nothing to do with what we're talking about – your foolish, harmful, pointless pursuit.'

Umberto was studying him as though he were an insect.

Jonathan was astounded. 'You knew and you allowed your daughter to risk her life stealing hams from a bunch of blood-thirsty cut-throats? You – the protector of little children!' Jonathan jumped up; he was struggling with the handcuffs. 'Save the children! Mr Hak – you're a hypocrite!'

Umberto smiled condescendingly.

Jonathan couldn't control his outrage. 'Then you try to make *me* responsible for Beatrice's death. Since I walked into this town you've tried to blame me for everything that's happened!'

'Mr Bradshaw . . .' Umberto's voice was calm, reasonable. 'Sit down, Mr Bradshaw. Many people have been jealous of me. You're nothing new. Jealous of many things.' He returned to his desk and settled himself wearily in his chair, as though he were obliged to state again a self-evident truth he had already repeated many times over. 'They're jealous of the spirit – that I have a job and manage to hold a dying town together. They know I do it at great personal cost. They're jealous of my beautiful wife and my attractive friends. They're jealous that I'm able to operate in this scum hole on a level that would rival the sophisticated societies in any capital of the world. They're jealous of superstar time, Mr Bradshaw. You in your own subconscious may be jealous of the intimate friendship I've had with your father, that I've known him years longer, much better, more personally than you ever can or ever will. I have his *past*, Mr Bradshaw. It's mine. You can't change what happened between us or the years we spent to-gether. Twenty-five years you wish you had, but they're mine. You're jealous and you want them back, but it's impossible because the past can't be undone. Our past. Years he gave me because he didn't want to give them to you or to your mother or to your smug, predictable world.'

Umberto smiled weakly. 'You must come to terms with your jealousy, Mr Bradshaw. You must realize how *dangerous* it is, how it forces you to try to hurt me – the terrible sorrow and tragedy it has already caused.' A mood of sombre resignation came over him. 'For both our sakes, and for the well-being of our town, which is my first concern, I must put you in prison.'

'Prison?' Jonathan cried. 'What for?'

'For being an accomplice in a murder.'

'But you can't put me in prison without a trial!'

'For your own protection as well. And please understand, Mr Bradshaw, I don't hold this against you. Under different circumstances, I believe we could have been friends . . .' Umberto's face was again changed by a humble, gracious smile.

'Mr Hak, you've completely distorted the reality . . .'

'Try to control your jealousy, Mr Bradshaw. I have many people to think about . . .' He looked away thoughtfully. 'To protect. I'll release you when the next boat arrives and make sure you're escorted safely aboard. Until then you'll be under police protection, and there'll be no further trouble. You know, many people in this town are blaming you . . .'

'Mr Hak, please let me go. I'll leave town today . . .'

'Oh?' Umberto asked mildly. 'And where will you go?'

'The swamp.'

'Mr Bradshaw, you don't seem to have understood me. First, there's no way you could possibly survive, or find your way into the swamp, let alone out of it. Few people have ever been able to do so. But that's not really the point. Your father deserted you. You must consider what that means and respect it. A man's desire for liberty is fundamental. It was his choice, and you'll never change that. As I said, your foolish courage can only cause fresh disasters. By putting you in prison, I'll be protecting you, and him. All of us.'

Jonathan opened his mouth to plead his case, but Umberto cut him off.

'Mr Bradshaw, let me tell you one more thing! This town is built entirely of wood. Consequently, all of us who dwell here fear fire, and to me you're more dangerous than a demented arsonist in a match stick town! *Get it?* All that's left now is my son Salvador. He calls me father, he's all I have . . . I have to protect him from your arrogance and your innocence. Do you hear? And here, this just arrived.' He handed Jonathan a telegram.

Jonathan was still shaking his head in bewilderment as the police boys came up behind him, seized him by the elbows, and dragged him away.

12

The Coop

The prison was another spectral, converted customs building built on pilings over the water. Rising from their mattresses, Jonathan's cell mates greeted him with friendliness and not a little curiosity. When these black men shook hands, palms and fingers touched but did not squeeze. And they, being big strong fellows, welcomed him with refined civility and gentleness as though they were in their own homes and not confined to a prison cell. They did not presume a show of strength which the firmness of a handshake is meant to convey. When Jonathan recalled the lectures he used to receive as a child – that the character of a man should be assessed by the strength of his grip and the shine on his shoes – why, these men didn't even own shoes. Certainly Jonathan, athletic though he was, would have had his hands full in a physical test with any one of these fellows, whose bulging muscles could not be hidden by rags.

As Ambrose, the eldest, later told him, they were four brothers from a place called Nile Town. Without doubt they were the most cheerfully naive fellows Jonathan had ever met, and apparently their present confinement was not of the slightest worry to them.

Jonathan climbed on a wooden box and looked out the window. There were the palm tops and the free swirl of vultures. Somewhere nearby women were laughing and talking as they pounded manioc. Although the prison stood by the sea, the window faced the town. As he was attempting to get his bearings, something flashed in his eyes. The flash was repeated and there, framed between two drooping palms, he made out the upper corner of Foo's establishment. The source of the flash was not a sun reflection off the tin roof. Foo himself was watching, and the sun was glinting off the telescope. Jonathan made a few signs, hoping to convey his helplessness. He took an empty cigarette packet from Ambrose, held it up and crumpled it in his hand.

All this his companions followed with the greatest interest, and when Jonathan got down from the box, Ambrose made a place for him on his mattress. Jonathan shared the last of his cigars with them.

'This is about the friendliest welcome I've received so far,' he said. 'You fellows almost make me feel glad to be in prison.'

He learned they'd come over from Nile Town in their boat loaded with rum to sell to the petroleros. Umberto had confiscated the rum and impounded the boat when he'd caught them sneaking ashore without paying customs duty. When Jonathan told them who he was, all four brothers rolled their eyes and whistled and clapped their hands.

'Is that why Umberto put you in jail?' Ambrose asked. 'Because his wife ran off with your father?'

'Do they punish sons for the sins of the fathers down here? There was a fight – that's how I got these stitches.'

At four o'clock in the afternoon came a tremendous crash as another thunderstorm swept over the town. Palm trees whipped back and forth as the rain advanced like a solid grey wall. In twenty minutes it was all over. The air cleared, the sky brightened, and all was quiet but for the sound of water running and dripping everywhere. It was at that hour, with the departing clouds turning pink and orange and the first tentative notes of a marimba becoming audible, that Jonathan sat on his mattress with his head in his hands and wept.

He remembered the telegram Umberto had given him. He took it out of his pocket and read: TOP PRIORITY FIND JONATHAN BRADSHAW STOP UNITED STATES PASSPORT 2770539 STOP URGENT REQUEST BY SENATOR ROBERT HOLLENBERG STOP BRADSHAW BELIEVED TO BE IN VICINITY OF PUERTO GUSANO STOP BRADSHAW FAMILY DEEPLY CONCERNED FOR HIS SAFETY AND WANT HIM HOME IMMEDIATELY.

The telegram comforted Jonathan for a few minutes. His family would stop at nothing to find him, but Granny, Henry and his mother seemed a million miles away.

Not much later the door opened and the turnkey entered with a bucket of water. Through the door one of the police boys could be seen leaning back in his chair, cradling a machine gun in his lap and picking his nose.

Jonathan removed his bloodstained suit and washed himself. The brothers gazed at his nakedness with undisguised curiosity.

The food pails were brought in, and Jonathan, who hadn't eaten all day, discovered tortillas, black bean mush, and a piece of fried fish – each wrapped neatly in a banana leaf package. He was wondering who it could be that took such care with the prisoners' food, when, in the bottom of the pail, he discovered a small corked bottle of rum, and, strapped to it by an elastic band, a packet of cigars.

DON'T WORRY BOSS were the words scrawled in a childlike hand on the side of the packet. Jonathan went directly to the window, where he got another flash from Foo. Then he sat down and ate his food with the others and felt a little better.

After dinner Jonathan handed around the cigars. They all had a smoke and a swallow from the bottle. The pails were lined up, the drinking glasses were carefully filled to various levels with water, tin spoons were handed out, and the concert began. The primitive instruments gave off a deafening racket, and the music and chanting went on far into the night. From time to time Jonathan returned to the window and looked out. The hotel was dark, but through the trees he could make out the glittering rim of the ferris wheel. All through the night it went on turning to the scratchy voice from the victrola.

> 'But that was long a-go:
> Now my con-so-la-tion
> Is in the star-dust of a song.'

Breakfast was coffee and sweet potatoes. Each time Jonathan showed himself at the window he got a flash from Foo. In the evening following the rain, he found a lump of charcoal in the bottom of his food pail. Ambrose snatched it from him and hid it beneath the mattress.

That night the music was louder than ever. It had to be in order to drown out the noise Ambrose was making as he rubbed one of the bars with a hacksaw blade that had arrived embedded in a melon. With one bar gone, he directed one of his brothers to rub the charcoal on Jonathan.

Jonathan was getting the clicking rhythm now, and he was learning the repetitive chanting. As the musicians pounded away in the dim light that entered under the door, his white skin was fading away. He smiled: he was becoming one of them. The music reached its most deafening pitch as he climbed through the window and lowered himself into a waiting canoe. A figure holding a pole was seated in the stern.

'Bertha,' he asked, 'is that you? I've wanted to talk to you, to tell you how miserable I feel about . . .'

'Don't say anything.' Her voice was unsteady. 'Please . . . '

'Why are you helping me?'

'For Beatrice,' she whispered. 'You tried to save her. Shhh.'

The concert drew to a close as the brothers piled out of the window one by one and dropped like cats into the canoe. Ambrose came last. He picked up a paddle in the bow, and in another minute they were gliding through a maze of stilts that supported the houses built out over the water. Right above their heads people were talking and arguing and walking around, putting their children to bed and eating dinner. Light was shining down between cracks in the floorboards, segmenting the stilts and casting ribboned patterns on the surface of the water.

Bertha sat alone in the back of the canoe. The laddered light shining from above seemed to isolate her from the others. A rosary was draped across her lap, and her lips moved silently, as she paddled. Jonathan could not bear to look at her.

A light was flashing up ahead, and in another minute they were passing beneath Ricardo's café. Stepping from the doorway, a man walked to the end of the pier and leaned against a piling while he relieved himself.

'Ah, this weakness I feel – it's like *death!*' A loud voice addressed the night. It was Umberto, bathed in the red light of Santa Petrolina, talking to himself. Jonathan, terrified by this silent proximity to his jailer, crouched lower in the canoe. Looking up through the stilts, he could see the Chief of Police – a lonely silhouette against the flaming sky. Umberto spoke in a loud stage whisper, shaking his fist at the gods and complaining bitterly of his fate. 'This fatigue . . .' he moaned. 'This heat . . . encouraging sloth, greed, alcoholism . . . are *these* to be my companions for life?' He leaned through the window and shouted to the people inside. 'What about it, you miserable sons of bitches!'

He was answered by guffaws and drunken mutterings from within.

'They don't care,' he mumbled. Facing the flames, he was talking to himself again. 'This heat of hell . . . boiling the sea with foreign filth, driving the turtle onto the beach, cracking the pelican's egg.' His voice trailed off. 'In my petty revenge I allowed her to be sacrificed,' he cried, unaware the canoe was gliding soundlessly beneath him. *'Beatrice!'* he shouted at the stars. *'Beatrice!* Oh God, forgive me!'

There was such agony and loneliness in this outpouring of sorrows that Jonathan felt his tears come and Bertha pressed her face into her lap to stifle her moans as the canoe slid away into the night.

13

The Island

Nobody spoke a word. They were at sea – a sea that was asleep. Darkness covered them with a shroud; silence accompanied them like a mournful presence no one dared disturb. Bertha's repetitive prayers droned softly through the night. Her voice would crack, and she would begin to cry once more.

The only other sound was the monotonous stroke of the oar. Ambrose had replaced Bertha in the stern. The thrust from the oar working against the chock sent a shiver through the canoe – a faint reminder that they were still moving through the void.

Dawn found them still close to the shore where the forest came down to the water's edge. Bertha was seated behind Jonathan in the canoe. He'd been afraid to talk to her during the night, but when he awoke he was ashamed to discover that his head had been resting against her knees. Her face was puffy with fatigue, and her eyes were dull. She looked weary and older.

The spell of silence was broken by the sound of a distant motor. A black dot had intruded upon the green rim of the horizon, and it was coming on fast. The pace of Ambrose's stroke quickened. Jonathan's eyes were riveted on the rapidly enlarging dot which had grown curves of white water on either side. A shadow fell across the boat, and he looked up. They were passing beneath a low branch festooned with beards of Spanish moss. With one powerful stroke Ambrose neatly propelled the canoe between two trees, and suddenly – miraculously – they were inside the forest. Ambrose rested on his oar as the canoe slid deeper into the shadows. Outside, the noise increased, and through the receding columns of trees they glimpsed the motor launch passing. A machine gun was mounted in the bow, and several armed boys were scanning the shore through binoculars.

'OUT OF MY TOWN! OUT OF MY LIFE! OUT! OUT! OUT!' It was the voice of Umberto, addressing the forest through a bull horn. 'BEN, MARIE, BERTHA, TOO! GOOD RIDDANCE TO SLOP TIME! TELL THEM TO STAY AWAY FROM PUERTO GUSANO IF THEY VALUE THEIR LIVES!

DO YOU HEAR ME, MR BRADSHAW? TELL MY WIFE THE
CURE . . . IS WORKING. THERE ARE SIGNS THAT . . . THE
PIGMENTATION IS BEING RESTORED. AND NEVER SET
FOOT IN PUERTO GUSANO AGAIN . . . DO YOU HEAR
ME? STAY OUT OF MY LIFE – ALL OF YOU!'

The motor noise faded with the sound of Umberto's voice
ranting at the jungle.

Bertha put her hands over her ears.

'Hear you? she cried. 'How can we not hear you, you mad fool!'

Her voice startled a pair of water birds. Pale wings flapping,
they flew off without a sound among the trees and were swallowed by shadows.

'Little Beatrice not yet cold in her grave, and he's already
sending messages to that woman! He's so bewitched by Marie, not
even the death of his daughter can calm the fury.' She spat
contemptuously into the water.

Her hatred for Umberto's wife renewed her vitality and briefly
relieved her pain. She patted Jonathan's arm and looked away.

By degrees his eyes adjusted to the gloom. The trees were of
monumental proportion, their roots like flying buttresses that
joined the massive trunks far above their heads. The roofing
branches blotted out all but a few patches of blue. Through these
rents in the foliage the sun, which had leapt up from the horizon,
poured with the intensity of searchlights, illuminating with
chiaroscuro effect the lifeless tangle of hanging lianas. These
shafts of light descending through leafy heights made luminous
pools afloat on the watery forest floor.

As the canoe had entered this liquid domain so surreptitiously,
with hardly a ripple from the shiny black bow, the forest birds
seemed unaware of the presence of strangers. A pair of scarlet
toucans hopped sedately from branch to branch. From somewhere came the screech of a macaw, to be answered from another
part of the forest. In spite of the occasional animal cries, the
overwhelming atmosphere of the jungle was one of brooding
silence, as though the world had not yet begun. The birdcalls
themselves – hoots, squawks, hollow croakings – all sounded
oddly inchoate and echoed discordantly like the first expressions
of fragile life awakening in a sullen universe.

A great fish rolled in the water near the bank and jetted beneath the canoe.

'Tarpon.' Ambrose said the word.

The canoe slid along a black water creek winding through the trees. The forest floor was lumbered with the wreckage of the fallen. Wherever one of the giants had come crashing down, a chamber of light had been created. The broken vines hung like harp strings against the variegated foliage and stroked the water. Clouds of glittering yellow butterflies were blowing together like petals or confetti. The sunlight, sifting through a tangle of leaves and branches, sprinkled the canoe as it glided by.

Presently the canoe emerged from the forest and entered upon a wide lagoon of clear water. Schools of fish could be seen swimming many feet below. The sail was raised and the sculling oar trailed in the water and served as a rudder.

Bertha wiped away her tears with the back of her hand and picked up a pineapple. 'It wasn't your fault. Don't go blaming yourself. You didn't know.'

Jonathan wiped his nose on his sleeve. 'I was drunk and tired.'

'Don't cry like that. She'll just have to be a sweet memory. Here, eat some fruit and feel better.'

He couldn't help it – he felt as weak as a child.

'Stop it, boss. Stop it!' she commanded. 'I'm the one who shouldn't have let her done it!' She shook him roughly by the shoulder. 'Umberto got his satisfaction from seeing those petroleros accuse each other and fight. Panadero made a little money selling the hams, but little Beatrice . . . she thought it was just a game.'

'If I hadn't been there, it wouldn't have happened.'

'She loved you, boss. She didn't play with everyone. She didn't sit in everyone's lap. From the moment she laid eyes on you, you made her feel good. That's why you don't belong in jail. We're all more to blame than you are!' Her eyes flashed. 'If anyone's at the bottom of it, it's parrot woman!' She bit ravenously into a piece of pineapple. 'If she'd behaved like a *wife* instead of an *exhibitionist*, Umberto would never have come running to me for love, and little Beatrice would never have been born . . . just to be killed like that.' She angrily snatched a knife from the basket. 'You heard him, didn't you? Screaming at the trees and alligators! Tell my wife this! Tell my wife that!' She sniffled loudly and cursed under her breath. 'She's been gone five years, but she's *still* got him! As if she never left.' She wiped away the tears with the back of her hand

and began to attack another pineapple, but she was too distracted to do it properly. She was making a mess out of it. 'He still loves her, and he still wants her back. She drove him crazy walking naked around the house, but when it came to bedtime – uh uh, *nothing doing.* Oh, she knew he was running to me all right.' She hacked viciously at the pineapple. Most of the fruit went into the water with the husk. The rest she crammed into **her** mouth.

'But Umberto gave me a detailed description of their sex life . . .'

'Lord, boss! Umberto tells everybody she crawled on her hands and knees, begging for love – because he wants to *believe* it's so. But that doesn't make it so. Whenever they went out she dressed up so everything was showing. Made Umberto wild. She came to me complaining the men wouldn't leave her alone when *she* was doing the chasing – right down the middle of the road!' She handed him another chunk of pineapple. 'You know what's funny? She doesn't like going to bed with a man. Told me so herself.'

Jonathan's eyes were red, his mouth was full of pineapple. 'Bertha, Umberto told me that he and Marie had a passionate marriage. Then my father came along and he had to make the sacrifice . . .'

'Umberto will knock anyone flat who messes with his memories, but that don't make them real. The fact is she never loved him – she ain't got love in her! Vision and purity and truth . . .' Bertha spat into the water. 'He wouldn't know the truth if he stepped on it.' She dug into the basket. 'Here take this.'

Jonathan was sick of pineapple. He passed it to the brothers in the bow.

'Vision and truth . . .' Bertha was engaged in a bitter monologue with herself. 'One night he walked clean through my screen door calling her name. He didn't even know what house he was in. Marie! Marie!' Bertha put her hands over her ears. 'You know why there's no chairs in my house? He broke them all cursing parrot woman.'

The canoe sailed placidly on. Great flocks of geese and ducks got up from its path. There were multitudes of cormorants and herons, and kingfishers by the dozen flitted over the water. Their tameness amazed Jonathan. Where he came from, all wild animals ran for their lives at the approach of man.

'That child had hardly been born when Marie went off to Nile

Town. Said she was going for a week to visit her folks and left Umberto alone with that infant for four months. You know who looked after Salvador?' She rapped herself hard on the chest. '*Bertha*. Let that woman see a beetle cross the road and she'll stop the traffic. She'll even get down on her hands and knees and hurry it along. But do you think she ever cared for her own child? Lord, that cold blooded woman gives me the creeps!'

'What's my father doing with her?'

'The swamp is where she belongs. She's not civilized yet, unless your daddy's done it. Better watch out. She'll be after you for sure!' Her daughter's death had unhinged her. 'She'd do *any-thing* to get attention. Parrot in her hair. An iguana on a leash. No underwear. Dressed so any man could see what he wanted. *Anything* to make a man look at her. And if you *did* look . . .' Bertha crossed her arms and sat back. 'She'd put her nose into the air, stick out her chin, flip that eyeglass of hers, and stare down at you as though she smelled something bad.'

Even though it was her hatred for Marie that did it, Jonathan was gratified to see Bertha's spirits revive.

'What does Dad see in her?'

'Heaven only knows! She had never seen anything like your daddy. Umberto welcomed him ashore like he was a king, and within hours they were friends. Umberto cut back on his drinking. He took long swims in the morning, lost weight and looked younger. The two of them were together all the time, talking, laughing, taking trips into the jungle, dreaming up schemes and wild projects to make them rich.

'Only one person was jealous of that friendship – parrot woman. She was on that boat from the start, pretending to look after the anteater. The way she paraded around town with it, so proud, you'd think it was Ben Bradshaw himself she had on the leash. He resisted her at first – he had to raise the gangplank at night to keep the bitch off the boat. But later, after he'd sold the boat, and Santa Petrolina had come, she followed him to the swamp. It was where she wanted to be.'

'So my father and Marie *both* deserted their children?'

'Uh, huh.'

An island was floating like a mirage on the liquid horizon. Tall trees were growing there. As the canoe sailed closer Jonathan could make out huts beneath the trees. The island was an evenly shaped mound, and the sides sloped symmetrically up from the water to meet at a low summit. The big trees loved the high ground so much, the island appeared top heavy beneath their broad spread.

'What's this place?' he asked.

'A special island, – nature favours it. Even Doc says it's a place where folks his medicine can't cure can come to get well. It calls down light and power from the sky. Wounds heal faster. You'll see – if your head hurts now, it'll feel better here.'

They tied up at a jetty. Bertha, followed by Ambrose and his brothers carrying baskets, hurried directly up the hill and entered the huts. Left to himself, Jonathan shed his clothes and jumped off the jetty. The water was warm, and he rubbed himself all over. The charcoal dispersed in a grey cloud. For a few minutes he floated on his back in the clear water, and then for nothing better to do, he reconnoitred the island. He soon discovered it was as wide as it was long – a perfect square. The surrounding water must have been fifty feet deep, which made the island an even greater wonder, poking its head so cleanly as it did from such a depth. Noticing a rocky outcropping above him, where even the rocks seemed to have their own geometrical shapes, he climbed up to investigate. Turning over a stone in his hands, it suddenly dawned in his aching head that these weren't ordinary stones at all but ancient masonry.

Elated by what he considered to be a major archaeological find, he ran back to the hut.

'Hey, Ambrose!' he shouted. 'This island's a pyramid! We could make a fortune . . .'

Ambrose put a finger to his lips and barred the way.

'What is it, boss?' Bertha's voice came from within. 'Let him in,' Jonathan heard her say.

Ambrose stepped aside, and he went inside.

It was dark in the hut, and it took a few seconds for his eyes to adjust. Bertha was squatting on her heels beside someone stretched out on a mat.

'Bertha,' he said, glancing uneasily at the prostrate man, 'you were right, this is no ordinary island.'

The man on the mat began to writhe in pain. *'Perdido!'* Pointing at Jonathan, he called out in a raspy voice, *'Perdido! . . . Perdido!'*

'Shhh.' Bertha wrung out a cloth and laid it across the man's forehead. He was twisting on an axis of pain that seemed to be concentrated between his legs. Jonathan sensed that his presence in the hut aggravated him. Somehow he was making the poor fellow's agony worse.

Suddenly the man threw off the blanket that covered him. Ambrose, who had been standing in the doorway behind Jonathan, went to retrieve it, and light flowed into the hut. Jonathan beheld the colossal naked torso, the filthy bandages, the thighs and belly streaked with blood. A hand was pointing at him, and the raspy voice repeated: '*Perdido . . . Perdido!*'

It was Panadero.

14
The Aphrodisiac

'Something terrible may have happened to Ben – it could happen to you, too. *Worse!*'

With Granny's warning pounding in his ears, Jonathan staggered from the hut and leaned against a tree. Murder and mutilation – these were acts of destruction that could never be undone. He understood Umberto's yearning to turn back the clock. The sins of the son had already exceeded those of the father.

He stumbled down the hill and stood on the end of the jetty. He was gazing across the lagoon, mirror of passing clouds, home of birds and fish, and untouched – but for the monument on which he stood – by the hand of man.

Perdido, he had called him. The lost one. The one who didn't know where he was or what he was doing. Granny was right, he should never have come here. What had been accomplished, besides murder and . . .

'*Castration!*'

The word carried across the water like a shot, shattering the silence and startling a flock of ducks to flight.

'Boss?' It was Bertha, standing behind him. She exuded an odour of fresh fruit and tobacco. 'Come on, boss, it's getting dark. I'm going to give you something to eat.'

'I can't go in there, Bertha.'

'He don't hold it against you, boss. He knows – we all do – you didn't know any better.'

'How can you forgive so easily? If I hadn't intruded upon your lives, none of this would have happened.'

'Just by being Ben Bradshaw's son you were mixed up with us the minute you set foot on our shore. Umberto put you in prison . . . well, to protect you. There ain't no one in Puerto Gusano who hasn't got strong feelings about what happened at Ricardo's, and he didn't want you walking around free and easy. We brought you away because it wasn't your fault.'

'Will he die?'

'If he wants to live, he will. If he don't, he won't.'

A lamp was burning in the hut, and Ambrose sat cross-legged in the corner. His eyes were wide open and staring straight ahead. Covered by the blanket, Panadero lay by the wall, breathing deeply. Otherwise, there was silence in the hut. Jonathan sat down. The lamp flickered in a draft from the door, and shadows leapt about.

When Jonathan looked again, Ambrose had rolled his eyes up into his head. Only the whites were visible.

Bertha entered carrying a brazier of glowing coals, which she set on the ground. Beside Jonathan she placed a bottle and a glass.

'What are they doing, Bertha?'

'They're trying to help Panadero.'

'Why do they roll their eyes up?'

'That's their way.'

She went out, and Jonathan poured himself a glass of aguardiente. The brazier had begun to produce clouds of smoke, and he guessed that Bertha had sprinkled some incense on the charcoal, although he hadn't seen her do it. The smoke smelled sweet. Ambrose had not moved but was breathing deeply, inhaling the smoke through his nostrils. Jonathan followed his example, and the effect was electric. The smoke entered his brain like an arrow and bounced off the back of his skull. The initial wave of dizziness subsided, and he felt relaxed and clear in the head. The aguardiente seemed less interesting now, and he put down the glass. Over by the wall, Panadero had begun to stir.

Bertha returned with a bowl, which she carefully set on the brazier. Jonathan found himself following her movements with cat-like intensity. She placed a plate of fruit beside him, but he didn't look at it. What aroused his curiosity were the contents of the bowl. He had to suppress a desire to crawl over and sniff at it.

'You all right, boss?'

Her voice came from miles away, and he didn't bother to answer. Ambrose's hand was groping like a blind man's for the bowl. He found it, carried it to his lips, and drank. Jonathan watched, consumed by a morbid jealousy and fear he would be left none. He also experienced a simultaneous sense of relief that he had not been obliged to drink first.

Jonathan's turn came next. The liquid was warm and oily and tasted bitter. Carefully, he replaced the bowl on the coals and looked down at the fruit by his knee. Now was a good time to eat the fruit, he thought. It was an avocado, but the meat was blue, with a large red nut resting in the centre. He could not take his eyes off the miraculous fruit, when a bolt of lightning flashed before him. Shaken from his reverie, he sat up straight and looked at the others.

Their eyes were wide open and staring at Panadero, who had moved into a sitting position. Jonathan felt a twinge in his testicles. Without having seen him do it, he realized Panadero had already tasted the liquid. He also knew that Bertha was sitting just outside the door of the hut, unseen but just a few feet away, and that she was making something with her hands she would give him later.

Another bolt flashed, with such force that it almost knocked him over. It was a physical stroke, like an electric shock, but a feeling of warmth followed immediately afterwards, especially in the testicles. They felt like they were growing. Strength was flowing into him, and he squeezed his bulging calf muscles.

The flashes were rolling at them in progressively shorter intervals, knocking Jonathan this way and that, while the others twitched and bucked, as though they were being buffeted by a pack of invisible devils. Only Panadero remained steady; his greater bulk resisted the blows. He was struggling back and regaining strength. He gripped his knees and bowed his head to the ground. Sweat was pouring off his shoulders.

They were reaching a peak, and Jonathan was convinced his testicles were swelling. This both pleased and embarrassed him, and he covered his crotch with his hands. He dreaded the moment he would have to open his trousers to free them for further growth. But his strength was ebbing; his head felt numb. The others were rubbing their bellies and vomiting. He shut his eyes and felt like vomiting, too. The pressure within his testicles was becoming painful, and he wanted the whole thing to stop. He fell over on his side and vomited.

Thunder was rising in his ears, like the grumbling of a distant storm. Bertha was tugging at his arm, trying to make him sit up and drink from a cup. Ambrose had departed, but the brothers had rushed in and were greedily lapping up what was left in the bowl. Panadero was sitting alone with his back to the wall of the hut, pounding the ground with his great fists, raising the dust and roaring like a bull.

15

The Swamp

The next thing Jonathan heard was the sound of water slapping. He had a glimpse of stars overhead; he was lying in the bottom of a canoe. Bertha wasn't there – it was just he and a shadow in the stern – going somewhere in the night. Swish . . . bump . . . swish . . . bump . . . It was Ambrose plying the long oar, propelling them to a new destination. Jonathan was in a daze, and indifferent to his fate.

Later on the canoe bumped against something, and he woke again. Stars were visible, sliding behind a ragged framework of branches. The canoe had re-entered the forest. Everything was deadly silent but for the sound of the oar, which reverberated eerily, as though they were splashing down the bowels of a giant sewer.

A violent wind rose up before dawn. Above the hollow roar of the gale the great trees could be heard groaning and grinding against one another, and massive branches came crashing down. The storm ceased as abruptly as it had begun. Dawn came on by degrees, slipping silently among the columns on the effulgent mist.

As if at a signal, the birds began to croak and hoot. The vegetation was thick, and they were gliding along a tunnel-like creek overhung by low branches heavy with Spanish moss. Ambrose sculled on and on.

By mid-morning the trees had thinned out. The heat became intense, and Jonathan wished he had brought a hat along. They were encountering great patches of sudd in the water. Jonathan worked with his hands in the bow, clearing away the weed, while Ambrose heaved from behind. The canoe was only about eight feet long, with just a few inches of freeboard; and Jonathan was obliged to bail with a calabash the water that constantly slipped in. The water weed swarmed with insects. He could not touch a leaf without a small army marching aboard his arm. Contact with the canoe brought them over the side in legions. Clouds of mosquitoes whined about his ears, and black spiders as big as his hand

dropped off the trees into the canoe. They were tremendously
fast and had to be killed instantly. Ambrose swatted at them with
his hat as more water slopped in.

From the recesses of a weed-choked pond, an animal was
sounding a mournful note. Jonathan spotted some large, turkey-
like birds hopping from branch to branch of a dead tree, hooting
lugubriously.

Ambrose, who was in no hurry, was chuckling to himself over
the prospect of a canoe load of fish.

'Many fish here, boss.'

Indeed, the swamp so teemed with them that he had only to
throw an iron-tipped spear blindly into the water. A *klunk* meant
he'd skewered yet another prehistoric creature with the hide of
an armadillo.

'Are there snakes, too, Ambrose?'

'Many.' He put down his pole. The bottom of the canoe was
alive with flopping fish.

'Alligators?'

'Plenty. Big ones.'

'Piranha?'

'*Claro*. Thousands.'

A hairy vine swatted Jonathan across the face.

'Ambrose!' he shouted. 'Let's get the hell out of here!'

Ambrose was pushing with all his strength, but they were
stuck. Jonathan thought that the heat and insects would
drive him out of his mind, but somehow they managed to shove
the canoe through.

At last they entered a shallow river. The blue sea glistened not
more than a mile away. They tied up in the shade of a tree.

Jonathan was relieved to be rid of the vegetable stink of the
jungle. 'What's going to happen now, Ambrose?'

'Big boat coming soon.' Ambrose was merrily counting his fish.

The river was sandy-bottomed. Jonathan wanted to swim and
wash himself, but Ambrose shook his finger. Dangerous sting
rays made their homes in the sand, he said. The river was also the
home of the candiru, a tiny fish that liked to dart up a man's penis
or anus, implanting itself with sharp spikes.

'You want to swim?' he giggled. 'Maybe lose prick.'

'I guess I'll sit this one out.'

Late in the afternoon a sail hove into sight – inland! For several minutes they watched it tack back and forth through the swamp as it followed the meandering course of the river. When it rounded the last bend and bore down upon them, Jonathan was amazed by the size of the towering lateen sail.

Ambrose dug into a basket and pulled out Jonathan's revolver.

'Where'd you get that?' Jonathan asked. He checked to see if it was still loaded.

'Bertha.'

There was no time to discuss the matter. Jonathan shoved the revolver into his coat pocket as Ambrose hailed the boat.

The tall sail was pulling strongly in the breeze, the boat was moving downriver at a good clip, and Ambrose had to pole furiously to keep pace with it. Black arms hoisted Jonathan aboard. When he looked back, Ambrose and the canoe were already fading away into the shadowy wall of the jungle.

'Ambrose – hey!' Jonathan waved. 'Thanks for the lift! Come visit me in New York!'

This was a large ship – forty feet in length, and very broad abeam. The deck was piled high with produce from the forest – bales of bark, lengths of hardwood lumber, sacks of nuts, and animal skins. The ship was moving at a terrific rate through water that couldn't have been more than four or five feet deep.

The skipper was an ancient greybeard, naked to the waist, displaying a bony torso. The crew was of varying ages – young blacks dressed in faded denim shorts and tattered shirts. They were all as muscular as gladiators, but they lounged about the deck in languid poses, as though they'd never done a stroke of work in their lives.

The ship shussed swiftly on the ebbing river to the open sea. The skipper barked an order, and the ship swung south along the coast as men leapt into the rigging and hauled in the sail.

They detoured around a fish trap where giant grey herons fed off the remains of the night's catch. Brilliant sunlight reflected off the immaculate white beaches, as smooth and hard as tennis courts. Orange crabs in their millions stared at the ship as it flew by.

How many shades of turquoise could Jonathan discern, where the waters faded or darkened over the pale sandy bottom? Gauzy nets had been set out to dry, and ragged kestrels patrolled the sandy wastes. Lines and lines of water birds were racing the ship home across the pastel plains – their cries spooked the wavering, eye-deceiving horizons. This was white space and blue time, where pink dolphins played side by side and dove beneath the ship. The water was so clear, they might have been flying down there below the keel.

16

Nile Town

At dusk the ship slid quietly into Nile Town harbour. Strings of lights illuminated the pier, the warehouses and customs sheds, the palm trees and row-boats. All reflected dreamily on the dark waters.

A bustle on the quayside greeted the ship as it tied up. Dark forms leapt aboard, and the unloading commenced immediately. Swathed in stupendous African costumes, the ladies of the town paraded ostentatiously back and forth. Conversing among themselves in a twittering, bird-like language, they encouraged the labouring men and competed openly for the sailors.

Jonathan stepped ashore and heaved a sigh of relief. A young man in military fatigues checked his passport and crisply summoned a boy who led him to a hotel.

Opening the door, he found himself in a cavernous lobby. At the far end a lamp burned and a number of black people were seated, listening to an organ recital. With the sound of Bach in his ears, Jonathan approached the circle of light. The audience numbered half a dozen. The ladies were lavishly dressed, and the men wore dark suits. All appeared to be completely absorbed in the music being played by a black organist about twenty-five years old. He was a handsome young man whimsically attired in a striped shirt and wing-tip collar. A piece of Christmas ribbon served as his bowtie, and scarlet suspenders held up his tuxedo trousers.

An old gentleman looked up, and with a friendly nod waved Jonathan into an empty chair, as naturally as though he had been a tardy guest. This certainly was a step up from Puerto Gusano, Jonathan thought as he gratefully sat down. With a twinge of regret he remembered his clean suit hanging in Foo's closet. The elegant attire of these music lovers put him to shame. The sole of one boot had come loose in the swamp, and the upper hung about his ankle like a grotesque spat. His necktie he was using as a belt. In prison his hair had filled up with fleas, so he had to refrain from scratching like a monkey. The bald spots on the top of his head were sewn up like baseballs. His jacket was stained with blood and encrusted with mud and muck from the swamp.

The music came to an end, and there were murmurs of approval and light conversation among the guests. The old patriarch swivelled around in his chair.

'Mr Bradshaw? Welcome.'

Jonathan cleared his throat. 'Thank you. That was a great concert! I hope you don't mind that I'm not dressed for the occasion. You can't imagine how *glad* I am to be here.' He was scratching at the stains in his suit with his fingernails. 'Uh, how do you know my name?'

'There is an article in the newspaper about your ingenious escape from prison. Everybody is talking about it. Now, permit me to introduce you to my friends. They are anxious to meet a celebrity.'

Jonathan shook hands with Misses Ruth and Annabell, Mr Boston, Mr Jackson, and Mr Madison Jones.

'And this is my son Randolph.' He patted the young organist on the back.

Judging from the way he dressed, in smoking jacket and cravat, Jonathan saw that the old man was well aware that he still cut a handsome figure. When father and son stood side by side, the resemblance was obvious.

Randolph limply extended his hand, and they touched finger-tips. 'What ho, old cock!'

'What?' Jonathan glanced anxiously at his fly. 'You know, you'd be asking for trouble if you said that in some parts of New York.'

'Ripping!' Randolph exclaimed. He slipped into the Ali shuffle. 'I love a bit of the old one-two.' His Christmas ribbon necktie was held in place by a pearl stickpin. His white silk scarf had tassels, and the front of his dress shirt was pink and white stripes. His starched shirt cuffs had been meticulously turned back; from one dangled the corner of a speckled silk hanky.

'Yeah, well, the old one-two isn't as sporting as you think north of 125th Street. It's a far cry from the playing fields of Eton.'

'I dare say, old sport, you look a far cry from Eton yourself.'

'Randolph!' his father said sternly. 'Mr Bradshaw is our guest.'

'No offence, old bean. A mere jest.'

'Yeah, well, please excuse this intrusion. You gentlemen don't know what a relief it is to be here!'

'Well, buck up. You can chuck off what's left of your boot and relax here.'

'Say, this is a great hotel, reminds me of the rambling Victorian boarding houses in Cape May, New Jersey. And the way you play the organ I thought it was Arthur Rubenstein or somebody. No kidding: I met the maestro in the Yankee Kitchen on Madison between 75th and 76th Street. I'd just read a big article about him in the *Daily News* and, *there he was*. Sitting on the stool right next to me. He reached in his pocket and his wallet had been stolen, so I had to pay for his two glazed doughnuts and a cup of coffee. He gave me tickets to his concert at St Patrick's Cathedral. I had a flat tire coming back from the races. One of my stepfather's horses had won at Monmouth Park, so I only got there for the last two chords, too. I'm really sorry I didn't hear your whole concert.'

'I say, thanks awfully, old bean – sorry I missed yours.'

The old man went off to bid his guests goodnight. Randolph took out a package of Benson and Hedges. 'Congratulations on the splendid getaway,' he whispered, snapping open the top of a gold cigarette lighter. Everything he did had a casual sweetness about it. 'Umberto's jail is kind of leaky, but that bust-out was simply first class.'

He pulled a newspaper clipping from his pocket.

'5 FLY THE COOP ON SAMBA BEAT'.

'You're a celebrity, old boy, but you're safe here, Umberto has no authority in Nile Town.'

'Since you know who I am, you probably know I'm trying to locate my father.'

'*Tiens, tiens.* Believe me, we know *all* about it. My dear, I'm agog to think of you in that primitive jail. No wonder you looked bushed! You're welcome to stay on with Big City as long as you like.' He motioned over his shoulder with his thumb and giggled.

'Say, how did you know I was coming?'

'They call me Big City because I've lived in most of them,' answered the old man, returning. 'And Randolph here is following in my footsteps. Already he's spent two years studying music at the London Conservatory, and just recently he's been awarded another scholarship.'

'I figured with that Oscar Wilde accent you must live in London.'

Big City looked admiringly at his son. 'He just arrived a few days ago for a holiday,' he said.

'Summer hols – just like you, Johnny.'

'Not only that . . .' the old man continued in an expansive mood. 'One of Randolph's elder sisters lives in Paramaribo, where she has a string of movie houses . . . another is in Georgetown running the pepper trade.'

'What about parrot sister, sir? She's the one that he'll be wanting to hear about.' Randolph winked at Jonathan.

'Ah yes, Marie . . .' The old man sighed.

'You mean Mr Hak's wife?' Jonathan looked incredulously from father to son.

'In a manner of speaking.'

'Marie is Randolph's other sister . . .'

'I say, go on and tell him, sir.'

Big City frowned. 'Not tonight . . .'

'Father dear, you'd be too beastly to drop it! Why do you think he's here?'

'Randolph, please control yourself!' The old man drew himself up – he really was quite a dignified chap – and looked Jonathan straight in the eye.

'I, uh, am sure you are an educated man, Mr Bradshaw . . . you will understand a father's desire to see his children lead useful lives, and that education and travel constitute essential training. The two older girls have turned out well. Randolph here has immense musical talent, and it is not only I who say so. His teachers in London . . . the very fact of this new scholarship . . . Marie married at a very young age. I regret she has caused so much unhappiness. I personally have the greatest sympathy and compassion for Umberto . . .'

'Let's not overkill the sympathy and compassion, dear father. Umberto was hardly an innocent bystander. After all, he baited his hook with her.'

'What? Huh?' Jonathan looked from son to father.

'I, uh, have nothing against your father, Mr Bradshaw . . . but Marie's present situation in no way conforms, uh . . . her education is far from complete . . . she *is* intelligent, you see, quite capable of leading a useful life . . . but in the Great Swamp . . . I do not see . . .' The old man's voice cracked: it distressed him to think about his daughter. Randolph came over and stood beside him.

'Marie is a beautiful girl, she's always done what she's wanted. You can ask Randolph – I didn't prevent her from marrying Umberto.'

Randolph placed an arm around his father's shoulder. 'By George, you pushed it from the beginning because you saw a profitable connection with Umberto.' He winked at Jonathan. 'There wasn't anyone in this town good enough for her. Her only prospect here was the local knife-sharpener. Lord, how you raised the roof when she left Umberto!'

'I guess I did.' The old man sighed and looked adoringly at his son.

'Big City – he can really raise the roof when he has a mind to. Whew! What a ruckus! That bloody sister of mine – she's crazy about white men. Loves to tantalize them, that is. Better watch out – keep your legs crossed!'

'Randolph!'

'Oh rot! It's better to warn him now. Look at the holes in his head . . .'

Jonathan gingerly touched the top of his head with the tips of his fingers. 'How do they look – all right?'

'Oh, la la.' Randolph turned his eyes away. 'We better have Mama look at those.'

'My wife knows something about medicine,' the old man put in. 'She studied briefly in Manaus before the war . . .'

'Before she went bonkers, you mean. Don't fret, Johnny – she'll take care of you – so long as it's not major surgery!' Randolph subsided in a gale of laughter.

'Oh God! I forgot! Can I get penicillin here to take to Dad?'

'Only witch doctors in Nile Town, old bean. You'd have to get that from Doc in Puerto Gusano.'

'I think our guest has heard enough talk, Randolph. Now, let's all go upstairs.'

Big City led the way with his slow, easy step. There were two upper storeys to the hotel, surrounded by screened-in verandas. The rooms opened onto the verandas. The floors, made of dark hardwood from the forest, gleamed in the lamplight. Tiger skins decorated the walls, and a life-sized cigar store Indian dressed as a cowboy – nickel-plated sixgun, lariat, leather chaps, silver spurs and all – sullenly guarded the door. A collection of ancient spears and Arabian sabres were thrust into a copper pot, like a bizarre flower arrangement.

'You've got some interesting things here, Mr City. I used to collect stuff like this on Madison and Park.'

The old gentleman lowered his eyes. 'I went to sea as a young man – for many years I was a cook aboard ships.'

'You could get a fortune for that Indian in New York.'

'Souvenirs of my younger . . . foolish days, when I carried something from each port to prove I'd been there.' Big City's eyes shone with remembered pleasure. 'Sentimental baggage to be sure . . . Don't we all drag it around with us in one form or another?'

Jonathan stopped beside a shiny brass spittoon. 'Hey this is just like the one at the gift counter at Brooks Brothers. They had these different crazy items on sale for Christmas . . . did you buy it there?'

'No.'

'Sometimes they would assign me to the gift counter when I was selling socks.'

'By Jove, a noble profession!'

'Yeah, well . . .'

'Come on, Johnny – meet the rest of the family!'

'Now Randolph . . .' Big City said with a note of warning.

Randolph grabbed Jonathan by the arm and led him running down the veranda. He opened a door and pushed Jonathan in ahead of him. There was a loud screech, and Jonathan ducked as a frying pan sailed over his head and crashed behind him. He found himself face to face with a wild-eyed crone.

Randolph went over and put his arm around her. 'I should have warned her you were coming, Johnny. She say's she's sorry – she didn't mean any harm.'

Jonathan smiled nervously and extended his hand. 'The pleasure's mine.'

The old woman cackled inanely.

'Why do you keep her chained to the stove?'

'During the day she wanders free and easy, don't you, mummy?' He gave her a squeeze, sending her into a fit of hysterics, until her cheeks were wet with tears. 'Only at night we got to keep her tied up like this. Poor mum.' The old woman grinned, displaying pink gums. 'She's pretty, isn't she? Can't you still see it in her? You should see her in the old photos.'

The old woman had returned to the stove, and was jabbering

contentedly to herself as she stirred the pots. A grimy lamp gave off an amber light.

'Big City's ashamed – he didn't want you to meet her.' The boy gave his mother a kiss on the cheek. She let out a loud whinny and went on with her work. 'He landed a beauty but she went wild – well, it can happen to anybody.'

While Randolph was talking, the old woman's watery eyes gradually brought Jonathan into focus. Dragging her chain, she came over to him.

'Don't be scared, Johnny dear.'

Tenderly, her hands took hold of Jonathan's face.

'She doesn't like the look of those holes in your head.'

Taking down a tin can from a shelf, she poured in a few drops of warm water from the kettle. Ingredients from other cans were added, which she stirred together. When the concoction was ready, she gently placed her hand on the back of Jonathan's neck and drew his head down.

'Don't worry, my dear – she knows what she's doing.'

She was applying an ointment to the top of his head. Jonathan felt the sensation of its warmth and the touch of her hands, which seemed to possess a healing power of their own. After a while he raised his head. His wounds were tingling. The woman had returned to her stove.

'You all right, Johnny?'

Whatever it was she was chewing – Jonathan had spotted her popping it into her mouth while she was brewing up the medicine – she'd breathed over him while daubing the stuff on his head. It had a slightly numbing and hypnotic effect, like a small dose of ether.

'I think so.'

'Come on, Johnny. I know you want a bath before dinner.'

During the meal Big City rambled on about his adventures around the globe. He was wearing a gold brocade vest with rhinestone buttons. His stomach put such strain on the cloth that Jonathan feared the vest might burst any minute and send a button flying into his eye.

'Umberto calls Puerto Gusano a prelude to hell. He says that all those children are his and – my father's.'

Randolph cleared his throat. 'Rather.' He reached across the table and tugged Big City's sleeve. 'Well, aren't he and Ben

Bradshaw to blame for the whole bloody mess? I mean, if it weren't for them, there wouldn't be Our Lady of Santa Petrolina, would there? And no army of orphans.'

'It's not quite that simple, Randolph. I think Mr Bradshaw here must be exhausted . . .'

'How can they be my father's children?' Jonathan asked.

'You see? It's monstrous not to explain! Tell him about the boat, sir!'

'Dad's boat?'

'Big City made a big pile of money for arranging the deal.' He winked at Jonathan in a conniving but friendly way and fluttered his scarf. 'How do you think I can afford to live in London like an English lord?' He began to sing. 'I get no kick from champagne . . . I'll never forget the sight of the *Pelican* low down in the water, gliding into Nile Town, loaded with guns.'

'Jesus, what was Dad doing – starting a war?'

'Rather! And that, my dear, was just the beginning. Wasn't it, sir?'

'Randolph, stop it.' Big City was puffing himself up with anger. Jonathan warily kept an eye on the rhinestone buttons.

'Notice how excited he's getting, Johnny? In other words, he admits the truth.' He slapped Jonathan on the back. 'That was a day to remember! The siege of Nile Town. Bullets buzzing and chickens running! Pure chaos! Mad! If only I could have reached the piano to play the 1812.'

'One thing at a time, Randolph. What happened?'

'You should have seen Ben and Umberto and Big City run for their lives while the guns blazed away!'

'Randolph, Jesus Christ, what guns?'

'They'd been *celebrating!* Lounging around the swimming pool, getting drunk on daiquiris, sitting on suitcases stuffed with dollars, when, my dear, all hell broke loose! The rebels were leaning out the windows, shooting at everything that moved! Pistols, shotguns, rifles, machine guns, even a bazooka – the lot! What a racket! The big wheelerdealers who'd been laughing their heads off jumped in the pool to save their lives!'

'Randolph!' Big City was swelling with disapproval. Jonathan, certain a button would come flying his way any second, put up a hand to shield his eyes.

'And, my dear, they stayed in the pool all day while that war carried on. You should have seen the place afterwards. It took the carpenters a month to plug up the bullet holes.'

'Your father was extremely correct, Mr Bradshaw.' Big City wiped his face with a napkin. 'He paid the workmen to repair my walls.'

'And so, does this war . . . have something to do with those orphans being my father's children?'

'Go on, sir. He has a right to know.'

'Mr Bradshaw, there are times when a man thinks he sees a shortcut to change,' Big City began solemnly. 'Yes, there are times when the way forward seems clear . . .'

'Father dear, aren't you being rather unspecific?'

'About ten years ago, Mr Bradshaw, everybody knew the end was near. Every day we heard it on the radio: Peaceful Banana had to go. Taking too much money out of the country, meddling in the affairs of state. The tide of popular resentment was rising, but who possessed the will to turn them out? It was common knowledge that officials in the highest places, while publicly braying for the removal of the octopus, were in fact on the company payroll . . .

'Your father and Umberto were close friends in those days. They foresaw that the departure of Peaceful Banana, no matter how distasteful its activities, or how corrupting its influence, would signal economic disaster for Puerto Gusano. Your father was even working for the company. He and Umberto, who spent all their evenings together, were secretly in contact with a group of certain "progressive personalities", who were hiding out in the swamp near here. How should I describe them – an odd assort-ment of exiled army officers and deported university professors – all relatively young, and inexperienced. They were feverishly plotting to overthrow the corrupt government in the capital. Your father and Umberto hoped to influence them.'

'Jesus! I'll have to show Dad my white paper on the alternative to Communism.'

'He and Umberto wanted to protect Puerto Gusano from economic collapse.'

'Rubbish! It wasn't just a humanitarian gesture, sir! They had their eyes on a mountain of money!'

'That was *not* the most important motive!' Big City snapped. 'Mr Bradshaw, your father and Umberto sincerely believed that by aiding the exiles, Puerto Gusano could be saved. We all did. Their programme, called "guns and beans," did not demand the expulsion of the octopus, only its regulation and taxation. They planned to give the country an industrial base by building factories and refineries. Their main target was the vast wealth of the church – they were going to tax it. All they lacked were arms.'

'Umberto had 'em – a whole warehouse full,' Randolph grinned.

'That's correct. Arms from America were awaiting trans-shipment to the capital. The arms conveniently disappeared. The meeting was arranged to be held in this hotel, and your father and Umberto arrived in your father's yacht, loaded with modern American weapons. The entire lot, yacht and all, was turned over to the young men who'd been waiting so impatiently. Just as the transaction was concluded, a military patrol boat appeared on the scene. Everybody was very tense, you can imagine, and accordingly quite drunk. They panicked, the shooting started, and the patrol boat was blasted out of the water. The result of all this, of course, was the famous Poker Revolution.'

'Hey! I remember hearing about the Poker Revolution on the radio after I got back from Bolivia!'

'The night of the coup, our jittery young friends forced their way into the presidential palace, where they found the President and his cronies at cards. The incumbents were offered, the story goes, first-class air tickets to Switzerland, so they might be near their bank accounts. The offer was immediately accepted, and there was a shared sense of relief with bear hugs all around.'

'*Very* civilized, the Bear Hug Revolution, wouldn't you agree, my dear?'

'The government freely surrendered their chairs, and the new leaders sat down in their places. And the game, as it were, goes on. In one hundred and sixty years of independence, this country has suffered two hundred and thirty-one changes of government.

'We soon learned, however, that Peaceful Banana wouldn't co-operate. When threatened with taxation and corporate responsibility, the company quietly moved its operations elsewhere. Price Waterhouse was brought in to audit the finances of the church. Hundreds of rural parishes closed down, and priests like Odorico went mad.'

'Jesus Christ!'

'My dear sir, haven't we forgotten one tiny detail?' Randolph, despite his effeminate manner, could be very stern. 'Wasn't the most important part of Ben's and Umberto's agreement with the junta that, once they were in power, they would build Our Blessed Lady of Santa Petrolina, from which Puerto Gusano would profit? My dear, this was supposed to make up for the loss of jobs and revenue if Peaceful Banana got kicked out or left.'

'True – factories and refineries were built in various parts of the country, and, in the case of Santa Petrolina, the result has been a nightmare.'

'Jesus, I just can't believe it – Dad and Umberto are responsible for the refinery?'

'That's right, Johnny. Thanks to Ben and Umberto, Santa Petrolina was built. The oil was brought in from the outside in tankers, refined, and sent away. Not a drop, except what comes ashore in slicks, ever reached Puerto Gusano. It wasn't long before the beaches turned black, and the fishermen began to complain their catch was dropping off. Our dear Lady has polluted the sea, fouled the air, turned night into day, and driven everybody bonkers. What's more, all proceeds go directly to the capital. And, if that weren't enough, not a single Gusanero was hired to work in the refinery. Some Dutch, some Portuguese, but mainly mixed-blooded thugs were imported from the islands to operate the refinery. You ought to know – that's how you got those holes in your head.'

'But, people in Puerto Gusano talk about Dad like he's some sort of *saint*.'

'They don't know it was his arms deal that brought Santa Petrolina to Puerto Gusano. And along with it, my dear, came the stench and the mess, the prostitution and the closing of the church. Thus your plague of children – all sons and daughters of Santa Petrolina – and therefore Umberto's and your daddy's. The Gusaneros still blame the politicians in the capital. If they knew Umberto and your daddy were the ones behind it . . . they'd be forming lynch mobs. Am I not right, sir?'

For a minute Jonathan sat staring at the toe of his boot, looking worried and lost.

'Johnny?'

'Oh yeah . . . so the *Pelican* started a war? The guys at the yacht club will love it. My stepfather will say, "*Well, what did you expect?*"

But nobody here knows?'

'Doc knows. People who know keep their mouths shut because they're afraid of what might happen to Umberto. Odorico knows something, but he's crazy and nobody listens to him.'

'Hellfires and a plague of children – it sounds like something out of the Bible. And poor Umberto's left with the mess. And he lost his wife . . .' Jonathan looked sympathetically at Big City. 'Your daughter.'

'I daresay, that's not an historical fact, Johnny.'

'Huh?'

'Umberto practically *gave* Marie away, didn't he, papa? Hoping . . .'

'Randolph, enough! Not another word under my roof!'

'Come on, Johnny dear. Off to bed. *Allons-nous.* You look absolutely bushed.'

17

Rio Gusano

Next morning Jonathan followed Randolph down to the shore where the vultures were squabbling with pariah dogs over the intestines of slaughtered tarpons. The beach reeked of slime and rot. Dugout canoes and sailing pirogues, in various stages of decay, rested on the mud among rafts and logs and other wreckage from the forest. Except for a few fishermen, who were flinging their nets into the dull, silvery water, nobody was around. The hot, oppressive silence was broken only by the dry rush of wings and the welcoming snarls of the mongrels as more vultures sailed in to join the feast.

Randolph's canoe gleamed like polished ebony; a voluminous sail was furled neatly along its boom.

'Step lightly on my boat, Johnny dear.'

He raised the sail. Jonathan didn't dare move for fear of capsizing the fragile craft. How the slender mast supported the broad lateen rig was a miracle. The sail, made of a light, gauzy material like mosquito netting, billowed out in the first breath of air. They glided toward the mouth of the river that tunnelled away into the jungle. Ahead, gloom awaited, where the trees crowded down to the water's edge. The tall sail cleaved the slot between the overhanging branches. This was going to be tricky business, Jonathan thought; he'd already spied bits of tattered cloth caught in the foliage. Black water rippled softly under the bow. The trees joined in a tangle over the river, blocking out the sky. Jonathan sat back and watched as they sailed away into the forest.

By degrees the trees thinned out, giving way to a thick growth of reeds, and they entered upon a broad watery savannah. Extending in all directions as far as the eye could see, the plain was dotted here and there by mounds of solid ground. No more than floating islands they seemed, or sailing ships becalmed on an inland sea where the tall trees had taken root, flourished and died. Many of the trees were still standing – grey trunks with gnarled branches like arthritic fingers clutching at the sky.

Vultures and fish hawks circled relentlessly. Every dead tree contained a predator.

Jonathan felt he was moving not only across a fresh landscape but backwards in time to the era of the Great Swamp. The vastness of it was eerie. Except for the dead islands floating on the horizon, there was nowhere he could have put his foot down. There was nothing but mud and water and a seething mass of vegetation. Ibises and spoonbills, taking wing through the reed beds, filled the swamp with departing cries. Fish jumped; a cayman eyed the approaching sailboat and silently submerged.

Randolph, in a fancy safari outfit, navigated the interminable loopings of the river with perfect ease; he made passages where the water was only inches deep, so the round bottom of the canoe left a shallow furrow in the liquid mud.

With the sun flaring down from directly overhead, it became oppressively hot. Neither spoke for hours; even Randolph was subdued by the heat and grandeur of the swamp.

In the afternoon clouds assembled, lightning cracked, and they were pelted by a driving, chilling rain. It could have been a recurrence of the beginning of the world, as the swamp took on weird, iridescent colours. Jonathan imagined a dinosaur heaving itself out of the slime, or a lightning bolt jabbing the fertile ooze to release a million wiggling things.

In the clarity of air which followed the rain, Randolph pointed out the Bitch's Tits Mountains. Like a row of grey-pink toads squatting on the horizon, they presided over their soupy surroundings from which they had been so inexplicably thrust.

Before dark they re-entered the forest.

'Randolph, I'm starved!' Jonathan was pointing to a tree loaded with red bananas. 'Let's stop and pick some.'

'Not here, Johnny.'

'It won't take long.'

'No.'

'Why not – snakes?'

'No.'

'Quicksand?'

'No!'

'What then? What's the matter?' Jonathan suddenly grew alarmed. 'What do you see?'

Randolph pointed. 'There.'

Among the trees on the river bank to the right, shadows were moving. A pack of wild dogs was loping along, noiselessly following the passage of the canoe. Randolph was using the oar to steer the canoe to the opposite side of the river, which was no more than thirty yards wide.

Jonathan gripped the side of the canoe. 'Jesus Christ! I hope they can't swim!'

The river curved to the right, and the loping shadows momentarily vanished. As Randolph navigated the bend, Jonathan saw that a sandbar had formed up ahead, effectively cutting the width of the channel in half. And there were more dogs lying on the sand. Their jaws hung open, and their tongues lolled out. As the canoe approached, they slowly got to their feet. There was a big red dog with black stripes across its back, two greys with dark heads, so identical they must have come out of the same litter, and a smaller black one. A yellow bitch with long dugs was lapping water by the river. Jonathan gasped at the sight of them. As big as stags they seemed, with broad chests, powerful legs and tapering hindquarters, and long pointed noses. They looked as though they had been specifically bred to chase and destroy.

'Are they going to try to come aboard?'

'Get out that pistol, Johnny!' Randolph was coolly inserting a long knife into a slot in the oar handle. It fitted snugly in, and he bound it with twine. All this he did automatically, without ceasing to steer the canoe.

Fortunately, the breeze had freshened, and the canoe moved into the narrow place at a good clip. Randolph kept an anxious eye on the sail, which was already grazing the high branches. As the canoe glided past the sandbar, Jonathan crouched down, braced his elbows on the edge of the canoe, gripped the pistol in both hands, and aimed. The bitch must have stood well over three feet high at the shoulder. Her head and neck were a mass of livid scars. Her ears were torn, and she exuded a powerful odour.

In anticipation of shooting, he felt a surge of crystalline power. When he pulled the trigger a horrifying scream erupted.

The pack of running hounds had invaded the beach and attacked the others. They seized the black dog and were pulling it to pieces. The big red was fighting for his life against a huge blue dog that had hurled itself into him. The pandemonium was frightening, but the canoe sailed cleanly through the narrow strait. In another minute they cleared the bend, and open water lay ahead. The battle ceased as abruptly as it had begun, as the hounds fled into the forest. The bitch lay writhing at the river edge, howling and dying. The canoe swept away into the shadows.

'Jolly good shot!' Randolph shouted exultantly. 'By jove, you know how to use that thing!' He was unlashing the knife from the oar. 'If you hadn't blown her to bits, I would have spitted her myself!'

Darkness descended quickly, and an island loomed ahead. A dog barked and a light flashed – there were people living in the swamp.

The canoe bumped gently against the bank where a man was standing, holding a lantern. Randolph lowered the sail and stowed the steering oar. They followed the man through the trees to a primitive encampment. A fire was burning, and two other men in loincloths sat on their haunches. Lines of fish, strung like laundry among the surrounding trees, exuded a nauseating odour. Jonathan had a look at his first piranha, which had been drying all day in the sun, prior to being eaten.

An hour later he was in a hammock, snoring peacefully, and the fire had died to a mound of glowing coals. Out in the river the frogs were whispering, and Jonathan was dreaming. A man and a small boy were crossing a golf course. The sun had just risen, and dew glistened on the grass. The man walked ahead with the fishing poles over his shoulder. The grass under their bare feet was icy cold. They came to a pond. The man rolled up his trousers and waded into the water, urging his son to follow. The boy refused – he hated the mud slithering between his toes and feared the slippery creatures he imagined lived there. Sadly, he trudged along the edge of the pond and cast his line into shallower water. His father, meanwhile, had hooked a bass. The rod bowed and the fish was jumping. Farther out, a pair of swans floated regally.

Jonathan in his sleep was becoming vaguely aware of a subtle motion in the air around him. Soft and nearly soundless, like the invisible fluttering of feathers, it had a soothing effect upon him. The dream images faded, and he slept more soundly.

Suddenly he snapped wide awake. All was pitch black. The moon had sunk, and thick foliage blocked the stars. The fire was out. He could see nothing – it was like waking up dead. His neck was wet with sweat – or so he thought – and he was shivering. He drew the blanket around him.

A long howl erupted from somewhere out in the swamp. Jonathan's heart nearly stopped; he felt for the revolver. He lay in the hammock, stiff with fear. It came again – louder and closer.

'Randolph!' he whispered. 'Did you hear that?'

'Not to worry, my dear,' came a voice from the dark. 'They can't make it onto this island. That's why these fishermen make their camp here.'

The sound of another human voice was reassuring.

'Haven't those dogs ever heard about man's best friend?'

Randolph laughed. 'Stay where you are, dear. Go back to sleep.'

There was another howl, and the camp dog let out a couple of whimpers. The howls were becoming fainter; the pack was moving away.

'What are your sister and my father doing living in a place like this? Are they crazy?'

'Excellent question, Johnny my dear. Ask them when you see them. Then we'll all know. Now let's get some shut-eye.'

'Randolph, what was that business of Umberto baiting the hook with Marie . . .?'

'*Mañana*, Johnny.'

Ben must be deranged, Jonathan concluded as he drifted off to sleep, the disease must have affected his brain. Stingrays, candiru, and now these wild dogs. To have staked out a position so remote implied renunciation in the extreme. No one back home ever imagined anything like this.

Gradually, the yelps and howls receded, and he was able to shut his eyes. The gentle vibrations began to hover about him once more, lulling him back to sleep.

18

The Scarecrow

Randolph's face registered an expression of mingled pity and disgust. 'Hey, Johnny! Wake up!'

Jonathan's collar was streaked with blood; so were his hands and feet. He couldn't see the tiny punctures in his neck, but they were plainly visible on his fingers and toes, just beneath the nails.

'Jesus Christ, what's been gnawing on me?'

'Bats, I fear.'

'*Bats!* Did they bite you, too?'

'Dear me, Johnny, dear me . . . not even bedbugs bite me. Bats have their preferred victims, and I'm not one of them.'

'We've just escaped the dogs, and now *bats!* Look at these bites – I'm their number one customer. *Rabies!* Have you ever seen anyone die of rabies?'

'Dear me – no.'

'I heard on the radio it's one of the most awful deaths imaginable! In Bolivia they hand a man dying of rabies a gun just to be kind. Do you think Doc has the injections?'

'I should think so. Do you want to go back?'

'Back to the dogs? Back to Umberto? I'll never see Dad . . .' Jonathan swung out of the hammock and paced back and forth, his hands plunged into his trouser pockets. 'If I can make it to where Dad is, he'd be forced to take me back to Doc. He wouldn't let me die of rabies.' He stopped and cast a worried look at Randolph. 'Or would he?'

'No, but Marie would.'

Jonathan punched his digital watch. 'Is this the final irony – son gets killed finding long lost father? But maybe these bats aren't rabid. Maybe there isn't any risk. Jesus! I've heard that victims tear their own flesh, foam at the mouth and would rather die than be brought near water. And here we are on a river!'

'Do you really want to take the chance? Surely, Johnny, we must turn back.'

'Wait! I heard it on the Bernard Meltzer show one night I was driving out from New York. I remember it distinctly, the man from the Atlanta Rare Disease Center said you have a week to begin the shots.' He thought for a minute. 'Do you think I'm doing the right thing?'

'*No*. I'm taking you back, old boy.'

The fishermen had paddled off to the fishing grounds, and they were the only ones on the island. Sunlight was streaming into the glade, and the drying fish were beginning to cook up a stench. Jonathan went down to the river to wash away the blood; when he returned, Randolph handed him a cup of coffee. They squatted on their haunches next to the fire. Not a breath of air stirred.

It was hot, but Jonathan was shivering. 'Thanks, Randolph – this is good coffee.' His hands were shaking; he could hardly hold the cup.

'Don't worry, Johnny – you'll be all right.'

'Yeah. Well. I might turn back now and step on a banana peel outside Doc's office and break my neck. You know, like that astronaut who walked on the moon, splashed down in the shark-infested Pacific, then got back to his quiet house in the suburbs and slipped on a bar of soap in the shower and was forced to retire to a wheelchair for the rest of his life.'

'That's better than rabies, old man.'

'I guess this is the point of no return. Beatrice is dead. Panadero . . . the jail, the dogs, the bats. My family must be berserk with worry, but I can't go back now! That's the Rubicon behind us, Randolph – we've got to go on.'

'Johnny – I say turn back!'

'No!'

'You know I can only take you as far as the landing. If parrot sister sees me, you won't have a chance.'

'Randolph,' Jonathan cried in desperation, 'you can't leave me in the jungle!'

'But we agreed to that condition in Nile Town.'

'That was before the bats.'

'Believe me, your only chance with Marie is if I'm not there . . .'

Jonathan thought for a moment. 'I'll stick by my word.'

'I'm against it, but it's your neck, old boy!'

'I dread to think what's next.'

'Marie is next.'

'She can't be more frightening than wild dogs or bats. At least I can *talk* to her.'

'Dear boy, the first thing you have to understand about Marie is that nobody *talks* to her. Discussions are simply out of the question. It's even difficult for her own father to get along with her since she beat up Mummy.'

'You mean she physically beat up her own mother?'

'That's right.'

'From the picture I'm getting of Marie, it's hard to imagine what charms my father finds in her.'

'It happened right after the big shootout. Everyone was celebrating. Ben brought in the musicians and Umberto was hopping around like a child, passing out flower chains and brand-new twenty dollar bills.' Randolph adjusted his cuffs and poked the hankie out of sight. 'And, of course, Marie was determined to put on one of her shows. I was agog. My dear, I'm not one of these people who spends all his time at harp recitals, but I do believe in certain refinements. Really, that sister of mine uncrossed her legs, let down her hair, and let it all hang out. She likes to turn people on, *en masse.* Definitely a crowd stimulator. Hips shaking, tits jumping, hair flying, she danced in her peacock green frock. We were all on the hotel terrace. I was sitting beside Ben and Umberto. Everybody was clapping with the music. The drums beat louder and faster, and Marie's body pulsed and writhed as though a wild animal had woken up inside her. Stark naked, mind you, under a thin layer of silk. Big patches of sweat under her arms. My dear . . .' Randolph wrinkled up his nose. 'Frankly I'm opposed to perspiration, though some people find it sexy.'

'Yeah, well, her dance sounds sexy.'

'Her face was shiny, and she was spraying us with sweat as she tossed her head. One hand was wrapped around her backside to accentuate the movements of her bum. Umberto and Ben couldn't take their eyes off her – no one could.'

For a moment Jonathan forgot his bat bites. 'She'd be a big hit at the Brasilian Ball in New York.'

'Arms over her head, eyes closed in ecstasy, hips gyrating – in other words, raw sex! I was agog!' He giggled. 'Damned foolishness. Even I, her little brother, was turned on! Everyone was mesmerized. She had a big red hibiscus behind one ear. I remember thinking, if she doesn't stop, this crowd's going to leap aboard and gangbang her right on the terrace! My dear, she was seducing everybody. I was *astonished!* Everybody knows Marie hates sex and won't let anyone touch her. But you wouldn't have known it that night. I'm ashamed to say that even Big City was licking his lips. Mummy had been set loose for the occasion. She saw Marie dancing and she wanted to join the fun. Suddenly she appeared out of nowhere, poor dear, throwing back her head and pretending she was a young woman again. She moved close to Marie, and, of course, she looked ridiculous. People began to laugh. When Marie heard the laughter, she opened her eyes a split second, saw Mum, and *Wham!* Down came her arm! She walloped her own mother on the back of the neck and knocked her flat!'

'My God!' Jonathan exclaimed.

'Poor Mummy crumpled to the floor. We ran to help, but Marie didn't miss a beat, and Umberto and Ben went on clapping. They were in a trance, too. You could have passed your hand in front of their eyes. They never saw the cruelty.'

'How did Umberto bait my father with Marie?'

'She was willing enough, Johnny. Let's say Umberto used her to make Ben more content in Puerto Gusano. You know, when he was thinking about leaving.'

'You mean Dad intended to come back home?'

'I remember arguments, drunken talk, Umberto's voice droning on till dawn . . .'

'Why was he so anxious to keep my father from leaving?'

'Look, old bean, when a desperately lonely man puts a lot of stake into someone, he doesn't give up easily. I don't know all the facts, but after the arms deal there was a lot of money around, and Ben was about to push off. Umberto used every argument and ploy to keep him. He saw to it the money was spent on parties and circuses until it was gone. He gambled his wife away, and ended up by losing them both . . . Johnny dear, how're you doing? You look rather pale.'

'Yeah, well. My nerves haven't agreed with my decision yet.'

A movement of air disturbed the branches above their heads, and the column of smoke rising from the fire began to waver. The breeze had arrived.

Randolph got to his feet and pulled Jonathan up by the shoulders. 'Come on, old chap, we've got a long way to go.'

That morning the Bitch's Tits Mountains were never out of sight. The reed beds were finally left behind, and they followed a sinuous waterway that threaded a maze of islands. The islands were infested by a species of nervous little parrot that never stopped screeching or flying about, apparently mindless of the snakes looped like bicycle tyres in the trees. Jonathan was terrified one of the snakes would drop into the boat.

The afternoon passed. They were back in the jungle. The tall sail cleaved the gloom like an alabaster blade. The river, meanwhile, continued to narrow. The terrain became more hilly, and the riverbanks were twenty feet high. As the current quickened the canoe's progress upstream became tediously slow. In the late afternoon they came to a landing. Some crude steps had been hacked into the bank, and a stake had been driven into the mud. A canoe was attached.

Randolph's canoe nosed the shallows, and Jonathan jumped out. 'Is this where he lives – this wilderness?'

'Well, almost.' Randolph remained seated in the canoe, holding the oar across his knees. 'The trail begins at the top of the bank. Take it and walk for an hour or so.'

Jonathan grabbed the bow of the canoe, which was beginning to drift. 'Randolph!' he pleaded.

'Johnny, dear, this is crazy. Come back with me and get those shots.'

'I can't. *Please* come with me!'

'If I come, Marie will kick us both out. If you go alone, she can't force you to leave, because she knows there's no way you can find your way out of the swamp except with her and Ben. Ben will have to look after you now.'

Jonathan let go of the canoe and stood up. 'What about those dogs?'

'No hounds this far upriver, Johnny. Not to worry. Never have been. If there were, Ben couldn't live here.' Randolph was using the oar to manoeuvre the canoe into the current. 'I'm really frightfully sorry to abandon you like this.'

The current caught the bow and turned it downstream. A breath of air filled the gauzy sail, and the canoe was moving away.

Jonathan scrambled up the greasy bank and stood at the edge of the forest. The canoe was rapidly growing smaller.

'Cheerio, old bean! Best of luck!' Randolph called. 'God speed.'

'Hey Randolph! You're a great guy! I'll see you in Carnegie Hall!'

'OK, Johnny.'

'*Randolph!*'

'Yes, Johnny?'

'Say a prayer for me.'

In another minute Randolph was no more than a silhouette against the sail. As the canoe rounded a bend in the river, the sail luffed lightly – a flutter of farewell – and it was gone.

Standing on the riverbank, with the whisper of the river in his ears, Jonathan was transfixed by the suddenness with which solitude had been thrust upon him. Within the pregnant silence of the forest, pierced by an occasional bird call, the pink and green blobs appeared before him. His mother and grandmother were jumping up and down on the dock at Martha's Vineyard, shrilly pleading with him not to take the pistol. Jonathan laughed, thinking of their horror if they could see him now – alone in the middle of the jungle, pursued by wild dogs, bitten by bats, and dressed in rags. They'd be thankful he had brought along the pistol. He turned from the river, found the trail, and set off through the jungle.

The ground was soft and spongy underfoot – a carpet of leaves and moss. Feeling like an ant in a vegetable garden, he made his way along by a dim luminosity that seemed to come from nowhere. So dark and silent were those woods the only shapes near at hand seemed real; all else lay deep in shadow.

For an hour he walked through the chambers of the neglected, the abandoned accumulations of the dead. The roots belonging to the massive columns snaked over the jungle floor like ancient lava flows. Here was a region dismally removed from the world of light and space. The history of the forest was recorded on its floor, which was littered with the corpses of the fallen. This garden, for all the stink of new life stubbornly emerging, was the ruthless work of death.

After a while he came to a glade where corn was growing. Jonathan stood still and held his breath. These could only be his father's silent plantings – grains of corn pressed one at a time into foreign soil within a forest so dark and foreboding people back home would think him mad. How far he'd ventured from the path of familiarity! Perhaps, Jonathan thought, this was what his father had discovered after all the years – silence. Perhaps he'd reached a point where he'd resolved to arrest the tumultuous disorder of his life by removing himself from humanity. Fatigue and remorse could have finally driven him to seek absolution, not from men, but through the vast impartiality of nature.

Beyond the clearing the land began to rise. Coming to the brow of a hill where the trees had thinned, Jonathan saw a small open valley ahead where more corn was growing. Out of the middle of the valley stood a scarecrow.

The sun was lowering between two spires of the Bitch's Tits Mountains. As he scanned the cornfield for some sign of habitation, his eyes kept returning to the scarecrow, finally fixing on it. Did it move? In the fading light he couldn't be sure. Had the wind disturbed its tattered garments? Behind him in the forest total silence reigned. The sun was resting like a glowing plum in a crack between two peaks. Then the scarecrow moved again – not a wind movement – it seemed to be shifting its feet! The sun went out, and the scarecrow began to walk.

'Hey!' Jonathan yelled. 'Dad?'

The scarecrow had not heard. It hobbled off through the corn and disappeared. The wind sent a chill through Jonathan.

Emerging from the edge of the forest, he waded through the corn. The breeze rustled the drying stalks. Coming to the place where the man had stood, he discovered a path that led over the brow of the hill to two wattle huts. He stopped on the hard-packed yard between them. They exuded the musty smell of woodsmoke and human habitation, but there was no light – no sign of life.

'Anybody home?' His heart was pounding.

At the bottom of the hill the frogs began to groan, and the wind would not stop moving the corn. The ghostly whispering of voices was the only response.

'Dad!' he called out. 'Anybody in there?'

No answer.

Ducking his head through the low door, he entered the hut. It was pitch black inside. He lit a match and held it aloft. There, in the corner, a man was seated. Jonathan jumped back. The man was staring directly at him. His eyes glittered in the dim light.

'Dad?'

'*Quien es?*'

It was the voice of a complete stranger. Jonathan had never heard it before. The match burned down to his fingers, and he threw it to the floor. Once more they were plunged in darkness.

'It's Jonathan – your son! I've just outrun a pack of man-eating dogs and vampire bats. Jesus Christ, it's good to be here.'

'Dios mio — eres mi hijo?'

'You still speak English, don't you, Dad?'

Jonathan was so bewildered by this reception that for an instant he entertained the absurd notion that this was not his father at all; that by yet another stroke of ill luck he had stumbled into the hut of a native.

A loud hearty laugh filled the hut. 'Damned right I do, Johnny! You've got to excuse me, but this is quite a surprise! Where are those matches? Step over here so I can see you. Is that really you?'

Jonathan was fumbling for a second match when the sound of a voice – a woman's – reached his ears. She was singing right outside the hut, setting something heavy on the ground. There was the sound of water sloshing. A figure appeared in the door- way.

'Oh!'

'Tenemos huesped! Mi hijo de los Estados Unidos,' came the jubilant voice from the corner. 'Johnny, by God. Welcome! What a surprise! Can you believe it, Marie?'

Without saying a word, she moved quickly to a shelf and lit a lantern, which she brought forward and set on a table. Around her towering mass of hair a bright-coloured bandana was bound, and she wore a white cotton blouse. A swath of blue Java print material was wrapped about her waist and fell to her ankles. She went barefoot and was smoking a pipe.

Jonathan held out his hand. 'Hey. Jonathan Bradshaw. Sure is good to be here.'

She abruptly whirled around to face Jonathan. What he saw made him speechless. She was much blacker than he'd expected. He was surprised by her tobacco-stained teeth, the wrinkles around her eyes, and the leathery hand that gripped a candle. He also detected elements of her former beauty – the high cheek- bones and the sharp symmetry of features and the graceful movements. She was about thirty years old, but life in the swamp had aged her.

'Yeah. I'm glad to meet you,' Jonathan mumbled awkwardly. He was beginning to sweat. 'I've heard a lot about you.'

He waited for a reply. None was forthcoming and he dropped

his hand. They were both approximately the same height, but Marie, with her tall mane of black hair, seemed to stare down at him from a higher elevation. Her nostrils flared and Jonathan involuntarily shrank back a step. As he did so he noticed something moving in her hair. A small green parrot was looking incuriously at him. Bits of droppings were tangled in the curls.

To break the silence, Jonathan tried another opening. 'I met your father in Nile Town.' He laughed nervously. 'And your brother Randolph. He brought me here. Great guys.'

No answer. She was still staring fiercely at him.

In desperation, Jonathan forced a cough and addressed the parrot. 'Polly want a cracker?' As soon as he said it he felt ridiculous, but Ben was laughing. Suddenly it occurred to Jonathan that she might not understand a word he was saying. 'Do you speak English?' he asked as politely as he dared.

'Of course I do!' she snapped. Brushing past him, she quickly left the room. The parrot fluttered its wings and hung on for dear life.

Jonathan cleared his throat and turned toward his father. Ben Bradshaw may have gone to hell inside, but somehow he managed to look trim. That he was clean-shaven and his hair was neatly combed conveyed the impression that he still cared about appearances. The shirt and trousers were faded from repeated washings, but the mendings were neat. He wore sandals, and a crudely made gold tooth gleamed in his mouth. He occupied his chair in an attitude of the utmost tranquillity. The blue eyes fixed Jonathan with an expression of curiosity and amusement as he leisurely inserted a home-made cigar into his mouth and struck a match.

'Jesus, Dad, you look so urbane, distinguished, and sophisticated. I was expecting someone going to pieces in the tropics. You know, Humphrey Bogart in *The Treasure of the Sierra Madre*.'

Ben laughed and blew out a cloud of smoke. 'Welcome, Johnny. Haven't you learned yet to expect the unexpected?' There was something mischievous about him as he raised one eyebrow to size up his son; it would be difficult to surprise or shock him. 'How about a drop of moonshine?' He waved at a bottle on the table. 'Made it myself.'

'Dad, you look *great!* You can't imagine how happy I am to see you!'

'The same goes for me, Johnny.' Ben was pleased to see his son; he was in a jovial mood. He waved at an empty chair. 'Make yourself at home. *Mi casa es tu casa*. Talk about *Du Temps Perdu* – are those my parachute boots you're wearing?'

'Yeah, they came in handy down here. One of them fell apart in the swamp, but I had it fixed in Nile Town. Hey! This stuff is pretty good!'

'Distilled from cashew fruit. I found a bat floating in the tank and had to throw the rest away. Damn pity.'

'Are you kidding?' Jonathan's hand went to his throat, but his instincts told him not to mention the bat bites yet. 'Jesus – uh, for a minute there I thought you had forgotten how to speak English. Cosy place you've got here.'

Besides the table and chair where Ben sat, there was one other chair. Shelves attached to the wattle walls held Indian pottery and terracotta figurines. Like the frieze of an ancient temple, a gigantic snakeskin ran all the way around the upper part of the hut. Pegs supported a pair of hunting rifles, binoculars, assorted fishing rods and straw hats. There was a display of shark jaws, Indian blow pipes and fishing arrows six feet long. The effect was primitive but artistic. A pair of hammocks had been slung up out of the way over a rafter. Carpeted with animal skins and festooned with chains of monkey teeth and bunches of aromatic herbs, Ben's hut resembled an upholstered cave.

Jonathan was admiring the snake skin. 'It looks like you've had a lot of adventures out here, Dad.'

'That anaconda was thirty-two feet long. It was the toughest thing I'd ever had to wrestle with since Granny.'

They both laughed.

'Marie and I used to go on safari once a year. On our last trip we were fording a river when a black panther appeared on the opposite bank. It is one of the rarest creatures in the jungle, and the sight of it nearly took my breath away. I was shoulder deep in water and couldn't get my gun ready. It walked to the river edge, took a few sips, calmly looked at me floundering around, and disappeared into the jungle. I went to the place where it had been drinking, and there, beside one of its footprints, was a gold nugget the size of a golf ball. I reckon it was the panther's gift to me for not shooting.'

'Does Marie like it here?'

'Marie loves being busy with the business of survival – taming animals and looking after them, growing food, sewing, building, mending clothes – the basics. She's a natural savage, my cave-mate.'

'I feel like a philistine wearing my digital watch. You know, like the first astronaut to walk the moon throwing down chewing gum wrappers and beercans. I guess you've adopted the "less is more" approach to life. Granny always says. "Too much is not enough".'

Ben laughed. 'This fur-lined fox-hole isn't exactly to Granny's taste, but she'd probably settle quite happily in. She's an adaptable old goat.'

'I see you still keep in touch with the outside world.' Jonathan had noticed a radio beneath Ben's chair.

'The old Zenith Transoceanic from the *Pelican*. No modern hermit would leave home without one. How the devil did you find me?'

'The *Pelican* turned up in Panama. I don't think you'd want her now – she's a complete wreck. The insurance company found her . . .'

'You mean, they're *still* looking for me?'

'*But do you know how I recognized The Pelican?*' Jonathan emphasized each word with enthusiasm. Remember that Chinese alarm clock you brought back from the war? The one with the chicken's head that pecked out the seconds? Smashed, but still screwed to the bulkhead!'

'How's your mother?'

'Granny claims Mom's headaches ended the day you left. But she says she'll need a brain transplant to stop worrying about me.'

Ben laughed and smiled at everything Jonathan said. 'So Granny hasn't lost her charms?'

'The latest on Granny is that she has an English beau. She went over to a reception at Buckingham Palace to honour his one-hundredth birthday. She has gotten terribly short-sighted but refuses to wear glasses. At the reception she was approached by a woman whose face seemed familiar but whose name she couldn't remember. They stood together making polite conversation. "Isn't it a nice day," she said. "Isn't it?" Granny agreed. And so forth. Suddenly Granny realized the woman was wearing a magnificent diamond necklace. Turns out it was the *Queen!* And she began, "Yes, Ma'am," and "No, Ma'am" and finally had to say it: "Sorry, Ma'am – I didn't recognize you without your crown." And she and the Queen had a big laugh together.'

'Are you going to talk all night, or can we have dinner now? Ben has to eat.' Marie had reappeared carrying a large steaming bowl which she placed on the table with a bang.

'I guess I have been talking too much.' Jonathan apologized.

'Nonsense.' Ben held out his glass for another drink. 'Johnny and I have a lot to catch up on.'

Jonathan had an uneasy feeling that Marie had been listening outside the door. 'You must excuse me, Marie. I haven't had a decent night's sleep since I arrived.'

Marie frowned at him.

'It's probably nervous exhaustion . . . the excitement of being here and all. I'm sorry.'

'Well, you should be. People can't just sit around waiting for you to indulge yourself. We're busy. We've got work to do. This isn't a holiday camp.' As she laid the table she accompanied each gesture with various bangs which Jonathan found unnerving. While the men watched, she carried a stool from outside and planted it with a thud some distance from the other two. There was a wildness about her which made her sullenness threatening. Her proprietary attitude embarrassed Jonathan; he felt that he was intruding. Everything she did was confident, purposeful, and efficient. She didn't waste a movement.

'You must be starving,' Ben said. 'Go ahead and start.'

Jonathan was ravenous but said, 'Just a bite for me, Marie. I'm not really hungry.' He waited for her to be seated. 'Are you sure you have enough?'

'*Please sit,*' she snapped. Standing by the table, she was looking expectantly at Ben. He made a motion to rise and suppressed a grimace of pain. She caught him lightly by the elbow, and he got to his feet with a grunt. Standing rigidly erect, an exaggerated uprightness because he could barely stand at all, he took a few stiff, swinging steps to the table. She quickly drew the chair behind him. With another grunt he sat down.

Until this moment Jonathan had completely forgotten Ben's affliction. He felt a surge of affection for his father. Crippled and older, it was still the same Ben. It was as though they had never been apart. He wanted to put his arms around him but didn't dare with Marie present.

'Is that enough?' Marie ladled out a bowl of cornmeal and handed it to Jonathan.

'Yes, thanks.' Jonathan looked with disappointment at the size of his serving. To make matters worse, the parrot had hopped onto the edge of his bowl. The cornmeal was too hot, so it pecked angrily at Jonathan's spoon as he tried to eat. He didn't dare shoo it away and Marie ignored it.

She ladled out much larger portions for herself and Ben. Another dish contained peppers. 'Have one,' she said, pushing it Jonathan's way. Having finished his cornmeal, he turned hungrily to the peppers. 'Jesus Christ!' He began to cough and choke and his face turned bright red. To his amazement, Marie devoured the peppers one after another, with a loud crunching noise.

'How do you like the Great Swamp, Mr Bradshaw?' she asked.

'Pretty hostile . . .' Jonathan was discreetly vying with the parrot over a bit of cornmeal that had fallen under his bowl. 'The environment, I mean. Uninviting.' He smiled weakly. 'Call me Jonathan. I'm sure it's just a bad first impression. Those dogs don't exactly make a person feel welcome.' With the end of his finger he nudged the half-eaten pepper towards the parrot.

'How dare you!' She snatched the parrot away and placed it on her shoulder. 'Feed that to an innocent unsuspecting creature!'

'How'd you get around the dogs?' Ben asked. 'They're killers.'

'Luckily, Randolph knew what to do . . .'

'Randolph's a fool. He thinks the jungle's a big ashtray, just like all foreigners.'

Remembering Randolph's advice about Marie's lack of sisterly feeling, Jonathan changed the subject. 'That's delicious cornmeal. Did you plant all the corn yourself, Dad?'

'My last crop.' Ben chuckled. 'I'll let the grim reaper take in the next one.'

'That's not funny.' Marie quietly disagreed. She put her hand over Ben's. Her voice, Jonathan noted with relief, could be soft. He experienced a warm sense of gratitude that her mood had changed. Moreover, the evil little parrot had burrowed into her hair and fallen asleep.

'What he means is,' she continued in a note of resignation, 'he's no longer able to spend twelve hours a day on his feet, working with the hoe.'

'Doc told me . . . yaws.'

The word popped out of Jonathan's mouth and hung over the table like an obscene bubble.

'Curable,' he added hastily. 'Easily curable. Doc told me himself. I meant to bring you penicillin, but I had to leave Puerto Gusano in a hurry. All you have to do is go back there and he'll give it to you right away.'

'You came all this way and *forgot* the penicillin? That's pretty stupid.' Marie's eyes drilled into him as she expertly filled her pipe and lit it.

Jonathan searched for another subject. 'Remember that butter and sugar corn, Ben? There's nothing better than Jersey corn, or a Jersey tomato. Remember that time we bought twenty-four ears and shucked them on the back porch and ate the whole lot ourselves? That was the summer of '54. The year the Yankees lost the pennant.'

'Yeah.' Ben thought for a minute. 'And Joe DiMaggio married Marilyn Monroe. I used to see them at the Stork Club.' He looked at Marie. 'Great tits! And John Kennedy was still in the Senate. I threw a party for him on the *Pelican*. Granny came. When she saw him she turned purple and muttered how her father would never have Irish in the house, not even as servants. But she was a big buddy of Black Jack Bouvier.'

'Granny took me to Europe that year. All anybody wanted to talk about was the Supreme Court decision and Dien Bien Phu . . .' Jonathan stopped in mid-sentence.

Marie had produced a gem-encrusted lorgnette which she flicked open and held up to her face. The unexpected appearance of the delicate eyeglass held in her leathery hand unnerved Jonathan. She was peering at him through it. 'Have you ever been married?' she asked.

'What? Why? No. You sort of surprised me, Marie. Do you have to look at me through that microscope? Your answer is no. But I met a girl called Micheline the other night at the Hunt Club during hockey practice.'

'Well,' Marie asked impatiently, 'are you going to marry her?'

'Jesus, Marie, you make me nervous looking at me through that thing. Do you think this is the Westminster Dog Show or something? I didn't think people still used lorgnettes, except in movies based on historical novels.'

'*Why* aren't you married?'

'Because I don't want to get married until I have a job.'

'You don't have a job?' Marie raised her eyebrows above the lorgnette. 'Are you what they call *a bum?*'

'Just because I've been out of work for twenty years, does that make me a bum?'

'You haven't worked *twenty* years? *Twenty years?*'

'Yeah, twenty or so . . . well, how long should it have been? Are you what they call an actress?'

'*No!*'

'That's a shame because I'm a talent scout and I'm looking for someone like you.'

Ben laughed out loud. Jonathan chuckled nervously, and Marie put away the lorgnette.

'There, that's better, I did have a job last year, Marie. I worked at Brooks Brothers in the pre-Christmas rush, selling socks.'

'And what did your mother and Granny think of that?' Ben asked.

'Yeah. Well, there was this big fiesta over New Year's at the Winslows,' Jonathan said to Marie. 'You know they own half the land in Somerset County. And everybody was over there having drinks. And my grandmother tells this story how I'd been asked to stay on at Brooks Brothers for the January sale. And my mother started to *cry* she was so happy. And my stepfather was so proud he said, "*Well what'd you expect?*"'

'Socks?' Marie said it with a sneer, addressing the parrot.

Ben was chuckling as he poured Jonathan another drink.

'And I knew that it was all bogus, you know, because they ended up asking everyone to stay on, then they fired all of us. It was just a *pro forma* thing. They'd say "Gee, wouldn't you like to stay on?" and you'd say, "Yes," and then they'd say "*You're fired!*"'

'Johnny, you know, I haven't laughed like this in years.' Ben looked at his son with affection and not a little pride.

Jonathan felt that his father's laughter was creating a bond between them; it was also isolating Marie.

'Listen, Marie, if I seem drunk, I haven't been drinking. It's this fatigue . . .'

'Is this something new?' She blew out a cloud of smoke. 'Do you think you're the only one who's tired?'

'What do you mean, *the only one?* I happen to be, maybe other people are, too, but I've had a hell of a trip. Your answer is no. I don't have a job. I've been working on a novel about my life.'

'What's it called – *The Mess?*'

Wounded and uncomprehending, Jonathan blinked several times.

'Is your life so interesting, then?'

'It might be to *somebody*, Marie.'

'Who? Your mother? Or your *father?*' She looked from Jonathan to Ben. 'Your father's expressed a great deal of interest in your life, don't you think? Ah! Ha! Ha!'

Jonathan was stung by these words. 'I don't understand you, Marie. Are you trying to hurt me?'

'Of course not. Can you please lower your voice,' she suggested. 'Didn't anyone ever tell you it's rude to shout?'

Jonathan's face went red, and he turned to his father. 'So anyway, I have a new idea for a story based on life on the rink. I have this friend of mine I played hockey with at Hotchkiss who gave me the idea. I think I can make a fortune with this book. The guy's name is Basil Kerner. Remember him, Dad? His father was president of one of those big sugar companies on the New York Stock Exchange. Both Basil and his younger brother ended up out in Menninger's Clinic out in Topeka, Kansas. They played for the Menninger's hockey team . . .'

'Is that all you ever do – sit around and tell silly stories?' Marie commented.

'Maybe I should write a book about you, Marie. Do you think there's any chance of our coming to some sort of amicable relationship? I mean, we're sort of stranded here together. I don't think you and your bird like me.'

'You should take a look at yourself. You come barging in here covered with blood and mud and muck.'

'Yeah, well I said I had a rough trip. There was a big fight at Ricardo's and someone hit me over the head with a bottle. Umberto threw me into prison . . .'

'Umberto! How dare you!' Marie slammed her hand on the table. The parrot began to squeak.

'Get that goddamned bird out of here!' Ben commanded.

She turned over the stool as she fled from the room.

'Did I say something wrong?'

'Don't worry, Johnny. It's been a long day.'

'Listen, Dad, I've got to tell you what happened in Puerto Gusano!'

Ben listened to his son describe the murder in Ricardo's bar until Jonathan, weary for sleep, finally went outside and fell into a hammock.

19

Parrot Woman

At dawn Jonathan tottered sleepily from his hut. During the night the mosquitos had drilled through his clothes. His blood, mined by the insects, mixed with the now familiar patina of perspiration. He shielded his eyes from the sun. The day was already half dead with heat. All was still but for the ceaseless shrilling of insects.

There was no sign of life from the main hut, so he followed a path through the corn and came to a pig pen near the edge of the jungle. They were long, lean, hairy beasts. As Jonathan approached, they rushed to the barrier, thrusting their snouts between the slats, and grunted expectantly. He counted three sows, a litter of four half-grown ones, and one boar. This last, a huge, semi-wild beast with yellow curving tusks, looked strong enough to break down Ben's enclosure if it had a notion to. Head lowered, it menacingly patrolled the perimeter of the fence until Jonathan retreated.

The path led on. Not far away a stream flowed. Kneeling on a smooth stone, he took a drink and splashed water on his face. The course of the stream intrigued him. It tumbled out of the forest in a series of deep, clean pools, showed a sunny bank to the clearing, and flowed back among the shadows. For nothing better to do, he decided to follow it. Flowering bushes had taken root among the rocks; their flowery sleeves trailed in the current and tugged in the waterfalls. A pair of fluorescent blue butterflies floated aimlessly through the dull green gloom of the jungle, like two lost souls from a distant, glittering age.

After a while he turned back, stepping from one glossy boulder to the next as the dark water spilled among them. Stopping near a flowering bush, he froze at the sight of Marie through the leaves. Carrying two buckets, she had just come down to the stream. Jonathan held his breath. He wanted to retreat, but she had set the buckets on the ground and had already begun to undress. She was going to bathe. Jonathan didn't want to watch, but he couldn't move without giving himself away. With a single motion she unwrapped the cloth from around her waist and dropped it on a rock. She wore nothing underneath. Next the blouse came away, and she stood naked at the edge of the forest. The colour of her skin blended perfectly with the woody surroundings.

Her breasts swayed and sunlight dappled her body as she submerged herself in the swirling waters. Only her head, still bound in the bright bandana, was visible. Jonathan feared the little parrot would spot him and sound the alarm, but it sat quietly in her hair, cleaning its feathers in the sunshine. Presently she emerged, her limbs and body glistening. She found a sunny boulder where she sat down. Setting the parrot on a twig, she spent some minutes arranging her hair, then lay down seductively on the rock.

When she'd dressed, Jonathan stepped from his hiding place.

'Good morning!' he called out. 'I've been back in the jungle following this stream,' he announced in a voice too loud for the scene. 'Mighty clean water. Anyone who supposes that jungle water must be foul and stagnant certainly is mistaken!' His words escaped as a shout; he couldn't control them. 'But it has a funny, chemical taste, like sulphur. Probably full of minerals.'

'Who do you think you're fooling, sonny-boy? I saw you hiding behind that bush. You've been watching me swim.'

Jonathan's mouth dropped open to protest, but nothing came out. 'It's true,' he admitted. 'I *was* watching. I did see you naked – only because it was too late to turn away. But I didn't mean to spy on you.'

'You expect me to believe that?'

'Take it easy. If you knew I was there, why did you take off your clothes in such a hurry?'

'This is my private bathing place. I'll undress if I please.'

'Why didn't you call my name? Why didn't you say, "Hey, Johnny, I see you!" or come back and bathe another time if you didn't want me to watch?'

'Nobody tells me when to swim.'

'I think you did it on purpose. You took your clothes off so I *would* watch.'

'That's not what your father will think.'

'Wait! This is a complete mistake. You can't tell him about this!'

'I can if I want to,' she said, placing her hands on her hips and provocatively pushing out her belly. 'Are you going to try to stop me?'

'Go ahead if you want to.' Jonathan challenged her. 'Bertha said you were an exhibitionist.'

She yawned. 'I don't think it would please your father to know sonny-boy isn't a man after all . . .'

'What do you mean?'

'Just an impotent peeping tom looking for thrills. I keep forgetting nobody taught you how to behave.'

Although stung by her insults, Jonathan swallowed his pride. He wanted to avoid fighting with her. He was also afraid she would tell Ben. He tried to change the subject.

'Did I tell you that I met your mother? She put something on my head which healed the cuts. At least, I think they're healed . . .'

'May I see?' she asked softly.

Muddled by her abrupt change of mood, Jonathan submissively bent his head forward. Once more he felt that gentle touch and inhaled the same hypnotic breath that had emanated from her mother. His face was but a few inches from the dark breasts, to which drops of water still clung. He was about to shut his eyes when he felt twinges in his scalp: she was taking out the stitches.

After what seemed a long time he raised his head, and she showed him a handful of tiny knotted threads. She smiled and put away a long knife she'd had concealed somewhere on her person.

Her strange behaviour put him at a loss for words. 'Your father wants you to complete your education,' he remarked idiotically. 'Maybe you should go to medical school.'

She was filling the buckets. The parrot perched in her hair and was eyeing him inimically. 'If Big City had his way, I'd be spending the rest of my days in school,' she said wistfully.

'You know how old folks are – he's probably afraid he'll never see you again. Want me to carry those buckets?'

'Think you're strong enough, sonny-boy?' she arched her eyebrows and smiled saucily.

'Yeah!'

With Marie leading the way, they entered the corn. When they came to the yard, she made him stop, took the buckets from him and carried them into the hut. Jonathan loitered about the perimeter of the hard-packed ground. He was hungry and he wanted his breakfast. From within the hut he could hear the sound of their voices.

'Where's Johnny – have you seen him this morning?'

'Oh, I saw him all right – crouched behind a bush. His excuse was he'd been off in the jungle, exploring.'

'Excuse for what?'

'Can't you guess? He was watching me take my clothes off. He was spying on me while I bathed. The impertinence! That's right – your own son. I tell you he has no manners. There's no privacy anymore – not even here.'

Ben made no reply; for a minute they were silent.

'He said he had a message from Umberto.'

'A letter?' Ben asked. 'Let's see it.'

'No, a message. He said Umberto told him to tell me that he still loves me and wants me back.'

'Well, Umberto has certainly changed his tune.'

'He wants me to be his wife again. He's ready to forgive and forget.'

'What makes him think you'd go back?'

'If that son of yours talks you into leaving here, he knows I'll go, too. Salvador asks for me every day. They need me and the past will be forgotten.'

'Well, Marie, in that case . . . maybe you should go back.'

'Oh – so you want to get rid of me, do you?'

'You know I don't, Marie,' Ben said softly.

'Do you know what else sonny-boy said? He said Umberto swore to kill you if you ever set foot in Puerto Gusano again.'

All of a sudden Ben began to groan.

Jonathan, who was about to protest Marie's fabrications, walked to the hut. Ben was seated in his chair with his back to the door, so that his normally surveillant eye did not notice his son standing just outside. His trousers were hanging over the other chair, and Marie was down on her knees before him, unwrapping the bandages from his legs. Although she removed them with care, the bandages were encrusted with scabs, and Ben cried aloud as they were ripped from his legs, revealing a mass of sores. A sour odour of pus issued from the hut.

Jonathan stepped through the door.

'Dad!' For the first time he saw the agony his father endured. 'You've *got* to see a doctor.'

Ben was caught totally by surprise. His hand, which was resting on Marie's head, went to cover his crotch.

'That's the most repulsive sight I've ever seen! There must be *some reason* why a civilized man would permit this disease to go so far. Is this a manifestation of what's wrong with your soul? Are you so pessimistic you just don't care any more? Or do you refuse to receive treatment out of some principle or cynicism? If I go home and tell people I found you living in a hut, miles from nowhere in the middle of the jungle, totally isolated and cut off from the world . . . and you're dying a slow death from a hideous tropical disease, and the best remedy you can think of is to wash your legs with water . . . *nobody would believe me!*'

'Is that what you're afraid of, Johnny – of not being believed? Is that why you want me to go back – to prove to the world that your mission has succeeded?'

'I want to take you to Puerto Gusano because you're my father and you're sick. Jesus Christ. You can be cured and live a long life – here or wherever you like. I've waited twenty-five years for this. I've missed you. I've needed a father. You owe me *that* much at least.'

'What? To live a long life?'

'No. To let me help you.'

'Are you claiming rights on my soul?'

'You short-changed me, Dad.'

'Is that what you came all this way to tell me?'

'I have a hell of a right, too – if that's what I did come to say. That and a lot more. Twenty-five years of pain, humiliation and uncertainty – wondering what happened and why.' Jonathan's voice cracked; his face was wet with sweat and tears. 'Jesus Christ, some guy decides to dump his family and – wham! – down comes the curtain. Maybe you raise it again, maybe you don't. I'd have a right to put a bullet in you.' Jonathan suddenly stopped talking. 'I'm sorry, Dad. I didn't mean that.'

'Maybe you don't know how you feel about me, Johnny.'

'Maybe I don't. Can you blame me for having mixed emotions? But I know that I want you to get well.' Jonathan began to pace the floor. 'What about pain?'

'Sounds like you think I deserve it.'

'This is the worst thing I've ever seen. Aren't you afraid of death?'

'The cage door is always open.'

'Jesus Christ, is that what you think life is – a cage?'

'Johnny, please let Marie finish what she's doing.'

Jonathan retreated from the hut. He went and lay down in the cornfield and covered his eyes.

A few minutes later a shadow fell across him. He opened his eyes. It was Marie.

'Come with me.' She placed a finger across her lips. 'Don't say anything.'

Jonathan followed her to the pig pen. She had changed her clothes. In place of the long skirt and cotton blouse she wore a pair of denim overalls. Her arms and shoulders were bare, the colour of ebony, and Jonathan could see the curving edges of her breasts. The colourful bandana had gone, and a mass of thick, springy hair rested on her shoulders and framed her face like a mane.

She opened the gate and urged the pigs out with loud guttural cries. Jonathan stood aside as the boar charged out and led his family trotting into the forest. Why does she tell me to keep my mouth shut, he asked himself, while she goes around shouting at the top of her lungs?

Marie was standing at the edge of the forest, beckoning him forward with a stick.

There was a path of sorts. As the jungle closed behind him, Jonathan could hear the pigs grunting and crashing through the undergrowth as they foraged hungrily beneath the trees. Occasionally one of them would bolt across the trail, causing him to stop dead in his tracks. He feared the boar. Marie's voice, uttering hoarse cries or whistling shrilly, sounded to the right or left, and he caught glimpses of her chasing after the pigs and beating the bushes with her stick.

The boar, running its snout over the ground like a vacuum cleaner, never left her side. This was her natural domain, and she was deliberately showing off her superior agility and stamina. Like a child, thought Jonathan, as he plodded glumly along. Normally, he would have taken up the challenge. He regretted being overweight and out of shape.

After a while she suddenly appeared on the path ahead of him. Planting her stick, she struck an exaggeratedly seductive pose. Her bare shoulders were back, her belly and breasts thrust forward, and her chin was in the air. Her denim overalls and blue-black skin effectively camouflaged her within the jungle gloom.

The bright green parrot ornamented her hair. It was an absurd posture, mocking his slowness.

'Marie, can we rest for a minute? I didn't get any breakfast, and I'm feeling kind of weak.'

But she was gone again, without a sound.

The ground began to rise, further slowing Jonathan's progress. He was famished and dizzy from hunger. For another couple of hours he pulled himself up the steep, mouldy slope. Grasping at roots and rocks, he tried to forget his fear of snakes. As the sound of the pigs receded deeper into the jungle, he began talking to himself again. 'What the hell does that bitch think she's doing? This is the craziest girl I've ever known.'

In the middle of the afternoon he stumbled into an open place high on the side of the mountain. A grey stone cliff fell away to a thick canopy of trees fifty feet below. A massive, egg-shaped boulder was poised on the edge and divided the cliff. He leaned against the rock and listened in vain for the pigs. He called Marie, but there was no answer. After a while he pulled a handkerchief from his pocket, wiped the dirt and sweat from his face, and took in the view.

Deep within the ocean of air a solitary vulture sailed. Twisting its raw head this way and that, it scanned with an obsidian eye the vast rumpled sward of the rain forest. The yellow elbows of the Rio Gusano, like the gleaming folds of a jaundiced serpent, marked the river's course to the horizon. All about the cumulus airships ranged, aiming down slanted shafts of rain at the green disk of earth. And there, at the bottom of the valley up which he had trudged, Jonathan could make out Ben's homestead – two huts standing in a bright field of corn hollowed from the jungle.

A sound caused Jonathan to whirl around and there, not ten yards away stood the boar. Its head was down, its yellow tusks curved threateningly, and its jaw and flanks were flecked with foam. Jonathan sucked in his breath and flattened himself against the boulder.

'Help!'

The boar was pawing the ground. The vulture swooped; its shadow raced across the space between them. For a few seconds time seemed to stop.

Just as it seemed that the boar would run at him, Marie's voice sounded.

'Dickie! Dickie! Dickie!'

The boar wheeled, scattering dirt beneath its hooves, and plunged into the forest.

Smiling, she stepped from behind the boulder. 'I don't think he likes you, Johnny.'

'Hey!' Jonathan's breath came out in a gasp. 'That pig is dangerous!' His heart, which had almost stopped, began to beat high in his chest. 'Have you been there the whole time?'

'Dickie! Dickie! Dickie! Come, my pet!'

The pig charged out of the woods again, stopping just a few feet from Jonathan, who jumped back against the edge of the cliff. He nearly slipped, sending a small landslide of dirt and pebbles cascading into the trees below.

'Take it easy with that pig, Marie.'

'You're not scared, are you?' She was fondling the pig's ear.

Jonathan glanced apprehensively from the pig to the long drop behind him. 'Oh no. Nothing I like better than having to face down a wild boar with my back to a cliff.' He tried to sound sarcastic, but it didn't work. The boar scared the daylights out of him.

'Poor little sonny-boy. Is that why your face is twitching?'

'Listen, Marie . . .' Keeping the boulder behind him, he edged away from the cliff. 'You and I have got to talk.'

'Talk? What does talk accomplish? You talk too much – all of you. We don't understand talk.' She patted the pig's backside. 'Do we, Dickie?'

'You've got to help me convince Ben to come back for treatment.'

'He's old enough to make up his own mind, isn't he?' She was pretending to concentrate her attention on the pig.

'If we don't get him to a doctor right away he's going to die,' he said. He wanted to add, *'you black bitch!'* but didn't.

'We're all going to die someday, aren't we, Dickie?' Marie laughed. She seemed to think her statement settled the matter. 'You don't give your father much credit for being tough, do you? He can still dance circles around you, sonny-boy.'

'This isn't a question of being tough. The disease has got to be cured. He can't last much longer.'

'He may get better,' she commented blandly. She was staring off into space. 'Besides, if he's as sick as you think he is, would he survive the trip?' Her arm was around the pig.

'It's a risk worth taking. Otherwise he'll die for sure. We've got to get him out of here.'

'Why? He's happy now. Isn't that a spectacular view? It's paradise in the jungle. Isn't it, Dickie?'

The pig, which had been pacified by her caresses, snorted contentedly.

'Paradise? What kind of weird utopia do you think you're living in? You thrive in this environment, while he dies a slow death. You don't want him to see a doctor, do you? What have you two made, some sort of suicide pact? What is keeping you here — it's insane!'

'Honestly, sonny-boy, *must* you be so rude — even here? *Must you shout?*'

Jonathan tried to recompose himself, but it was no use. He didn't know how to talk to this woman, and frustration was getting the better of him. 'Do you mind if I sit down?' he asked. It was a ridiculous request, but he felt as though he were in her house. Randolph was right: it was impossible to talk to her.

'Please do,' she replied, taking him at his word. 'These rocks are for everybody.'

'I'm really tired.'

He sat down on the edge of the boulder and rubbed his eyes with his hands. She took a seat nearby. For a moment they were quiet. When Jonathan opened his eyes again, one of her breasts had partially slipped out the side of her overalls. He blushed as she unhurriedly pressed it back inside. He didn't know what to make of her or anything she did.

'Don't you miss your family?' he began. 'Randolph and your father?' He hesitated before adding: 'Umberto and Salvador?'

'Umberto talks too much — like you. Besides, there was nothing to keep me in Puerto Gusano.'

'How can you say that?' he asked bluntly. 'Salvador's your son. Wasn't that enough to keep you?'

'Have you ever given birth to a child?'

'Of course not.'

'Then what do you know about it?'

'I know about it from the son's point of view. If you love my father you can't let him die!'

'If you continue to shout, you'll frighten the wild animals away.

They're very timid, you know.'

'Do you love my father, Marie? Look, I'm not trying to take him away from you. I just want him to get well. I can't stand to see him this way.'

'I look after him, don't I?' she replied in a petulant tone of voice. 'How long do you think he'd last if I didn't take care of him? How can you be so stupid to think that I don't love him, when I wash his legs every day! I feed him. I help him in the field and grind his corn meal like a slave! I look after the pigs. I mend his clothes. I cut his hair. I do everything.'

'Just like you did for Umberto?' Jonathan couldn't resist saying it.

'Umberto doesn't hoe corn,' she answered right back.

'And Salvador – who's taking care of him?'

Marie slapped him hard across the face. 'That's none of your business!'

The force of the blow brought tears to Jonathan's eyes. 'Hey, take it easy,' he gasped. 'I'm sorry – I didn't mean that.' His heart started pounding again. He could see he was losing ground. His chest heaved. He thought he'd ruined his chance to reason with her. 'Listen, Marie. I'm appealing to you. You're an intelligent woman . . .'

She had taken the parrot from her hair. As it perched on her finger she spoke to it in a language Jonathan could not understand. The parrot convulsed, sent a stream of excrement to the ground, and shrieked triumphantly.

'No, I'm not intelligent. I'm just a simple, silly woman.' The confession brought a coy smile to her lips. Her eyes glittered with amusement.

'What's so funny?' Jonathan wanted to know.

'You sure do need my help, sonny-boy. You need me to get out of here alive. You couldn't possibly find your way out of this forest. You'd drown in the swamp and wind up as a meal for the alligators.' With the tip of her finger she was tickling the parrot's cloaca. 'Can he, Chita? He can't leave without Marie. Ever think of that, Johnny?' The parrot raised its tail feathers and uttered soft peeping sounds.

'I can't leave him like this. What about you? You don't want to bury my father and live here alone, do you?'

She put the parrot back in her hair and took Dickie's snout in both hands. 'I'm not alone, am I Dickie?'

The sight of Marie, with her breast exposed once more, shame-lessly kissing the pig on its snout, made Jonathan uneasy. He remained silent while she continued to fondle the pig in a way that disturbed him. He tried to prevent his imagination from running wild, but her caresses were arousing him.

'You know, Marie, if we go back to Puerto Gusano, maybe I could talk to Umberto and reason with him . . .' Jonathan was desperate enough to use any argument. 'He still talks about the days when the three of you were together.'

She glared at him. 'That's my husband you're talking about. My *husband*. So you think you know him better than I do?'

'I didn't say that.'

'My husband, and you're going to speak to him for me, are you? And for Ben, too?' She laughed sarcastically. 'Besides,' she added, 'I don't believe in tit for tat.'

This remark confused Jonathan. 'Tit for tat?'

'Tit for tat. I help you, you help me. Tit for tat. Tit for tat. Tit for tat. I don't like it.'

If she'd said the words one more time, Jonathan felt he would explode.

I'm not bargaining with you, Marie . . .' he began again. 'I'm appealing to your better judgement . . .' She was now making a show of rubbing Dickie's belly. 'Ben is weak, he's . . .'

'Weak? He masturbates three times a day!' She laughed. 'You call that weak? I call it excessive!' Dickie squealed with delight.

Jonathan was stunned. 'I don't want to hear disgusting insults about my father. How can you say such a thing?'

'Oh? Maybe you don't agree it's excessive, is that it?' She muttered something unintelligible in the pig's ear. The parrot clung to her hair and studied Jonathan through its invisible lorgnette. 'I suppose compared to what you do it's nothing.'

'Jesus, Marie!' What have I gotten myself into? he thought. Who is this woman? What does she want? How can I get through to her? He realized that he probably couldn't even find his way back to the hut by himself. He was dependent on her for every-thing, and he wasn't getting anywhere. When he looked again, Marie had gotten to her feet and had straddled Dickie. Rocking back and forth, she was giving the pig a back rub between her thighs.

'Good, Dickie . . . good,' she crooned.

Christ in heaven, Jonathan said to himself. Even the parrot looked jealous.

'Johnny?'

'What?'

'Do you miss having a woman out here?'

'No.' He couldn't help noticing the shape of her ass as it slid back and forth on Dickie. The pig groaned contentedly. Inside her denims, the flesh of her thighs rolled as she rode him harder.

'Why not?' she asked defiantly. 'Don't you like women?'

'It just so happens my father's dying.'

'You know, if anything happened to Ben, you and I would be here alone . . . with Dickie.'

Jonathan nearly choked. 'What the hell are you talking about? I've been bitten by bats. I *have* to go back!'

She climbed off Dickie, put her hands on her hips and laughed. 'Bats! So sonny-boy's scared? Don't take things so seriously. You don't like to be teased, do you?'

Her comment flustered him. 'I don't mind being teased,' he insisted, 'but we're talking about life and death.'

She sat down beside him and placed a hand on his knee. The pig moved closer. 'Look at Dickie's balls,' she said. 'Aren't they huge?' Jonathan reddened. 'Think of all the sperm in there waiting to come spurting out. You should see the size of his penis when he's aroused,' she went on. 'Do you know it's bright red and shaped like a corkscrew?' One long pendulous breast had slipped completely out of the side of her overalls this time. She let it stay. Her hand slid down toward his crotch.

'Marie, stop it!'

Jonathan tried to stand up, but her hand held him. She was laughing idiotically. They slipped to the ground and were rolling in the dirt together, dangerously near the edge of the cliff.

'Marie – stop!'

But she wouldn't stop laughing or kissing him. Her hand grabbed his crotch – a hard, unfriendly grip. The pig was dancing around and squealing excitedly, and the parrot flew up. Jonathan was terrified they would roll over the cliff.

'Let go of my penis!' Jonathan, furious now, punched her in the leg and jumped to his feet.

Marie, still on her knees, immediately got her composure back.

'Do you always come on this way with women?' she asked.

'Me? I feel I've just been raped in Macy's show window.'

'That's not what Ben will think.'

'You already pulled that once on me today. Hey, don't do that.'

She unbuttoned the flap of her overalls and her pendulous breasts fell free. Seizing his arm, she forced him to pull her to her feet, and they struggled briefly again. Jonathan managed to push her away. They were both breathing hard.

'Oh, I see you're one of those,' she said contemptuously.

'One of what?'

'You don't like women.'

Jonathan stepped forward and slapped her.

'Stop it! Stop it!' she cried. She crumpled to the ground and began to sob.

Jonathan leaned against the boulder. He was exhausted and dizzy from lack of food. For a minute he covered his eyes with his hand. He couldn't imagine how things had gotten so bad. Marie was still on her knees, and her shoulders shook. Her face was covered by hair. The parrot fluttered back and landed in it. Dickie trotted nervously about. Oh my God! Jonathan's lips moved, but no sound came out. What will she say to Ben now? He must try to reason with her again, plead . . .

He moved forward and patted her hair. 'I'm sorry . . . Marie.' It was a child's gesture.

Marie raised her head, but he couldn't see her face. With a swift movement she seized Dickie by the tail and wheeled the pig around to face Jonathan.

'Wait a minute!' Jonathan backed off against the boulder. The cliff was right behind him.

Through her tears Marie was smiling. It was a smile that frightened Jonathan out of his wits. She was brutally twisting Dickie's tail. The pig was squealing in pain and fright and straining to be freed. It was aimed right at Jonathan. Only a few inches separated Jonathan from the edge of the cliff. If she released her grip now, both he and the pig would be carried into space.

If only he had eaten he wouldn't feel so weak. He had a vision of the roast beef on his grandmother's table in Martha's Vineyard and remembered her warning: 'This could be foolish and dangerous.'

'Don't please!' he shouted as the pig charged.

He leaped forward and kicked Dickie in the snout as hard as he could. The pig shrieked, turned away, and crashed into the jungle. He dodged to one side so Marie, still on her hands and knees, was between him and the cliff. Push her over! a voice inside him said. You'll be doing yourself a favour – the whole world!

'It's you, Marie! It's you!' he heard himself yelling. 'You control everything, don't you – Umberto, Ben, me, everyone!'

She let out a witch-like cackle. The laugh stopped him like a wall. He had her cornered, but he was afraid to touch her. He wished by all means to avoid grappling with her again.

She got to her feet and pulled herself up to her full height. 'Let me pass,' she said, brushing by him. 'You're a gentleman, aren't you? How dare you kick an animal! Where are your manners?' She was composedly buttoning up the front of her overalls. For a second she managed to make him feel embarrassed for having saved his own life.

'Manners?' Jonathan lay back against the boulder, shut his eyes and laughed.

Before he knew what was happening he heard the parrot screeching. He opened his eyes and saw it circling in the air above the boulder. Marie had jumped.

He threw himself down and looked over the cliff at the clods of earth and stones crashing through the canopy of trees far below.

'Marie! *Oh my God!* Marie!' He lay there for a few seconds, paralyzed by the realization of what she had done.

The parrot would not stop screaming as it flew in wider and wider circles. Its cries echoed from the stone face of the cliff.

He ran back and forth along the edge of the precipice, looking for a way down. The cliff looked sheer and dangerous, but she might have survived the fall.

'Marie!'

No answer. She might be unconscious with a broken leg.

'Marie!'

Groping for toeholds, he lowered himself over the edge of the cliff. Sweating and scared, he gripped the rock. Had he been in his right mind, he would never have attempted such a descent. It was suicidal.

About half way down he stopped. With the toe of his boot he felt the rock below him but could find no niche. A kind of tingling numbness passed through his body. There seemed no way up or down. Pressing his cheek against the rock, he took two or three deep breaths, shut his eyes, and waited for the dizziness to go away. Beatrice – dead. Ben – dying. Marie – probably dead. Panadero. Now a hundred foot drop awaited him. For a second he contemplated letting go and putting an end to this nightmare. He opened his eyes and looked up. The sky was blue. A fly landed on the sweat mark that his cheek had left on the rock and walked around.

'Marie!' he screamed. 'Oh God I'm sorry!'

His voice reverberated off the cliff and died in the jungle.

Edging sideways along the rock, he found a diagonal crevice where the cliff had split and followed it down through the trees to the ground.

For the next hour he searched for Marie among the jumble of mossy boulders and fallen trees that littered the jungle floor. Hoping the branches had broken her fall, he scanned the treetops for her body. Shattered and confused, he left the area when daylight began to fade. He was afraid of not being able to find his way back in the dark.

The sun had set by the time he stumbled out of the stream and emerged from the jungle into Ben's clearing. He was out of breath, his clothes were soaking wet, and he was nearly faint from hunger and exhaustion.

'Beatrice. Now Marie. My fault,' he muttered over and over again as he fell and slid over the rocks. Ben would never leave now.

He'd run the whole way back, but suddenly he stopped in his tracks. Something was moving through the forest, or so he thought. The light was failing, and he couldn't be sure. He strained his eyes to see, and it moved again. This time there was no mistaking the swift diving shadows, loping effortlessly between the corn and the forest wall. In another second they vanished without a sound, and Jonathan was racing up the hill toward the huts.

The lanterns had been lit and gave off a soft, romantic glow. The little hut, for all its rudeness, seemed a cosy and safe abode. Ben was sitting in his chair, cup in hand. He was talking to himself, or so Jonathan thought.

'Come on in, Johnny!' He beckoned as soon as he caught sight of his son in the doorway. 'Been on a wild pig hunt? You must be worn out.' He waved magnanimously at a bottle on the table. 'Have a drink.'

'Ben . . . something terrible has happened . . .' Jonathan leaned heavily against the doorway. He raised his eyes and blinked. There at the back of the hut, dressed in blouse, long skirt, red bandana, parrot and all, was Marie, candle in hand. She smiled at him without opening her mouth, and, touching one candle to another, lit it. In the softly expanding light her face appeared to be suffused with mirth and self-confidence. A serene and saucy black madonna, she arched her eyebrows and cocked her head for Jonathan to see, and held up the candle before him like a mock offering to the dead.

'Listen, Ben . . .' The sight of her made Jonathan's knees buckle. She'd tricked him somehow – jumped down somewhere he couldn't see, arrived ahead of him and even had time to change for dinner. His enemy was standing right in front of him, and he hardly had the strength to speak. 'Ben, you better get those rifles down.'

'Why?' Ben's joviality vanished in an instant. 'There's no ammo!'

'We're going to have to protect ourselves.' Jonathan was trying to decide whether he ought to tell him about the revolver. At this point he was equally prepared to use it against Marie or the hounds.

'From what?'

Jonathan felt like he was eighty years old. 'The hounds.'

Ben started from his chair.

'I saw them running through the trees a minute ago . . . the bottom of the field.'

'Impossible!'

'I couldn't believe my eyes, either. Randolph said . . .'

Just as Jonathan was beginning to wonder if his eyes had deceived him, the answer came. A rising crescendo of howls and barking issued from the forest. Ben was clenching his fists. They were all staring like maniacs at the door, as though it were a dark windy opening in time.

By degrees the howls faded and were replaced by the faint mewing of frogs. Jonathan still vacillated – should he use the pistol now to shoot the hounds, or keep it as protection against Marie?

Marie launched herself toward the door.

'Wait, Marie! Johnny . . . you're going to do something now . . .' Ben announced through his teeth. 'Go with her. Now. Help free the pigs. Otherwise the hounds are going to kill them. The only chance the pigs have is to be free in the forest.'

Jonathan had made up his mind. There were four bullets in the revolver. He would use it in self-defence against whoever attacked first.

'Hurry, Johnny . . . help her set the pigs free before it's too late.'

The tone of his voice was tender, and Jonathan again experienced a rush of warm feelings for his father. He wanted to throw his arms around him, but there was no time.

There it was again – the long howl – and he flung himself out the door behind Marie. He dove into his hut and scrabbled frantically on his hands and knees in the dark, but he couldn't find the pistol. Who'd taken it? The fact that the gun was missing panicked him as much as the arrival of the hounds. The breeze was rustling the corn. The moon was far away but very bright, and the shiny corn leaves glittered like sharpened spears. The frogs down by the stream would not stop their peevish wailing. Then the noise came – a wild confusion of screams – the voices of hysterical terrorized animals confronted by certain death. He caught up with Marie jut in time to see the silvery forms hurdle the barrier of the pig sty. The pandemonium was monstrous – a thing upon which his nightmares would always be founded.

20

The Slaughter

At first light Jonathan crawled across the floor of the hut and found the revolver exactly where he'd hid it – lying in a depression beneath the palm frond mat.

The sun was already high in the sky when he kicked away the stick he'd propped against the flimsy door. Shielding his eyes from the glare, he looked about. The corn stood motionless in the heat, frozen by the maddening shrill of the insects.

'Ben!' he called.

There was no reply.

A shadow swept the yard. Daintily, with a little hop, the vulture landed on the roof of Ben's hut and folded its wings. Alert, like a dog waiting for a command, it cocked its head and regarded Jonathan with insolent prejudice. The bold blank eye wanted the man dead. A stone went whistling past, and with an ungainly flap it took to the air and soared away over the corn.

He followed it. In their hundreds they had come, lured by the prospect of an unprecedented feast. The boughs of the trees along the edge of the forest were so laden with them that the arrival of one forced the departure of another. Many more were parked on the ground, and the rails of the pig sty were packed solid.

Jonathan ran and shouted; he threw stones and scattered them.

Like a thousand simultaneous unfurlings of old umbrellas, with much grunting and croaking, they struggled to get themselves aloft. For a minute the air stirred with the dry beatings of wings. A few more branches were blackened, but they didn't fly far. The more intrepid ones merely hopped out of his way. The intrusion only delayed the mission which they had come so far to carry out, for which they had been created to faithfully perform.

They'd not yet begun to eat because Dickie was still staggering about among the family of carcasses. The blood glistened where it welled up through the rents in his hide. One eye hung by a tendril from an empty socket; the other had been caked shut by a flow of blood. The jungle boar had been blinded during the battle. Part of his snout was torn away and hung uselessly, exposing tusks and teeth.

With the exception of Dickie, all the pigs were dead. One had been made a meal of: another had escaped or had been carried off. One hound had also met its match, however, and it must have been an horrendous struggle. In the end, Dickie had got in under it and ripped its insides out. The guts had caught on the fence, and, with the boar rooting in its belly, they'd spilled out over the lot. But what a magnificent specimen it was, even in death. It was the size of a great dane, all muscle and sinew. Its ears were missing and its jaws were clotted with gore and pig bristles. Dickie staggered over and gave the corpse a final thrust, just to make sure.

'Shoo, you damn birds! Move!' Jonathan ran about clapping his hands. 'Hungry devils, greedier than pigs,' he muttered and returned to the fence. But it all came their way in the end. They'd get what they wanted. Nothing could ruffle their smug acquaintance with death. The final swing of the pendulum always wound up in their mouths. Then the ants would arrive to finish the job. Wonderfully efficient system that it was, the unsentimentality of it affronted Jonathan.

There was a vulture movement as Marie came out of the corn. She stood beside him at the fence and grimly surveyed the carnage. To the vultures she paid no attention. Dickie was squealing pitifully. She vaulted the fence, long skirt flying and approached her pet, who wobbled faithfully toward her. Pulling the knife from her blouse, she took hold of the helpless brute by a mangled ear and neatly plunged the blade up to the hilt in its throat. The blood spurted out in a crimson stream, and the boar collapsed with a groan, kicked a few times, and was dead. A tremor of delight simultaneously coursed down the corridors of vultures.

Marie was wiping her blade on Dickie's hide. As she climbed the fence she shot Jonathan a look of such hatred that made him shudder and shrink back.

'And now *you!*' she said.

For a second Jonathan thought she meant to use the knife on him. The birds were sighing ravenously.

She wheeled to face him, hands on hips, her face an African mask – wooden, pitiless, imperial. 'This is all *your* fault,' she said, and walked off through the corn. Jonathan ran after her, and the birds, with a rush of wings, descended on the pigs.

He caught up with her in the cornfield and grabbed her arm and whirled her around.

'How can you? Jesus. My fault? That's unfair, Marie! You can't say this is all my fault.'

Grunting, she pulled herself free. She was strong. 'Everything's your fault. You interrupted our lives. You ruined our peace. You brought the hounds.'

'Peaceful Banana brought the hounds.'

'You brought them *here*. And they'll be back.' Impregnable, she glared at him, and ran off. He let her go. There was no way he could make her listen. Besides, he had an awful feeling that she was right.

The corpses of the pigs were shrouded by a shimmering, quivering blanket of feathers. The beating of wings raised the dust as the birds struggled for the fresh pork and entrails. Mesmerized by the sight, Jonathan's mind went blank. For a minute he couldn't recall if he'd ever had a life before this. He had to shut his eyes in order to bring back the reassuring vision of the shingled house on Martha's Vineyard. The American flag fluttered above the tennis court where he had slammed serves not so long ago, where his father had played before him.

He opened his eyes. The forest wall loomed ominously above him. More birds sailed in to join the feast. If the jungle, the bats or the hounds didn't kill him, Marie would. Even Puerto Gusano seemed a lifetime away – safer and better.

He walked back to the huts.

Ben and Marie were arguing in muffled tones. Jonathan entered his own hut, deliberately leaving the door open a crack so he could see what was going on outside, and lay down in the hammock. A few minutes later Marie emerged with the buckets and went off to the stream.

The day was stoking up; not a breath of air stirred. It was hot in the hut, and he could feel the sweat leaking over his body, soaking into his filthy clothes. He tried to lie quietly and gather his wits, but he itched all over. The unrelenting scream from the insect world stifled any effort to think clearly. He heard someone coming and felt for the revolver.

She came back through the corn. She'd been bathing. Beads of water glistened in her hair. The damp blouse clung to her breasts and stretched taut across her shoulders as she carried the heavy buckets.

Salty tears blurred his sight. He had aimed the pistol at her as she went by.

'Don't go berserk,' he warned himself. 'Don't make any more mistakes.'

He put the pistol away. He wiped his face with his hand and tried to breathe deeply. He could hear their voices – low, indistinct murmurs from the other hut.

After a while he smelled food. He slipped the revolver into his pocket and stepped outside.

From the exposed roofbeams of Ben's hut yards of gauzy bandages were flying. Although they'd just been washed and were still wet and dripping, the stains had not been entirely removed. The bandages had been used over and over again.

Barely conscious of his feet touching the ground, Jonathan drifted toward the hut. A grotesque cackle stopped him a few feet from the door.

'Oh, *now* I see. You want to go back to Puerto Gusano, do you? Now you think like *he* does. Like father, like son. Umberto's no longer a threat, is he? Have you forgotten he swore to kill you?' A banging noise accompanied her words. 'If we go back, I'll leave you and go straight to Umberto!' The parrot shrieked at the banging. 'We were all right until he came here!'

'Marie, why don't you admit it – we were never all right.'

'I left my child for you. I gave up everything.'

'If you love me, why don't I feel it? Besides, you were determined to come . . . You weren't thinking about Salvador then, were you? If you love me, you'd want me to go back.'

Holding his breath, Jonathan waited outside the door. He guessed this was a conversation they had had many times before.

'You never wanted me any more than you wanted Umberto,' Ben commented bitterly. 'You wanted to get away from Puerto Gusano, away from everything you knew. You were ready to abandon civilization – if you can call it that – even your own son. I was your ticket out. And now you want to stay here, even if you have to bury me to do it. Don't tell me you were passionately in love with me.'

'You know I can't respond that way . . .'

'Why not, Marie? Why not?' Ben asked hopelessly. 'Are you capable of feeling love at all?'

Jonathan blushed to hear these intimacies, but he didn't dare move.

Marie's voice softened, too. 'We wanted to be happy, didn't we? We tried . . .'

'We were happier there – in Puerto Gusano.'

'I've been living with you five years, Ben, and when you say "*we*", you still mean you and Umberto!'

Ben laughed out loud.

Marie was in a rage, '*I'm going to make you suffer!*' she cried hoarsely.

The laughter stopped. 'As if you haven't already.'

'It's *his* fault! It's all Johnny's fault!' Once more the clanking noise punctuated her words, and the parrot protested.

The smell of hot corn meal crazed Jonathan. If he didn't eat right away, he would faint. Marie stormed out of the hut and collided with him. He grabbed her wrist, twisted her arm behind her back, and pushed her inside. A clay pot full of the steaming corn sat on the table. A battered ladle lay beside it. Without letting go of Marie's arm, he thrust his free hand into the pot but withdrew it immediately. The corn meal was scalding hot.

Ben was attempting to rise, but couldn't. 'What are you doing, Johnny? Let her go!'

Paying no attention to his father, Jonathan tipped the pot, dumped the corn meal on the table and smeared it about with the ladle. He scooped up the cooling gobs with his fingers and crammed them into his mouth.

Marie cried out in pain. Ben's arms lifted him from the chair, but he couldn't move his feet. 'Stop it! Let her go!' he commanded, making another futile show of strength.

'She tried to kill me, Dad!' The corn meal spattered from Jonathan's mouth.

Marie grunted. 'Look at the way he eats,' she cried. 'Like a pig!'

'She tried to kill me once and she'll try again. I was bitten by bats coming here, and I can't sit around like Hamlet wondering what to do about it. I've got to see a doctor quick and you do, too. I don't want to die and I don't want you to die. This woman will kill us both, or the bats will, or the hounds. The vultures are waiting outside for the next course!'

'Bats?' Ben said. 'My God, Johnny, why didn't you tell me?'

Jonathan's mouth was full of corn meal. He forced Marie down and placed his knee across her back, crushing her cheek against the floor of the hut. The violence he was committing erased the confusion from his mind, but he had not forgotten the knife. Even while kneeling on the floor she could slash his legs.

'Throw the knife out the door!' Jonathan was amazed how threatening he could sound. *'Throw it!'*

Marie didn't move. He increased pressure and forced another cry from her.

'Johnny, stop it! Don't you dare hurt her!' Ben threatened. He tried to move from his chair. There was a machete on the wall, but out of his reach.

'My instincts tell me if you play around with hostile people you get hurt! I'm not playing with her any more.'

He put all his weight on Marie's back and forced her arm upwards. She didn't make a sound; she was thinking whether to use the knife on him. Jonathan knew it. If she did, he'd shoot her. He'd already made up his mind to do it, even though it would mean the end of everything.

'Throw the knife, Marie.' Ben's voice was reassuringly steady. 'Johnny's out of his mind. Let him eat. He's starving. He doesn't know what he's doing.'

Jonathan and Ben watched as her hand slowly travelled to her bosom. Jonathan forced the arm harder, but he was frightened. The knife was razor sharp. One slash and she could cut his arteries or tendons and he'd never get out of the swamp alive.

Ben must have been thinking the same thing. 'Throw it, Marie, I'm asking you . . . throw it . . . *please.*'

A wave of relief surged through Jonathan as the knife flew out the door.

Ben relaxed and sat back in his chair. 'Now let's all calm down. Let go, Johnny. You're hurting her.'

Jonathan released her arm but moved to block the door. For once, the advantage was his, and he was determined to press it to the limit.

'We're going back. All of us.' His pulse was racing, and he spoke without thinking. 'She cornered me on the cliff and sent her executioner in to finish me off. Not every woman trains her pigs to kill!'

Marie was rubbing her shoulder. She glanced at him, her nostrils flaring, then faced Ben. 'Your son's afraid of everything in nature.' She threw her hair back. 'The jungle, the pigs, the night, heights . . .'

'What I want to know, Dad – were you in on it, too? When I came back here last night, I heard you laughing. Was this some kind of murderous joke you two planned together?'

Ben shifted his eyes from one to the other. 'What are you talking about, Johnny?'

'I just managed to escape, and she jumped over the cliff. I thought she'd killed herself, I nearly broke my neck looking for her. I ran all the way back here to tell you . . . to find you *laughing!*'

Marie drew herself up to her full height. 'That's *sonny-boy's* story. What really happened was . . . he tried to rape me!'

'That's a lie. Like those messages from Umberto – all lies.'

'I tried to fight him off, and he pushed me,' Marie said. 'I had to jump down to the ledge to escape.'

'Jesus, Marie, is there anything you won't do? She started to take her clothes off and grabbed my crotch. When I pushed her away she called in the pig. She said disgusting things about you – things I can't repeat.'

Marie stiffened. 'Believe what you want,' she said.

Ben covered his face with his hands.

'He exposed himself and attacked me – the dirty little queer! Your son's a queer . . .'

Her voice faltered, and Ben looked up. Jonathan was holding the revolver in his hand. His hand shook.

'You wouldn't dare, you little queer.' Marie glared at him out of the corner of her eye.

Jonathan cocked the revolver and placed it against her temple, infuriating the parrot. It resolutely waded through her hair and pecked at the gun barrel.

Ben was staring wild-eyed at his son. His mouth was open, his features rigid, as though he feared the slightest movement would make the gun go off.

'We're going back,' Jonathan's voice was firm again. 'Even if I have to kill her.'

'Without me you'll never make it out of the swamp. Bye bye sonny-boy, a meal for the alligators.' Marie said it coolly, but her mouth twitched.

He held the revolver in both hands to keep it from shaking. 'I'm not waiting around for the vultures to finish us off.'

For a few seconds the metallic click of the parrot's beak against the barrel of the revolver was the only sound in the hut. A moaning noise distracted Jonathan.

'Stop it, Johnny! You've got to stop it!' Ben's face was deathly pale.

Still keeping his pistol aimed at Marie, Jonathan took a step toward his father.

'Dad, I'm sorry.' He lowered the gun and went down on his knees by his father's chair. 'Dad, I know I'm upsetting your life. I'm not trying to pay you back for ruining mine. But you owe me something, Dad, even now. I've been bitten by bats. For my sake, we've got to get out of here.'

The parrot fluttered from Marie's head to the table and began to peck at the corn meal.

'Marie,' Ben said softly, 'We're leaving. Johnny has to have rabies shots.'

21

The Way Back

At dawn the crickets cranked their wild motors; and Jonathan was out in the jungle with a machete, hacking a pair of crude crutches from the branch of a tree.

Ben turned to survey his land for the last time. Beneath a sky that was immaculately blue, where a few vultures still circled at great height, the little homestead seemed a quiet and welcoming abode. The corn was ripening and the thatched roof of the hut was just visible over the brow of the hill. For an instant Jonathan experienced a twinge of regret about removing his father from his refuge, but doubt faded with the light as they moved off into the jungle.

In the afternoon they reached the river. Soon a fire was blazing. Marie went off with the machete and returned with an armful of slender poles. From these she erected a dome-like frame which she roofed with banana leaves. A fish was tugging on the line she had set. She dragged it in, gutted it, wrapped it in leaves and buried the bundle among the ashes and embers. While she worked, father and son sat by and watched but did not speak. Jonathan offered to help, but Marie refused.

Darkness came on with a rush. When the fish had been eaten, Marie crawled inside the shelter. A murky silence prevailed in the bowels of the forest. Jonathan and his father stayed outside by the fire.

Someone was snoring softly – a feminine snore.

'Dad,' Jonathan whispered. 'How are the legs holding up?'

'Not so good.'

'I thought you did pretty well today – walking all that way without stopping. Didn't you want to sit down?'

'My legs would have swollen.'

'Are they swollen now?'

'Yes.'

'Tomorrow we'll be on the river. You can give them a rest.' Jonathan cracked a branch with his hands and fed the pieces to the fire. 'Dad, do you hate me for doing this?'

'I could never hate you, Johnny. Do you hate *me?*'

'I used to, I guess. Mostly I hate myself.'

'Me, too.' They both laughed. 'Did you bring that revolver down here to kill me?' Ben asked.

'Maybe. If you had been different – mean or callous or ornery. I had no idea what to expect. Granny was convinced that if you were alive you would have become a criminal. I thought I might have had to shoot my way in, or out. As it turned out, it was a nightmare looking for you.'

'Granny never lost her faith in me, did she? She never stopped thinking I was a bastard. I admire her for that. You are like her – you have her persistent streak. You don't give up.'

'We did have some good times when the family was still together, didn't we, Dad? Do you remember that time when I was about ten you took me fishing on Blair Lake and I caught a two-and-a-quarter pound pickerel on a fly rod?'

'There was never a happier face. Your mother used to have the photo on her dressing table.'

'Umberto has it now, with all the other things. Why did you give him your signet ring?'

'Oh, the humidity gave me eczema on my fingers, and I couldn't wear it. I didn't want to leave it lying around in case one of the servants walked off with it . . . he said he'd like to have it.'

'Jesus Christ! He's created a whole mythology about you and him, he's built a shrine to your past, and he's practically assumed your identity. He wears your clothes!'

'Typical of Umberto – his passionate devotion.'

'Mom said that when you were in the Philippines she used to write you every day because she had this feeling that you would just forget all about us and never come home.'

'I have never forgotten you or anybody, Johnny.'

Jonathan poked the fire with a stick, and the sparks exploded.

'I *had* to come looking for you no matter who was going to get hurt . . . even if it was only to grab you by the throat and say, "I'm your son, you no good bum, why in the name of hell did you run out on us?" '

Ben looked up but said nothing.

'They all had this crazy idea that I would bring you back,' Jonathan added hopefully. 'Back to the United States. Granny and Mom swore that if I did, it would ruin their lives all over again, but I thought, well, they'll be all right. But I'm not so sure any more. It seems that some things are better left undone.'

'Your mother and Granny were right, Johnny.' Ben cast a long worried gaze into the fire. The fire crackled; he was silent for a moment. 'Poor Bertha . . . Umberto must be tearing his hair out. He must be keeping the whole town awake with his monologue of despair.'

Jonathan pulled a blazing stick from the fire and lit one of Ben's homemade cheroots. The flames briefly illuminated his furrowed brow. 'Two people's lives ruined and a little girl killed. All because of my selfish hunt for you!'

'That brawl could have happened any night, even if you had never come.'

'Umberto thinks I'm to blame, and now the hounds . . .' Jonathan threw more wood on the fire.

'We all make mistakes, Johnny. I made up my mind not to go back to you and Bea because I was afraid that my mistakes would only hurt you more.'

'*More* than you hurt us by leaving us? That's not good enough, Dad. You ruined me.'

'I'm sorry you feel that way. I wanted to save you, not ruin you.'

'You left us to save us? I wanted you *there*. I didn't care if you were drunk in a gutter, or brought chorus girls home. I wanted *you. You ruined my life*.'

'Is my having left you sufficient reason for your life to be ruined?'

'*Yes*.'

'It sounds to me as though you let it ruin your life. The blame has to stop somewhere. You should have stopped blaming me twenty years ago and gotten on with something else.'

'How could you have left us standing on the dock knowing that you would never see us again?'

'It didn't happen that way. I didn't mean to go away for ever.'

'What?'

'I sailed the boat to Florida as planned – not for a winter berth but to make some fast money. I met this fellow on an elevator in New York. He turned to me and out of the blue said, 'Do you know anybody with a boat in Florida?' I said I was about to take mine down there. He needed someone to smuggle weapons into Cuba. It was an opportunity to make a lot of money, and I agreed to do it. Granny was refusing to finance any more of my projects. This would be a quick job that would get me off the hook. I knew that it would be dangerous, so I took out that insurance policy before I left. But it was an adventure that suited me. I had a wife, of sorts, in Cuba, and a little girl. Angelita. She was about two years old then.'

'Jesus!' Jonathan felt a pang of jealousy and possessiveness. 'Did Mom know about this?'

'No one knew. I had been going over to Cuba for years – Havana was a fantastic place in those days. I met Puri on the beach and I found her irresistible. We made love on the beach, in gardens, in cars, standing behind doors just out of sight of crowds of people – it was outrageous and wonderful. We never stopped. I had been married nearly twenty years, and Puri was a kid, but sex with her was a revelation. Goethe discovered sex in Rome at the age of thirty-six, and I discovered it at forty in Havana. She loved me passionately. We never married, but I loved her.'

'Like you loved us?'

Ben looked straight at his son. 'Yes.'

There was a crash in the forest. A wild pig was foraging on the other side of the river.

'I picked up a cargo of weapons in Key West and sailed across. It was just before Castro's disastrous revolt of December, 1956, when only twelve men, including Raul and Che Guevara escaped to the mountains. I dropped the guns off near Santiago and sailed back to Havana to see Puri. I was planning to stay a week. It was a chaotic and lawless time in Havana. Although the revolution was still three years away, one sensed that the end was near. No one could be sure who was on who's side, and informers were everywhere. One night Puri and I came back to the boat to find gunmen aboard. They were looking for the cash box. They held their guns on us and ordered us not to move . . .' Ben stared into the fire. He was having difficulty speaking. 'They told us not to move, but Puri panicked. She screamed, "Where is my baby?" and dove into the cabin. They shot her in the back and killed her. They shot me in the stomach . . .'

'My God, Dad . . .'

'They gunned down everyone on board. Puri's grandmother, the baby – murdered by the same guns that I had brought to Cuba . . .'

Jonathan's vision blurred when he saw the tears on his father's face. 'I didn't know it would be like this.' He reached over and placed a hand on Ben's shoulder.

'I spent three months semi-comatose in the hospital. Another six months or so passed in a drunken daze. When I woke up, nearly a year had gone by, and I realised that you must have given me up for dead.'

'But, Dad, for *five years* every time the phone rang Mom thought it was you!'

'I sailed the *Pelican* out of Havana without any idea where I was going. I considered jumping overboard and making a meal for the sharks. I went to places where I wasn't known. Haiti. Columbia. Peru. Brazil. Dozens of places . . .'

They sat for a long time in silence. The river was audible – a soft rippling passage.

'That was all a long time ago, Johnny. I'm tired now. I'm going to lie down.'

'Dad, I never stopped wanting you back. I'm sorry I thought all those things about you.'

Ben laughed. 'Didn't Auden say, "Only those in the last stages of disease can believe that children are the true judges of character"?'

'What did he mean by that?' Jonathan asked.

But Ben had begun to snore. For a long time Jonathan gazed at him. His head was full of things he had waited twenty-five years to say, but sadness and exhaustion overwhelmed him, and he fell into a deep sleep.

All the following day Ben lay in the bottom of the canoe. His eyes were shut, and he said nothing. Jonathan rolled his coat into a pillow and made him as comfortable as he could; but his complexion was chalky white, and his lips were grey. From time to time he felt his father's pulse and finally allowed his wrist to rest limply in his hand. Through the hot hours of the day, while Marie sat in the stern and steered the canoe, he shielded Ben's face from the sun with a straw hat.

'Marie, do you want me to sail a while so you can rest?'

She shook her head and looked away.

Jonathan secretly enjoyed this silent communion with his father. Here was the hand he had longed to hold, and at last it was his. The father he had needed to turn to for guidance and support

rested with his head in his lap. For however long this lasted, he had
a father. Here was the physical man; to be able to touch him after
so many years of separation produced in Jonathan feelings of
profound tenderness. It was a luxury to be able to comfort and
support him.

Marie followed a course through the swamp that was unfamiliar to him, but Jonathan hardly noticed. When he was not gazing
down into the face of his father, he was staring straight ahead at a
single point, and weighing the meaning of everything that he had
done, and considering what his father had revealed to him.

In the late afternoon they entered an area of desolation that
had been ravaged by some mysterious pestilence. Animal and
bird life were non-existent. The only sounds were made by horse-
flies, as big as a man's thumb, that buzzed constantly around
them. Gigantic columns of gnats were stacked up over the water,
and the sky was filled with red light.

The moon rose, languidly picking its way through the leafless
branches of dead ceibas. When it cleared the forest what was
revealed was a graveyard of dead and dying trees. Fallen trunks
made navigation hazardous. The wind had died, the sail hung
loose, and Marie was using her oar as a pole.

The bow of the canoe nudged a sandy bank. Jonathan jumped
out and with the help of Marie carried Ben ashore and settled him
on the sand. Jonathan collected firewood and tried to make
himself useful. Marie got a fire going right away – there was
plenty of dead wood about. On this bleak shore, Jonathan began
to feel a kind of grim camaraderie for Marie. He was grateful that
she was there, that she knew what she was doing, and that she
wasn't frightened of the swamp.

The next thing they did was to get out the bottle and have a
drink.

Jonathan squatted down on the sand across the fire from his
father. 'Randolph didn't bring me this way. Look at these trees,
Dad, what's been going on around here?'

'Some disease. It looks like the same disease that got me.'

'*We're lost!*'

'Lower your voice, Johnny, and you'll feel better.' Ben tried to
comfort him.

It was true; the sound of his voice made him more frightened.
Jonathan's hands were shaking. Grasping the cup in both

hands, he tried to control them but couldn't. He sank forward on his knees, placed the cup on the sand and hid his face. His body was trembling, and there was nothing he could do about it. There was nothing he could do, it seemed, about anything.

After a while he raised his head and wiped his eyes. Ben was calmly gazing at him through the flames.

'Feeling better?'

'A little. You don't think it's – the beginning of rabies?'

'I think it's the end of a long trip.' He offered the bottle. 'Have some more of this.'

When the cornmeal was ready, they helped themselves to two bowls each. A few minutes later they were back in the canoe. The tall sail leaned before the rising breeze, and the flickering mound of coals was left behind.

Hours later, Jonathan was awakened by the sound of water slapping against the bow. They were out in the middle of a lagoon. The canoe was scudding along before the wind. The moon had sailed over the horizon, and the night was awash with stars.

The island loomed ahead. Jonathan bounded ashore and ran up the hill.

'Bertha!' he called out. 'Hey, Bertha! Bertha! Bertha!'

The thatched roofs rattled in the wind, and a door bumped and bumped.

The wind whistled through the rigging. The sail was flapping, and the waves were slapping against the jetty. Everything was cold and wet, and Ben lay unconscious in the bottom of the canoe. There was no choice but to press on to Puerto Gusano. Jonathan lifted his father's head and embraced his shoulders to keep him warm.

As the night wore on, Jonathan began to dream of freedom – from this time and place, from the deathly pale face of his father, from Marie's hatred, from Umberto's accusations and Bertha's tears, from Beatrice's frail arms and Panadero's helping hand – from everything that had happened, and everything he had learned . . . these nightmares of his conscience.

The absence of suffering, physical and mental; the end of decisions affecting other people's health and happiness; and an end to guilt: these seemed to constitute the elements of happiness. He longed for a quiet Sunday afternoon in New York with

nothing to do but read the *Times*; for Brooks Brothers shirts
freshly ironed by Tilly; for a game of tennis at Henry's beach
house in Hobe Sound; for clams and beers with the 'losers' on
the Vineyard.

He thought of the avenue of apple trees that led to the
entrance of his grandmother's house in New Jersey. Horses
grazing in the bucolic setting belied the proximity of New York
City. The massive, maternal, ivy-draped citadel was built of local
stone; it was a fortress of strength – of ancestors, heirlooms,
preservation and family continuity.

And here lying in his arms was his father. Around them was no
protective structure, no tangible or material proof that their bond
existed. No past and no future. All they had was this moment
together, which was already fleeing.

Jonathan thought of Tolstoy: 'Well, Leo, I'm your perfect
archetype – at war and peace with myself.' He had a premonition
that this period of 'captivity' (which was how he had begun to
define his search for his father) would prove to be the mould in
which the rest of his life was already being shaped. *If* he survived,
the remainder of his life would be dominated by these moments
of pain and joy, the spiritual peace and torment, the inner freedom and bondage – the culmination of a lifelong quest for his
father.

With the wind behind them like a gathering force they could
not control, they raced across the lagoon and re-entered the
forest. Jonathan tried to fight off sleep, but it was useless. When
he opened his eyes again, he thought he was dreaming.

They were gliding quietly along a canal. Lights made halos
in the filmy morning mist. One of Ben's own rickety draw-
bridges creaked and opened wide to let the sailboat pass. By
threading the maze of canals that once served the banana plantations, Marie had managed to bring the canoe to Puerto Gusano
by the landward side.

Just as the first streaks of light were appearing in the sky, the
bow nudged the bank only a few yards from Doc's house. They
carried Ben to the front door.

'Doc!' Jonathan whispered as loudly as he dared. 'Let us in!'

A light glowed within and Doc, clad in a night shirt and cap,
held up a candle and squinted sleepily at them through the screen
door.

'It's me – Jonathan Bradshaw. I've brought my father!'

'Ach! Bring him inside. Quick! Quick!' The door opened. 'My God – you've brought the woman, too? Wait!' He rushed inside and snapped an order to Adam. A door slammed and he returned.

They carried Ben into the bedroom and laid him down. He was filthy and soaking wet. One leg had swollen and filled his trousers. Doc was listening to his chest with a stethoscope.

'How is he, Doc?'

'Alive.'

'Please help him!'

Marie looked ancient with fatigue. 'Do you have a place for her to sleep?' Jonathan asked. 'She's been sailing the canoe for nearly twenty four hours.'

Doc attempted to coax her to a couch in an adjoining room, but she lay down on the floor at the foot of the bed and fell instantly asleep. The parrot had hidden itself in her hair.

'What about Adam?'

'No worries.' The doctor patted Jonathan's arm. 'Always order in my house.'

'What can I do to help?'

'Many things.'

They got Ben's clothes off, dried him with towels and pulled the covers over him. He was as cold and as grey as a cadaver. Jonathan was relieved that Doc was going to leave the bandages in place for the time being; he didn't think he could bear the sight of those legs. While Doc was taking Ben's pulse, he noticed a quick movement through the door.

'Doc – Adam's out there!'

'Yes, yes,' the old man replied. Taking Jonathan by the arm, he led him to the veranda, where a hammock was slung. Jonathan rolled in, and Doc covered him with a blanket.

'Is Dad going to be all right?'

'Ach! Who can say? Sleep now – in the morning we will know more.'

'Doc, I forgot to tell you! In the jungle I got bitten by vampire bats. Do you have the injections against rabies?'

'Ach! What next? Yes, yes of course I have them.'

22

The Telescope

It was midday when he awoke. Padding into the house, he came upon Adam crouching outside the door to the room where Ben lay. The door stood open a crack, and Adam had been so intently observing whatever was happening inside that Jonathan's appearance startled him. He jumped up and bounded off into the kitchen.

Marie was sitting by the bedside. She was stroking Ben's arm. His eyes were shut and his head was propped up on pillows. She had combed his hair and washed him. He was receiving the drip in both arms.

Jonathan went over to the bed and whispered, 'How're you feeling, Dad?'

Ben raised an eyebrow but did not speak. He was very pale. Marie's hand passed gently over his forehead, and wiped away a few beads of perspiration.

A few minutes later a small figure in white emerged from the forest. Jonathan met him on the steps.

'Ah, Mr Bradshaw.' Doc wiped his brow with a handkerchief. 'This heat! The worst of all tropic complaints, is it not? You slept well, I think?'

'I just went in and looked at Dad . . . Doc, can you save him? Should I have brought him back?'

The doctor thought for a minute. 'The left leg, I think it can be saved, but the right . . . Do not excite yourself, Mr Bradshaw.' He patted Jonathan's arm. 'Let us see how your father progresses. We will know more later.'

In the middle of the afternoon two men dressed in white arrived at the house – Doc's assistants from the clinic. Jonathan helped them lift Ben from the bed while Marie held the bottles high.

A nauseating stench drifted from beneath the disturbed sheets. Part of the man had died and was rotting – the part that Doc would cut away. He was wheeled into a small operating room at the rear of the house – primitive by modern standards, but clean enough, with scores of gleaming instruments arranged in rows.

Jonathan returned to the verandah, sank into the hammock and restlessly propelled himself back and forth. The bright-coloured birds were singing just outside the window, through which the perfumes of flowers and ripe hanging fruit and the faint notes of a marimba floated. One man was using his skill to save the life of another, when each knew that the jungle would eventually claim them both, as it had already taken possession of their souls.

At the edge of the forest, something moved. Raising himself up, Jonathan saw a man standing beneath the trees, beckoning to him.

For an old man of undetermined age, Foo scurried over the trail with remarkable speed. Jonathan had to hurry to keep up with him. They crossed the bridge and entered the hotel by a back entrance. Foo led him directly up the stairs to his room. There was his unslept-in bed veiled with mosquito netting, and the suitcases. The clean suit hung in the closet.

'Mr Bradshaw.' Foo was calling him from the balcony. 'Look, look.'

By aiming through a division in the trees, Foo had focused the telescope on Doc's house. Jonathan peered through it and saw the police boys approaching the door. It was as though they were ten feet away.

As they were hammering on the door, he twisted a knob and rode the view down the side of the house to the window of the operating room. Ben lay on the table, his face as gaunt and white as a death mask. At that very moment Doc, with a tense, vexed expression on his face, looked up from what he was doing. His mouth formed the teutonic syllables. One of his assistants abruptly left the room.

Turning the knob again, Jonathan rode the view back to the front door just in time to see the police boys recoil in panic and draw their pistols.

Adam had been sent to answer the door. For a minute it looked as though they might shoot him, but they handed him a letter. Backing off, they beat a hasty retreat into the forest.

Refocusing on the operating chamber, Jonathan viewed again the profile of his father. Doc worked methodically, with an intensity only surgeons know. From time to time he would snap out an order, an instrument would appear in his hand, and an assistant would move to a new position. It was impossible to see just what they were doing, for their hands were busy behind an obstruction of white cloth. Nor did Jonathan want to see. As Doc worked his lips moved, as if in silent prayer. Tears came to Jonathan's eyes, and he prayed, too – for Doc's skill, and for the life of his father.

Foo took over the telescope. Swinging the barrel around, he expertly refocused and invited Jonathan to look again. Framed by the feathery, exploded fronds of an out-of-focus palm tree, Jonathan realized that he had a clear, unobstructed view of Umberto's house. The foreground teemed with gardeners and workmen making last-minute preparations for the Night of Sacrifices. Even as he watched, Jonathan could hear the distant cacophony of hammering, sawing, and shouted orders.

Many small trees had already been cut down. The branches of larger ones had been trimmed, and the Spanish moss was being thinned out. Strangling vines were losing a duel to machetes. Flower beds were being laid out beneath the balcony where only days before a maze of tropical vegetation competed chaotically for light and air. The weeds had been levelled and came to resemble grass. The workmen were securing hammock ropes to the limbs of a mango tree; they were also putting up swings, loops, and bars for the children to play on.

Umberto's house had never looked more inviting. For years the trees had blocked the light from reaching the verandah. Now the square yellow building with its blue shutters and white upper balcony seemed secure and comfortable and sunny within its leafy surroundings.

Umberto appeared on the balcony to shout orders down to the gardeners. His physical appearance had altered dramatically. He had lost weight and bore all the signs of a man who has just visited his barber. His thick mass of curls had been trimmed and brushed. Instead of shabby tweeds, he wore a double-breasted linen suit, a black arm band, and a purple bow tie. His shoes were shiny, and Jonathan could almost smell the cologne. The naive, expectant expression made him appear younger than his years; indeed, he looked boyishly handsome.

He was waiting for something, and began to pace and smoke. All of a sudden, he wheeled about and stared fiercely into the telescope; and Jonathan experienced the absurd panicky sen-

sation that he had been spotted. The police boys bounded into
view, and an animated discussion ensued. Umberto abruptly
dismissed them with an angry wave of the hand. Simultaneously,
he barked at the men below, who began to gather up their tools
and leave. He disappeared inside the house, and a minute later
Bertha came out and, with a vexed expression on her face,
hurried off through the garden.

Swivelling the telescope, Jonathan peered into all the windows
of the house and finally found Umberto downstairs, inspecting
the living room. A great deal of attention had been given to its
arrangement. The Bradshaw silver was gleaming, and the cocktail shaker and ice bucket were prominently displayed on the
sideboard. Yellow and red hibiscus flowers in blue china bowls
adorned the tables. Nevertheless, Umberto went about the room
meticulously straightening and touching each object. Stopping
before the photographs of himself with Ben and Marie, he
examined each one with a furious drag on his cigarette.

He wound his watch and walked to the mirror. Characteristic-
ally, he ran a hand up through his curls, sucked in his cheeks and
puckered his lips; for a minute he studied himself with a critical
eye. He was comparing himself to his portrait above the fireplace.
Pouring himself a drink, he gulped it back and glanced toward
the door.

It was Marie. She had entered the verandah. She, too, had
made an effort to look her best. Her customary white blouse was
knotted at the waist. A length of red flowered material swathed
her hips, and her hair was done up in a matching bandana. She
struck a defiant and provocative pose by the door. With the tiny
green parrot perched in her hair, the effect she created was more
savage than sexy.

Umberto walked toward her with long, flat steps. With a toss of
her head, Marie regally extended her hand for him to kiss. The
gesture stopped Umberto in his tracks. He stared at it in bewilderment. He seemed stupefied by the sight of the hard and
leathery hand, transformed by five years of hard labour in the
jungle. Finally he took it without enthusiasm and shook it limply.
His face was a mixture of friendly and challenging looks.

For a few minutes they stood talking before Umberto prevailed
upon her to go inside. Turning the knob on the telescope,
Jonathan followed them back into the living room to find Um-

berto in a rage. The parrot had flown straight to his portrait, perched on the frame, and sent a stream of excrement slithering down the centre of the picture, right across his face.

Umberto ran to the mantel, frightened the bird off, and began to wipe up the mess with his handkerchief. Marie was convulsed with laughter. The bird flew to the ice bucket and began to peck at its reflected image. Umberto knocked it away. Marie walked around the room, arbitrarily rearranging Umberto's objects and slamming the photographs face down. Umberto turned on her with a look of pure fury. Jonathan thought that they might start fighting when Salvador appeared at the door. Beatrice's kinkajou was clinging to his arm.

Marie stared at him and burst into tears. Salvador ran to his father who gathered him in and held him securely by the shoulders. For a few minutes they watched Marie, who sank to her knees and bowed her head. The mane of black hair covered her face.

Gradually Marie raised her head. She was beckoning and calling to the kinkajou. Salvador watched with fascination the bird in his mother's hair. She leaned forward to kiss him, but the boy gripped his father tightly and turned his face away. Umberto tried to coax him, but Salvador refused. At last Marie lured the kinkajou away and began to kiss and fondle the little creature. She let it loose in the room and began to chase it around. In another minute Salvador had joined the game.

The kinkajou ran out of the house and into the garden. Umberto followed, smiling; the sight of his wife and son playing together had softened his mood. Suddenly Marie grabbed Salvador and started dragging him out the garden gate. Umberto ran after them, seized Salvador by the arm, and for a second there was a tug of war with the poor boy in the middle. Jonathan expected the knife to appear any instant, but it was Umberto who snatched the parrot from Marie's head and held it up before her in a trembling hand as though he would crush it. Jonathan was sure he was going to kill the bird. Marie's face froze. She looked as though she had stopped breathing, and she was coiled to strike. When the police boys appeared on the other side of the gate, blocking her escape, she released Salvador, and Umberto grabbed him. Mother and father stood exchanging threats and insults until Umberto hurled the bird into the air. It flew off into the jungle, and Marie disappeared after it.

For the next hour or so Jonathan concentrated on cleaning himself. Slipping out of the tattered garments that had once been his suit, he took a shower, shampooed his hair and shaved. His body was covered with red welts that itched horribly. Jungle lice. He put on clean underwear and a shirt. The clean suit looked baggy on him. He'd lost a lot of weight in the jungle.

He reloaded the revolver, slipped it under the mattress and hurried back to Doc's.

Ben had not regained consciousness and was shivering from the effects of the anaesthetic. A protective arch beneath the sheet sheltered his legs. One leg now. From time to time he trembled and muttered or groaned. Marie was crouching on the floor at the foot of the bed. Jonathan took a seat and waited. The night was warm, and the sick room lapsed into a peaceful somnolence. A candle burned on the bedside table. The tiny flame danced bravely in a breath of air from the window, but could not dispel the darkness that was gathering in the corners of the room.

Ben's chest rose and fell beneath the sheet. Beyond the open window, fireflies danced, and a marimba was sending limpid notes into the tropical night.

Doc entered and took Ben's pulse.

'What do you think?' Jonathan asked. 'Is he going to live?'

'This night is important.' He released Ben's wrist. 'He is weak, your father – weak, weak. Stay by him now, watch the bottle with the urine. The kidneys give me worry. The whole system is weak, weak. He can die of one of many weaknesses. But we do not give up hope. You go to the hotel, and sleep.'

Jonathan's heart sank. 'Shouldn't we pray for him or give him the last rites or call a priest?'

'I'm praying for him, Mr Bradshaw. At this hour Odorico is always drunk. He would be no help.'

Jonathan sat down again as a storm broke. Lightning flashed and the palms were thrashing in the windy darkness. The candle flame fluttered in the draughts of air, and the room rocked. From time to time a loud snuffling noise could be heard at the base of the door. Adam was lurking just outside.

As rain drummed on the tin roof with sporadic effect, Jonathan dozed and dreamed that birds were flying. Umberto's pelicans, in ragged V formation, were flapping and gliding away into time past.

'Goddamnit! The birds!'

Ben's eyes were staring, and his chest heaved. **His** wrists were straining against the gauze ropes that held them. The arm muscles distended, and it looked as though the needles might jump out of his veins.

'Get those birds out of there! Throw rocks, sticks – anything!'

Jonathan rushed to the bedside. 'Dad, what's wrong? What's he talking about?'

Marie was wiping the perspiration from his brow. 'The birds that came . . .'

'They're eating the corn!'

'Birds from the swamp . . . black birds . . . one time they came . . . thousands.'

'Can't you throw, woman? I told you to keep an eye out for the birds!'

'Ben . . . Ben . . .' she pleaded.

'Adam! For God's sake, *Adam!* Help me!'

The door burst open, and Adam leaped into the room. Marie recoiled as though from a snake, and her hand went to her blouse. Adam was leaning over Ben, panting and trembling with excitement.

'Free the pigs, Adam! Set them loose!' Ben was writhing on the bed. The gauze cords were about to snap. 'Follow them into the jungle, Adam! You're the only one who can do it!' He was raving.

Adam's perplexity was total. As he strained over the body of his former master, he brushed up against Jonathan, who placed a hand on Adam's shoulder and gently pushed him from the room.

Jonathan felt sorry for Adam, who seemed utterly alone in his elemental humanity. No expression of pity lived in the eyes of Marie, however; she continued to regard him with glowering hostility until he had gone.

At length Ben's struggles ceased. Marie placed her smooth brown cheek next to his pallid one. The tension went out, and his arms dropped to the bed.

'Marie, is that you? Where are you?' he called out. His voice was as gentle as a child's.

'I'm right here, Ben . . . here.'

'Marie, Johnny's come . . .'

'I'm here, Dad.'

'Johnny's come . . . at last.' His chest was heaving.

Something inside Jonathan contracted, and he stifled a sob. Marie, meanwhile, was bending over Ben, running her hands over his chest. Her blouse had come open. In the dark crevice between her breasts stood the white bone handle of the knife. That was the image Jonathan would retain of her: the deadly weapon concealed by the softness of flesh. He slipped out the door and left the house.

Following the rain, the night air was hot and moist. The moon, hurrying behind low flowing clouds, cast an indefinite green light. Rising from the damp earth, from the puddles and canals, the mist glowed with an eerie phosphorescence. The tropic night jangled with choruses of insects. Following Doc's orders, he returned to the hotel to sleep.

23
Death

The sun was just floating up from the horizon when Jonathan removed the cover from the telescope. Doc's house nestled in deep shade. The sun had not yet invaded the clearing among the trees. All was quiet. He was about to turn the telescope away, when the front door opened and Doc stepped outside. What light there was seemed to gather about the diminutive man dressed in white. His hands hung loosely at his side, and for several minutes he remained immobile. Raising his hands, he wearily ran them through his hair. He leaned against the wooden railing and covered his face with one hand. The gesture brought tears to Jonathan's eyes. His father had died.

Suddenly Doc whirled around and faced the door – something happening within the house had alarmed him. He rushed back inside, and the telescope became a useless instrument.

Dashing into his room, Jonathan drew the revolver from its hiding place. In another second he was on his way down the stairs. His heart was beating madly as he ran through the forest, but something made him stop beneath the trees at the edge of the clearing.

Doc's house was silent. Nothing moved. Everything seemed to be perfectly normal. It was six o'clock in the morning, and the parrots in the branches were noisily breakfasting on mangoes. The treetops on the opposite side of the clearing had turned emerald green in the sunshine. At turquoise altitudes vultures cruised.

The door slammed open, and Adam lurched drunkenly from the house. His neck was glistening with blood. Red foam bubbled at his lips. He was in a killing mood and he was looking for something. Jonathan, half faint with fear, stepped behind a tree and prepared to shoot. But to his relief Adam turned away and with a piercing whimper bounded away into the jungle.

No sooner had he disappeared than there was a swift movement to Jonathan's left. He whirled to meet it, and the knife, which was to have entered his stomach, sliced through his coat that billowed out as he spun. It was the only chance Marie got. Jonathan took a step backwards, cocked the pistol and took aim.

Her arm had been clawed and was dripping blood. He looked at her in horror, but he didn't pity her. He even felt the absurd urge to apologize, but she didn't give him a chance. Implacable as ever, she turned her back on him, and, regal as a black swan, glided away through the trees.

The room was a shambles. There was blood on the walls, as though two children had gone berserk with paint pots, and bloody footprints tracked the floor. The narrow bed had been overturned, the bedclothes were stained and spattered with blood. The body had tumbled to the floor, dragging the tubes and bottles with it.

Doc was sitting in the chair, shaking his head.

Jonathan went down on his hands and knees by the body, which he hardly recognized. The corpse bore little resemblance to the living man. It was horribly emaciated.

'Savages . . .' Doc sighed.

Ben's eyes were shut as if in sleep, but the jaw hung open. The gold tooth gleamed like an obscene Aztec jewel. Jonathan pulled out his handkerchief and fastened it about the head so the mouth would stay shut.

Doc was talking to himself. 'Marie and Adam fought over the body like the old Greek warriors . . .'

Jonathan righted the bed. After detaching the needles from the arms, he lifted the body and placed it back on the bed, and sat down. Unless his eyes were deceiving him, Ben's face had transformed. It reminded him of an old photograph taken of his father many years ago when he had won a tennis tournament. While admirers clustered about and fixed him with looks of eager admiration, Ben held a trophy aloft. His own eyes were half closed, his face smooth and mystically serene, as though his thoughts were lost in some exotic contemplation and he cared nothing for the game.

That was the look, Jonathan reflected, that frightened his mother and made her write a letter every day during World War II. It was the look that Granny distrusted. Within minutes of death, an almost identical youthfulness had reappeared, and Ben bore the expression of a man at peace.

Jonathan knelt by his father's bed. Doc went out and quietly closed the door.

24

The Night of Sacrifices

With Bertha and Foo walking beside him, Jonathan returned to the hotel.

'You've got to get some rest,' Bertha was saying.

'When will the funeral take place?' Jonathan asked. He was enveloped by the dull hopelessness of his father's death.

'We can't put your poor daddy in the ground. Not today, that is. Today is Umberto's party and everybody's taking time off, grave diggers included. No way you can get them to work.'

'Won't Umberto call off the party when he hears that Dad is dead?'

'He can't, honey. The children are counting on it. They've been waiting a whole year.'

They got Jonathan upstairs and into bed, and he slept. In the late afternoon he awoke to the sound of marimbas, and Doc arrived to give him another rabies injection.

'Doc, does Umberto know that my father is dead?'

'We've been looking for Umberto all day, but nobody can find him.'

Doc told Jonathan that a bushmaster had been discovered in Umberto's garden that morning. It had been living in sinister symbiosis with a capybara, a giant rodent. The capybara had dug its hole, and the bushmaster had moved in to guard it. The serpent, whose length exceeded fourteen feet, had been instantly hacked to death by a bunch of terrified gardeners. The portly burrowing rodent, shrieking pitifully, fled and was not seen again. Everybody said it was a bad omen. Waldo had been looking for Umberto high and low to tell him about it. Now the party was in full swing, and the host was still missing.

After the doctor had gone, Jonathan dragged himself from bed and went out onto the balcony. For a while he surveyed the town through the telescope. Aiming it out to sea, he spotted a sail. It lay about a mile away on the ribboned, tropic sea and was making little progress on the windless afternoon. In the stern sat Marie. Crouched beside her was a small boy. It was Salvador. They were sailing away to Nile Town.

The screen door slammed as Jonathan ran down the street.

The wind had come up, and torches flickered. The palms were rattling. A large flock of migrating birds, thrown into confusion by the flares of Santa Petrolina, was circling anxiously over the town. As Jonathan reached Umberto's gate, they were settling in the trees of the garden. He stepped aside as a crowd of mothers led their protesting children away.

'Don't go in there, sonny!' one of the women called. 'It's a mess!'

A pig was squealing and tearing around with a dozen urchins in pursuit. The torches had taken on gauzy haloes from the dust that had been stirred up by the dancers. The marimbas were in full swing, and the illuminated area beneath the trees had become one big yellow cloud. Someone had let the petroleros in, and they were consuming all the drinks. A gang of ragged children was gathered about Bertha's pots of curry. They were eating it with their fingers and throwing it at each other.

Jonathan spotted Bertha and grabbed her.

'Help, let me go!' She wheeled around, slapping his hand. 'Lord, boss, what are you doing here? You scared me to death!'

'Bertha,' he pleaded. 'Where's Umberto?'

'He'd skin you alive if he found you here. Just look at his party. Typical of Umberto – disappears the day everybody needs him. First that snake, and then Odorico was in here shouting that this was the garden of evil and that the Lord had cursed us with Santa Petrolina because Umberto closed the church. He said that Umberto and Ben sold guns to the capital. That's why Peaceful Banana left and Santa Petrolina came crashing in here. He blamed Umberto for everything – the petroleros and the whores and the children. It ain't true, is it?'

'I don't know.'

'When Odorico started on Santa Petrolina, the petroleros got mad and there was a fight. What we have to do now is to get this mess over with and tell everyone to go home!'

The church bells suddenly began to ring. Bertha looked up in astonishment; the bells had not been heard in years. All through the garden people stopped whatever they were doing and started saying, 'Shhh!' and 'Listen!' and pointing into the air and making the sign of the cross. The music died away. The running and shouting stopped abruptly as people stared into the darkness and tried to comprehend the meaning of the smothering peal.

'Father forgive us!' Bertha said out loud and crossed herself. Some people near her dropped to their knees. No one knew how to interpret this miracle.

There was a loud explosion, and the sky flooded with light. People screamed, thinking the church had blown up. Then they clapped and shouted with excitement. The rockets were popping overhead, and plumes of twinkling sparks were cascading down. While everyone oohed and aahed, the bells began to fade, and an awestruck silence greeted the blazing sky. The children were singing. Attracted by the sound of their voices, the crowd moved toward the house. A spotlight come on, and all eyes centred on the balcony above Umberto's front door.

'Angels,' Bertha muttered with relief. 'Come to save us.'

All Jonathan could see was a line of glittering animals assembled along the balustrade. It was Umberto's little cripples dressed in circus costumes. Some sat in wheelchairs. Others were hanging onto the railing for dear life. He recognized Simplicio's face framed by a huge white-petalled daisy collar. Little Eusebio perched on the railing, his truncated body adorned by a green parrot outfit, tail feathers and all. Beside a chicken sat a rubber monkey with no arms. A cow with a jangling bell round its neck came next. Jorjito couldn't stop grinning, he was so pleased with his cowboy suit. Jonathan couldn't see who was behind the monster masks, but Carlos's face peered over the railing. He had a bone in his nose and wore a grass skirt.

These children seemed to be saving the world from itself. The cripples had taken on the ornery crowd and charmed it. Even the petroleros were silent. Some had doffed their hard hats and were holding them reverently against their chests as they listened to the alphabet song.

'A is for Anteater, from the most graceful yacht afloat.
B stands for Ben Bradshaw, captain of his boat.
C is for the Children, victorious in the end.
D is for the Dinosaurs, who will rule this earth again.
E is for Everybody who listens to our song . . .'

An errant rocket, spinning crazily and spitting flames in all directions, caromed off the side of the house, landed on the roof and burst in an explosion of blue sparks. 'Look!' 'How beautiful!' The audience applauded.

The sparks were drifting gently downwards when the flock of birds that had been roosting in the trees took flight. In all their hundreds they launched themselves as one. They veered sharply right, then left, with white breasts flashing in the eerie blue light. The night air shivered with the myriad beatings of wings. In one great motion they wheeled full circle above the garden and vanished over the roof of the house. Flapping frantically to catch up, a few confused stragglers darted after them.

'*Fire!*'

The roof of the house had burst into flames. The rocket had landed in a nest of dry leaves, twigs and branches – years of accumulated fall-out from the surrounding trees – which ignited instantly. As the flames shot up, the crowd in the garden drew back. There was a loud crackling noise as a sheet of flame raced through the dead branches of an adjacent tree. A torrent of firey twigs cascaded to the ground. The entire roof of Umberto's house seemed to be ablaze. The dancing flames cast a lurid glow through the garden. The children on the balcony began to scream.

'Get them down!' Bertha shouted. 'Save the children!'

Jonathan ran to the house. All around him people were fleeing. He could smell smoke and feel the heat. Above the clamour of the crowd, the children were crying for help. He saw Umberto, followed by Waldo, come racing through the rear of the garden and dash into the house by the back entrance. He ran through the house and met them in the kitchen.

'Where's Salvador?' Umberto's eyes flashed like a madman's. 'What are you doing here?' he shouted at Jonathan.

The kitchen table was overturned; school books and breakfast dishes were scattered about.

'It's Marie!' Jonathan said. 'She had a fight with Adam! She kidnapped Salvador!'

Umberto roared in anguish and pushed him aside. 'The children!' With Waldo on his heels he ran upstairs. 'Get outside! Help me!' he yelled to Jonathan. 'I've got to save the children! Catch them!' He disappeared into the smoke billowing from the top of the stairs.

Jonathan rushed outside just as Umberto appeared on the

balcony. The children clamoured about reaching for Umberto as the flames leapt up. Suddenly a small child hurtled through the air. Jonathan made an attempt to catch him, but the child bounced off his chest, hit the ground and lay still. The flower collar framed Simplicio's face. His eyes were shut, and Jonathan was sure he was dead. Another child tumbled down, screaming, and hit the ground. It was the monkey. Umberto was running along the balcony, picking up the cripples from where they were, then throwing them over. The ballerina came flying down, and Jonathan with arms outstretched collided with Bertha. The pink flurry fell through their arms. Eusebio in the parrot suit thudded to earth and writhed about. People were running this way and that, frantically attempting to catch bodies as they plummeted out of the smoke.

'No. No! Let me go!' It was Jorgito.

'I'm saving your life!' Umberto bellowed.

Jorgito came pinwheeling through the air. Dolores, who was blind, didn't understand what was happening. Dressed in a clown's suit, she fell from the balcony with a smile on her face and crumpled against the earth.

'Umberto!' Jonathan called out as he ran among the fallen bodies. 'You're killing them!'

'Stop it, Umberto, stop it!' Bertha cried. 'The fire is out! Look behind you! *The fire is out!*'

It was true. The accumulation of twigs and leaves, years old and tinder dry, had ignited instantly and burned quickly. The flames, which were leaping six feet into the air a minute before, had already reduced to glowing embers licked by a few shrinking tongues of fire. The corrugated tin roof glowed red but did not burn. Little if any damage had been done to the house.

Jonathan looked down at the parrot. He was still, and blood trickled from his mouth. The chicken moved a bit and groaned. He saw movement in several others and knelt beside the ballerina, who was whimpering. He felt the ground. It was soft. The children had landed in a freshly turned flowerbed. The lights had gone out, but he could see them stirring and regaining consciousness.

'Mother of God!' Bertha whispered. 'Maybe they're all right!'

People were stumbling about, stamping out embers. Waldo was trying to convince Umberto the fire was out. Jonathan was holding a child's head. Dark forms gathered about. 'Poor dead children,' someone said. 'Umberto killed them.' Nearby a child convulsed on the ground. Another tried to raise himself but failed. A few torches still flickered among the trees. The crowd, which had fled in terror, began to draw in.

'Murderer!' someone shouted. 'They're all dead!'

'Hush!' Bertha growled. 'They're alive!'

Umberto spoke from above. His voice was flat, without expression. 'Oh God, I killed them.'

People were moving about in the dark, hissing. 'He killed the children!'

'*He killed them*!' echoed an angry voice. It was Odorico.

Jonathan was cradling the ballerina in his arms. 'They're all right!' he protested. 'The ground's soft! Look if you don't believe me!'

There was a confusion of voices and threatening shouts.

'*Murderer!*'

'No, No! They're alive!' Jonathan wasn't sure of this. Round about him the little bodies were strewn; not all of them had begun to stir.

'He threw them down and killed them!' There was a rising chorus of angry voices. 'Get him!'

'Mercedes, are you all right? It's me – Bertha.'

The little ballerina opened her eyes. 'My head hurts.'

'Thank God – she's all right.' Now the parrot was moving, and the monkey. They'd been knocked unconscious by the fall, but they weren't dead.

There was the sound of scuffling from above. Umberto and Waldo were arguing on the balcony. 'You did what you could, boss!' Waldo was pleading. 'The fire is out and the kids are all right.'

'*I killed them*!' Umberto yelled hoarsely.

Jonathan could see him now, leaning over the balcony, shouting into the night.

'*Murderer!*' came Odorico's reply. 'Admit you closed the church! Admit you brought Santa Petrolina! He's the Devil!'

From a babble of confused comment of those gathered in the dark, voices began to scream.

'Kill him! Get him! Get Umberto!'

'No! No!' Bertha's face was flooded with tears. She fell to her knees and hugged a child. 'They're alive!'

'*Sal-va-dor!*' Umberto's voice filled the darkness. The front door of the house slammed.

'*Sal-va-dor!*' he bellowed and ran off into the night.

Jonathan crouched down beside Bertha.

'They're all right, boss. All of them. Tell Umberto!' she begged. In the flickering torch light they could see the children moving.

'Where's he going?' Jonathan asked. 'What's he doing?'

'He's going for his boat! He's going to save Salvador! *Tell him the kids are alive*! Tell everyone the kids are alive! Get Doc!'

Petroleros dashed past brandishing beer bottles. 'Murderer!' they were shouting and running after Umberto. Jonathan was lost among them. Trying to stop them, he turned around and ran backwards. His arms outstretched, he tried to gather them in. 'Stop! Stop! The kids are alive.' He reached the gate and stumbled over the anteater. It was dead. The camera lay smashed on the ground.

The town was alive with the sound of breathing and the pounding of feet. With the mob of petroleros on his heels, Umberto ran down Main Street past Foo's hotel. They were about to tackle him in front of the church when everyone was distracted by a terrific rattling in the sky. Lights were flashing, and the branches of the mango trees were thrashing in the wind. A helicopter was circling the town, searching for a place to land.

The mob stopped in amazement. As one man they suddenly changed direction and began to follow the helicopter. Jonathan, who had been running along behind, stopped in his tracks as the petroleros stampeded past him. They had completely forgotten Umberto who, no longer pursued, was running along behind the mob. Everyone streamed through the trees and gathered in Cathedral Square as the helicopter touched down in a cloud of dust. The crowded parted to let Umberto through. He was there by the helicopter when the blades stopped swinging and the door opened.

Jonathan, who was craning his neck from the back of the crowd, was pushed to the ground in the crush. He put his hands up to protect himself as people stepped over him. The world began to spin in front of his eyes. Just before he passed out he heard an authoritative voice declare:

'Who's in charge here? Where's Jonathan Bradshaw?'

25

The Funeral

'Johnny dear, for heaven's sake, wake up!'

Jonathan blinked as he opened his eyes to a red blur and familiar smell of talcum powder and gardenias.

'Granny!'

Granny Terry was leaning over him, dabbing his forehead with a wet cloth. Her red flowered dress, rosy cheeks and cherry lipstick gave off a warm glow. 'I knew you were too ornery to kill!'

'Jesus Christ!' Jonathan grabbed the beloved braceleted arms. 'Granny – is it really you? How in the . . . ?' He began to cough and splutter. 'How did you . . .? I don't, ugh . . . *I don't believe it!*' He shouted with joy, 'Jesus, My God! Are you really? *I'm so glad to see you!*'

Granny laughed, kissed her grandson, and embraced him. Her white hair was smoothed back in satiny waves. She wore a pearl choker with red stones, and matching earrings. Her face was sun-tanned and sprinkled with the usual crop of summer freckles. 'Mr Hak answered the State Department cable. Your mother squawked like a smashed cat when she heard where you were. Henry's only comment was, "Well, what'd you expect?"' Granny mimicked Henry's grumpy tone of voice. Although Granny was cheerful and busy fussing with his sheets, she eyed Jonathan with concern, and couldn't resist feeling his brow. 'You *are* all right, aren't you?'

With Granny there, it seemed to Jonathan that the door to the Old Terry Place had been thrown open and the red carpet on the stairs was welcoming him home to roast beef and clean shirts.

'Granny!' Jonathan gripped her hand. 'Do you remember that time Dad took me for a moonlight skate on Blair Lake? And the ice broke, and he was in up to his shoulders in the freezing cold water? The ice kept breaking as he tried to climb out, and I had to slide forward on my belly and push my hockey stick toward him to grab on to? And when he got home he told everybody I had saved his life! Granny, he was glad I came down here and found him, I'm sure he was. But so many terrible things have happened, things I can never . . .'

'Shush! Don't talk about it. Bertha and the doctor and Mr Hak have told us everything. It breaks my heart, but we can't think about that right now. Henry and Senator Hollenberg are out with Mr Hak, touring the town. Those poor orphans, something simply has to be done.'

'Jesus Christ! Henry and Senator Hollenberg?' Jonathan scratched his head. 'This sounds like Congressman Ryan and the Jonestown commission. Did you think I was being held prisoner?'

'We didn't know what to think! Henry says this town was invented by Hieronymus Bosch. He goes around saying "grassy-ass" to everyone. It's the only word of Spanish he knows. But he's very impressed by Mr Hak. Senator Hollenberg thinks Mr Hak should come to Washington and run for president. He says Mr Hak is a born politician. I must say, he *is* full of charm. He makes you feel he's so *interested* in you. I never thought I'd find such an attractive man in a place like this. And he lives in such an attractive house. He has taken such good care of Ben's photographs and silver that I didn't have the heart to remind him that they all belong to you now. Of course, I am sure he understands that we will have to take them all with us when we go home.'

'O.K., O.K.' Jonathan scratched his head and sat up. 'Who's going to throw the first stone? Which one of you is going to start hurling blame at me for everything that's happened? Dad is dead, I've got bat bites, Mom is worried sick, the State Department has had to conduct a man hunt. Senator Hollenberg has come all this way, and Henry's spent *all this money*.' Jonathan stopped. He had a pained expression on his face. 'And Beatrice is dead.'

There was a knock on the door, and Bertha entered carrying a breakfast tray. 'Good afternoon, boss! Feelin' better?'

'Hey, Bertha, what is this?' On the tray sat a package of cigars and a rumpled copy of *The New York Times*.

'From Mr Harrison.' Bertha went to the window and flung open the shutters. The sun poured into the room. 'We've got your suit mended, cleaned and pressed.'

'What time is it, anyway?'

'Nearly two.'

'Bertha, I was just about to tell Johnny that from the air it looked like the whole town was after Mr Hak last night. My word, I've never seen such a mob!'

Bertha poured out the coffee. 'It's happened before. They get so mad at Umberto, like they're going to skin him alive. But they never do. They come back feeling shamefaced and silly. And he'll yell at them that they're rednecks, and this is jerk time. He'll let them have it at Ricardo's tonight, all right.'

Granny sank into a chair and began to fan herself. 'I nearly leapt out of the helicopter when I looked down and saw the flames and a man throwing little children off a balcony. Henry took one look and said, "This looks like Ben Bradshaw's kind of town all right. We've come to the right place." Then he saw the mob. But tell me, why was everyone chasing Mr Hak?'

'Some people thought he'd killed the children by throwing them down,' Bertha said, 'when he was only trying to rescue them from the fire and smoke. When he started running they figured he was trying to get away.'

'Are the children alright?'

'Those flower beds saved their lives, I reckon.'

'Well, that's a relief. Henry sent the helicopter to Nile Town this morning to bring back Mr Hak's son,' Granny said.

Bertha clapped her hands and grinned. 'The trouble was, and I told Umberto myself, too much Hak House punch. Besides, he scared the wits out of everybody ringing those bells. First time folks heard the bells in years!'

Waldo walked into the room and doffed his hat. 'Everybody thought it was the Lord, but I knew it was the boss. He busted in,' Waldo said with pride, 'to light a candle for your daddy. When he heard Ben was dead, he went straight to church, broke down the door, and lit a candle.'

'Heavens, Mr Hak must be a very religious man!' Granny exclaimed.

'Well, ma'am, he said his prayers for the first time in years, then passed out on the cold stone floor of the church. Lay there all day where it was peaceful and cool, where no one bothered him. First good sleep he'd had in weeks. When he woke up he started ringing the bells. I came running and found him. He said he was ringing them for Mr Ben and Princess Beatrice.'

'That's a very sweet thing to do,' Granny said, trying to comfort Jonathan and Bertha.

Jonathan began unwrapping the cigars. 'You know, I've been thinking about Puerto Gusano and the children. Granny, do you remember that idea I had for a Meaning of Life Conference?'

The church bells began to toll.

'Jesus Christ! What now?'

'Henry and I have some ideas, too.' Granny walked over and touched Jonathan's cheek. 'We have been discussing them all morning with Mr Hak. But get dressed, angel, we're going to bury your father. Everybody is waiting.'

'But . . . but . . . I need more time to think. It's too soon.'

'Shhh . . . now. Mr Hak has made all the arrangements. He won't want us to be late.'

Bertha signalled for Waldo to leave. 'We're going to have a real nice funeral for your daddy, honey.' They quietly closed the door behind them.

'Granny . . .' Jonathan would not let go of his grandmother's hand. 'I've been thinking about writing a book about finding Dad. I keep seeing Michelangelo's frescoes on the roof of the Sistine Chapel. God's hand reaching out to Man. Father to son. Fingers almost touching . . . you know, electricity shooting back and forth, passing the gift of life. The Alpha and Omega. The story of creation.'

'We'll talk about all that later, Johnny. It sounds like a wonderful idea.' Granny turned and frowned at her pink dress in the mirror. 'It just goes to show,' she said with a sigh, 'you should always travel with something black.'

The bells were still tolling when Jonathan, Granny and Bertha arrived at Cathedral Square to find that the entire population of Puerto Gusano had gathered beneath the mango trees.

'Well, I never in all my days!' Granny put on the spectacles which hung on a chain around her neck and looked up into the tree. 'Johnny! What on earth?'

Perched in the branches, the children were looking down at them. When they caught sight of Jonathan and his grandmother, they stopped whispering, and within a few seconds the giant mango tree was silent. Then, on cue from Sox who stood below, the children began to sing.

> 'Swing low – Sweet Char – i – ot,
>   Coming for to carry me home!'

Granny took a handkerchief from her bag. Her cheeks were flushed. Ratero appeared and led them through the singing assemblage:

> 'I looked over Jor – dan,
> and what did I s – ee?'

On the back of a wagon lay a coffin. It was draped with the green and yellow flag that Jonathan recognized from Umberto's office. Huge bunches of red, orange and pink hibiscus flowers and long sprays of purple bougainvillea were arranged on top.

> 'A band of angels coming after me'

Sox's throne was strewn with crude bouquets made by the children. A large photograph framed in black and decorated with flowers was attached to the tree. It was a picture of Ben in uniform, wearing his purple heart. Beneath the tree a grave had been dug.

Umberto approached wearing a black armband, a dark suit and a sombre expression. He shook hands soberly with Jonathan and smiled at Granny. Jonathan felt a hand grip his shoulder. Henry embraced him in a bear hug. Behind him was Senator Hollenberg, who clasped Jonathan's hand in both of his.

> 'Coming for to carry me home!'

Umberto led Granny and Senator Hollenberg to their chairs. Everyone was holding flowers. Jonathan, Henry, Waldo and Doc stood by the coffin. A murmur went through the crowd, and Jonathan was astonished to see that Adam was joining them as a pall bearer. His neck was bandaged. Henry stared incredulously at him.

'That was Ben's companion in the jungle,' Jonathan whispered. Henry and Adam exchanged nods.

> 'Swing low, sweet Char – i – ot!'

When Jonathan felt his father's weight upon his shoulders, he could not restrain his tears. They carried the coffin from the wagon and lowered it onto two beams that spanned the open grave. Umberto then motioned for the pallbearers to sit down. Jonathan looked around at the familiar faces. Foo, Ricardo, Ambrose and his brothers, the police boys, Rosa, Doc's assistants, the ragged children – they had all come to pay their last respects to Ben.

Sitting among the roots of the mango tree was Umberto's little band of cripples. They were leading the chorus of the song.

'Coming for to carry me home!'

When she spotted Adam, Granny adjusted her glasses and poked Henry in the ribs. Randolph and Big City, elegantly slippered and attired, took the last seats next to Bertha. They nodded to Jonathan.

As the song ended, Odorico, in clean cassock and shorn of lottery tickets, carried an incense burner to the throne.

'*En nomium de padri et filie et spiritum sanctum*', he intoned and made the sign of the cross.

The entire crowd crossed themselves and answered in one voice: 'Amen.'

Vigorously waving the incense burner back and forth, Odorico continued his version of the Latin requiem for several minutes. The incense partially dispelled the pungent odour from the latrine. Suddenly his voice broke, and, pointing a finger at the refinery, he croaked, 'Save our town! Save our children from Santa Petrolina! A million! A million! A million!'

Some of the children began to snigger. After an awkward struggle Doc and Umberto dragged him from the throne.

Granny and Henry exchanged glances as Umberto mounted the podium with a paper in one hand. Running his hand quickly through his hair, he surveyed the respectful crowd, and with a slight bow acknowledged the visitors. His face was solemn and tragic; his lips were pursed as though to hold back the tears. He began:

'Benjamin Winchester Bradshaw knew the wonders of God and man.' Umberto paused here. He was addressing the small number in the crowd who spoke English. The ones who did not stood silently, hats in hands watching intently, as if they understood every word. 'He hiked in the Andes and scaled Mt Kenya. He ventured to the forbidden city of Smara in the Western Sahara and swam among the coral reefs of the South Pacific. He prayed in Notre Dame de Paris and St Catherine's Monastery in Sinai.' Henry cleared his throat and glanced quickly at Granny. 'He had tea in Andorra.' A smile flickered across Granny's face. 'He skied in

Chile, in the Atlas Mountains, at St Moritz, and in Vermont. He crossed the Atlantic on the *Normandie*, floated down the Amazon on a balsa raft, and walked the gangplank of an Arab dhow off the Mozambique coast. He drove his prized BMW 500 from Munich to Mombasa. He visited Djerba, Odysseus' "Island of the Lotus Eaters" in the Mediterranean, and the ancient Roman cities of Sabratha and Leptus Magna. He scratched his initials into the top of the Great Pyramid, climbed the Acropolis and explored the Caves of Hercules. He knew the sunset of the Sahara, and the moon over Morocco. He shot an elephant in Kenya and a jaguar in the Matto Grosso. He experienced the passion and anguish of love. He lunched at Maxime's.'

Umberto's voice had dropped to a loud stage whisper. Staring sternly at his audience, he stopped to let the effect of his words sink in. Granny took out her handkerchief, began fanning herself, and glanced nervously at Henry who was trying not to laugh.

'Ben Bradshaw was the son of Admiral Gardner Bradshaw of Boston's North Shore and Elise Merriweather Dandridge of Kentucky. Born August 5th, 1916 in Ithaca, New York, he wandered the earth like a former King of Ithaca. His restless creative life was the envy of all who met him. He was equally at home in Paris, Rome, London, Cairo, Marrakesh, Hongkong, Manila, Lima, Rio, Buenos Aires and finally Puerto Gusano – where he left for another world.'

Umberto raised his eyes as though expecting Ben to wave from heaven. The children in the tree craned their necks to search the sky. Umberto's band of cripples sat in rapt attention among the sprawling roots of the tree. Eusebio's face was scratched, Jorjito wore his arm in a sling, and the tiny hunchback Simplicio needed a crutch; but they all had dreamy looks on their faces as they imagined the magical places where Ben had travelled.

As always, Umberto mixed truth, nonsense, brilliant insights, wishful thinking and blatant lies into an intoxicating potion for his followers. Incredibly, this was the same man who only the night before had been chased through town by an angry mob that had included many of those present. Senator Hollenberg's face expressed appreciation for an inspiring and wily leader.

'Ben studied at The Hotchkiss School, Princeton University, the Sorbonne in Paris, and taught briefly at the University of San Marcos in Lima, Peru. He was caned by British school masters and rapped on the knuckles by French nuns. He learned the Spanish of the Conquistadors, the French of Molière; before he died he studied Quechua and the ancient tongues of Central America.' Umberto stumbled over these last words. Disconcerted, he cast an angry stare toward the kiosk. There was Marie, dressed in black, strangely elegant and demure.

'During his distinguished university career, Ben majored in aeronautical engineering and ancient Greek. He wrote his senior thesis on the Battle of Marathon. A classicist and engineer, he was inspired by the truly great Headmaster George van Santvoord who sequestered him for running a taxi service for girls and booze from Hotchkiss to New York in his Stutz Bearcat. Ben loved equally the language of Joyce and W.S. Burroughs. He smoked pot with Burroughs in Pucallpa, he drank tequila with Malcolm Lowry in Cuernavaca, he armwrestled with Hemingway in Havana, he swapped yarns with Borges in B.A. He was a friend of John Kennedy and Fidel Castro.'

'Henry sat up straight and gave Granny an incredulous look.

Umberto had recovered his composure. 'He loved music, too – from marimba to Mozart. He was an habitué of the '21' Club, which had formerly been his grandparents' New York residence.'

Granny put on her spectacles to study Umberto more closely, and Henry slumped grumpily in his chair.

'Ben was a superb athlete and championship tennis player. Princetonians will remember him for leading the Princeton–Harvard team that defeated Oxford and Cambridge for the Prentice Cup at Wimbledon. After Pearl Harbor he joined the U.S. Army and accompanied General MacArthur on his triumphant return to the Philippines.' Henry began to cough loudly. Granny waved her finger to silence him. 'For heroism in battle he was personally decorated by PRESIDENT ROOSE-VELT!' As Umberto's voice soared, the children cheered and soon the whole assemblage was applauding. Henry had doubled over and Senator Hollenberg was pounding him on the back. When he sat up, his face was bright red. Granny shook her head fiercely to make him behave.

'But, it was as an international yachtsman that Ben Bradshaw achieved world fame. In search of adventure and spiritual fulfilment he single-handedly piloted the *Pelican* through the Panama and around South America.' Again there was a burst of cheers and clapping. 'This act of releasing himself from the bonds of the past in the pursuit of perfect freedom was the culmination of a lifetime based on purity and vision.' Granny looked like she would explode. Henry patted her hand with a sly smile. 'During this period of his life, his adventures are too numerous to re-count. He panned for gold in Peru, he had a pepper farm in Brazil, he ran a nightclub in Valparaiso. He always yearned for respectability, and he died a respectable man.'

Henry let out a groan.

Umberto's arms were raised in triumph. 'It is fitting that Ben Bradshaw will rest here. In a letter to a girl named Flo that he wrote but never mailed, Ben called Puerto Gusano "the closest thing to a hometown I have ever known". He will be at peace here, next to my own beloved daughter, Beatrice, whom I laid to rest only two weeks ago. The day after Jonathan Bradshaw arrived. Princess Beatrice will welcome Ben into the next world.'

'A – men!' someone shouted.

'And neither of them will be lonely!'

Umberto's face indicated quiet. 'Like all of us, Ben Bradshaw has long been waiting for Godot. Before many of us, he has found him. In the 1960s Ben signed his letters: "Peace. Ben." Thus peace, Ben, and adieu.'

No one moved or made a sound. Umberto suddenly began again in a loud voice:

'Ladies and gentlemen, distinguished guests, Mrs Averill Dillon Terry, Mr Henry Heiskell Harrison, and Senator Robert Hollenberg, and dear people of Puerto Gusano:'

At a signal from Umberto, Waldo leaped upon a box and began translating for the crowd. A simultaneous translation was already being whispered through the trees.

'Ben Bradshaw died without a will.' Granny and Henry looked at each other. 'But he did not die without a legacy. He did not come to this wild outpost like a fortune seeker or conqueror, to rob and plunder and carry away our treasures. Instead he brought riches to *us*. To a town at its wits' end, he brought hope. To orphans with no future, he imparted a vision of the world they would never see. To a down-and-out town, robbed of its natural beauty and dignity, he brought the spirit of America. He opened our eyes and aspirations as no Peace Corps or diplomatic mission or ambassador has ever succeeded in doing. To people stripped to their souls, he gave his love. The people of Puerto Gusano are deeply indebted to Ben Bradshaw for giving us our self-respect! For giving us the ability to dream!'

Thunderous applause followed until Umberto raised his arms again.

'The people of Puerto Gusano are also indebted to Ben Bradshaw . . .' Umberto suddenly switched into Spanish, 'for bringing us his *son!*' Jonathan jerked forward as though he had been hit and looked nervously around him. Granny smiled and squeezed his hand.

'I am here to tell you, people of Puerto Gusano, that Jonathan Bradshaw is *not* what you think! It took great *courage* and self-sacrifice to come here searching for a father he hadn't seen in twenty-five years. It took exhausting perseverence and passion to endure the hardships in pursuit of a father he hardly knew, and who probably didn't recognize him . . . a father who hadn't thought of him in over two decades.'

Jonathan was beginning to feel anxious. Umberto's words were uncomfortably familiar, yet his tone was almost tender.

'It took dedication to carry his filial bonds to a father who had embraced a new freedom and life of independence!' Umberto's voice had again soared with these words. 'It took great faith to expect a man who had learned to walk on water to return to the dirty polluted shore,' he whispered. 'I know you have misjudged him, people of Puerto Gusano, and I am here to beg you to change your minds. Jonathan Bradshaw is not what you think! He is not the clumsy, selfish oaf who came to inflict pain upon this town, to shed the blood of innocents!'

Every eye was on Jonathan. He suddenly felt very hot and wanted to loosen his collar, but he was afraid that any movement would be incriminating.

'I beseech you, people of Puerto Gusano, do not think he came here only to start a brawl that would end in murderous brutality.'

Jonathan began to panic. Surely Umberto wasn't going to incite the crowd again. Was he going to set the mob against him and Granny and Henry and Senator Hollenberg?

'Jonathan Bradshaw may have arrived with his shirttails hanging out, his belly showing and a cigar in his mouth, a wise-cracking innocent abroad, confident that he was doing the right thing. But, believe me, people of Puerto Gusano, he did not *mean* to leave a trail of havoc and pain. He did not *mean* to heap upon our town more despair than we already suffer with our homeless children, our mutilated natural resources, and the satanic flames of Santa Petrolina.'

Umberto looked like a man who has just announced the end of the world. Jonathan was scared, but Granny and Henry were calmly listening. No one moved or even seemed to breathe.

'*No!* People of Puerto Gusano, Jonathan Bradshaw did not *mean* for his good intentions to hurt us or to upset Ben's life, or inflict suffering and death upon his father.' Umberto's voice was becoming threatening. '*No!* People of Puerto Gusano, Jonathan Bradshaw is no terrorist or assassin. He is no revolutionary or anarchist determined to sacrifice others for his own selfish goals. No. People of Puerto Gusano, I lay before you the overwhelming evidence in his defence: Jonathan Bradshaw *simply didn't think!*'

Umberto's voice drifted away. All eyes in the crowd were trained on Jonathan, whose head swam with fear, anger and embarrassment.

'But before you judge him too harshly, good people of Puerto Gusano, I submit to you that Jonathan Bradshaw has in fact given us a great deal. Here with us today are his highly esteemed grandmother, step-father, and a United States Senator who heads the Senate Foreign Relations Committee.'

Umberto clapped his hands and the crowd cheered.

'This is *superstar time*, and I wish Ben Bradshaw could be here to enjoy it!'

As Umberto jubilantly shouted these last words he flashed a smile and Jonathan relaxed.

'These are not just any ordinary people, dear friends! These are caring people who have seen our plight and who are going to dedicate themselves to helping us. It is with great humility and sincere gratitude that I can announce to you today that the first Meaning of Life Conference, ever to be held anywhere in the world, will take place next year in our town! Upward! Onward! Forward together!' He held up a clenched fist to the sky.

A wild cheer followed and the children took up the chant. 'Upward! Onward! Forward! Together!'

Umberto silenced them, and, with a smile to the personages in the front row, continued:

'Thanks to the generous donations and sponsorship of Mr

Henry Harrison and Mrs Averill Terry, ecologists, environ-
mentalists, philanthropists, charitable organizations and the
World Wild Life Fund and many private individuals from the
United States and all over the world will visit Puerto Gusano and
study our problems!'

Jonathan grabbed Granny's hand, but she had turned and was
smiling and waving and acknowledging the applause and shouts
of *'Gracias!'*

'Television cameras will show the world the evil of Santa
Petrolina! Mrs Terry and her friends will see that our unfor-
tunate homeless and crippled children are adopted by families
who will love and care for them in the United States of America.'

A wild whoop went up through the mango tree. Foo ran forward and embraced Bertha, who stood applauding, with tears in
her eyes, and blowing kisses to Granny Terry. Soon everyone was
standing and shouting *'Gracias!'*

'Senator Hollenberg will recommend to the Senate Foreign
Relations Committee that aid be sent to Puerto Gusano for a
hospital.'

Doc stood up to shout 'Bravo' and 'Thank You!'

'Senator will also ask that an American School be founded in
Puerto Gusano to *educate all our children!'*

The joy in the branches of the mango tree was a sight Jonathan
would never forget. The crippled children began to laugh and
sing. Jonathan hugged Granny, Henry and even Senator Hollenberg. Umberto finally managed to quiet everyone down.

'Let us never forget what we owe Ben Bradshaw, his son and
our guest from *Heaven!'* He shouted, *'Gracias, señores!'* and the
crowd took up the cheer.

Suddenly Odorico barked, 'What about my church?'

'We'll get the church opened!' Umberto roared.

Bertha made the sign of the cross and knelt. One by one, all the
people followed her example.

Umberto crossed himself. 'And now, dear people and friends
of Puerto Gusano, if the pall bearers will come forward, in this
time of our happiness and celebration for what he has done for
us, we will silently thank Ben Bradshaw as we lower him into his
grave.'

Jonathan, Henry, Doc, Waldo, Senator Hollenberg and Adam
took hold of the straps.

'Let us all bow our heads and thank God for our dear friend, Benjamin Winchester Bradshaw.'

Umberto was about to step down when he suddenly remembered something. 'I forgot to announce one more thing. As a token of their gratitude, the people of Puerto Gusano will dedicate a memorial to Ben Bradshaw,' he said in English. 'It will be *permanently* housed in my very own home, and will include *all* his memorabilia – his photographs, his silver, even *this ring* – for us to love and remember him by.'

Granny's face turned purple. It looked as though her choker would pop. Words of protest were forming on her lips, but Umberto had stepped between Jonathan and Henry to help pull on the straps. The crowd took up a final chorus of *Swing Low Sweet Chariot*. The wooden beams were removed, and Ben Bradshaw was lowered into the ground.